Exiles of a Gilded Moon Volume 1: Empire's Wake

Exiles of a Gilded Moon, Volume 1

Dustin R Cummings

Published by Shadow Spark Publishing, 2020.

EXILES OF A GILDED MOON VOLUME 1: EMPIRE'S WAKE

First edition. November 17, 2020.

Written by Dustin R Cummings.

For my mother Sheree, for my father Wayne, and for my brother Don. For my family, and for my ancestors.

Chapter One

Darshima walked steadily under the shrouded glow of the night sky. Before sunrise, he had diverged from the rest of his hunting party to track and kill one of the many fearsome beasts that roamed these lands. He had spent his entire day trudging through the soggy marshes and was sure that he remained the only one left in the woods. Evening had fallen long ago, and everything around him was cast in shadow. Alone and empty-handed, he looked out over a large quagmire just ahead. A thick, roiling carpet of white mist spread over its tangled vines and matted grass.

During the previous days, his companions had succeeded in their hunt and avoided this treacherous place. Darshima hadn't caught anything, and he was desperate. The hunt was the most important rite that a boy needed to complete to be considered a man in the eyes of his family and peers. He walked forward and mustered his remaining strength, the thin soles of his leather moccasins clinging to the sodden ground.

He hoisted his wooden bow and dark fabric quiver upon his shoulder, which seemed to grow heavier with each step. Rivulets of sweat poured down his face and into his eyes, blurring his vision. Darshima pressed his palms against his forehead, and shuddered momentarily amid a wave of dizziness. His tongue stuck to the roof of his dry mouth, and he grimaced at the sour taste. He stumbled to a stop and briefly glimpsed down at his abdomen, covered in a layer of grime and perspiration. His empty stomach growled, and he grimaced as it twisted itself into an aching knot.

Darshima let out a weary sigh and collapsed onto his hands and knees. The damp red soil oozed over the bronze skin of his fingers, staining the black leather gauntlet fastened to his right forearm. He shivered as the mud soaked through his red linen breeches, gripping his skin in a flash of coldness. His quiver and bow fell to the ground beside him with a clatter. Head hanging downward, Darshima drew in a tired breath. His heart pounded with a creeping sense of despair. Memories of hunting seasons past flooding his mind, he wondered if he could accomplish this task. A stiff breeze swept through the carpet of grass surrounding him, pricking the bare skin of his torso. He swept back the locks of his wavy brown hair with a muddied hand and looked up to the sky. The veil of clouds slowly parted, revealing the heavens beyond. A triplet of moons hung in a bold arc amid the swirls of stars, their brilliant light casting a soft glow around him.

Darshima's head drifted back to the ground, when something in the mud caught his attention. He moved closer and saw a ray of moonlight glimmer upon a water-filled impression, cast in the shape of a hoof print. Pulse bounding with excitement, his gaze darted toward a set of tracks leading into a small grove. Darshima grabbed his bow, slung his quiver over his back, and leapt to his feet. He peered into the darkness and carefully stalked through the wet blades of grass, trying to hush his footsteps upon the damp ground. Moments later, he arrived at the secluded edge of a dark pond amid a stand of stout trees, their gnarled branches casting ominous shadows around him. Fatigued, he hunched over, drawing in deep breaths as he looked ahead.

Darshima eyed two particularly large, four-legged beasts standing at the opposite end of the pond. A triplet of white, crescent-shaped horns adorned their fur-covered foreheads and curved around their pointed ears. They waded at the pond's shallow edge and bent their necks for a drink, taking in loud gulps with their stubby snouts. Beads of water trickled down the thick grey fur of their jowls.

A sharp pang of fear coursed through Darshima's chest as he observed the pair. Known as powilix, these beasts were among the most ferocious animals that roamed these lands. Incredibly strong, their muscular frames were covered in a boldly striped, silver and white pelt. With a stature a bit taller than a man's waist, they traveled in pairs and could easily kill either a hunter or beast brave enough to challenge them.

Darshima clenched his jaw as he watched them. He reached for his quiver and ran his fingers along the feathery arrow tails, contemplating his next move. His attempts at hunting an animal during the previous days had failed. Tonight was his last chance before returning home with his party, and he remained without a kill. An anxious sigh escaped his lips as he realized that he had no choice but to go after these beasts alone.

Darshima drew in a measured breath, snuck closer to the water's edge, and crouched behind a large boulder cast in shadow. The animals continued their drink undisturbed, howling raucously between draughts. He slowly rose from behind the boulder and peered at the beasts. Arm trembling, Darshima unfastened a pocket in his leather gauntlet containing a powdery resin. He dipped his fingers into the white substance, then massaged it into his palms.

With his right hand steadying the bow, Darshima loaded one of the gleaming, metal arrows and drew back upon the silken bowstring with his left arm. His glinting cobalt eyes narrowed, Darshima aimed at the beasts, exhaled a nervous prayer, and let go. The bow shuddered under the release of the tension, vibrating in his hand. The arrow vaulted forward, spiraling on an errant path through the air. It then skipped along the surface of the water before diving below the ripples.

Startled, the beasts jerked their heads up from the pond. They rudely lurched about, searching for the source of the disturbance, the sounds of splashing water echoing around them. Their gaze fell upon the boulder where Darshima hid. His knees trembled as the creatures approached from the pond's edge. Fear seizing him, he dropped to the ground and pressed his back against the cool stone surface.

The deep thud of hoofbeats grew louder, then stopped abruptly. Darshima glanced upward and his eyes met the wooly gullets of the pair, quivering with each rumbling breath. Their heads raked sharply to the left and then to the right as they searched for him. His mind racing, Darshima realized that this may be his only chance to kill them.

He deftly withdrew another arrow from his quiver and loaded it into the bow. Steadying himself upon one knee, Darshima looked upward and then aimed at the beast to his left. The bow creaked under the tension as he pulled back. With an earsplitting crack, the weapon shattered, sending a hail of splinters in every direction. The arrow misfired into the sky and sailed right between the two creatures, spiraling out of sight. The recoiling bowstring sliced open the skin of his thumb and he yelped at the stinging pain. He clasped his hands over his mouth to muffle his cries, but they were drowned out by the angry roar of the beasts.

His heart seized with terror, Darshima leapt to his feet. He dashed toward the trail leading out of the grove and back into the marsh. The beasts' instincts took over as they chased him. The vengeful pair charged closer, letting out fierce growls as their hooves pounded against the ground. Darshima ran as fast as his legs would carry him, his quiver striking against his back with every frenzied stride. He jumped over upturned roots and charged through muddy ditches, the beasts galloping only a few paces behind him. He tore desperately along, the surrounding terrain but a dark blur.

The steady drum of hoofbeats filled his ears as he ran. Darshima shot a glance over his shoulder and met the gaze of the two angry creatures. Their fiery-red eyes locked onto him, and they let out ghastly howls that echoed through the night. His blood surged at the frightful sound, and he snapped his head forward. He dashed down a grassy slope and into another marsh, the murky waters lapping about his waist.

As Darshima trudged ahead, he felt a vine catch his foot. He tried to move forward, but abruptly tumbled face down into the tepid water. Disoriented, he thrashed about, briefly slipping beneath the surface. He struggled to regain his footing upon the soft, clinging silt. Lungs aching as he held his breath, he coughed loudly. His nose and mouth filled with the foul, brackish water, pungent with the odor of decaying vegetation.

Darshima gripped his ankle and desperately yanked at the vine, splashing about as he freed himself. He jumped to his feet, hastily cleared his throat and looked around him. He tried to make sense of the shadowy marshland before him, but couldn't recognize anything. The beasts' screeching yelps filled his ears, and a bolt of terror shot through him as he struggled to regain his bearings. He frantically trudged onward, his feet slipping upon the mud.

Darshima scrambled back onto drier ground and darted through the stiff grass, glancing at the unfamiliar lands ahead. Eyes widened in fear, he tried to find some feature he could identify, but he was lost. The growing sound of flowing water filled his ears, and his heart rose with a glimmer of hope. If there were indeed a river in the distance, he would be safe. Powilix were deathly afraid of moving water, and would abandon their pursuit if they had to tread across anything swifter than a meandering brook. He ran forward, the sound steadily drowning out the bellowing howls of the beasts.

Darshima emerged from the field and stumbled to a halt at the rocky ledge of a steep bluff. He drew in a fearful breath as he looked out onto the vista before him. The raging waters of the river crashed violently through a jagged network of rocky canyons far below. The air around him echoed in a deafening, disembodied roar. He shivered as swirling gusts of cold mist rose from the crag and drenched him.

Darshima turned back around to see the two beasts emerging from the field, their low angry grunts rising above the sounds of the water. Their brawny shoulders and haunches moved rhythmically as they stalked closer. They bared their sharp teeth and let out fierce snarls, strands of saliva dripping from their prominent jaws. Muscular haunches rippling with tension, they stood ready to charge. Darshima backed up to the ledge as much as he dared. His pulse bounding with fear, he stared at them and struggled to maintain his balance.

The creatures let out menacing growls and lowered their heads, their smooth horns glinting in the moonlight. Without warning, they reared up on their hind legs, then burst into a sprint. The ground trembled under their hoofbeats as they approached him. Overwhelmed by an acute sense of dread, Darshima threw up his hands as they rushed forward.

Just as the beasts were about to tear into him, several sharp whistling sounds sliced through the deafening roar. From seemingly nowhere, a volley of silver arrows pierced their flanks. The beasts abruptly stopped their charge and let out mournful cries. They took several staggering steps as if intoxicated, then collapsed beside each other in a quivering heap. Dark red blood oozed from their wounds and soaked the grass at his feet.

Darshima stood quietly as he watched them expire, afraid that the beasts might still attack him as their lives faded. When they exhaled their final breath, he sank to his knees, overcome by a wave of exhaustion. A nascent sense of relief rose within him, and he let out a sigh. His heart thudded in his chest as he realized just how close to death he had come. The sound of the water enveloping him, Darshima sat down, drew in a haggard breath, and tried to calm himself. The terrifying chase, combined with an entire week of hunting had thoroughly exhausted him. He wanted nothing more than to rest beside the river for the remainder of the night.

The sharp sound of a snapping twig, followed by the plodding thud of footsteps broke through the din of the roaring water. Too fatigued to stand, Darshima lifted his head toward the noise, his chest tightening as the fear returned. The form of a man emerged from the tall blades of grass. Darshima's pulse slowed, and he calmed down when he realized that it was his older brother, Sasha. He walked into the clearing toward the ledge and came to a stop in front of Darshima. Sasha stood silently, his amber eyes peering at him with a discerning gaze. His lips curled into a sympathetic smile and he extended his arm. Darshima clasped his brother's hand, then pulled himself up to his feet.

"Are you okay?" Sasha gently shook Darshima's shoulder.

"I'm fine." Darshima peered at the beasts between tired breaths. "Thank you, Sasha." He then cast his eyes downward, avoiding his brother's stare.

Sasha looked around the ledge, his eyes lingering upon the beasts.

"That was a very close call." Sasha let out a sigh. He ran a hand through his thick mop of silky, shoulder-length black hair. "Stay here and rest for a bit, you've been out all night."

Sasha walked toward the carcasses, his moccasins padding softly upon the damp soil. A large metal bow strapped across his muscular back shifted rhythmically as he moved, glinting in the moonlight. He knelt beside one of the beasts and examined it. Freshly killed, the creature's eyes had not yet glazed over. He yanked the gleaming arrows from the powilix's hide and placed them back in the rawhide quiver slung over his shoulder. Sasha's fingers gently unfastened the leather gauntlet upon his right arm, decorated with spiral patterns of glowing glass beads. He pulled it off, tucked it in the waistband of his red breeches, and then untied a length of thick rope hanging from his belt. He crouched next to the beast and methodically bound its three-toed hooves.

Darshima approached Sasha as he worked, and his lips wrinkled into a frown. His heart thudded with a rising sense of anger as he watched Sasha secure the animal's legs.

"Sasha, I was the one who tracked those powilix. Why didn't you let me kill them?" he huffed, his voice brimming with exasperation. Sasha's brawny shoulders froze as he listened. He then rose to his feet and faced Darshima. His tall, athletic frame towered over his younger brother, who was leaner in stature.

"If I'm not mistaken, those animals had you running for your life." Sasha's brow furrowed in a look of confusion. "If it hadn't been for me, you would've been their dinner." He stepped away from Darshima. Sasha knelt beside the other beast, pulled the arrows from its flank, and stowed them in his quiver.

"It isn't all my fault." Darshima shook his head, stuttering as he searched for the right words. "My bow broke as I aimed at them. They were startled by the noise and then chased after me." Sasha continued to work, shrugging his shoulders as Darshima spoke.

"That bow worked fine when I used it on the last hunt," he muttered.

"Is that all you have to say?" Darshima's face grew hot with frustration.

Sasha finished tying the hooves of the second carcass, then looked over his shoulder.

"I'll have something more to say when you admit that you were completely unprepared this evening, with no strategy for the hunt. You should've known better than to go after a pair of these beasts alone."

"I tried my best to prepare." Darshima bowed his head as he listened to his brother's rebuke. A discouraged frown crossed his lips, and he let out a sigh. Sasha's stern gaze softened as he saw Darshima's expression grow more somber.

"We should move on, daybreak is approaching." Sasha turned back to the brightening horizon. The copper-red sun slowly ascended, its brilliant disk steadily illuminating the dark skies.

Sasha picked up one of the heavy carcasses and hoisted it upon his broad shoulders, its bound legs draping over his bare, muscular chest. He moved away from the cliff and walked toward the grass, the early morning light reflecting off the smooth, brown skin of his back.

Darshima grappled with the other beast and tried to get a proper hold of it. With a heave, he lifted the warm carcass upon his shoulders. A shiver ran down his spine as the stiff, damp fur of its belly prickled against the skin of his neck. He followed Sasha into the field and they began their long trek back to the camp. As he scanned the muddy trail before him, his mind swirled with thoughts of what had just happened. He had been on the verge of killing those beasts, but then they had him running for his life. As usual, Sasha had rescued him from the brink of disaster. Darshima shook his head as a mixture of disbelief and disappointment rose within him. The load upon his shoulders seemed to grow heavier with each step. He looked up at the brightening sky, and a lump formed in his throat. He had failed yet again.

Chapter Two

Darshima trudged forward amid the thick, woody underbrush, carefully balancing the carcass upon his weary shoulders. He walked in silence, the exhaustion of the hunt and the humid morning air steadily sapping his energy. Sasha led, and Darshima followed, their path cutting through a dense patch of forest. Though unfamiliar, it was more favorable than the one Darshima had traveled the day before. He squinted his fatigued eyes against the sunlight. Fiery orange rays shone through the leafy forest canopy, casting the worn trail in soft shadow and brilliant flecks of silvery green light.

Darshima was relieved that he had survived his nearly fatal encounter with the powilix the night before, but it was overshadowed by a deep sense of failure. He was eighteen years old - among the oldest in the hunting party, yet he remained unable to achieve this significant milestone. Darshima had been on hunting trips in seasons past, but no matter how hard he tried, success eluded him. In addition to providing much prized wild game for one's family, hunting the powilix was a rite of passage and an important tradition.

Killing this ferocious animal was considered the ultimate test of strength and ability. Once a boy killed a powilix, he was considered a man. The need for hunting and gathering had long been replaced by ranching and farming, but the ritual endured as a cherished tradition. His thoughts drifting, Darshima pulled his gaze from the ground and looked at Sasha, who marched even further ahead. Darshima hurried his pace and tried to cast the worries from his mind.

By mid-morning, they reached the edge of the forest and arrived at a large clearing. The air rippled with the boisterous shouts and playful chants of members of the hunting party. Darshima's heart leapt at the sound of the familiar voices, then sank as he realized they would soon ask him about his night. He didn't know how he would explain it to them. Staring at the crowd of young men, he followed Sasha into the camp, and their chatter abruptly ceased. Like Darshima and Sasha, they were bare-chested, dressed in simple linen breeches, and stood either barefoot or wore leather moccasins. Several of the young men whooped in delight as they approached.

"What is this?" asked a young, copper-skinned man, his voice ringing with surprise. He rose from the grass and approached the two. His name was Seth, and he was one of Sasha's closest friends. Tall and slender in form, he wore tan breeches, and his silky black hair was fashioned in a thick braid that ran down his back. Before Darshima could reply, Sasha began to speak.

"It's amazing isn't it?" A toothy grin spread upon his face. "Darshima killed them both at the same time." Sasha lifted the dead powilix from his shoulders, rested it upon the ground and stood before the group. Darshima nervously eyed the other hunters. He briefly knelt upon the grass, and placed the carcass he carried beside the other.

Everyone in the group listened intently as Sasha spun an increasingly complicated tale. Darshima shook his head in disbelief as he listened to his brother's lie. When Sasha finished, the young men let out a raucous cheer.

"You've finally succeeded! I didn't know you had it in you." Seth's cloud-grey eyes lit up as he stared at Darshima. He slapped Darshima on the back and drew him into a friendly embrace. The others congratulated him, letting out excited howls of approval.

"Sasha helped me greatly, and I couldn't have done it without him." Darshima's face grew flushed with embarrassment. Sasha had already told the tale, and everyone had heard. Darshima knew it would appear even worse if he contradicted his brother's words, so he said nothing more. He tried to deflect the compliments and looked over to Sasha, who had already walked to the shaded end of the clearing. He sat at the foot of a large tree and gave Darshima an earnest smile. Sasha then rested against the knobby trunk and closed his eyes.

The crowd moved away from Darshima and settled back down. Many of them had just awoken and were tidying up the camp for the day's trek. Hunting knives in hand, the younger members of the party skillfully field dressed the fresh carcasses. They drained the remaining blood and buried the organs in a pit beyond the perimeter of the camp. The young men placed wooden tags around their horns, and Darshima cringed as he saw his name neatly written upon them. He knew that Sasha's name belonged upon those labels, not his.

The young men then secured the powilix in brown cloth sacks, infused with a mixture of pungent herbs to preserve the meat for the trip home. Darshima thanked them, then walked to a secluded area at the edge of the clearing. He sunk down at the foot of an old tree, and rested his weary back. He stared at the others as they readied their things, his eyes burning with exhaustion. Though he hadn't rested since the previous morning, he could not sleep. The harrowing memories from the night before left him feeling anxious. A chill ran through him as the images of the charging, fiery-eyed beasts flooded his mind. He had been so close to capturing them, but like so many times before, his chance had slipped away.

The rough bark scratched his bare skin, but he paid little attention. Sasha's false tale tugged at his conscience. Just when Darshima thought he had figured him out, Sasha did something unexpected. He had always been a good brother, and despite Darshima's current frustration, he knew that Sasha was only trying to protect him.

Sasha had been like this since they were children. When Darshima faced taunts as a young boy, Sasha was the first to defend him. When their father was harsh toward him, Sasha often spoke up on his behalf. When Darshima faced dangerous situations on previous hunts, Sasha had always come to his rescue. If he was having a rough day, Sasha tried his best to cheer him up. Darshima looked over to his brother, who dozed peacefully against the tree. A contrite smile crossed his lips, and he sighed. Darshima was proud of him. Sasha was the leader of their group and had managed to keep them all safe. He looked on as the others finished clearing the camp, then rose to his feet and put his equipment away.

After Sasha's brief nap, the entire hunting party, twenty members in all, set out from their camp. With the calm wind at their backs and the sun lighting their path, they began the journey homeward. The only things encumbering them were their equipment, camping packs and the heavy animal carcasses. Wrapped in the cloth sacks and strung along a wooden pole, two hunters carried a pair of carcasses upon their shoulders. They marched along trails that guided them amid the humid forests, over meandering streams and through vine-covered tunnels carved into the rocky hills.

These paths had been worn into the lands by the footsteps of generations of hunters who had long preceded them. At their current pace, they would make it home by that evening. To pass the time, they chatted amongst themselves, their voices rising boisterously with tales of ferocious beasts, narrow escapes, and decisive kills. They trekked onward as the sun traced a fiery arc across the immense sky.

As dusk approached, they reached a grassy hilltop overlooking the river. They were now only a moderate distance from their home, the city of Ardavia. Darshima's heart stirred as he peered out over the waters, his eyes lingering upon the majestic, spiraling turrets and gleaming oblong domes. Ardavia was far and away the largest city among the settlements scattered across the largely unspoiled surface of their home, the moon Gordanelle. The center of government, commerce, and culture, the city had long played an important role in the moon's history. Ardavia had been established thousands of years ago upon a chain of large island plateaus at the mouth of the surging, freshwater Eophasian River. Gordanelle's longest river, the Eophasian carved a serpentine path through much of the moon's northern hemisphere. Just beyond the pentad of principle islands, the river ended in a wide, curving waterfall that crashed into the sea below.

The winds picking up around them, Darshima looked at the clouds above. The sky grew darker, and a dense fog rolled in from the surrounding hills and palisades, spreading over the river like a blanket. The change in weather had been unexpected. They had intended on returning that evening, but the reduced visibility would make the trip home too dangerous. The hunting tradition dictated that they must return solely by ship. With the hazardous weather, maritime traffic would be suspended.

"The fog is getting thicker. We will have to wait until morning to travel home," said Sasha as he settled upon the grass. Darshima and the others followed his lead and sat in a semicircle around him.

The light of the setting sun cast a diffuse glow upon the heavy fog. The ancient temples and stately palaces disappeared as the billowy wisps enveloped them. The royal palace, adorned with soaring red and white stone towers stood boldly atop the highest hill of the city, appearing as an island unto itself amid the fog. The skies above Ardavia hummed with fleets of aerial passenger and freight ships, their angular fuselages carving through the mists. The filamentous bridge spans linking the islands glowed with the pinpoint lights of bustling terrestrial traffic, shuttling between the districts of the city. Unlike sea traffic, air and road traffic were rarely disturbed by changes in weather.

"There is still some daylight left, so we should continue," said a young man, his voice rising above the chatter. His name was Ero, and he was about a year younger than Darshima. Brown-skinned with curly black hair, he sprang to his feet and hastily dusted the grass from his tan breeches. Sasha rose and faced him. Surprised by the exchange, Darshima pushed himself off the ground and stood beside Sasha.

"There is no rush, and the visibility is poor. No ship would dare to take us across the river in this fog." Sasha pointed toward the shore in the distance. "We've worn ourselves out enough for one day. Let's rest while we can." As Sasha turned away, Ero let out a frustrated groan.

"Why must we wait? Most of us are ready to leave now. We can set up camp at the riverside." His amber eyes narrowed as a brooding expression crossed his face.

"This is my decision to make. The fog is too dangerous and we could get lost. You must think of your fellow hunters." Sasha rested his hand upon Ero's shoulder. "We will continue in the morning."

"I am ready to leave..." he began, but Sasha shook his head and Ero grudgingly fell silent. Sasha was responsible for all of them, and the young hunter had no choice but to obey him.

Ero stared at the city, let out a dejected sigh and tore himself from Sasha's grip.

"I am more experienced than Darshima, yet you treat me like a child and him as a man." He shot a cruel glance toward Darshima. "You say he killed both of those beasts at the same time?" He smirked, then let out a wry chuckle. Ero glared at Darshima and Sasha for a moment, then marched toward a vacant patch of grass, rudely brushing past them. Darshima's blood surged in anger at the slight. As he started toward Ero, Sasha stepped in front of him.

"Confronting him isn't worth your time. You mustn't let him provoke you." Sasha's hands clamped firmly upon Darshima's shoulders.

"You're right." Darshima let out a sigh as he composed himself. He drew in a deep breath and tried to let his anger subside.

The sun dipped below the horizon and the skies darkened. Sasha, Darshima, and several others set about building a fire with bits of dry brush and branches they had gathered from around the clearing. The temperature had decreased considerably, and the cool, humid air was a welcome change. Together, they piled the materials in a small pit at the center of the camp. Sasha then set it ablaze with a metal lighter he retrieved from his pocket. The pile rapidly transformed into a tower of bright yellow flame, casting the clearing in its warm glow.

The hunters partook in a simple meal of cured meat they had brought with them and gathered roots, grilled over the open flame. Though some were tempted to cook one of the prized powilix, tradition forbade the consumption of the beasts during the hunt. Darshima watched in silence as the others ate and chatted. His appetite had disappeared, and the thought of food made him queasy. Both the outcome of the hunt and Sasha's false tale weighed on his mind, settling anxiously in the pit of his stomach.

The conversations between the young men slowed as the exhaustion from their hike caught up with them. The hunters finished their meal and made their way to comfortable spots around the fire. They unrolled their woven fiber pallets and drifted off to sleep. Resting upon his side with Sasha nearby, Darshima tried to settle in for the night. Every time he felt himself drifting off to sleep, Sasha's lie resurfaced in the corners of his mind and jolted him awake. He let out a frustrated sigh, rolled onto his back and stared up at the night sky, the triplet of moons obscured by wisps of fog.

"Sasha, why did you do it?" whispered Darshima. Sasha stirred for a moment and drew in a sleepy breath.

"What are you talking about?" he asked groggily.

"Why did you tell everyone that I was the one who killed those powilix?" Darshima anxiously bit his lip as he felt Sasha processing his words.

"Don't worry about it. You will get your first kill soon enough," he murmured. Sasha's words failing to reassure him, Darshima drew in an anxious breath.

"I was so close. If it hadn't for that flimsy bow," whispered Darshima, his voice filled with frustration.

"You did find and stalk the beasts, so you did help kill them." Sasha turn onto his side and faced Darshima, his amber eyes gleaming softly in the firelight.

"I'm being serious, Sasha." Darshima huffed angrily. He rose to his feet, dusted himself off, and walked toward the edge of the camp. He shuffled to a stop, sat upon the damp blades of grass, and stared at the moonlit vista before him. The spires and domes of the city poked through the thinning shroud of fog. The river had calmed some, its waters gently breaking against the rocky banks in a hushed murmur.

Darshima stared at the water, taking comfort in the solitude of the night. The sporadic pop and crackle of the roaring fire teased his ears, and its radiant warmth spread against the bare skin of his back. He wrapped his arms around his knees and rested his forehead upon his wrists. He drew in a breath, the cool evening air mingling with the pungent odor of his sweat and the subtle, leathery musk of his gauntlet. The soft sound of approaching footsteps filled his ears. He lifted his head and looked over his shoulder to see Sasha standing behind him. He glumly turned back toward the river. Sasha sat down upon the grass beside him, amid the swirling mists.

"What's the matter with you?" he asked. Though Sasha was usually even-tempered, his voice held a note of frustration.

"It's nothing," said Darshima, his voice barely audible. As he began to stand up, Sasha gently grasped his arm and pulled him back down. Darshima glared at him, then turned toward the river. He looked away as Sasha tried to catch his gaze.

"You've acted strangely this entire hunt," said Sasha.

"I'm fine," whispered Darshima. His eyes lingered upon the currents rippling under the moonlight.

"You're not fine. Whenever you want to talk about it, I'm here." Sasha reclined upon the grass.

"Okay," muttered Darshima.

"We have a long journey ahead of us tomorrow. You should get some rest." Sasha patted Darshima's shoulder and let out a yawn. He rose to his feet, walked back to the campfire, and settled upon on his pallet.

Darshima gazed homeward, the light winds blowing his wavy locks before his eyes. He listened to the sounds of the surging waters, trying to find a sense of calm. His mind was much too restless for sleep. His chest tightened as renewed feelings of failure came over him. It was his third time trying and his third time failing. He couldn't understand why success continued to elude him. He had blamed the faulty bow, but he was beginning to believe that it was something more.

He couldn't understand what faults within him kept holding him back, when so many of his peers had long ago succeeded. Darshima stared into the night, his thoughts lost amid the billowing mists. He didn't know what he would tell his parents about his latest attempt. They would surely be disappointed, but his own disappointment was much greater.

Chapter Three

The loud, clear blasts of a horn roused Darshima from a fitful bout of sleep. He lifted his head from the ground, then settled back down. The horn sounded a second time, and Darshima jolted upright to see Sasha standing with the curved bronze instrument pressed to his lips. Darshima looked around him and realized that he had fallen asleep where he rested the night before. He sat up and stretched the muscles of his back, which ached from reclining upon the stiff ground. Sasha blew the horn a third time, letting out another powerful, earsplitting note. Darshima rubbed his bleary eyes, rose to his feet, and shook the damp blades of grass from his hair.

Instrument in hand, Sasha stood in the center of the camp beside the fire pit. The blaze from the night before had extinguished itself, and only the smoking ashes remained. He looked across the river, with his gaze fixed toward Ardavia. The fog had cleared and the early morning sunlight shimmered upon the rippling waters. A loud fanfare from the direction of the city returned his call, the brassy harmonies just audible over the rushing current.

By the end of the communication, everyone was up and moving about, preparing for the journey back home. Darshima rolled up his pallet, grabbed his equipment, and placed them in his camping pack. With their belongings secured, they set out toward Ardavia. The city's bejeweled domes and gleaming palaces shone brightly under the blazing sun and seemed to beckon them.

Led by Sasha, they marched in a single line upon the steep trail. Darshima followed closely behind his brother as they descended, carefully stepping upon the rocky ground. With the strung carcasses balanced upon their shoulders and their hunting gear stowed upon their backs, they made their way through the valleys, toward the rugged banks of the river. To break the tedium of the journey, they chanted lyrics from ancient tales about the fabled hunt. Like all Gordanellans, they learned them as children and the words stayed with them.

Darshima half-listened as they trekked, his thoughts consumed with the turmoil awaiting him back home. His mind searched for some way to explain the events of the hunt to his father and mother. As they walked, Sasha's deep, melodic voice rang out with a particular lyric that caught his attention.

"...The beasts wouldn't relent, and they failed in their attempt. Their efforts were brave, their honor saved," sang Sasha. The other hunters echoed him as he continued. "Gracious in defeat, they prepared for harder trials they would yet meet." Darshima lifted his head, his heart rising into his throat as he listened to the words. Sasha briefly glanced over his shoulder at Darshima and offered a conciliatory smile. Many of the fables weren't about victories, but of defeat. Darshima returned his brother's gesture with a timid nod. He walked onward, shouldering the load with Sasha, the lyrics giving him some solace.

By late morning, they arrived at the water's edge. Sasha led them along a narrow stone jetty, where a large, spindle-shaped wooden sailboat piloted by a uniformed mariner awaited them. The craft bobbed gently amid the ripples, and its freshly painted, red hull gleamed in the sunlight. The mariner, a thin-framed man with ear-length black hair, copper-colored skin, and amber eyes, wore a traditional sleeveless orange tunic, black breeches and a white and silver billed cap.

Traveling by sea was quite a novelty for the young men, as air travel had been the standard mode of transportation for ages. Tradition dictated that they return to Ardavia by sea. Waterborne craft were only used for the heaviest of freight and for ceremonial occasions such as the hunt. The men who piloted the ships for the hunting parties were experienced volunteers. They were revered for their knowledge of the river and for upholding this important Gordanellan custom.

The hunters loaded the carcasses and their belongings at the rear of the large craft, and settled upon the rows of rough wooden benches. The mariner yanked a lever between his bare feet, which pulled up the anchor, then released the mooring ropes tying the boat to the jetty. The boat rocked gently back and forth amid the ripples. He then pulled a silver cord that unfurled a hexagonal array of giant, red sails along its single mast. The stiff breeze filled the angled cloth panels, and the craft lurched away from the shore, heading into the choppy blue waters.

Darshima took his seat next to Sasha and drew in a deep breath of the crisp air. He cast an eye ahead, barely making out the opposite shore of the wide river. The silhouette of the city appeared atop the line of imposing pillars just upon the horizon, growing larger as they approached. In the distance, he spied a dozen other sail ships, filled with hunters traveling in the same direction. The voyage back was perhaps his favorite part of the hunting trip. Darshima closed his eyes and let the sound of the flowing water fill his ears. He could feel his pulse slow down and his worries dissipate.

The ship drifted along the river, bobbing with the churning currents. The mariner deftly tugged upon a web of silver cables, and maneuvered the gleaming copper steering wheel before him. The complex array of sails changed subtly, their geometric forms rotating with the wind. As they drew nearer to the city, its cluster of towering island plateaus loomed overhead. The colossal, rocky formations blotted out the sunlight and cast immense shadows upon the river.

The ship glided past a curtain of cascades gushing from the rock faces above and jostled violently in its wake. The passengers huddled together and braced themselves against the turbulence. Some grew visibly sick, and others gripped tightly to the sides of the craft. Neither Darshima nor Sasha were bothered by the commotion. Darshima caught a glimpse of Ero, who looked worse than the rest. Drenched in a cold sweat, he retched and shuddered as the ship skimmed the choppy waters. Seated beside him, Seth's eyes widened in concern as he observed Ero's condition.

"We're almost home, Ero." Seth put an arm around his shoulder and drew him nearer, trying to comfort him. Darshima felt a pang of empathy for Ero in his moment of vulnerability and chided himself for their tense interaction back at the campsite.

Darshima stole a glance at Sasha, whose face bore a look of serenity as he gazed out upon the water. Darshima peered up at the city towering over them, its spires shimmering against the bright sky. As he beheld the majestic sight, a creeping sense of dread rose within him. His chest tightened as he contemplated his parents' possible reactions to the outcome of the hunt.

When they had set out earlier that week, both he and Sasha had assured their mother and father that he would succeed. They would certainly be pleased with Sasha for leading another successful expedition. Under his guidance, the hunting party had killed forty powilix, a record number. Darshima didn't know what his parents would think of him. He would once again be coming home empty-handed. He needed to find a way to explain the dangerous predicament he had faced, and why he had failed yet again. Darshima vigorously shook his head as the memory of the two beasts chasing him hung vividly before his eyes. As he reflected upon the events of that evening, the meaning of Sasha's words only became clearer. He had been unprepared.

The steady gust of wind from the waters rippled against Darshima's breeches and pricked the bare skin of his back, rousing him from his thoughts. With a steady hand, the mariner skillfully guided the ship around the jagged rocks and treacherous, churning whirlpools. He spun the wheel and the craft made a wide arc, veering toward the rugged, granite cliffs of the central plateau. The ship rocked as they approached a misty line of cascades, its turbulent waters veiling the entrance of an immense cave.

The sound of the flowing currents steadily grew into a deafening roar. Torrents of water spilled into the craft, tossing it violently back and forth. The hunters grasped tightly onto its sides as they sailed under the waterfall. They tumbled about, holding their breath against the thunderous deluge. The force of the cascades overpowered several of the young men, who fell from their seats and into the surrounding waters. Amid ripples of laughter at their clumsiness, Darshima, Sasha and the other hunters reached out and pulled them back aboard.

"Come on everyone, we're almost there. Try not to hurt yourselves," said Sasha, his voice ricocheting throughout the dim chamber.

The craft soon steadied and they drifted deeper into the cave. Catching his breath, Darshima found himself both calmed and disoriented by the echoing rush of the cascades. They settled themselves back into their seats and checked to see that their prized cargo remained intact. With their cupped hands, Darshima and the other hunters reached below the benches and bailed the water from the bottom of the ship. The light gradually faded to darkness as they moved away from the entrance, and the roar of the water diminished. Darshima could barely see the other passengers amid the shadows.

"Please prepare yourselves for the ascent to Ardavia." The mariner brought the craft to a gentle stop. He pulled down the sails with a tug of the cord. With a hushed mechanical whir, the mast telescoped downward into a recess at the center of the ship.

Darshima drew in an anxious breath and awaited the next moments. The mariner picked up a long copper rod from the bottom of the craft and probed the darkness. He tapped firmly against the rock face beside the vessel and waited patiently. Just above the lapping noises of the water, a faint rapping sound echoed throughout the cave in response. The mariner tapped against the wall once more, mimicking the same steady rhythm. He rested the rod neatly between his feet and sat down upon his bench. He then faced the young men, the groan of clicking metal gears and grinding stone filling the silence between them.

Darshima's pulse thudded in anticipation as he looked around. In the dim light, he could just make out the features of the mariner's stoic face. The echo of the gears faded, followed by the loud, deep thud of a closing door reverberating throughout the chamber. The sound of flowing water started as a trickle and steadily grew louder.

"Please secure yourselves," shouted the mariner, his voice barely audible above the roar. The young men followed his order and fastened the thick fiber ropes bolted into the benches around their waists. They grabbed onto the handles hewn into the sides of the craft and braced themselves as a torrent of water surged into the chamber.

The ship jolted upward under the thrust of the rapidly rising current, scraping against the rocky faces of the shaft. Darshima clenched his teeth and narrowed his eyes against the icy spray. The deafening rush overwhelmed the narrow space, and the hunters held on tightly as the craft ascended. The only thing that remained motionless as they careened upward was the stern expression of the mariner, barely visible amid the shifting shadows.

Darshima held his breath, and a momentary grin spread upon his lips. His heart pounded in his chest as they vaulted up the passage. Though others typically dreaded this part of the journey, he found it exhilarating. It almost felt as if he were flying. The darkness steadily receded as the craft rose atop the column of water.

Before long, he could see the walls of the shaft moving rapidly all around them, giving him more reason to hold on even tighter. His soaked breeches flapped in the violent gusts as they shot upward. The light grew brighter, and the speed of the rushing water slowed to a soft gurgle as the ship reached the top of the well. Darshima breathed a sigh of relief, and several others let out excited yelps and howls.

They emerged through a portal and into a large, tiled circular basin, located at the center of an airy terminal. The current from the water gently nudged the vessel toward the rim. The mariner secured the mooring cables to a stone bollard and extended a wooden plank onto the basin's edge. Darshima and the other young men unbelted themselves and gathered their belongings. They thanked the mariner and then disembarked along the plank. With the wrapped carcasses upon their shoulders and their gear and equipment in tow, they walked toward the entrance of the building. The sound of rushing water filled the air of the cavernous structure as several other basins received ships from the river below.

Though Darshima had been here many times before, he was nonetheless amazed by this place. A small smile crossed his lips as childhood memories of standing beside these very basins came to him. Like Sasha, their father was a skilled hunter and led many trips during his youth. As children, Darshima, Sasha along with their mother would await their father's return from his hunting trips beside the basins. Darshima's smile dissolved as feelings of inadequacy welled up within him. Like their father, Sasha had been able to complete the hunting rite and lead others in the tradition. Darshima realized that he was nowhere near to achieving such an accomplishment.

Trying to ignore his thoughts, Darshima lagged a few steps behind the others and focused on the varied architectural details of the building. His eyes lingered upon the chipped marble tiles and the forest of enormous, fluted stone pillars supporting the multi-hued glass canopy. He craned his head upward to see a flock of colorful birds flying high overhead, their flapping wings, and whistling breaking through the din. They darted skillfully among the finely carved arches supporting the ovoid roof, making their way to their nests tucked between the worn stones.

"Darshima, you're falling behind," said Sasha, his voice echoing loudly through the terminal. Darshima snapped his head forward to see Sasha and the others rolling their eyes at him. Embarrassed, he cast his gaze toward the ground. Struggling with the heavy sacks upon his shoulders, he walked faster and caught up with them.

The group of hunters moved past the grand, circular colonnade of the entrance and into the humid afternoon. Darshima drew in a breath as a gentle breeze carried the fresh scent of the river, offering a momentary respite from the heat. He waited with the other hunters under the stone arches, the large shadow of the building shading them from the intense rays of sunlight. A triplet of gleaming domes loomed overhead, appearing to nudge the billowy white clouds aside.

"Congratulations to you all on a successful hunt this season." Sasha nodded earnestly toward the young men as they surrounded him. "I am sure your families will be proud of you." They applauded, let out an enthusiastic cheer, and thanked him.

"We couldn't have done it without you," exclaimed one of the hunters. Several of them shook Sasha's hands, and a few reached over and embraced him. A reserved smile crossed Darshima's lips as he saw how much the young men respected his brother. Despite his own frustrations with the hunt, he couldn't help but be proud of Sasha.

The young men worked in pairs, claiming their carcasses and hanging the thick fabric sacks upon the wooden poles. They lingered in conversation, reluctant to part ways. The hunters had bonded during their time together and shared many unforgettable memories. Darshima stood silently as they relived their successes. Their words echoing in his mind, he anxiously bit his lip and mulled over what he would tell his parents.

The afternoon sun moved slowly across the sky, and the group parted ways, but not before promising to meet up again someday soon. Sasha and Darshima were the last ones to leave the terminal. They grabbed their belongings, balanced the carcasses between them, and set out for home. Darshima followed Sasha through the teeming crowds, and they wove their way through the heavy foot traffic upon the dark cobbled stones of the sidewalk. Gleaming, four-wheeled metal vehicles rumbled in the streets beside them, the low hum of their engines filling the air.

Crowds of brown and copper-skinned people moved along the narrow streets between the richly carved, pale stone buildings, taking care of their daily errands. They made purchases and haggled with the crush of vendors stationed in colorful wooden stalls lining the road, engaging in lively bursts of conversation. The men were dressed in simple fabric breeches, in hues of black, red and tan. The older men wore vests with the arms exposed and the younger men were mostly bare-chested. Their hair, colored in varying shades of black and brown, was shorn at different lengths between the neck and the shoulder.

The women were dressed in vividly patterned robes that draped their calves, and embroidered blouses that exposed the shoulders and the midriff. The younger women wrapped their necks in bright fabric scarves that fluttered in the lazy afternoon breeze. They fashioned their dark, silky hair in a thick braid that hung down their backs, and they wore glittering jewels and gold studs in their earlobes and noses. Some of them carried infants upon their backs, wrapped in multicolored swaddling cloths. Many of the older women wore thick gold bracelets upon their wrists and ankles that clinked delicately as they moved.

Darshima and Sasha, laden with their hunting gear and the carcasses, bumped against the crush of pedestrians as they walked home. People looked upon them with admiration, cheering as they passed, shaking their hands and jovially slapping them upon their backs. Sasha offered an earnest smile and thanked as many of them as he could. He looked over his shoulder and winked at Darshima, who returned his gesture with a frown. Sasha's lie was weighing upon him, and it grew heavier as they neared home.

The exhaustion of the journey caught up with Darshima, and he felt weary under the withering heat of the afternoon. Despite his effort, he lagged a few steps behind Sasha.

"Darshima, you must keep up or else we are going to drop our things." Sasha shot a frustrated glance at him.

"I'm sorry, but I'm tired. Maybe we can hire a coach to help us," muttered Darshima. He knew the tradition dictated that they carry the carcasses home by foot, but fatigue and frustration had loosened his tongue, and he asked anyway.

"You already know the answer to that question. Don't be so impetuous." Sasha let out a groan. "I'm tired too." Sensing his brother's growing discontent, Darshima picked up his pace and remained silent.

They arrived at a rectangular field near their home and walked upon the inviting green lawns. Darshima breathed in deeply at the scent of the freshly cut grass and looked around him. The field was home to a pair of majestic, hexagonal stone temples that stood in the center, opposite one another. Their gleaming white, carved marble domes loomed over a web of cobbled pathways and gardens. The temples were a focal point for the neighborhood and hosted many religious ceremonies, both festive and solemn. It was a peaceful place that had seen many an impromptu gathering. It was a place that Darshima and Sasha had known since they were young.

The grounds hummed with activity amid the humid afternoon. Small groups of bearded priests wandered barefoot upon the stone paths among the crowds. They wore vivid orange robes with the right shoulder exposed and wrapped their long hair in white turbans. Delicate chains of glass beads, in hues of blue and red, hung about their necks, glistening in the sunlight. The dark copper skin of their arms and shoulders was covered in intricate, flowing patterns of ochre and red inks to commemorate a recent holy observance.

The priests chanted prayers as they walked, stopping to greet many of the visitors. They carried silver, cylindrical censers on chains that billowed fragrant red smoke, and they wore bronze bells upon their ankles that chimed softly with each step. They gently swayed the censers over the men and women seated upon the marble stairs of the temple, and the groups of people reclining upon the lawns. This gesture was a common rite of benediction for those that entered this sacred space.

Darshima and Sasha picked a vacant spot upon the grass and gently lay down their cargo. Darshima sat upon the verdant carpet, and Sasha settled beside him. Darshima let out a deep sigh, thankful for a moment's rest. A contemplative frown crossed his lips.

"I can tell that your mind is somewhere else. What's troubling you, Darshima?" Sasha's brow furrowed as he noticed Darshima's subdued mood.

"Honestly I'm fine." He shrugged.

"You're not fine, and you've been sullen this entire trip. We're almost home, but we're taking a break on your account." Sasha looked intently upon him. Darshima stared at his hands, trying to avoid his brother's gaze. He could tell that Sasha was growing more frustrated with him. Darshima imagined that the exhaustion of the hunt and the long journey back home had eroded his usually abundant patience.

"You lied to everyone about what really happened during the hunt. What are we going to tell mother and father?" Darshima stared at him, then looked around furtively to make sure he hadn't been overheard.

"We will tell them what I've been telling everyone." Sasha reached toward the ground, grabbed a blade of grass, and idly twisted it between his fingers. "Anyhow, it was both of our efforts that led to a successful kill."

"Father will be able to see through any of your tales." Darshima folded his arms across his chest.

"Mother and father will be disappointed in you, Darshima. You have failed again this hunting season." A concerned frown crossed Sasha's lips.

"There will be other seasons." Darshima shook his head and tried to avoid his brother's stare. "I just need another chance."

"This is your third try. What makes you think that you will succeed on a fourth or a fifth hunting trip?" asked Sasha, his voice bearing a note of exasperation. Darshima shot an angry glance at him and scowled.

"I will succeed somehow!" Darshima firmly struck the ground with an open hand in frustration.

"Calm yourself." Sasha winced at Darshima's sudden change in countenance.

"It's an old-fashioned tradition anyway." Darshima shook his head and muttered under his breath, but he could tell that Sasha had heard him clearly.

"It's an important tradition and a matter of family pride." Sasha's eyebrows arched in disbelief. "What will father and mother tell our family when they learn that you haven't yet killed a powilix?" he sighed.

"I'll think of something," whispered Darshima.

The hunt was more than an old tradition to most Gordanellans. The success of a young man or lack thereof reflected upon the standing of his entire family. Darshima's failure on the hunt was considered an embarrassment to his parents and their relatives. Young men who didn't succeed on the hunt were frequently overlooked for work. They were not considered eligible suitors, often remaining isolated and unmarried. Neither children nor men, they struggled at the margins of society.

"You will have to take it more seriously next time." Sasha shook his head, then pointed to Darshima's arm. "The hunt is over, why are you still wearing your gauntlet?"

"I'll take it off then." Darshima's eyes drifted to the dark leather garment upon his arm. He let out a frustrated sigh as vivid images of the beasts chasing him through the marshes appeared before his eyes, and then evaporated. Another hunting season had concluded, and again he had nothing to show for it.

Darshima slowly unfastened the round metal clasps along its seam and removed the gauntlet. He then reached over and placed it into his camping pack. He settled back down and stared at the fine, flowing lines inscribed upon the skin of his right arm. The deep blue marks began subtly at the bases of his fingernails and grew increasingly bold as they wound in an intricate, tessellated pattern up his forearm, stopping abruptly at his elbow. He idly traced the lines with a finger, and gazed at the scene before them.

"Doesn't their disappointment ever upset you?" asked Sasha. Darshima didn't know how to respond. Though it weighed upon him, he had grown accustomed to his family's displeasure. He felt that failing yet another time wouldn't change much.

"It does, but what can I do?" Darshima shrugged his shoulders. Sasha stared at the grass around him and shook his head in frustration. He opened his mouth to speak, but fell silent.

Darshima gazed toward the pair of shrines to see a trio of priests approaching them. They came to a stop beside them and chanted softly, their voices mingling with the steady winds and the chatter of the crowds. Their arms extended, the priests waved the censers over both of them and the carcasses. Darshima and Sasha closed their eyes and bowed their heads in deference as the priests offered their blessing.

Amid the chanting, Darshima furtively opened an eye. He glimpsed at the billowing cylinders, swinging slowly between him and his brother. They moved in exaggerated and opposing arcs, like gleaming pendulums. He drew in a deep breath of the sweet, charred aroma and let out a sigh. Through the tendrils of smoke, Darshima saw a solemn frown spread across Sasha's lips as he murmured a prayer. He could sense that Sasha was growing weary of trying to help him, but he didn't know what else to do. The priests issued a rousing, harmonious shout to conclude their blessing, and then moved to another group.

As the haze cleared, Sasha threw the bits of grass back to the ground and patted Darshima's shoulder.

"Let's get going, we've spent enough time here." Sasha jumped to his feet and dusted off his breeches. Darshima rose up and joined him. They gathered their belongings and continued home in silence.

Chapter Four

The late afternoon sun burned brightly as it drifted toward the horizon. The triplet of moons hung high above, their bold crescents glowing against the darkening sky. Darshima eyed the neat rows of modest brick and stone two-story houses lining the path. Their large sloped, slate roofs offered shade to the small gardens surrounding each dwelling. A gentle wind stirred the drooping branches of the gnarled trees lining the cobblestone road.

They walked along the worn stone footpath leading to the porch of their home, protected by the roof's broad eaves. Darshima's chest tightened as a wave of anxiety came over him. With the carcasses and their packs in tow, they trudged up the wide stairway. Darshima caught a glimpse of his distorted reflection in the pane of beveled glass encased in the wooden front door. The polished surface shone a brilliant shade of orange in the fading light.

As they laid down the carcasses and their packs, the door creaked open and their father, Sovani stepped onto the smooth tiles of the porch.

"Welcome home," exclaimed Sovani. A tall muscular man, his skin was a deep shade of copper. His black breeches and red armless tunic rippled in the steady breeze. His arms resting at his sides, he cast an appraising look upon his sons. His brow knitted in a contemplative expression, he knelt beside the brown sacks and carefully untied them. His amber eyes burned intensely as he inspected the carcasses.

He swept his shoulder-length locks of black hair from his face. "They are quite impressive." A discerning frown crossed his lips as he ran a hand along the hide of one of the animals. Darshima eyed Sasha, who rhythmically clenched his jaw as he looked at their father.

"Darshima did an excellent job during the hunt," said Sasha, the confident tone in his voice faltering ever so slightly. Sovani rose to his feet and faced Sasha.

"Darshima caught these you say?" He turned to Darshima, an astonished smile crossing his lips.

As Sasha spun the tale of Darshima's success, Sovani's smile steadily dissolved into a weary frown. He raised his hand, and Sasha fell silent. "Sasha, we both know that this incredible tale did not happen. Only the most experienced hunters can kill two powilix at once. Tell me the truth." He let out a resigned sigh.

"You are right father, I had no choice but to kill the beasts. Darshima spent the whole evening tracking them, but they charged him. He came so close this time." Sasha bowed his head, his face drawn in a somber expression.

"I tried my best," stammered Darshima. His stomach sank as he registered his father's disappointment. Sovani looked to the sky and put a finger upon his temple. He pursed his lips and then turned back to Sasha.

"I am not upset with you, Sasha. You did what any good brother would do." Sovani gently nudged him under the chin. He then turned to Darshima and narrowed his eyes in a harsh stare. "Darshima, you're lucky to have a brother who is willing to risk his life to help you, despite your failures." Sovani grabbed Sasha's camping pack and hoisted it upon his shoulder. Sasha then reached for Darshima's pack and lifted it from the ground.

"You mustn't do everything for Darshima. He should carry his own things." Sovani's brow wrinkled in frustration.

"Really it's fine, father. He's exhausted from the trip." Sasha pulled the pack over his shoulders.

"Don't just stand idly there, Darshima. Take the carcasses to the storeroom," muttered Sovani as he glared at him. He rested a hand upon Sasha's back and ushered him through the door. Sasha looked over his shoulder and tried to catch Darshima's gaze, but Darshima turned away and avoided him.

Sovani and Sasha stepped into the hallway and shut the door firmly behind them, slamming it with a thud that sent a jolt through Darshima. He stood on the porch and faced the closed door, his heart thudding as the tense encounter replayed in his mind. He had expected their father's disappointment, but it somehow felt worse this time.

Darshima knelt beside the sacks, unstrung them from the wooden poles, and gripped the cumbersome items. He then dragged them down the porch stairs, along the cobbled footpath beside their home and into the walled garden behind the rear entrance. His hands gripping the rough fabric, he placed the sacks in front of a stone storehouse. With a heave, he opened the wooden door, brought them inside and rested the poles against the wall. After every hunt, he was responsible for preparing the carcasses for storage, a laborious task which he loathed.

Darshima held his breath and closed the door behind him as he stepped into the low building. Dark and humid, the stench of smoked wood, rank flesh and stale blood from hunting trips gone by filled his nostrils. Gagging on the pungent odor, he retched and briefly put a hand up to his mouth. As Darshima acclimated to the smell, he removed the carcasses from the fabric sacks and lifted them onto a scuffed stone table. He grabbed an old hunting knife from his belt and began his task, the dull blade making tough work of skinning and carving them.

After he finished dressing the carcasses, Darshima cleaned the knife upon the fabric of his breeches and stowed it back in his belt. He grappled with the heavy slabs of meat and bone, and carried them toward the back of the storehouse. Darshima pried open the metal shutters of the smoke locker, its aromatic heat radiating against his sweaty face. He fastened the glistening, sinewy portions upon a row of metal hooks, then firmly closed the shutters. His task finished, Darshima hurried out of the storehouse, and the heavy door slammed behind him. He walked back to the house, entered through the side entrance, and stepped into the washroom.

Darshima looked at his clouded reflection in the speckled, oval mirror and sighed. His gaze lingered on the streaks of mud caked upon his forehead and the circles of exhaustion around his eyes. He turned on the faucet and splashed a handful of cold water upon his face, shivering as the refreshing jolt coursed through him. He scrubbed the mud, blood, and grease from his hands and face with a cake of gritty soap beside the sink, but the scent of wild game still clung to him.

By the time Darshima made it to the dining room, Sovani, Sasha, and their mother, Dalia had just finished their meal. As he walked toward the rectangular glass table, Sovani abruptly rose from his seat and stomped out of the room, brushing past Darshima without so much as a glance. His pulse thudding, Darshima tried his best to ignore the slight.

Darshima pulled out the wooden chair beside his mother and sat down. Slender and of medium height, her smooth bronze skin and youthful, fine-featured face yielded nothing of her age. She wore a bright orange robe that revealed her shoulders. Her shiny, dark brown hair was fashioned in a thick braid that hung down her back.

Sovani stood at the threshold and glared at them.

"Dalia, Sasha let's retire to the garden for the evening." He motioned for them to join him. Sasha obediently rose from the table and walked toward his father, hesitantly avoiding Darshima's stare.

"You both go and I'll stay here." Dalia smiled curtly at them. She wrapped her arms around Darshima's weary shoulders. Sovani stood in the doorway, his jaw set and his muscular arms folded sternly across his chest.

"Dalia..." he began, but she interjected.

"Darshima hasn't eaten yet. I will join you both in a little while." She firmly rested her hands upon the table. Sovani's frown softened slightly as he stared at her, seated beside Darshima.

"I will wait for you." His eyes lingered upon her for a moment, and then he left, ushering Sasha ahead of him.

Darshima let out a long sigh and slumped forward, resting his forehead upon the table's cool surface. Light from the setting sun flooded the dining room windows and cast shimmering rays through its thick glass, giving it a subtle glow. He drew in a deep breath as the stress from the hunting trip eased a bit. His mother's presence always had a way of calming him down when he was anxious.

"Your father is in one of his moods today." She gently rested her hand upon the back of Darshima's tense neck.

"He is never in a good mood when I'm around," muttered Darshima. He lifted his head and gazed sullenly at her.

"How was the hunt this time?" She knitted her brow in a contemplative expression.

"I failed again." Darshima let out a soft groan and rested his forehead back upon the table.

"What happened?" she asked, her voice rising with concern.

"I don't know. I did everything I could, but I wasn't prepared," he whispered into the glass, his breath fogging its smooth surface.

"I'm sure you tried your very best." She gently rubbed his shoulders. Dalia then rose from her seat and headed into the adjoining kitchen, her robe flowing behind her.

The sound of an object clinking against the table pricked Darshima's ears, and his nostrils filled with a delicious, spicy odor. He lifted his head to see a clay plate heaped with sizzling meat and vegetables. She placed a glass of water beside the plate, handed him a copper fork, and then resumed her seat beside him. Darshima tucked into the plate, hastily shoveling the food into his mouth. He hadn't realized how hungry he was.

"You clearly haven't eaten these past few days," she murmured.

"I didn't have time," he said, speaking in a garbled voice between bites.

"You look like you've lost weight." She gently pinched the back of his arm and he winced at the sensation. Her eyes widened in modest surprise as she watched him steadily clear his plate. A wistful frown crossed her lips, and she sighed softly.

"Your father may be upset, but he cares about you, Darshima." She fidgeted with the delicate silver bracelets upon her wrist. "He would never admit it, but he can be sensitive at times." Darshima ruminated on her words as he finished the last scraps of food.

"He's really disappointed in me. I wish he knew how hard I tried this time," whispered Darshima. His chest grew heavy with a sense of despair as he thought anew of his failure. His eyes growing damp, he pushed his empty plate across the smooth glass, rose to his feet and started toward the door.

"Darshima, wait," she said firmly. Her voice held a familiar resoluteness that caught his ears, and he turned toward her. She stood up from the table and calmly approached him. She looked at him with her large amber eyes, rested her hands upon his shoulders, and stared at him as if searching for something. He avoided her gaze and looked to the scuffed stone tiles at his feet. "You will succeed when the time is right." She nudged him under the chin, stepped back toward the table and picked up his plate. "Someday you will make your own path and be recognized, just like your brother." An earnest smile crossed her lips. Darshima stood silently and stared at her as she worked. His heart thudded as a wave of disappointment rose within him.

"Why must everything be such a struggle for me?" he asked, his voice heavy with sadness.

"Have patience, Darshima. Your day will come, but you must keep trying." Her lips wrinkled into a concerned frown as she saw the change in his countenance.

"I will try, mother." Darshima's shoulders slumped as he contemplated her words. He then joined her at the table, and they finished clearing it together.

Chapter Five

The cloudy skies cast a muted grey light over the cityscape, and a damp shroud of mist hung in the warm air. His gaze aimed downward, Darshima trudged along the street amid the bustle of the late afternoon crowd, his leather moccasins sliding upon the slick cobbled stones. It had been a long day of lectures on imperial civics and Gordanellan geography. In his first years as a student, he found the subjects interesting. He was nearly at the end of his formal studies and now found these lectures somewhat interminable.

Darshima stifled a yawn as he walked briskly among the crowds, shaking his head to stave off the fatigue. He hoisted his cloth satchel upon his shoulder as he wove his way through the throngs of harried pedestrians in their colorful attire. The mists soaking him, he adjusted the thin red fabric of his damp armless tunic and tugged at the worn leather belt supporting his black breeches. Still exhausted from the hunting trip, he had struggled to stay awake for the lectures and was simply thankful to be heading home. Most of his classmates had also taken leave to go hunting, and during class, he had listened to the accounts of their adventures.

He walked upon the wet grass of the temple grounds, the pair of marble domes partly obscured by the cloudy skies. His eyes narrowed as he recalled the impressive stories he had heard throughout the day. People his age were leading their first expeditions, not participating in them. Their success made him acutely aware of his failure, and he had kept quiet during his classes. It would be only a matter of time before his peers found out what had truly happened during the hunt. Ero and the other members of the party had seen through Sasha's tale and had drawn their own conclusions about Darshima and his abilities. He was sure they would eventually reveal the truth.

Darshima walked slowly along the winding path through his neighborhood and reached home. He stood upon the paved walkway and drew in a nervous breath. A day had passed since his return from the hunt, and he hoped that his father would be in a better mood. He trudged up the stairs of the porch, through the front door and into the dim hallway. His moccasins padded softly against the dull tiles as he headed toward his room at the back of the house. As he passed by the kitchen, he ducked his head into the doorway.

"Good evening, mother and father." He offered a brief wave to his parents, who sat at an oval wooden table in the midst of a conversation. Sovani wore black breeches and a beige armless tunic. He lifted his head and offered a curt nod, the lines of his face drawn in a stern expression. Dalia, wearing a red robe with the shoulders exposed, greeted him with a bright smile.

"How are you, Darshima?" Her brow furrowed with concern as she saw the tension upon his face.

"I'm fine," he replied softly. Not wanting to further interrupt them, he continued down the hallway and opened the door to his room. He closed it softly behind him and then collapsed onto his bed, not even making the effort to remove his damp clothes. He lay still and basked in the moment of calm.

Darshima looked up lazily at the ceiling, the white plaster covered in a thin film of dust. Soft beams of reddish-grey light filtered through the small windows above his bed, casting the modest space in a dull glow. The muffled sound of his parents' conversation crept under the wooden door. His pulse quickened when he heard his father mention his name. His eyes darted toward the door, and he held his breath. His mind raced as he tried to think of what chore he didn't finish or detail he had missed. Despite his best efforts, he often fell short of his father's expectations.

Their conversation quieted down, and Darshima exhaled a sigh of relief. He reluctantly rose from the bed, removed his moccasins, peeled off his damp clothes, and threw them onto the floor. He grabbed a clean pair of grey linen breeches from an old wooden wardrobe braced against the wall, pulled them on, and lay back down. He let out a contented sigh as he felt the cool bedsheets against the bare skin of his back.

As he drifted off to sleep, the walls unexpectedly shuddered under the boom of a harmonious fanfare. His heart thudding, Darshima jumped to his feet. He slipped his moccasins back on, and opened the door. He cautiously walked down the hallway to see Sovani and Dalia standing at the front entrance.

Sovani gripped the door handle and looked through the glass pane, his eyes widened in an expression of curiosity. He slowly pulled it open and a gust of wind entered, rippling over their garments.

"Greetings Mr. and Mrs. Eweryn," called several deep voices. Three tall, lanky men ascended the steps and stood before them. Their smooth, dark skin was the color of midnight and their heads and faces were shaven. They beheld Sovani and Dalia with their piercing, cloud-grey eyes. Their striking features revealed them as visitors from the neighboring moon, Ciblaithia. Wearing long blue embroidered tunics with the sleeves folded, white trousers trimmed in gold thread, and polished leather boots, they each carried rectangular leather cases at their sides. A troupe of a dozen men and women in similar dress stood at attention on the sidewalk behind them, holding curved silver horns in their hands. Their fine costumes indicated their status as official messengers of the royal family.

The clouds had parted, and the late afternoon sun hung above the misty horizon, glowing softly above the stately lines of steeples and domes in the distance. Sovani eyed the group, and an unexpected smile crossed his lips.

"Good evening." He offered a polite nod.

Case in hand, the lead messenger stepped forward. The chiseled features of his square-shaped face bore a serious look, but his rich, baritone voice exuded a sense of cheer.

"Good evening sir, madam. We come bearing a message of goodwill from The Vilides for Mr. Sasha Eweryn," he said. Sovani looked over his shoulder and excitedly motioned for Darshima to summon his brother. Darshima turned around, trudged up the staircase and pounded on Sasha's door. Moments later, they bounded down the stairs and joined their parents at the entrance. Sasha, dressed in a simple red sleeveless tunic and black breeches, stepped in front of his family and faced the men. Realizing who they were, he hastily adjusted his garments.

"Good evening Sasha, we are messengers sent on behalf of the Prince of The Vilides." The lead messenger bowed politely. Sasha nodded cautiously as he listened to the man's pronouncement. He reached into his case, retrieved a finely engraved golden cylinder, and gently placed it in Sasha's hands.

"The prince has requested your attendance at his annual birthday celebration. Your peers have recognized your intelligence and leadership and have nominated you to attend. The prince would be honored by your presence." Sasha's eyes widened in incredulity as he carefully cradled the golden vessel.

"Thank you, I gratefully accept." Sasha held the invitation tightly to his chest and humbly bowed his head. Dalia and Sovani clasped the messengers' hands and thanked them.

The group bid the family farewell, then walked down the footpath toward the road, their forms disappearing in the fading sunlight.

Sasha gently closed the door and turned around to meet the delighted expressions upon his parents' faces.

"Open it, the vessel must contain the invitation." Dalia excitedly gripped Sasha's arm. A look of surprise flashed across his face and dissolved into an embarrassed smile as he peered at the object.

Dalia and Sovani ushered Sasha to the dining room and guided him toward the table. Carefully cradling the gleaming cylinder, he sat in a chair near the window. Darshima trailed behind them and stood in the doorway. Their parents sat on either side of Sasha and put their arms around his shoulders, warmly embracing him.

Sasha carefully turned the cylinder in his hands, and an expression of genuine surprise spread upon his face.

"It's exquisite." He hefted the polished vessel as he inspected its details. Cast from an ingot of pure gold, its intricately filigreed surface shimmered in the waning rays of reddish sunlight. Sasha's name was engraved in flowing script upon the large, sturdy clasp.

"It's from the Vilidesian royal family, so it must be." Sovani's eyes narrowed appraisingly.

"I think this vessel must be the finest object in our house," whispered Dalia, her voice exuding a sense of awe. Sasha unfastened the clasp along the side of the hinged cylinder and pried its halves open. He pulled out a rich, blue fabric scroll and gently unfurled it upon the table. His fingers glided along its lustrous silk edges as he looked over its features. The embellished Vilidesian script appeared to be printed, but upon closer inspection, the words were embroidered with fine golden thread. It read:

Prince Khydius of The Vilides,
Master of Ciblaithia, Defender of Iberwight, Scion of the Royal House of Fyrenos, heir to the Vilidesian Realm, cordially invites Sasha Ewеryn, and his parents to a celebration marking his seventeenth year of life, to be held at the Royal Palace in The Vilides.

The invitation went on to describe the schedule of events and ceremonies. Sasha, Dalia, and Sovani eagerly read the text, contemplating each detail aloud. A royal invitation was a true honor and incredibly difficult to obtain. The fact that Sasha had been nominated, let alone selected to go to The Vilides showed that he was held in high esteem by his peers.

"I am so proud of you," said Sovani, his voice filled with emotion. He beamed at Sasha and drew him closer.

"Even amid your studies at university, you have done so much to earn this invitation. I am so happy." Dalia leaned over and kissed him upon the forehead.

"Thank you mother, father." Sasha's cheeks flushed with mild embarrassment. Darshima stared at Sasha, his pulse quickening as a pang of envy shot through him.

"Congratulations, Sasha." Darshima's eyes lingered upon the invitation as he marveled at his brother's fortune. It was exceedingly rare for regular, working families like theirs to be invited to a royal function, let alone one in The Vilides. Darshima turned back to the threshold, then briefly glanced over his shoulder to see them still pouring over the scroll. They were preoccupied and hadn't even heard him. Darshima let out a sigh and stepped out of the room.

He wasn't proud of it, but Darshima found himself becoming more distant from his brother as they grew older. For as far back as he could remember, his parents, particularly Sovani had bestowed their praise and attention on Sasha. He sometimes felt invisible to them. Sasha's invitation to the palace served to highlight their differences even more.

His thoughts growing heavy, Darshima walked through the kitchen, pushed open the side door, and stepped out into the warm evening. He made his way down the narrow, shrub-lined path beside the house. The broad stones of the tall fence shone a dusty grey in the shrouded moonlight. He looked up at the surrounding brick and stone homes of their neighborhood. They cast long, amorphous shadows into the darkened street that seemed to loom over him.

Darshima continued onto the main road, his sadness about the hunt lessening only somewhat. He traveled along the winding, cobbled path until it ended at the edge of a large field. He plodded through the damp grass, the cool beads of evening dew soaking through his moccasins. The steady crash of churning waters thrummed against the tranquil evening air.

Darshima walked toward the field's edge, which ended abruptly at a cliff plunging toward the river's surface far below. The mists had cooled the air considerably and pricked the bare skin of his back, sending a shiver through him. He stopped at a jagged, tree-lined promontory, jutting from the edge of the cliff out over the water. He then continued along a narrow, gravelly path that led to the edge of the rocky formation. Pausing for a moment, he looked around, then sat upon the ground. The dewy grass soaked through his breeches, but he barely noticed.

Legs folded, he sat hunched over amid his roiling thoughts. He was proud of his brother and his achievements, but a part of him ached for some of the same fortune that seemed to surround Sasha. Sasha was only three years older than him, but they couldn't be more different. For much of his life, Darshima had lived in what felt like his enormous shadow. When he was a boy, he had found it comforting, but he was no longer a child. Darshima knew that he needed to stand on his own.

A sigh escaped his lips as memories of the failed hunt came back. He was not formally a man, nor would he be recognized as one until he succeeded. He stared down at the grass, unsure what his next steps would be. Realizing that he would have to try again the following season, his mind mulled over what he needed to do differently to succeed. The fatigue from his long day was steadily getting the better of him, and he reclined upon the grass. He drew in a deep breath and closed his heavy eyelids. Before long, the sounds of the river began to fade and his thoughts drifted.

The loud, mournful call of a bird pierced through Darshima's mental fog like an arrow. His eyes fluttered open, and he was greeted by the starry skies overhead. He sat up and wrapped his arms around his knees, unsure of how much time had passed. The stiff breeze dashed away the remaining fragments of sleep. He looked out upon the river and the sea just beyond.

Darshima lifted his gaze toward Benai, the planet that their moon orbited. Occupying the entire western sky, the glowing pale orb cast its reflection upon the rippling expanse of water. An impenetrable grey haze shrouded Benai's immense surface. Innumerable bands of dusty red and white rings framed the planet and dipped below the horizon, seemingly plunging into the sea.

From what he had learned as a child, an ancient disaster had rendered Benai uninhabitable. The planet's cities had been abandoned for ages, and all that remained were their legends. Explorers from Gordanelle and the other moons had attempted to voyage there, but Benai's gritty atmosphere damaged their ships well before they could reach the surface and glimpse its ruins.

Darshima looked toward the center of the sky, where the moon Ciblaithia hung low over the horizon. The closest to Benai, Ciblaithia stood out as a bold, gilded crescent. Enveloped in shimmering deserts of gold sand, it was arid, hot, and known as the gilded moon. Wispy clouds dotted the sunlit half of its surface. The glowing lights of The Vilides, its dense capital, shone like embers upon the dark side. Owing to its vast power, wealth, and location, The Vilides was informally known as the gilded city. The Vilides had ruled over Ciblaithia, Gordanelle and the other neighboring moons for centuries as an empire, known as the Vilidesian Realm. Tales of its splendor were well known among Ardavians.

Further west, Darshima spotted the moon Wohiimai. The third closest to Benai, its blue-grey surface was punctuated by great oceans and large continents with rugged coastlines. Jagged peaks, pristine lakes, and rolling hills were among its most notable characteristics. He narrowed his eyes, and spotted traces of its capital, Renefydis ensconced amid the vast plains. With agreeable weather and mild seasons, Wohiimai was said to have the most ideal climate among all of the moons. As such, its people cultivated the majority of the realm's crops and livestock.

In the eastern sky, Darshima spied the moon Iberwight. The furthest from Benai, it was by far the coldest, with a climate of perpetual winter. The color of snow, Iberwight glistened in the incandescent glow of Benai. Steep mountain ranges, immense glaciers, and patches of deep blue ocean enveloped its surface. The lights of the capital, Gavipristine, shone like a constellation upon the moon's icy face.

Despite the curiosity Darshima felt when gazing at the other moons, he felt the fondest for his home, Gordanelle. The second closest to Benai and the largest moon among the quartet, Gordanelle's surface was covered in a dense carpet of tropical forests, humid grasslands, and misty swamps. Broad rivers coursed through the moon's continents like watery veins, emptying into turquoise oceans that covered the remainder of the moon's surface. Active volcanos at its equator belched sulfurous smoke and glowing lava.

Darshima looked briefly overhead to see the angular silhouettes of Vilidesian trade vessels quietly plying the Ardavian skies, their bright beacons pulsing rhythmically against the night. He sat amid the silence, taking in the sights and sounds of the evening. This particular location had always drawn him when he was feeling sad. As he grew older, he found himself spending more time here. Darshima assumed that it was the sweeping view of the heavens that called to him, but he felt that it was something more. Having never traveled very far beyond Ardavia, this place was important to him. When he sat here, he felt transported to worlds beyond his own.

The chilly gusts blew through his hair, and his sense of calm dissipated. He shuddered as the feelings of disappointment steadily crept back. A sigh escaped his lips as he mulled over the mistakes he had made during the hunt. If only he were faster and stronger like Sasha, he would have surely succeeded by now. He was the age of an adult, but his failure would again delay the recognition that he desperately sought. He shivered as the winds picked up, tucked his arms under his legs, and rested his head upon his knees.

Over the distant hush of the crashing waves, he heard the sharp sound of gravel crunching underfoot. He lifted his head to see a flowing shape emerge from the darkness. A sense of apprehension filling him, he looked upon the approaching figure and then rose to his feet.

"Settle yourself Darshima, it's only me." Dalia peered at him from beneath the large, dark cowl shrouding her face. Her slender hands emerged from underneath the folds of her cloak and pulled it back. Her hair shimmered in the evening light as she looked around. She turned and faced him, her eyes narrowed in a worried expression. Darshima offered a contrite frown and sat back down upon the grass. Dalia settled beside him and adjusted the folds of her garments.

"It's a beautiful, but windy night." Dalia gazed up at the sky. She pulled a black woolen cape from under her robe and draped it over Darshima's bare, shivering shoulders.

"You'll catch your death out here, exposed like that," she chided.

"Thank you, mother." Darshima gratefully clutched the warm fabric and rested his head upon her shoulder. The starlight illuminated her face and gave it a subtle glow. They sat together in silence, listening to the sounds of the river. After some time, she turned to him.

"I can tell that something is troubling you. What is the matter?" she asked.

"It's nothing." He cast his eyes down at the grass around them.

"If nothing is bothering you, why are you out here by yourself? You only come to this place when you are feeling upset." She tapped him under the chin. "Look at me, Darshima." He lifted his eyes toward hers, and they met face to face. His heart rose into his throat when he saw how concerned she was. Her expression had lost some of its radiance and had a drained look.

"Don't worry mother, I am fine." He rested his hand upon hers, but she drew it back and folded her arms across her chest. She glared at him, her amber eyes glittering in the starlight.

"Be honest, Darshima," she said, her voice cutting through the chilly air. "You may no longer be a child, but I am still your mother and I know you. I hate to see you like this."

"I'm sorry," he stammered. "I am not trying to cause any trouble, It's just..." his voice trailed off as he struggled to find the right words.

"What is it?" she asked, the patience in her voice wearing thin. She looked at him as if searching for a sign. Darshima turned away from her and stared blankly ahead.

"I feel like I don't belong anywhere or to anyone. I can never do anything right. Though I try, I keep on failing," he blurted in a harsh and anguished tone. He turned toward her. A worried expression spread across her face.

"Why do you feel this way? Is it because of your father or your brother?" She folded her hands in her lap.

"I feel as though I'll never measure up to them," he sighed. "I really let them down on the hunt." His words came out as puffs of steam in the night air. Wispy clouds passed overhead, intermittently shrouding Benai. Darshima looked up to the sky, his gaze lingering upon the other moons.

"You mustn't compare yourself to your father or Sasha. You are different from them, and that's good." She rested her hand upon his shoulder.

"I just wanted to succeed and make them proud." A frown crossed his lips.

"Your time will come," she replied softly. He fell silent as he mulled over her words. "Darshima, "she exclaimed, drawing in an annoyed gasp. He felt her hand upon his wrist. Puzzled, he looked at her as she gazed intently at his arms at rest in his lap. His eyes darted down to see his fingers idly tracing the markings upon his right arm. He stopped and looked up at his mother, whose expression of worry changed to one of contrived calmness.

"Why must you play idly with that birthmark, you'll bruise your skin." She drew the cape over him, covering his arms.

"It's nothing," he said softly, trying to reassure her. He rested his hands upon his knees.

She gently pulled her hand away and stared numbly at the sky. A teardrop slowly rolled down her smooth cheek and glistened in the moonlight. She hastily dashed it away with her palm, but Darshima had already seen it. Heart sinking, he moved his lips, wanting to say something to comfort her, but no sound came forth. He hated to see her upset.

"I don't mean to be any trouble," he whispered.

"You could never be any trouble to me, Darshima." She cleared her throat. "You're growing older, and I worry about you."

"I'll find a way somehow," he sighed.

"I know you will." She cast an earnest gaze upon him. They looked toward the heavens in silence, until a thin arc of sunlight rose above the horizon.

"Let's go home." Dalia rose from the ground and beckoned Darshima, who grasped her hands. With a heave, she pulled him to his feet, and then he embraced her. "You're not too old to hug your mother?" she chuckled, then gently kissed his forehead.

"That day will never come." Darshima hugged her tightly, then let go. Under the brightening sky, they walked together along the path toward their neighborhood.

Chapter Six

Wide, smoky shafts of sunlight filtered through the dusty glass windowpanes, and Darshima felt the back of his neck tingle under the radiant warmth. The humid atmosphere rippled with the low chatter of restless students. Darshima slouched upon a wooden bench at the back of the large, circular auditorium. Heavily absorbed in his thoughts, he leaned his head toward the glazed window, lazily eying the bustling street below.

Today marked the last day of his formal education. Darshima had finished his examinations earlier that morning and was attending his final lecture, which focused on the history of Benai. Despite his best efforts, ancient history had always been a subject that he found uninteresting. The joy of being finished with school was tempered by the uncertainty hanging over his future.

He wanted to continue his studies, but his family had only the means to educate Sasha, who was already in his third year at university. Sovani had discouraged Darshima from seeking further education by reminding him of his rather undistinguished academic record. Darshima felt that he was intelligent, but his performance in school didn't always reflect it. Had he been more dedicated like Sasha, he believed that he would have achieved more as a student. Despite his present circumstance, a part of him vowed to continue to learn somehow.

His father worked as a foreman for a Vilidesian construction company in Ardavia and had pressed Darshima to join him as an apprentice. As his studies drew to an end, Sovani had given Darshima an ultimatum: he either had to accept a position working with him, or find a job elsewhere. If Darshima failed to find employment, he wouldn't be allowed to live at home. He didn't want to follow in his father's footsteps in construction, but he felt that he had no other choice.

Darshima had looked for work throughout the city, but he had received nothing but excuses and apologetic faces. The weeks of fruitless searching had left him doubtful and discouraged. Confronted with the difficult prospect of moving away from home and finding his own place to live, he reluctantly accepted his father's offer. Later that day, he would begin his apprenticeship at the construction site.

The familiar feelings of disappointment floated through Darshima's mind like an enveloping mist. As he mulled over his missteps on the hunt, he idly fidgeted with the worn hem of his red tunic. Maybe if he hadn't pulled so hard on the bow, or if he had chosen a different arrow, he would have succeeded. He wallowed amid his thoughts when he unexpectedly heard his name being called. Darshima lifted his head and peered toward the front of the hall.

"Mr. Eweryn, please stand up and tell me the correct response," said the woman at the lectern. Her name was Professor Elasa, an intelligent historian whose voice filled the entire room. She was well known among her pupils for her keen interest and scholarship in the history of the realm. She also did not take kindly to distracted students.

Darshima slowly rose from his seat under the intense glare of his classmates. His pulse thudded as a mixture of nervousness and embarrassment coursed through him. He hadn't paid attention to any part of her lecture.

"Mr. Eweryn, please tell me the answer," demanded the professor, her voice ringing with an authoritative tone. Her amber eyes glinted with a hint of impatience as she stared at him. Her skin was deep bronze in hue, and she wore her silky black hair in a braided bun. She rested a hand upon the lectern, her dark orange, armless robe moving as she shifted her weight. Darshima returned with an anxious stare and her expression softened a bit.

"Can you please repeat the question?" asked Darshima, mustering as much sincerity as possible. A fine sweat broke out upon his brow, and he prayed that the moment would soon end.

"Very well. How many kingdoms were on Benai before its demise?" asked the professor.

"Kingdoms on Benai..." he stammered, unsure of the answer. At that moment, he wished the floor would give way underneath him so that he could disappear.

"Please sit down, Darshima." She offered a polite smile and gestured toward his seat. "It is the last day of class and I can see that your mind is elsewhere. I'll save another question for you." The corners of her eyes wrinkled sympathetically and she let out a soft chuckle. Darshima sank into his seat, trying to ignore the glares of his peers. The professor looked around the class and called upon another pupil, who answered the question without hesitation.

She concluded her lecture and dismissed them at the end of the hour. Darshima picked up his fabric satchel and joined the crush of students filing past her on their way out of the hall. She stood at the doorway and bid each of them farewell, congratulating them on completing their last lecture. As Darshima walked past her, she gently gripped his arm and pulled him aside. He waited patiently as she saluted the last of the departing students. She walked back to the lectern, her leather moccasins padding softly against the stone tile. Darshima followed closely behind her.

"Darshima, you and I go back a long while." She leaned against the smooth marble podium and cast an appraising look upon him. Darshima had been daydreaming through her lectures on history and civilization for the greater part of his schooling.

"I apologize for not paying attention." He cleared his throat.

"I realize that this is your last lecture with me, and I know that you have more important concerns ahead of you." A spark of recognition glittered in her eyes. Darshima was one of the few students in the lecture hall who would not be continuing on to university. "This is our history. We must study and embrace it, no matter our station."

"I understand," he said hesitantly.

"You've used that phrase before, but do you truly understand?" Her brow furrowed.

"I guess I don't," he replied. Though her lectures were challenging, he couldn't help but respect her devotion to the subject.

"If you've learned nothing from my lectures, please take this thought with you: Even a great civilization is but a mere palimpsest of the one that preceded it." She stared at him, her eyes intently searching his.

"I don't understand what that means." Darshima shrugged, unsure what to make of the words.

"Though people might try to erase the history of those that preceded them, they inevitably build upon it. The two cultures are forever linked, and the former has an undeniable influence on the latter." A studious frown crossed her lips. "We are Ardavians, and we are also Vilidesian subjects. Even though it isn't always apparent, we cannot deny the influence of the old empires on Benai, the ancient civilizations on Ciblaithia, and their traditions upon our present experience."

"I see," he said cautiously. Darshima sensed the profoundness of her words but felt rather naive in trying to understand the complexity behind them.

"A civilization cannot endure if its people learn nothing from the struggles and triumphs of those that preceded them." Her eyes narrowed pensively.

"I will try my best to learn." Darshima nodded. "Thank you for sharing your words with me professor, but I must go." He slowly stepped away.

"Wait a moment." she held up her hand, then rummaged through a red fabric bag resting upon the lectern and retrieved two black books.

"I want to make sure that you take something away from this last lecture, even if it is heavy and bound in leather." Her fingers caressed the worn spines of the volumes. "These books are among my favorites."

"Thank you, but I couldn't accept them." Darshima stared at the faded covers. His mind ran through the names of his more attentive classmates, who were surely more deserving of the books than him.

"I insist, Darshima," she replied. "I certainly don't know why, but I've always sensed something more to you than meets the eye." She looked upon him with an air of curiosity. "I want you to have them. May they serve you on your journeys." She clutched the books to her chest, then handed them over to Darshima. Humbled by her kind words, he accepted them and thanked her.

"I will read them and learn as much as I can." He gently placed the volumes in his bag, bid her farewell, and left the hall.

Darshima bolted past the doors and out into the city, barely taking notice of his surroundings. He was due to meet with his father, but still had a considerable distance ahead of him. The early afternoon sun shone directly above, burning through the clearing mists. He walked upon the cobbled pavement, the sunlight glowing against the richly carved, pale granite edifices lining the streets. He moved amid the bustling crowds in the sparse shadows to avoid the intense rays. In the distance, he spotted a large, angular metal frame, towering high above the twisting spires and gleaming copper domes at the city center. Aerial freighters, like swarms of silver flies, hovered around the building, delivering their payloads to the workers hoisted upon the girders.

This structure was where Darshima would be working. Commissioned by a Vilidesian enterprise seeking to expand its presence on Gordanelle, the tower's incongruous and foreign design had engendered much controversy. Nearly all Ardavian buildings were crafted from exquisite, hand-carved, red and white hued stone from local quarries. The metal, Vilidesian-styled skyscraper was an unwanted intrusion and an affront to Ardavia's fabled architectural heritage. Ciblaithia, Gordanelle, Iberwight, and Wohiimai had been under Vilidesian imperial rule for ages, and despite relative peace, tensions among the four moons often simmered below the surface.

Darshima pushed through the crowded streets as he made his way toward the site, his shoulders squeezing against the frenetic crush of people carrying out their daily affairs. Though the scenery changed, the building seemingly imposed itself upon every view and angle. Out of the corner of his eye, he spotted the silken blue and gold invitations sent by the Prince of The Vilides. They hung prominently in several windows of the homes and offices along the road. His chest tightened as a pang of sadness coursed through him. Darshima cast his gaze toward the ground and tried to avoid looking at the scrolls.

His thoughts dissolved in the mechanical din of construction equipment as he walked onward. His mind filled with images he had seen of the palace in The Vilides, and what the Prince's celebration might be like. Darshima lifted his gaze toward the pale blue sky, his eyes lingering upon the faded golden crescent of Ciblaithia. He wondered what kind of rarified splendor his brother and the other invitees might witness upon that moon. His eyes drifted from the sky, back to the crowded, dusty street, and he shook his head in frustration. He had yet to achieve anything substantial in his life to earn such a coveted invitation.

As he approached the tower, his thoughts wandered back to that night when he attempted to kill the pair of powilix. Though it had been his closest chance, he had nearly lost his life. He wished that he had somehow found a way to kill those beasts, but he was thankful that Sasha had saved him. Nonetheless, a success that night would have meant so much to Darshima. He would have finally demonstrated to his family and himself that he was a capable young man. His lips briefly wrinkled into a frown, then he pushed the sad thoughts aside. He would have to wait yet another season to prove himself. There was no use mulling over his past mistakes. He needed to move on.

Darshima stopped along the congested sidewalk in front of the large, metal gates protecting the site and took in the harried scenes around him. Fleets of enormous four-wheeled vehicles roved past, hauling debris, uniformed workers, and materials. Their engines breathed trails of smoke and grunted under the burden of their cargo. His ears pricked at the sound of their large tires crunching against the gravel upon the road. The humid air enveloped him in a thick cloud of dust amid the frenzied activity. Darshima drew in an anxious breath, passed through the gates, and headed toward a large wooden shed at the foot of the structure.

He walked up the gritty stairs of the low building, opened the door, and entered the dimly lit interior. The conversation inside ceased, and he felt the stare of several pairs of eyes upon him.

"You are late," muttered his father. He sat behind a wooden desk in the corner and stared at Darshima, his arms folded across his chest.

"I walked as fast as I could..." he began. Sovani impatiently raised his hand and Darshima fell silent. He rested his bag beside the door with a soft thud and approached the desk.

The slightly disheveled office came into view as his eyes adjusted amid the darkness. Shafts of murky yellow light poured through the small, dusty windows and spilled onto piles of paper and haphazard stacks of boxes. He eyed Sovani's brawny form, clothed in a grey smock, loosely fastened over a red tunic and black trousers. His face bore a serious expression, partially veiled in shadow. There were several other men in work uniforms braced against the walls, and sitting upon groups of chairs arranged around the office.

Sovani rose from his chair, stepped out from behind the desk, his leather boots scraping against the wooden floorboards. He stood before Darshima, rested a hand upon his shoulder, and ushered him toward the door. With a glance, Sovani summoned his assistant, Ivan, who stood patiently off to the side. He was a sinewy, brown-skinned man with amber eyes, who stood a bit taller than Darshima. A round leather cap sat atop his head, hiding his black wavy locks, shorn just past his ears. A loose-fitting, armless grey tunic hung from his broad shoulders. He wore rough, black fabric work trousers and leather boots. Darshima couldn't help but notice a passing resemblance to Sasha.

"Let's get him started, Ivan." Sovani waved toward Darshima.

"Yes, sir." Ivan nodded vigorously.

"My junior foreman will be in charge of you. I want you to do exactly what he says, no questions asked. His word is law." Sovani glared at Darshima.

"Yes, father." Darshima clenched his jaw and his eyes narrowed in mild annoyance. One of the men in the office rummaged through a closet and gave Darshima a similar uniform as Ivan. As they waited, he hastily changed in a corner, then stowed his old clothes in his bag.

"Let's get started, we have much to accomplish today." Ivan put his arm around Darshima's shoulder and guided him out of the office, the door slamming behind them.

They bounded down the steps and back into the sunlight. Ivan walked briskly, kicking up clouds of dust as he charged forward. Darshima jogged to catch up with him.

They wended their way through the towering forest of metal beams composing the building's hexagonal foundation.

"We're all busy so you'll have to learn quickly," he shouted over his shoulder, casting an appraising glance at Darshima. Ivan turned back around and walked even faster. "That's one thing you will find around here, there's never enough time." His voice was nearly lost amid the cacophony. They walked through the maze of columns, past armies of workers, cascades of flying sparks, and bands of roving vehicles transporting supplies.

They arrived at the end of a walkway, and stepped inside a large construction elevator. Ivan punched a row of buttons along the door with an index finger, and the carriage shuddered to life. They ascended through the unenclosed shaft, and Darshima could see the levels disappear below them. The scenery melded into a blur, and the winds blew through his clothes as the carriage vaulted upward. Darshima barely heard the sound as the blood rushed from his head. His heart pounded, and a knot formed in the pit of his stomach. He gripped the railing of the elevator, steadied himself, and prayed for the ride to end.

The carriage shuddered to a stop, and they stepped out onto an unfinished stone floor. Ivan walked to one end of the expansive level, and Darshima followed closely behind him. His eyes swept over the army of uniformed men and women as they worked on various tasks. Ivan stopped at a metal cabinet and pried open the doors. He grabbed a leather satchel and a belt fitted with several tools. He then fastened the belt around Darshima's waist and draped the heavy bag over his shoulder.

"Your job is simple enough." Ivan led him toward the edge of the floor. "All you have to do is fasten the bolts in that bag to the girders on this level with a bolt gun." He pointed to the floor as he explained the importance of the bolts. They were meant to secure the soon to be installed walls. His outstretched finger traced a metal grid at their feet.

He then pulled a black, pistol-shaped device from Darshima's belt and grabbed a handful of large steel bolts from the bag. He knelt at the edge of the floor and carefully loaded several of the objects into the back of the gun. He twisted a pair of dials that let out a sharp tick, then pushed a row of buttons along the handle. The barrel emitted a high-pitched whine, followed by several jarring clicks, and then a pulsating white light.

"Now watch how I do it," he called over his shoulder. Darshima knelt beside him and observed intently. Ivan held the barrel of the gun against a marked circle upon the metal beam and pulled the trigger. The device gave off a loud popping sound, then generated a rapid sequence of flashing light. He pulled the device from the floor after the pulses dimmed, revealing a glowing bolt fastened to the beam. Darshima examined it closely, noting that it had been welded into a solid piece. He looked on as Ivan fastened several more of them along the beam.

"It doesn't seem too difficult." Darshima leaned closer.

"I'll ask about your thoughts after you spend a day up here," chuckled Ivan. "This job is more demanding than you might think."

Ivan handed the device to Darshima along with a small radio communicator for use in case of an emergency. They stood back up and Ivan led him to another part of the unfinished floor, their footsteps clicking upon the rough stone tile.

"You will be working here today." He gestured toward the edge of the floor. A steady gust of wind blew through, tugging at their clothes. Darshima squinted against the bright sunlight and followed the grey floor to its boundary at a black metal girder.

Having rarely experienced extreme heights, Darshima cautiously approached the edge and looked out upon the vista before him. He could see nothing but the dark building frame stretching far beneath his feet until it met with the city below. From his vantage, the streets and avenues looked like mere etchings upon the ground's surface. Through the faint mists, he could just make out the forms of the pedestrians walking along the pavement.

His heart thudded as he looked off into the distance, the city's buildings and bridges sprawling upon the other rocky plateau islands. Darshima drew in a breath and tugged at his leather cap as he tried to reassure himself. Under Ivan's watchful eye he knelt beside the girder, donned a pair of leather gloves from his belt, and set to work. He carefully placed the first few bolts in the same manner as Ivan, his hand shaking under the power of the device.

After Darshima had installed a dozen bolts, Ivan crouched beside him. His eyes narrowed in thought, Ivan inspected Darshima's work and gave him an approving slap on the back.

"So far so good Darshima, but you'll have to move faster," he shouted over the clangor of the equipment. With his gloved hand, he gestured to the grid at their feet and offered Darshima a few suggestions to ensure the bolts were properly welded to the girders. Ivan then jumped to his feet and left Darshima under the watchful eye of his more experienced colleagues, stationed nearby.

As he worked, Darshima tried not to look over the edge, but his eyes continually betrayed him. The altitude and the motion of the vehicles flying below sent his stomach into queasy knots. At one point, his nervousness was so strong that he had to set the device aside. Darshima sat still with his eyes closed until the feeling passed, the chilly gusts of wind offering some relief. Forcing his eyes open, he dusted himself off, picked up the bolt gun, and tried to acclimate himself to the height.

Though the task was straightforward, it soon grew tedious. Darshima's mind drifted to thoughts about his future as he methodically welded the bolts. His father had worked in construction for his entire career and had provided a stable living for their family. Darshima respected Sovani's work, but he imagined a different future for himself. He still didn't know what it would be.

As Darshima grew up, he tried to follow his brother's path, but it was difficult. Sasha was not only athletic, but also intelligent. He was talented with mathematics and studied engineering at Ardavia's best university. Darshima let out a forlorn sigh as he thought about how different they were. He and his brother had been close as children, but as they grew older, their diverging paths grew more pronounced. He feared that there would come a time when they would no longer relate to each other.

Darshima chased his errant thoughts aside and refocused upon the array of girders before him. Time passed slowly as he worked, the building's shadow crawling over the city like the hands of a clock. He made sure to follow Ivan's instructions, carefully welding the bolts to the outline upon the floor. Darshima had the suspicion that his father had offered him the apprenticeship with the expectation that he would fail, so he worked even harder. He observed the laborers around him, learning from them and asking questions as they methodically and efficiently fastened their bolts to the girders.

Darshima wasn't even sure why his father had insisted he work with him. He suspected that his mother had asked Sovani to give him a chance at the construction site. She had been firmly against the idea of him moving out of the house if he failed to find a job. On several occasions she let Sovani know of her displeasure at the harsh ultimatum.

A smile crossed Darshima's lips when he thought of his mother. She had been a source of reassurance during his fruitless search for work. For as far back as he could remember, Dalia always stood by him whenever he struggled. She took his side when his father was tough on him. When he doubted himself, she encouraged him and cheered him up. She saw things in him that he didn't see himself. He did not want to disappoint her and vowed to work even harder at the job.

The sound of a whistle pierced the din of his thoughts. Darshima lifted his head to see the other workers summoning him. The workday had finished, and they were preparing to leave. Darshima rose to his feet and stepped away from the ledge. His legs ached from kneeling upon the floor, and his stiff joints popped as he moved. He shuffled back to the cabinet with the other workers and deposited his tools. He joined the crowd of tired men and women and stepped onto the elevator for the shaky ride back to the ground. His tunic damp with sweat, he shivered amid the gusts during the descent.

Darshima bid farewell to the crew and walked back toward his father's office to retrieve his bag. He trudged up the grimy steps and ducked through the doorway. The other workers had already left, and Sovani sat alone at his desk, methodically thumbing through a file. He slowly lifted his eyes from the pages and stared at Darshima.

"How was your day?" he asked, his low voice, barely audible above the din of the machinery. His gaze drifted back down to the documents in his outstretched hand.

"It was good. I did everything that Ivan taught me," said Darshima. Sovani looked back up and offered a brief smile.

"He is one of our best foremen. You will learn a lot from him." He closed the file and set it aside.

"I will be on my way then, father." Darshima reached for his bag beside the door and slung it over his shoulder. He looked at Sovani for any hint of displeasure.

"I'll walk home with you." Sovani neatly shuffled the stack of papers, placed them at the edge of the desk, then rose from his chair.

Darshima waited patiently by the door as Sovani arranged his things and grabbed his leather case. His pulse quickened as a feeling of anticipation coursed through him. He hadn't expected that his father would want to walk with him. It had been a while since they had spent any time together, and he wasn't sure what to think.

Sovani joined Darshima at the door and they stepped into the fading sunlight. They passed through the gates and out into the bustling city district, its stone buildings shimmering in warm tones of beige and white. Darshima walked upon the cobbled road, his weary muscles aching with each step. The job had seemed simple enough, but a day's worth of hard work gave him a new appreciation for his father, who had done similar work at his age. Over the years, Sovani had worked his way up from a laborer to a tradesman, and finally a senior foreman.

Darshima followed Sovani through the crowded streets between the crush of vendors and their wooden booths, painted in warm, pastel hues. The boisterous conversations of customers making their transactions filled the air. They strolled along the rows of food stalls, the vivid sight of bright flames, charring fresh meat, and searing vegetables catching Darshima's attention. He breathed in deeply of the savory odors, and his mouth watered. His stomach rumbled, and he placed a hand over his abdomen. In his rush from the lecture hall to the construction site, he had missed lunch.

"I hear you, and I'm also hungry. Let's get something to eat." Sovani turned to Darshima.

They approached a stall selling large wooden skewers of roasted wild game. Sovani reached into his pocket, retrieved a few golden Vilidesian coins, and exchanged them with the vendor for two skewers. He handed one to Darshima, who hastily devoured a few of the sizzling morsels.

"Thank you," he mumbled between bites.

"Be careful not to burn yourself. It's as if your mother and I don't feed you," said Sovani. He laughed as he took a bite from his skewer. Darshima chuckled at his father's remark and chewed more slowly.

Darshima ate the grilled meat and walked with his father amid the crowds, enjoying the ambiance of the evening. To his surprise, Sovani asked him more about his day.

"It's only your first shift, but what do you think about the apprenticeship so far?" he asked, clearing his throat. Darshima pondered the question. Though the work was tedious, he wanted more than ever to prove himself.

"It is an important job and I won't let you down," he replied in a resolute tone. Sovani smiled, clearly satisfied with his son's response.

"You are probably meant for something else, but you must give it a chance. Working here will teach you something valuable." Sovani offered him a firm pat on the shoulder. His voice bore a serious note that caught Darshima's attention. "You are a young man, and I expect as much from you as I do Sasha." Darshima's chest tightened anxiously as he listened to Sovani's words.

"Father, I am sorry about the hunt this season." Darshima bit his lip. His heart rose into his throat as the feelings of sadness returned.

"I know you tried your best, but you must keep at it." Sovani looked at him, his eyes glittering with a flash of concern. He then gently tapped Darshima's chest with his index finger. "You are no less capable than Sasha, but something within you keeps holding you back." His gaze lingered upon Darshima, as if he were trying to read his thoughts.

"I will be more prepared next time, and I will succeed." Darshima looked toward the ground and his lips briefly wrinkled into a frown. He couldn't argue with his father's words. Something needed to change if he wanted to succeed the following season. He had yet to figure out what that change would be.

"Let's hurry home, your mother and brother are waiting for us." Sovani pointed toward the winding road before them, the long rays of the setting sun glimmering upon its dark cobblestones. They finished their meal and discarded the remnants of their skewers in a murky drainage canal flowing alongside the pavement.

They walked along the familiar streets of their neighborhood, trudged up the steps to their home, and passed through the entrance. The rich spices of his mother's cooking filled the humid air, but he was too exhausted to eat.

"Get some rest, and we will talk later." Sovani patted Darshima's shoulder and headed into the kitchen.

"Yes, father." Darshima nodded slowly. He continued down the dimly lit hallway and listened to the muffled sounds of his family preparing themselves for dinner.

Darshima entered his room and closed the door behind him. He took off his moccasins and shuffled across the worn tiles. His bag slid from his weary shoulder and fell to the floor, landing beside the wooden desk with a thud. He removed his cap, peeled off his sweaty work tunic and tossed them aside. Exhaustion getting the better of him, he collapsed onto the stiff bed and let out a long sigh. His head felt dull, and every muscle ached. His hair and skin felt grimy from the long day of work, but he couldn't muster the energy to bathe.

Darshima looked up at the ceiling, his mind adrift in thought. Bright beams of moonlight streamed through the open rectangular windows beside his bed, casting the room in stark light and shadow. A cool breeze wafted through, and it felt good against his damp skin. The soft, melodic chirping of the small nocturnal creatures outside had just about lulled him to sleep when he heard the sound of footsteps approaching. He lifted his head as the door creaked open, and peered at his mother's silhouette against the muted light of the hallway. She entered the room and stood beside the desk, her hand gently resting upon its scratched surface.

"Good evening." She looked at him, her eyes narrowed in concern.

Darshima sat up at the edge of his bed and offered a forlorn nod. She walked toward him, stepping over his clothes and a few other scattered items.

"Sorry for the clutter." He winced as she navigated the untidy space.

"It's often like this in here." A wry smile crossed her lips. Dalia sat beside him at the edge of the bed, the folds of her green robe fluttering as she arranged them.

"I haven't seen you at all today. How are you doing?" She gently rested her hand upon the back of his head. She tried to look into his eyes, but he avoided her gaze. She had a knack for reading his feelings and he didn't want to trouble her with his frustrations.

"I'm just a little tired," he mumbled as he fidgeted with his hands.

"You didn't even have dinner with us. You must be hungry, and you look like you need a bath." Her brow furrowed as her eyes swept over his sweaty skin.

"Father and I had something to eat on the way home. I promise I'll bathe later." Darshima let out a yawn and stretched his arms.

"How was your first day at the job?" Her fingers tapped softly against the bracelets upon her wrist.

"I tried at it, but I don't think it's for me." He shook his head.

"What do you mean?" Her eyebrows arched in surprise.

In one great rush, Darshima shared his unhappiness with the tedium of the work and lamented his predicament of not continuing his education like Sasha.

"It's only your first day. Give it some time, and the work will get better." She looked at him thoughtfully.

"What will I do if it doesn't?" he asked. His voice wavered as a frown spread across his lips.

"Don't be so petulant Darshima, you're no longer a child. You must try at something." She shook her head and sighed.

"You're right, mother." Darshima's cheeks grew warm with embarrassment. "I'll stop complaining."

"I understand that you're upset, but you will see this through. Your father and I have faith in you." Her lips wrinkled into an earnest smile.

"I'll go to the site and work hard every day." He glared at his hands, folded in his lap.

"I know you will." She wrapped an arm around his shoulder and drew him closer. "You are young and have many years ahead of you. Someday, somehow, I know you will make a way for yourself."

"Thank you, mother." Darshima turned to her. She kissed him upon the forehead and rose to her feet. She gazed at him for a moment longer, and left the room, gently closing the door behind her. Darshima collapsed back onto his bed, let out a frustrated sigh, and stared up at the ceiling. He caught a glimpse of the starlit sky shimmering through the window, and his sadness lessened some.

Chapter Seven

Despite his initial misgivings, Darshima continued his apprenticeship at the construction site. He worked hard and picked up extra shifts to help as needed. When he wasn't scaling the giant girders, he spent time in the tool crib amid the showering sparks of the grinding wheels, sharpening and repairing equipment. The months wore on, and he did his part to keep the project on schedule.

To his surprise, Darshima grew to enjoy working at the site. His apprenticeship had given him a needed and fulfilling sense of purpose. His work ethic gained him the respect of his older colleagues, and he even noticed his father treating him with more kindness. He had taken Sovani's words to heart and sought to learn as much as he could.

Darshima's work took up much of his day, and he was left with only the evenings to rest.

During his time off, he helped with household chores and tended to his mother's garden. He had never been one to make friends easily like Sasha and thus spent much of his free time alone. After work, he often wandered outdoors, the evening air bringing a sense of tranquility to him. Much to his mother's worry, he would hike along the surrounding forest trails, sometimes well after dark.

On one particular evening, he ended his stroll at his favorite promontory overlooking the river. His day at the site had been particularly exhausting. A late delivery of bolts had delayed him and his crew, and they spent the whole day working feverishly to catch up. He sat down and rested against a particularly old tree that had gotten to know his back very well over the years. He drew in a breath of the humid evening air and unbuttoned the collar of his tunic. The sounds of the flowing water filled his ears, and he could feel the day's tension lessen.

As he drifted off to sleep, his arm slid on top of his bag and hit against something firm, jolting him awake.

"What is that?" he muttered to himself, wondering if he had accidentally brought home a tool from the site. He curiously rummaged through his bag and retrieved two books. He held them under the moonlight and smiled to himself as the memories of his former professor came to him.

He brought the tomes closer, their gilt letters catching the starlight. The title of the first book read: *The Collective Histories of Benai and her Moons,* and the title of the second book read: *The History of The Vilidesian Realm.* Darshima opened the first book, taking care not to tear any of the well-worn parchment pages, and began to read. From that moment, the book captured his interest like no text ever had. He poured over the pages, contemplating the histories written upon them.

The recorded history of Benai and its moons stood as a turbulent amalgam of triumph and tragedy, spanning thousands of years. Long ago, Benai was ruled by Fidaxis and Jevidan, rival empires that spanned the continents and islands upon the planet's once watery surface. Both expansionist powers had long sought supremacy on Benai, and their designs of conquest frequently led them to the brink of war.

Dozens of uninhabited moons orbited the void beyond their skies, each possessing an immense wealth of unexploited resources. The empires gradually developed machinery that gave them the ability to travel into space and colonize these worlds. They grew in strength and fought viciously over the moons. At the close of a particularly bloody and protracted war, the dueling powers claimed all of the moons, except for Ciblaithia.

Ciblaithia was home to a unique people who called themselves the Omystikai. Their origins were mysterious, and their existence had been previously unknown to either empire. Details of their physical appearance and culture had been lost to the ages. Known as a peaceful people, they had been renowned for their wisdom, superior cognition, and alleged abilities of divination. Their secretive traditions were based upon ancient rituals and precise measurements of celestial movements. The Omystikai had established highly sophisticated civilizations on Ciblaithia, far older than the first known primeval settlements on Benai.

Apart from a large blue sea covering a third of its surface, Ciblaithia was arid and enveloped in immense deserts of fine gold sand. Beneath the valuable dunes, explorers had discovered prodigious quantities of normally scarce liquid fuel. They used this precious source of energy to power the engines of their aerial ships. With aims of exploiting its incalculable wealth, Jevidan launched an invasion of Ciblaithia and waged a brutal war against the Omystikai.

Though peaceful, the Omystikai were skilled fighters and proved to be fierce opponents. Both sides incurred heavy losses in the vicious battles between them. Seeking to gain a share of territory on the gilded moon, Fidaxis allied with Jevidan and they defeated the Omystikai. The empires divided Ciblaithia in half, with Fidaxis claiming all territories east of the meridian and Jevidan claiming all territories to the west.

The first centuries of settlement presented many challenges for the empires. Apart from Ciblaithia, the moons had remained completely untouched by human hands. The settlers worked to tame the lands and succeeded in establishing new cities, villages, and farms. Millions migrated from the overpopulated territories on Benai to find their fortunes upon the new moons.

The conditions on Ciblaithia remained difficult for ages. The Omystikai cities had all been destroyed by the war, leaving a large population of indigenous refugees who had survived the invasion. Rendered destitute, the Omystikai wandered as nomads amid the ruins of their moon. Violent clashes erupted between the settlers and the exiles as they sought refuge. Jevidan sent armies to the troubled territories and quelled the uprisings, forcefully expelling the Omystikai to prison camps in the unforgiving desert.

The Omystikai languished in these settlements for centuries, and many perished from starvation and illness. Alarmed at the cruelty occurring on Ciblaithia, the subjects of the two empires demanded a resolution. Fidaxis and Jevidan evacuated the camps and exiled all of the Omystikai to the frozen wastelands of Iberwight. Neither power had colonized the moon due to its inhospitable climate and therefore agreed to relinquish the frigid world to them. The Omystikai were resettled there without fear of interference or reprisal. Over the ages, they established new civilizations, but remained by most measures a marginalized people.

The dueling empires expanded the settlements upon their celestial territories until a cataclysmic event permanently altered the course of history. A hail of asteroids from the unknown depths of space collided with Benai and her moons. They struck the planet with a devastating force that gouged the surface, grinding its rotation to a virtual standstill. Debris spewed forth from the depths of the planet, permanently clouding its atmosphere. The cosmic bombardment pulverized all of the moons, except for Ciblaithia, Gordanelle, Iberwight, and Wohiimai. As ages passed, the remnants of the destroyed moons slowly assimilated with the planet's characteristic wide band of rings.

As Darshima read, the winds began to rise around him. The unexpected whisper of crunching grass underfoot filled his ears. Completely immersed in the book, he lifted his gaze from the text and remembered where he was. He peered over his shoulder toward the footpath, his pulse thudding as he saw a figure moving amid the shadows.

"Calm yourself, it's only me," said Dalia. A tan fabric satchel hanging over her shoulder, she emerged under the moonlight and walked toward the promontory. As she approach him, the folds of her red robe fluttered in the wind. She settled on the ground next to Darshima and placed the bag beside her.

"I haven't seen you since you left for work this morning, are you okay?" She rested a hand upon his shoulder.

"I'm fine, mother. I've just been out here reading." Darshima closed the book and rested it in his lap.

"I have never known you to be such an avid reader." The corners of her mouth lifted in a thoughtful smile.

"This book explains everything so clearly." Darshima gestured toward the volume. She gently picked it up, her brow furrowing as she eyed the letters under the moonlight.

"Ancient history. How interesting," she muttered as she leafed through the pages. "Written of course by the Vilidesians. They behave as if they know everything." A slight frown crossed her lips as she closed the book and returned it Darshima, who placed it beside him.

"There's so much I don't know." Darshima looked up at the shrouded atmosphere of Benai. He shook his head in disbelief as he pondered the ancient cataclysm that happened upon its surface.

"I am glad you are learning something. There are countless mysteries and untold stories on all of the moons." Dalia lifted her gaze toward the heavens, her eyes narrowed in thought.

"When you were a student, did they teach you about all of the strife that happened?" asked Darshima.

"We discussed both the struggles and the hopes of our ancestors, but we mostly learned about current events," she replied.

Dalia looked away from the skies and reached into her satchel. She brought out a covered clay bowl, a copper fork, and a metal flask of water, then handed them to Darshima.

"You missed having dinner with us again." Dalia shook her head and her brow wrinkled in a mild look of annoyance. She pulled a dark handkerchief from the satchel and placed it in his lap.

"I'm sorry, the time escaped me." Darshima eagerly held the warm bowl in his hands and removed the lid. He breathed in the savory aroma of seared meat and steamed grains. He hadn't realized how hungry he was, and proceeded to shovel a forkful of food into his mouth.

"Thank you," he mumbled between bites.

"I know how hard you have been working these past few months. You deserve to spend your free time as you like, but it would be nice to see you now and again." A wistful frown crossed her lips.

"I'll come home soon, mother." His heart sinking, Darshima offered her a contrite smile. Because of his busy schedule over the past several weeks, he had not been able to spend much time with her.

"Don't get so engrossed in the past, that you forget the importance of the present and the future. We can work to change them for the better." The corners of her eyes wrinkled as she nodded toward the book.

Dalia leaned over and kissed his forehead. She then rose to her feet and walked away from the promontory. Darshima's eyes lingered on her form until she faded into the shadows. He finished the bowl of food and stowed it back in the satchel. His mouth parched, he took a swig of water from the flask and then opened the book, eagerly picking up where he left off.

From the moment of the asteroids' impact, all contact between the empires and their colonies ceased. Chaos, death, and destruction ensued upon the remaining moons. Noble families of the former colonial era vied for power, waging fierce battles to gain territory and influence. Over the ensuing centuries, each moon fell under the control of one ruling family, descended from Jevidani and Fidaxian nobility. They built the capitals of Ardavia and Renefydis upon the ruins of former colonial cities. Gavipristine was founded on Iberwight by a powerful tribe of Omystikai.

The situation on Ciblaithia remained tenuous. Protracted disputes between the descendants of both empires stalled progress as they refused to accept each other's rule, resulting in a series of violent wars. The noble families eventually decided to intermarry for the sake of peace. As calm returned, they established their new capital, The Vilides, and built it upon the ruins of an Omystikai city.

Diplomatic relations between the moons declined further as the ruling families disputed trade routes and territorial rights. They levied tariffs, issued embargoes, and placed sanctions, to devastating economic effect. As time passed, tensions escalated into an all-out war amongst the four moons. Each struggled for power and fought to expand its influence. The vast armies of Ciblaithia, the most populous moon at the time, subdued all of the others and established its rule.

Ciblaithia's attempts at unification were short-lived. Rebel factions on Gordanelle and Wohiimai challenged their authority, reclaiming vast swaths of territory. The moons descended into chaos, culminating in the surprise invasion and sacking of The Vilides by armies from Gordanelle. Ardavia assumed power and ruled supreme over the four moons for more than a century.

Ardavian rule ended abruptly with the rise of a mysterious and previously unknown family of merchants and scholars, by the name of Fyrenos. Marshaling an army of their own, they ascended to power in The Vilides and recaptured the palace from Gordanellan soldiers. After this victory, their forces grew and they reconquered all of the lost territories. They destroyed the remaining separatist factions and worked to unify the disparate populations of the four moons.

The House of Fyrenos established the current dynastic order and ushered in the era of the Vilidesian Realm, which had endured for more than a millennium. They built military bases and constructed palaces of government in all of the cities and villages. The dynasty rebuilt the war-torn capitals of each moon and founded other important cities throughout the realm. They abolished tariffs and issued a common currency to facilitate trade. The dynasty employed legions of scholars who created universities, museums, and libraries on all of the moons. These renowned institutions flourished over the centuries, serving to educate and unify people under a common Vilidesian language and culture.

The House of Fyrenos expended significant effort in rebuilding the pillaged ruins of The Vilides. After generations of reconstruction, it stood transformed as a dazzling, cosmopolitan city of soaring glass, stone, and metal towers set against an expanse of golden dunes and blue sea. It served as the imperial capital, as well as the cultural and economic crossroads of the four moons.

The dynasty's tireless efforts were not without difficulty, but unlike their predecessors, they succeeded. From the ruins of total war, the Vilidesians had united Ciblaithia, Gordanelle, Iberwight and Wohiimai, and their billions strong citizenry as a cohesive empire. The war-weary peoples of the era were heartened by the stability and sweeping change brought forth by their new rulers. They accepted their place as subjects within the Vilidesian Realm, but strived to maintain their cultural traditions amid the pervasiveness of imperial hegemony.

Chapter Eight

Darshima lay still upon his bed. He folded his arms across his chest and let his legs dangle off the edge. He cast a hard gaze through the partially open door and glimpsed Sovani shuttling back and forth with the luggage.

"Are you ready, Sasha?" asked Sovani, his anxious voice echoing throughout the hallway. A large leather case in each hand, he lumbered toward the front entrance, the muscles of his forearms bulging under their weight.

"I'll be ready in a moment," shouted Sasha, his voice floating down the stairs from his room.

Darshima let out a long sigh. He slowly clenched and relaxed his fists, trying to diffuse some of the anger roiling within him. On any other day, he would have been at the construction site, working amid the girders. Instead, he rested upon the bedsheets, stewing amid his thoughts. Today, he and his family would be traveling to The Vilides for the royal birthday celebration. Darshima had been looking forward to some time alone at home while Sasha and his parents were away, but Sovani had made other plans for him.

Earlier that week, Sovani had insisted that Darshima join the family for the voyage. The Prince's invitation permitted maids and valets to travel with the invitees to attend to their needs during the week of ceremonies. Families without domestic help could bring younger siblings to serve as assistants. The Eweryn family, like many Ardavian families, was not wealthy enough to afford such a luxury. As Darshima was the younger brother, Sovani demanded that he serve as Sasha's assistant. Despite Darshima's protests, their father gave him no choice. Sovani canceled his schedule at the construction site that week and paid for his passage.

Darshima looked up at the ceiling, his eyes tracing an imaginary path upon the faded paint as he listened to Sasha's muffled footsteps thudding above him. His cheeks grew hot as a sense of embarrassment pushed aside his anger. It was bad enough that he had failed at the hunt. It was even worse that he hadn't earned an invitation to the ceremony, but to serve as his brother's assistant was too much for him to bear. He had pleaded with Sasha to convince their father out of the arrangement. Sasha tried his best, but Sovani had remained firm.

Darshima broke out in a cold sweat, and he pictured the guests laughing at him as he followed Sasha around the palace. The siblings assisting the invitees would be young children, and he would literally stand head and shoulders above them. He knew that Sovani wanted to save face in front of the wealthier Vilidesian families. He felt that it was unfair to be placed in such a situation, but his father didn't seem to care. His pulse thudded as a sense of helplessness washed over him. He had no choice but to follow through with his father's demand. Gordanellan tradition was strict regarding relations between parents and their children. A boy who disobeyed his father on such an important matter could be disowned or even disinherited.

Darshima lay amid his frustrations when the door creaked open. Sovani crossed the threshold, his broad shoulders filling the doorframe. He wore tailored black trousers hemmed at the calf, leather sandals, and a finely woven red armless tunic, trimmed in curlicues of white embroidery. Thick armbands fashioned of leather and Ciblaithian gold encircled both of his biceps.

"Please go help your brother with his things." He glared at Darshima.

"I don't understand why I have to go to The Vilides." Darshima's eyes lingered upon the ceiling as he avoided his father's stare. Sovani shook his head in disdain as he glanced around the modest space.

"Darshima, we have been through this before. Your brother needs you. Get up and get dressed." He let out a frustrated sigh and exited the room, firmly closing the door behind him. The door kicked up a flurry of dust and knocked the pair of books off the desk in the corner.

Darshima dragged himself out of bed and put the volumes back upon its scuffed surface. Thick beams of morning sunlight streamed through the small windows above his bed, diffusing through the dusty, humid air. Save for the desk, the bed a wardrobe, and a lamp in the corner, the room was bare. A forlorn frown crossed his lips, then softened as he looked around. Though simple, it was his space nonetheless. He never felt more at home in any other room.

He walked over to the closet, the soles of his feet tingling against the cool stone tiles. He pulled open the door and rifled through his clothes, most of which had been handed down from Sasha's old garments. He put on a pair of cuffed black trousers, a black armless tunic tucked in at the waist, and stepped into his leather moccasins. He adjusted his belt and glanced at himself in the mirror hanging from the door, smoothening the wrinkles in his outfit. His reflection stared back at him through the cloudy pane of glass. The clothes were slightly worn and fit him loosely. He peered back at the unsure young man, who seemed as ill-fitting and out of place as the garments draped upon his frame.

Darshima pried his eyes from the mirror and started to do the packing he had meant to do a week ago. He pulled a leather duffel bag from under his bed and hastily threw in a few pairs of trousers, shirts, tunics and a pair of leather boots. He approached his desk, pulled open the drawer, and retrieved a leather envelope heavy with Vilidesian coins, his travel documents, and a communicator. A gift from Sasha for his last birthday, Darshima held the glass and aluminum object up to his face. The rectangular, glowing screen flashed with images and scrolling lines of Vilidesian script. He rarely used the device, but figured it might come in useful during the trip.

Darshima eyed the books upon his desk, deciding whether to take them. He had finished the first one about Benai, but due to his busy work schedule, he had barely started to read the one about The Vilides. He grabbed the book and threw it in his bag along with the other items. Though he would have little time to himself during the week, he figured it might be nice to have something to read during the journey. He slung his bag over his shoulder, cast a final glance around his room, and closed the door behind him.

Darshima dropped his luggage by the front entrance with the other cases. He made his way up the stairs toward Sasha's room, then knocked lightly upon the door.

"What is it now?" Sasha pulled the door open. His frown disappeared when he saw that it was only Darshima. Sasha stepped aside and let him enter. Similar to Sovani, Sasha wore an elegant red tunic with gold trim, black hemmed trousers, and sandals.

Though it was only separated by a flight of stairs, Sasha's room seemed a world apart from Darshima's. The freshly whitewashed walls were decorated with a variety of colorful paintings. Large windows in the ceiling and the walls let in ample amounts of light and gave a view onto the tree-lined street below. Several large, powilix hide rugs covered the tiled stone floor. A wood-framed feather bed lay in one corner, and a polished dark granite desk stood in the other. The thin gleaming glass screens of his new computer and televisor sat atop the stone surface, reflecting brightly in the rays of the sun.

The wall above Sasha's desk featured the mounted, sun-bleached skull of a powilix, its triplet of curved horns adorned with chains of multicolored glass beads. Hanging below it was his metal bow and leather quiver. Darshima gazed at the ornament, biting his lip as he tried to stifle his envy. Memories of the failed hunt flooding his mind, he turned away and looked at the furnishings around him. It seemed that every time he went to Sasha's room, there was some new device or object.

"Father wants me to help you with your things," said Darshima.

"You can grab that case if you'd like." Sasha pointed to a cloth bag by the door, then turned back to a pair of leather valises open at the foot of his bed.

Darshima eyed the fine new tunics, trousers, and colorful ceremonial robes within them. The golden cylinder containing his invitation was carefully nestled between the garments. While packing, Sasha looked up at Darshima, whose lips were drawn into a frown.

"What's wrong now?" Sasha paused as he folded a robe. His calm voice betrayed a hint of exasperation.

"I shouldn't be going on this trip." Darshima stood by the door, his arms folded across his chest.

"Well, father didn't give you a choice." Sasha rested his arms upon his hips and let out a sigh. "You must come with us."

"But I really..." started Darshima, but before he could finish his sentence, their father shouted from below.

"We'll be late if you both don't hurry!" His muffled voice filtered up through the floor. Darshima pried his eyes away from Sasha. He grabbed his brother's case, descended the stairs, and bolted down the hallway. His ears filled with the thud of Sasha's footsteps behind him as they walked through the front door.

It was a humid morning, and the scent of rain permeated the damp air. A gentle breeze offered a refreshing chill, and the sun peaked through the puffy white clouds. The trees lining the street towered above the house, and golden beams shone brightly through their green foliage.

Dalia and Sovani waited for them on the front porch. Sovani paced anxiously, while Dalia stood patiently. Her hair was unbraided and swept up in an elegant style, held together by silver and crystal combs. She wore a rich blue gown with a silky texture that hugged her waist. Fine chains of Ciblaithian gold graced her neck and bare shoulders.

"You look lovely, mother." Darshima smiled as he eyed her glittering jewelry.

"Oh, these are just some heirlooms from your grandmother. I seldom wear them." The corners of her eyes wrinkled pensively as she clasped the delicate chains about her neck. A pair of thick gold bracelets clinked softly upon her wrist.

"Darshima, Sasha, take those items into the coach over there," Sovani gestured toward the waiting craft parked at the edge of the walkway. Oblong in shape, the coach's gleaming metal and glass facets gave it the appearance of a cut gem under the sunlight. The engines whirred gently as it hovered motionlessly above the cobbled street.

Darshima and Sasha eyed the large pile of heavy bags by the door and set to work loading them in the trunk at the rear of the vehicle. Atop the luggage sat a hexagonal wood and copper cage that contained a pair of colorful Ardavian songbirds. It was a tradition for those attending the Prince's birthday party to bring a special gift. Sasha had neither the time nor the imagination to think of anything suitable, so Darshima took it upon himself to come up with a present. Despite his schedule, he had found time during an evening after work to trap the birds. Dalia cared for them, and she helped him build the cage by hand.

With their luggage and the gift loaded, Sasha closed the front door and Darshima followed him. They boarded the rear passenger compartment of the vehicle with their parents, and settled upon a pair of opposing padded leather benches behind the driver's seat.

"What is your destination?" asked the driver. He was a brown-skinned man, with bright amber eyes and shoulder-length, black hair. The driver smoothened the wrinkles in his red tunic and glanced over his shoulder toward the family. The vehicle slowly rose from the street, and its doors slid closed with a mechanical whir.

"Please take us to the port at Arnesis." Dalia nodded politely toward him.

The driver offered a curt wave and then guided the craft upward above the canopy of trees. He banked sharply to the right and merged into a broad band of aerial traffic that stretched beyond the horizon. The craft accelerated to speed, pressing Darshima firmly against his seat.

The wind whispered softly over the sides of the vessel as they hurtled over the city, gliding past the surrounding airborne vehicles. A grimace upon his lips, Sovani held his head down and folded his arms across his chest. He had never liked flying and it showed. Dalia sensed his unease and gently placed her hand upon his arm.

"Don't worry, I am fine." He turned to her, mustered a grin, and held her hand as the craft gained momentum.

"Your face says otherwise," she chuckled. He drew in a deep breath and settled in his seat.

Darshima shifted to the side of the bench and eagerly peered through the large rectangular window. Having only flown a few times before, it felt like a novelty to him. A smile crossed his lips as he looked upon the familiar landmarks below them. Through the broken wisps of clouds, he spied the stately old parks and winding boulevards, bustling with early morning traffic. The ornate domes and gleaming spires spread before him in a vivid tapestry of colored stone and stained glass.

"Sasha, will any of your friends be attending the prince's celebration?" asked Dalia as she arranged the folds of her gown.

"Of course." Sasha nodded eagerly.

As he listed their names, Darshima's chest grew heavy with renewed anxiety. He recognized all of those people, and they would see him at the palace serving Sasha. They would know that he had failed at his latest hunting attempt. Before Dalia could say anything, Sovani called out to them.

"Sasha, Dalia, come and take a look." He waved his hand toward the window. Darshima remained in his seat as they joined Sovani at the large pane and gazed upon the vista, their noses pressed against the smooth glass.

"The building is nearly complete and when it's finished, it will be the tallest structure on Gordanelle." Sovani pointed straight ahead. Dalia and Sasha lingered at the window, their eyes widened in surprise. "Quite impressive, isn't it?" He jovially patted Sasha's shoulder.

"It is enormous." Sasha sat back down next to Darshima.

"Darshima, you are doing an excellent job on the building. The importance of your work shows." Dalia beamed at him.

"Good work, brother." Sasha gave him an approving slap on the back.

"His work is only a small part of a much larger project," muttered Sovani. His words were cut short by Dalia's piercing glare.

"Don't listen to him, what you're doing is important." She turned to Darshima as she adjusted the bracelets upon her wrist. "I would imagine that when one seeks to raise towers to the sky, no task would be deemed too small or insignificant." She cast a harsh gaze toward Sovani.

"Father, you can't deny that Darshima has worked hard these past few months," chided Sasha. He put an arm around Darshima's shoulder and pulled him closer.

"I didn't mean to diminish his contribution." Sovani stared blankly at his hands. He let out a sigh and turned to the window.

As he registered his father's words, Darshima set his jaw and stared forlornly at the ground. Out of the corner of his eye, he saw his father peer at the scenery beyond the window, avoiding Sasha's and Dalia's glares. Sovani's comment hurt Darshima more than his usual criticisms. He had devoted so much of his time and effort at the site. A sigh escaped his lips as he realized that his father's opinion of him would likely never change, no matter how hard he tried.

His pulse thudding, Darshima rose from his seat, stepped across the cabin, and peered through the window. He had spent so many hours working on that building and wanted to see what his labor had helped to achieve. His gaze fell upon the immense frame of structural steel. Even as an unfinished skeleton, it dominated the horizon. The Vilidesian design stuck out rudely from the low domes of the skyline as it pierced through the thick ceiling of clouds.

The bottom half of the soaring tower was fully clad in clear glass panels, but the upper half remained a giant steel web. He could see the crews of people working upon the thin girders, their tiny silhouettes imprinted boldly against the bright sky. Despite its unusual appearance, he was impressed by the building. Though he was an Ardavian and preferred their traditional masoned stone buildings, he was a Vilidesian subject like everyone else. Despite his father's insensitive comment, a feeling of accomplishment rose within him as he looked upon the soaring structure.

Darshima moved back to the bench and sat down. He stared through the window beside him onto the city below, trying to avoid the concerned gazes of his mother and brother. Bars of light and shadow draped over him as they flew past the colossal spires of the viceroy's palace. The craft banked sharply to the left and traced the perimeter of the immense, hexagonal stone wall. He pressed his face against the glass and looked closely, remembering the building's importance from the books his professor had given him. Long ago, it served as the center of governance during Ardavia's brief rule over the four moons.

As the realm was vast, the royal family appointed representatives to rule in their place on the other moons. The palace was home to the Viceroy of Gordanelle, the younger brother of the Vilidesian Emperor. His younger sister served as the Vicereine of Wohiimai. Under the aegis of the emperor, Iberwight was ruled by the sovereign of the largest Omystikai order. Through the wisps of clouds, Darshima spotted a large throng at the palace gates. Protests at the palace were commonplace. People demonstrated against various grievances, such as high taxes and burdensome laws. More recently, the protesters marched against the corruption and stagnation that had become worryingly common in Ardavian affairs.

The craft flew through a canyon of immense stone buildings lining a wide boulevard, their imposing colonnades moving swiftly by as they approached the port. They glided over the open water as they made their final approach toward Arnesis, a neighboring town situated on a separate island plateau further upriver. The town hosted the largest port on Gordanelle and its airspace was the second busiest in the realm after the port in The Vilides. The lofty stone spires, docks, and passenger terminals sat upon a narrow peninsula jutting into the Eophasian River. The surrounding skies teemed with passenger and freight vessels from all corners of the realm.

Through the panes of glass, Darshima could hear the low roar of engines and the deep wail of sirens. In a great rush, the craft descended through the dense belts of traffic and landed just beyond a line of red granite towers marking the entrance of the terminal. Dalia pulled a small leather envelope from the folds of her robe, retrieved several gold coins, and handed them to the driver. Darshima and his family exited the vessel and gathered their belongings. They hurried across the smooth pavement and entered the grand, airy terminal.

Giant fabric screens of blue and gold partitioned the opposite end of the hall, obscuring the view beyond. A large woven tapestry bearing the imperial seal of four stylized crescents encircling a golden shield hung from the ceiling above the reserved space. The prince's invitees were scheduled to travel to The Vilides aboard ships from his personal fleet. Royal staff members in white trousers, leather boots, and long, shimmering blue tunics with short sleeves milled about, greeting and attending to the invitees and their guests. The staff collected their bags and confirmed their invitations. As Darshima was not an invitee, Sovani had arranged for his travel aboard an ordinary passenger ship.

"Be sure to meet us promptly when you reach The Vilides." Sovani stared at him as he hoisted his bag upon his shoulder. "This is an important week for Sasha, and we want to make a good impression."

"Yes, father." Darshima nodded earnestly.

His family bid him a hasty goodbye and joined the growing group of invitees. Darshima raised his hand for a final farewell, but they had already walked away. He clung tightly to his bag and watched them mingle with the other elegantly dressed travelers, biting his lip as a pang of envy coursed through him. Trying to push aside the feelings, he turned away and started the journey to the other end of the terminal.

Darshima arrived at his designated gate and sat upon a wooden bench among the crowds of passengers. Though tired, he fidgeted nervously in his seat as thoughts of the coming days sifted through his mind. Sasha had been vague about the duties expected of him during the week of ceremonies. Darshima would help him dress in the ornate court attire and attend to his needs during the myriad of ceremonial rituals and purification rites. He would not be permitted to stay with his family, but would lodge with the other assistants in the valet chambers beneath the palace.

Darshima narrowed his eyes as he mulled over the days ahead. A shudder coursed through him as he imagined himself attending to his brother during the ceremonies. His mind pictured the other invitees looking down upon him, seeing him as Sasha's mere servant instead of his brother. He already struggled with the fact that his family didn't treat them as equals, but now their differences would be on display for all to see.

In the weeks leading up to the trip, Darshima had pleaded with his mother about the arrangement. She had protested to Sovani, but he refused to change his mind. Darshima knew she sympathized with him, but he sensed that she was secretly glad he would be joining them. Since he was a child, she always seemed to fuss over him more than Sasha. Whenever he ventured out on his own or didn't let her know of his whereabouts, she became noticeably worried. He never understood why.

Arms folded across his chest, he stared off into the distance and tried to think about anything else. His eyes lingered curiously upon the crowds of travelers steadily streaming past him. Their colorful and distinctive garments caught the shafts of sunlight cascading through the large, oval windows in the domed ceiling above. They were from every race, tribe, and creed of the four moons. A smile crept across his lips as he saw the diverse mass of humanity milling about. Despite their various origins and cultures, they all were from the same vast realm.

A low rumbling alarm interrupted the din of the passengers' conversations and the sleepy terminal came to life. People rose from their seats, secured their belongings, and headed toward the large gate at the opposite end. Darshima grabbed his bag, hopped to his feet, and joined them. Despite his misgivings about the week ahead, his chest tightened with a sense of anticipation. He had never traveled much further than the villages surrounding Ardavia, and this would be his first journey beyond Gordanelle's skies.

"All aboard for The Vilides," shouted a slender, copper-skinned man with shoulder-length black hair and a long face. He wore a uniform of leather boots, grey trousers and a tunic embellished with the signature white trim of the shipping line. The agent stood at the front of the gate, his amber eyes narrowed as he checked people's passes and ushered them through the parted doors. Darshima showed his travel documents and walked with the crowd onto a narrow, inclined steel footbridge leading away from the building.

Darshima glanced over the railing to see workers scurrying around the enormous ship. Its narrow, blade-like metal hull glinted in the afternoon sunlight, tapering into a quartet of massive cylindrical engines at its rear. With a soft drone, the craft hovered ever so slightly above the ground, and its rows of trapezoidal gravity shields oscillated subtly. Several crews milled beneath the large panels of the fuselage, loading cargo, connecting fuel hoses, and spraying down the dusty keel.

Darshima stared intently at the ship as they boarded. He had seen these Vilidesian craft ply the skies every day, but had never had seen one up close. His eyes lingered upon its gigantic proportions and he craned his neck as he tried to glimpse its full length and breadth. Despite his efforts, the ship's entire scale eluded his view. He stepped aboard with the crowds and was enveloped by the dark interior. A pair of hands held him by the shoulders and a stocky, uniformed attendant emerged from the shadows. His face was partially illuminated by the stark lights in the ceiling above, giving his features a hollow expression. The attendant examined Darshima's pass and shot an appraising stare at him.

"Deck sixteen." He pointed toward a waiting elevator at the end of a long corridor. Its curved clear glass panels opened as Darshima approached.

He joined a small group of passengers in the carriage and it made a swift ascent, stopping at each floor, letting people on and off. The elevator reached the sixteenth level and he exited. Sunlight poured through the large, cantilevered, trapezoidal windows, reflecting brightly off the polished metal floors. Passengers settled themselves in rows of steel benches lining the deck, stowing their bags beneath them.

Darshima approached a vacant bench beside a window, sat upon its hard surface, and rested his bag at his feet. He looked out upon the curving domes and spindly watchtowers of the sprawling port. Wispy clouds sailed lazily past the large orb of Benai and the other moons, their vividness faded by the daylight. The low din of the vessel's machinery gradually faded into a deep and pulsating rumble, drowning out the chatter of the passengers.

The deck shuddered as the ship slowly rose off the ground, groaning deeply under the sheer thrust of its powerful engines. Darshima's pulse thudded, and he reflexively gripped the armrests at his sides. He eagerly peered through the window, taking in every detail as the port steadily drifted away, and the cityscape beyond revealed itself.

A commotion of voices in the rows behind him drew his attention away from the window. Darshima looked to his side and saw a young Ciblaithian man searching for a seat. Lean in stature, his skin was dark brown, and he had a sympathetic, angular face, marked by smoke-grey eyes. His curly black hair was parted to the side and shorn just past his ears. He wore a fine white tunic embroidered in gold thread, black trousers, and polished leather boots. Holding large leather cases in both hands, he struggled to avoid dropping them as the floor shifted beneath his feet.

His eyes darted among the empty seats when the ship unexpectedly lurched forward. A bag escaped his grip and sailed through the air. It landed with a clatter, bursting open in a bright flash of rich fabrics and jewelry. The man chased after it, knelt down, and gathered his belongings. He hurriedly stuffed the items back into the case and looked around to see if he was missing anything. The other passengers looked at him as he scrambled, the ship continuing its ascent. Some chuckled, but none offered any assistance.

Darshima's heart fluttered with embarrassment as he saw the man rush to repack his bag. Though Gordanellans were usually kind, they were often envious of the Vilidesians for their prosperity and their seemingly ubiquitous influence. Many believed them to be overly concerned with money, possessions, and status. Gordanellans rarely missed an opportunity to take pleasure at a Vilidesian's misstep no matter how small. The man's appearance, with his expensive luggage and fine clothing, clearly marked him as a wealthy citizen of the realm's capital.

Darshima shot a disapproving glare at the laughing passengers and shook his head. They fell silent as he rose from his seat and approached the man. He walked toward the aisle, maintaining his footing while the ship rocked beneath him. Darshima knelt down and helped the man pick up the rest of his belongings. He offered a hearty thanks and looked up at Darshima.

"An Ardavian willing to help a Vilidesian? It must be my lucky day." He rolled his eyes as he briefly looked over to the other passengers.

"Pay them no mind. Most of us are more than obliging," said Darshima as the man refastened his bag.

"I guess I'll sit here." The man pointed toward Darshima's row. Darshima helped him stow his luggage beneath the bench and they took their seats beside the window.

"Thank you for your help." The man extended his hand toward him. "I am Sydarias Idawa." His cheerful voice had a deep tone, and his sharp, Vilidesian accent was unmistakable.

"I'm Darshima Eweryn, glad to make your acquaintance." Darshima grasped his hand.

As they belted themselves in, the ship rocketed upward. Their backs pressed firmly against the bench under the force of the take-off. The ground sank rapidly away from view as they hurtled upward, the streets and buildings vanishing under the veil of clouds. The vivid green canopy of the rainforests beyond the city came into view and merged with the bright horizon.

Darshima caught a glimpse of Benai and the other moons as the ship banked sharply. His head spun as a sense of dizziness overcame him, and he gripped the armrests as they pivoted. A deep vibration shuddered through the airframe, and his teeth chattered. His stomach sinking, he clenched his jaw and stifled his retching. Embarrassed, he looked around, unable to fathom how people got used to this mode of travel.

"Are you feeling okay?" Sydarias' eyebrows arched in concern. Darshima eyed him, impressed that he hadn't even flinched. Despite the turbulence, his clothes had somehow remained perfectly in place.

"I've never been on a voyage like this." Darshima brought his hands to his mouth, waiting for the nausea to fade. The acceleration slowed some, and his heartbeat resumed its normal pace. As he acclimated to the speed, the color steadily returned to his face.

"You're going to be fine. The ride on these older ships can be rough. Nearly everyone gets sick on their first voyage." Sydarias cast a sympathetic gaze at him and chuckled.

Darshima offered a timid smile and turned toward the window, figuring that he probably looked worse than he felt. The ship rumbled through a thick layer of clouds, and then the ride smoothened.

The sky steadily faded into the blackness of space as they hurtled forward. Darshima turned back to Sydarias.

"What brought you to Ardavia?" he asked, his voice just audible over the low drone of the engines.

"I was visiting my mother's family." Sydarias pulled his gaze from the window and turned to Darshima.

"Your mother is Ardavian?" asked Darshima, his voice raised in surprise.

"Yes, some Vilidesians and Ardavians do get along." Sydarias offered a wink and chuckled. Darshima rolled his eyes, laughing along with him.

Despite the contentious relationship between the moons, there were countless mixed families throughout the realm, with the mother from one moon and the father from another. Like these families, the diverse peoples found ways to get along and prosper, despite their differences.

"What brings you to The Vilides?" Sydarias stared inquisitively at him.

"I'm attending to some family business." Darshima fidgeted nervously, unsure of what to say. Fine beads of perspiration broke out upon his forehead.

"I'm sure you're going to have a wonderful time." Sydarias offered him a broad, toothy grin. Much to Darshima's relief, he changed the subject and spoke a bit about himself.

Sydarias had turned eighteen years old a week ago, and celebrated his birthday with his family on Gordanelle. Like Darshima, he recently completed his last year of school. An avid stargazer, he obsessively tracked and observed the celestial movements. He aspired to become an astronomer and would be attending a prestigious Vilidesian university later in the year. His father, a prominent businessman was dismayed by this decision. He implored Sydarias to work at one of the family's enterprises like his older brothers, but Sydarias had refused.

Darshima's eyes widened as he heard this detail.

"You went against your father?" he asked, his voice brimming with incredulity.

“Of course, it’s my life. I’m eighteen and no longer a child.” Sydarias let out a wry laugh. A puzzled frown crossed Darshima’s lips as he contemplated Sydarias’ boldness.

“I’m no good at hunting,” he blurted, his face growing hot with shame. Darshima cast his eyes toward the ground, unsure what had compelled him to share this embarrassing fact. His heart pounded like a drum as he realized that this was one of the few times he had admitted his failure aloud.

“My mother may be Ardavian, but I’m glad my father is Vilidesian. We have no time for the powilix hunting tradition.” Sydarias peered at him, his expression softening.

“Your mother’s family didn’t make you do it?” Surprised, Darshima lifted his eyes toward Sydarias.

“We Vilidesians are far too busy earning a living for those kinds of pursuits. Thankfully, we have none of those vicious pests on our moon.” Sydarias shook his head disdainfully.

“You don’t?” Curious, Darshima leaned toward Sydarias as he spoke.

“I don’t understand how a modern society can pin someone’s adulthood on such an outdated tradition,” he said bluntly.

Darshima’s jaw dropped as he listened to the words. The passengers around them sat with stunned expressions upon their faces as they heard Sydarias. Some exchanged surprised glances and whispers. Others shook their heads in thinly veiled disgust. Sydarias looked around them and chuckled softly. His calm expression made it clear that he didn’t care about their opinions.

Darshima looked at Sydarias and felt a smile creep across his lips. He had heard of the infamous Vilidesian directness, but witnessing it firsthand surprised him. They were a wealthy and industrious people busy ruling over four moons. Always seeking to change or improve something, they had no time to parse their words. Young men and women on Ciblaithia, especially those from the capital were known to be strong-willed. At age seventeen, they were considered adults and acted with full agency in their affairs.

To Darshima's surprise, conversation flowed effortlessly between them. Sydarias had a worldly and disarming air about him that Darshima found intriguing. He couldn't recall a time when he had spoken so much about himself. Their dialogue slowed some when they both realized how hungry they were. They left their seats and made their way through a maze of narrow corridors and into an airy cafeteria. They moved through the long line of passengers and picked up rectangular metal trays with plates of steaming food. Darshima found an unoccupied booth adjacent to a window and they sat across from each other upon the firm benches. They grabbed their utensils and tucked into the spicy Ardavian meal.

As he ate, Darshima's eyes lingered upon the ever-changing view just beyond the pane of glass. The sun steadily sank below the curvature of the horizon, and the mighty Eophasian River appeared as a mere scar slicing through the primeval forests. He could still make out the vast continents, green forests, belching volcanoes, and immense tropical seas. The ship steadily gained altitude and the blackness of space hung above, seemingly within arm's reach.

"It's truly your first time leaving Gordanelle." Sydarias' eyes widened in surprise as he saw Darshima stare intently through the window. He scraped his fork noisily at the remainder of his plate and Darshima's ears pricked at the grating sound.

"Indeed it is." Darshima's heart thudded in wonderment as he beheld the moon in all of its untamed beauty.

"Wait until you see The Vilides, it will make Ardavia look like a campsite." Sydarias snickered softly. Darshima shook his head, half annoyed, half amused at Sydarias' comment. Sydarias pushed his tray away and leaned back in his seat. A beam of light pierced the window and diffused softly over him.

"I hear that it's decent for a desert town. Too much steel and glass for my tastes." Darshima smirked as he slid his tray aside.

"It is no mere town. It is the crossroads of the realm. Pictures or stories don't even scratch the surface." Sydarias let out an incredulous laugh.

"Well then, what is it like over there?" asked Darshima, his voice edged with sarcasm. "I clearly know nothing about your language or culture. I'll be a mere foreigner on your gilded moon." A dry laugh escaped Darshima's lips as he finished his sentence. Like everyone in the realm, Darshima was fully aware of The Vilides and its inescapable, hegemonic presence.

"I'm only joking, Darshima. You Ardavians are a tough people." Sydarias offered a conciliatory smile, appearing to register the sentiment behind Darshima's glare. "You probably know more about the place than I do." He cleared his throat and let out a polite chuckle. Darshima couldn't help but laugh along with him.

They lingered at their table until only a few others remained in the canteen. Darshima's gaze wandered back toward the window. He felt the ship tremble underneath them as they vaulted through the blackness of space, venturing closer to Benai. The immense grey sphere floated before them, its vivid rings appearing as if they were just beyond the pane of glass. A curved sliver of the sun emerged from behind the planet, burning a bright orange against the consuming darkness.

"Did you enjoy your visit to Ardavia?" Darshima turned toward a drowsy Sydarias, who jumped slightly at the sound of his voice.

"I didn't mean to doze off, but that food could put a large animal to sleep." Sydarias shook his head and rubbed his eyes. He straightened himself in his seat, and a bashful grin crossed his lips. "My aunt invited me to spend a few weeks at her estate outside of the city. I always have a wonderful time when I visit Gordanelle. It's such a beautiful place." The corners of his eyes wrinkled thoughtfully as he beheld the bright emerald sphere, ensconced amid the infinitesimal points of starlight.

"So what kind of family business brings you to The Vilides?" Sydarias leaned closer. A wave of nervousness came over Darshima, the question catching him by surprise. Much to his astonishment, he began to recount everything about Sasha's royal invitation.

"The Prince sent him an invitation?" Sydarias' eyes widened in amazement. "What a rare and distinguished honor." He rubbed his chin in a contemplative manner and shot a quizzical stare at Darshima. "So you weren't invited either?"

"I haven't done anything to earn an invitation." Darshima shook his head. "I've never been invited and probably never will be."

"Neither I nor my brothers were nominated, despite our father's best efforts," said Sydarias, his voice sounding uncharacteristically downbeat. "There is always next year I guess." He shrugged his shoulders.

A bout of silence fell between the two, their eyes lingering upon the view beyond the window.

"So why are you joining your family in The Vilides if you weren't invited?" Sydarias turned back to Darshima, his brow furrowing in curiosity.

Darshima gulped nervously as he heard the question. He anxiously drummed his fingers upon the table and let out a sigh.

"I have to serve as my brother's assistant during the ceremony." His eyes darted around the cafeteria, and he looked to see if anyone had overheard him.

"Don't you have a maid or a valet to help him?" Sydarias leaned back in his seat, a look of surprise spreading upon his face.

"My family doesn't have any domestic help." Embarrassed, Darshima avoided Sydarias' gaze and stared at the floor.

"That is unfair. I am sorry to hear." Sydarias nodded sympathetically.

"I'm expected to take care of him like a servant. It will be so humiliating." Darshima shook his head in frustration.

"Then don't do it." Sydarias emphatically pounded the table with his fist, and their trays clattered against its steel surface. Startled, Darshima jumped at the noise.

"I couldn't possibly disobey my parents." Darshima's jaw dropped in disbelief as he contemplated Sydarias' suggestion.

"It's ultimately your decision." Sydarias leaned forward and studied Darshima's astonished look. "It's not right for them to expect you to serve your brother in such a way."

Darshima sat in stunned silence. The concept of going against his father had never entered his mind.

"What do you mean, it's my decision?" he asked.

"You may be considered a boy in Ardavia, but you are considered a man in The Vilides. Your opinion will count just as much as your father's." Sydarias firmly rested his hand upon the table.

"Are you telling the truth?" A frown crossed Darshima's lips as he pondered the stark difference between their cultures.

"Trust yourself, and make your own decision." Sydarias cast a discerning gaze at him.

"You Vilidesians have answers for everything. It's not so simple in Ardavia." He shook his head as Sydarias playfully rolled his eyes.

Darshima looked at Sydarias, a feeling of both incredulity and envy coursing through him. He had never met someone his age with so much confidence. He turned his gaze beyond the window toward the abyss, unsure what to think of Sydarias' incredible suggestion. If only he could muster the will to speak his mind, maybe people would see him as more than Sasha's aimless younger brother. He let out a frustrated sigh, realizing that even if he tried, they might not see him any differently. His gaze idly wandered through the points of starlight as he contemplated a way out of his predicament. He didn't know how he would make it through the week.

"We should go back to the deck, but this conversation isn't over." Sydarias offered an earnest smile and a resolute nod.

"If you say so." Darshima shrugged his shoulders, his thoughts preoccupied by Sydarias' bold words. They rose from their seats, returned their trays, and left the cafeteria.

Chapter Nine

The large speakers in the ceiling above crackled to life and Darshima awoke with a start from a fleeting bout of sleep. A booming voice echoed throughout the deck, announcing their descent to Ciblaithia. The floor rumbled beneath his feet as the ship applied its brakes. He peered around at the other passengers, who stretched and yawned as they roused themselves.

"Finally awake?" Sydarias playfully nudged his shoulder.

"Where are we?" Darshima rubbed his bleary eyes. As he straightened his clothes, he looked over to Sydarias who didn't appear the least bit disheveled.

"We're nearly there. The journey takes about one Ciblaithian day, or one and a half Gordanellan days." He glimpsed through the window.

"What does that mean?" Darshima shot a quizzical glance at him.

"The moons have slightly different lengths of day. Don't be surprised if you have trouble sleeping or if you feel tired," said Sydarias.

"I hadn't realized that even the time here would be different." Darshima shook his head in disbelief.

"We Vilidesians measure everything." Sydarias' eyes narrowed in a professorial expression.

"Every second matters here, doesn't it?" Darshima chuckled as he adjusted himself in the firm seat.

"Time and money are everything." A shrewd frown crossed his lips. "We are the bankers, the builders, the timekeepers..."

"And also the taskmasters, don't forget that." Darshima rolled his eyes sarcastically.

"The responsibility falls upon us to maintain order." Sydarias folded his arms across his chest.

Darshima let out a sigh as he heard Sydarias' words, reminding himself that he was no longer in Ardavia. Long ago the Vilidesians had created the calendar that all of the other moons followed. Timeliness, efficiency, and accuracy were an essential part of their culture and commerce. Combined with the might of their military, they were the unquestioned rulers of the four moons. Back on Gordanelle, life flowed at a less punctual, more spontaneous pace. It was normal to take breaks throughout the day or pay an unexpected visit to a friend's home. Ardavians often derided the Vilidesians for their obsession with time and money.

"If you're not too busy during your stay, come and visit me. It would be my pleasure to show you around." Sydarias' serious expression dissolved into a ready smile. He handed Darshima a crisp metal card. Darshima held the glinting blue object up to his eyes and examined its details. The front surface bore Sydarias' full name and address in flowing gold script. He turned it over and glimpsed the etchings of an unfamiliar constellation that caught the light with a curious shimmer.

"Thank you, but I don't have one to exchange with you." Darshima hefted the smooth card before stowing it in his bag.

"Don't worry about it." Sydarias looked at Darshima, the corners of his eyes wrinkling. "I'll be sure to remember you."

They gathered their belongings and made their way down the aisle toward the exit, bracing against the railings as the craft shuddered. As they waded through the crowd, Sydarias chatted casually about the city and places that Darshima should try and see while there. They took an elevator down to the main deck of the ship and waited next to a wall of windows. The large sphere of Ciblaithia occupied the entire view, and the abyss of space appeared as a faint black halo around its edge. The sun illuminated half of the moon's bright golden surface, and the other half was veiled in darkness.

"Look closely, and you'll be able to see some of the larger buildings." Sydarias pointed at the surface. What appeared as shimmering granules rapidly morphed into dense clusters of towers as the ship hurtled toward the gilded orb. Countless pinpoints of light illuminated the dark side of the moon, glittering like gems.

They dashed through the hazy atmosphere, the windows flashing bluish-white as they pierced through the vapor. The ship careened through the misty layers, its engines letting out a deep growl. They descended further, and the clouds faded into clear nothingness. Darshima stepped away from the window and shielded his eyes from the reflection of the gleaming, golden dunes.

Built on the ruins of an ancient Omystikai settlement, The Vilides was located upon a wide bay sheltered by a pair of opposing, curved peninsulas, extending like shields into the only ocean on Ciblaithia's surface. Inhabited for thousands of years, the sandy terrain had long been paved over by a mosaic of streets and boulevards. Grand tower blocks reached stupendous heights, piercing the clouds. The buildings here were far taller and more sophisticated than in any other city of the realm.

The ship slowed its descent and maneuvered its giant bulk into a swiftly flowing stream of aerial vehicles. Like long gleaming chains, innumerable bands of traffic filled the skies, winding intricately between the gleaming edifices of glass and metal. Darshima eyed the orderly grid of streets below, pulsing with the flow of terrestrial vehicles and pedestrians. The craft expertly glided through the levels of traffic and aimed toward the port.

A grand glass and metal hub built upon a triangular-shaped island in the bay, the port was barely visible amid the forests of gleaming skyscrapers. Far and away the busiest destination in the realm, it served as a crossroads for passengers and freight from thousands of cities and villages upon the four moons.

"It's enormous," whispered Darshima, his heart stirring in awe.

"All routes lead to The Vilides." Sydarias made a sweeping gesture across the expansive vista. Darshima had often heard that phrase as a child. As he viewed the frenzied activity, he finally understood what those words meant.

The ship made its final approach and then hovered beside a large terminal. The steel towers and arched docks loomed overhead, the light reflecting brilliantly off the gleaming pyramidal domes. With a great groan, the engines powered down and the craft landed with a gentle thud. Bags in tow, Darshima and Sydarias moved amid the bustling crowds on the deck. They crept forward through the exit, down a gangway, and stepped into the enclosed entrance hall. Darshima walked a few paces behind Sydarias and held tightly onto his bag.

"Follow me." Sydarias stepped assuredly through the diverse crowds milling about the vast space. He jostled through the swarms of luggage-laden humanity and made a path for both of them. Darshima's gaze wandered as they walked across the polished floor, its gleaming blue and white checkered tiles mirroring their reflections. Soft reddish-gold light from the afternoon sun poured through the immense glass windows. High above, he spotted flocks of birds gliding under the vaulted glass and steel canopy. The hushed flapping of their wings echoed softly against the ceiling.

The unexpected grip of a hand upon his shoulder snapped him out of his thoughts.

"Darshima, you're no longer on Gordanelle, you must keep your wits about you." Sydarias looked worriedly upon him. They stood still as the crowds moved swiftly around them.

"I'll be more careful." Darshima winced as he felt a wave of embarrassment come over him. As they resumed their trek across the terminal, he eyed the passengers in their colorful patterned tunics and robes, heading to various exits and quays. The Vilidesians viewed people from the other moons as rustic, unsophisticated, and easily fooled. Darshima hoped that Sydarias hadn't already developed that impression of him.

They moved through the crowds, toward the building's entrance at the water's edge. Darshima eyed the bustling cityscape just beyond an enormous colonnade of gleaming, arched steel gates marking the entrance. Intermittent peals of laughter, and joyous cries of travelers ecstatic to reunite with their kith and kin filled the concourse. Off in the distance, Darshima saw a small group of people emerging from a separate gate. He could make out the forms of his mother, father, and brother as they walked across the terminal. Sovani peered at the crowds, spotted Darshima, and approached him.

"Well, Darshima, I must leave. My family is expecting me at home for dinner." Sydarias hoisted his leather cases upon his shoulders.

"Thank you Sydarias, I would have been lost without you." An earnest smile crossed Darshima's lips.

"I am glad to help," said Sydarias. "Give me a call. If you have time, we should meet before you leave."

"I'd like that very much." Darshima nodded. Sydarias shook his hand, gave him a hearty slap on the back, and merged into the crowd.

Before Darshima could collect his thoughts, his father stood in front of him and clasped his shoulder.

"Darshima, please stop idling. We will be late if you don't hurry." Sovani frowned, his hushed voice brimming with irritation. Darshima's chest tightened in surprise as he saw his father's stern gaze. He handed a case over to Darshima, then walked toward Sasha and Dalia.

Darshima gripped the bag and stood still for a moment, bewildered by Sovani's anger. He didn't understand what had made him so upset, and presumed his father was anxious about the events in the upcoming week. After all, they would be in the presence of both royalty and the Vilidesian elite. Luggage in hand, Darshima followed a few steps behind his family as they made their way toward the exit.

His mind raced as he thought about the days ahead, fearing that things would only worsen between him and his father during the festivities. He didn't want their anger at each other to spoil Sasha's achievement. His stomach churned as a feeling of worry came over him. He didn't know how he would make it through the week. His eyes lingered upon the checkered stone tiles as they passed through the entrance and into the afternoon heat.

Chapter Ten

The Ewerÿn family, along with the prince's other guests boarded a large fleet of gleaming, imperial ships stationed upon a reserved airfield just beyond the gates. Waves of heat radiated from their angular fuselages as they shimmered under the midday sun. In a great rush of wind, the vessels ascended amid the brassy fanfare of the prince's ceremonial guard, standing at attention alongside. Clutching their silver horns, the troops issued rousing notes, their long blue and white tunics fluttering in the fleet's wake.

Darshima looked forlornly through the window as they zipped over the grand boulevards, amid the narrow canyons of soaring skyscrapers. Despite the astounding views spreading before him, his mind was still back at the port. For as far back as he could remember, Sasha was their father's favorite, but rarely had he been so open about it. Darshima had never let the distinction bother him before, but this time it felt different.

They traversed the bay and landed upon an airfield on the grounds of the royal palace. Perched above the city, the palace was built upon the verdant palisades of the western peninsula, which curved into the blue waters of the bay. The palace stood out boldly from the surrounding metal and glass skyscrapers that had risen around it over the centuries. Hewn from massive blocks of pearl-colored granite, its hexagonal base and chamfered stone spires stood elegantly against the shapeless clouds in the sky. Its lush, well-manicured gardens contrasted greatly with the rest of the region's arid terrain. Having been home to generations of emperors and empresses, its magnificence was widely renowned.

The passengers disembarked from the fleet of craft and walked upon the immaculate, white stones of the column-lined pathway toward the palace entrance. Darshima followed his family as they exited their vessel. Squinting his eyes against the brilliant sunlight, he was immediately taken aback by the suffocating temperature. The dry air had a slightly salty, metallic odor that he could almost taste. He had heard of the formidable climate on Ciblaithia, but nothing could have prepared him for it. Panting in the heat, he unbuttoned his tunic at the collar and eyed the other guests, who did the same. Gordanellan men usually went bare-chested in such heat. The Vilidesians were more formal in their dress and would frown upon such casualness, especially at the palace.

Sovani, Dalia, and Sasha mingled with the other invitees amid the leafy gardens. Darshima looked on as the three engaged in a lively bout of conversation with a group of old friends from their neighborhood back home. His pulse thudded nervously as his eyes swept over their familiar faces. His stare froze when he recognized Seth, Sasha's friend from the hunt earlier that season. Dressed in a white, embroidered tunic, black trousers, and leather sandals, Seth stood with a playful arm around Sasha's shoulder as he spoke to him. Without warning, Seth turned toward Darshima. Eyes widening in surprise as he recognized him, Seth offered a cautious wave.

Darshima's stomach sank as they exchanged glances, and he hastily waved back. He imagined that Seth and the others must have wondered why he had accompanied Sasha without an invitation. He was sure Sasha had already told them that he was serving as his assistant. A frustrated groan escaped Darshima's lips, and he clenched his jaw. His chest tightening with a wave of anxiety, he wished he could simply disappear.

Darshima walked to the rear of the craft, grabbed several bags, and carried them to a reception area near the entrance. Teams of porters dressed in tidy uniforms consisting of folded, white cloth headdresses, long grey tunics, trousers, and black boots, received the cases and brought them into the palace. After the first two trips, Darshima was already fatigued from the exertion and the heat. He knew that Sasha and their parents would require several kinds of costumes for the week, but the sheer quantity of luggage overwhelmed him.

Darshima lumbered back for a third trip, his tunic dripping with sweat. His arms laden with cases and the birdcage, he started back toward the palace. Just as the cage was about to slip from his grasp, a hand reached beside him and caught it. He looked up to see Sasha with the cage in hand and the birds unharmed.

"I'm sorry, I should be helping you with these." Sasha stepped beside him.

"You should go and chat with your friends," muttered Darshima as he grappled with the slipping baggage.

"Let me help you." Balancing the cage in one hand, Sasha reached with his other hand and took a bag from Darshima.

"Really, I'm fine." Darshima panted as he lifted the other cases.

"I understand that this trip is hard on you. Thank you for helping me." A gracious smile crossed Sasha's lips. Between breaths, Darshima offered a hasty nod and a grunt. He followed Sasha back to the palace with the last items in hand. As they approached the entrance, his frustration lessened a bit. He hadn't expected his brother to thank him.

Groups of royal staff members stood near the entrance and greeted each family. Like all Ciblaithians, they were slender with dark brown skin. Their smooth faces were marked by bright grey eyes and a serious demeanor. They either had shaved heads or wore their black woolen hair in various braided styles. Dressed in immaculate uniforms of blue, long-sleeved tunics with embroidered gold trim, white trousers and leather boots, they stood out among the crowd. Darshima marveled as they didn't seem to even break a sweat under the intense heat. The Eweryn family stepped forward, and the staff collected most of their luggage as they ushered them inside.

Sasha held onto the birdcage and Darshima carried one of his mother's small cases along with his own bag. Accompanied by their parents, they entered the palace with the rest of the invitees. Darshima looked around, his eyes widening in awe as they passed through the enormous, golden doors. A shiver coursed through him as he peered around the rarified space, his mind recalling the descriptions that he had read as a child. The palace stood at the proverbial center of The Vilides and in turn, the center of the realm. Over the ages, decisions of great consequence had been made within these walls.

He craned his neck up at the soaring glass and stone atrium. Magnificent tapestries hung from the gleaming walls. Lush green vines and vivid floral bouquets from Gordanelle festooned the vaulted stone arches. The air held a pleasing fragrance and carried a much-welcomed chill. The porters shuttled back and forth from the atrium to the inner chambers with the guests and their belongings, their soft conversation echoing throughout the grand space.

Lively music performed by an unseen orchestra permeated the tranquil atmosphere, the harmonious, airy notes brightening the mood. After examining each invitation, the royal staffers admitted the guests into the palace's inner chambers. Many of the invitees eyed the birdcage in Sasha's hand, voicing their admiration. The energetic pair with their colorful plumage, hopped about the cage, their sweet chirping attracting many delighted stares. No one else had thought of a gift so unique. Sasha accepted their praises and returned them with a humble nod. Darshima smiled to himself, pleased at their responses.

The sound of a slamming door followed by the sharp click of footsteps interrupted the festive ambiance, and Darshima lifted his gaze toward the noise. A figure emerged through a set of ornate wooden doors on the mezzanine above. His skin, a golden brown, glowed under the sunlight filtering through the windows. His cerulean eyes were narrowed and his nostrils flared as he breathed. His dark silky hair was fashioned in two thick, long jeweled braids that draped over his broad shoulders and rested midway down his back.

A fine blue shirt embroidered with rays of gold thread draped his sinewy torso. His high collar was fastened with an exquisite silver broach, studded with blue and white gems. A thick gold chain adorned with a hexagonal golden pendant hung at his neck, its finely engraved links glinting in the rays of sunlight. He wore tailored white trousers embroidered with curlicues of golden thread. His black leather boots, heeled with silver, clicked methodically against the polished stone. A cloak of shimmering dark blue silk, embellished with flowing ribbons of gold draped his broad shoulders, trailing behind him as he walked. He came to a stop at the front of the stone balcony extending over the crowd. One of his uniformed assistants, followed several steps behind, his blue tunic fluttering about.

"Your Highness," started the assistant.

"I'll attend to it later, now please take your leave." The man looked over his shoulder and glared harshly at his assistant, who fearfully scuttled away. The severity of his tone cut through the air like a knife. The crowd below ceased their milling about and stared up curiously at the balcony. The man looked out over the large group of invitees, his brow furrowed pensively.

Darshima's pulse quickened in surprise as he realized that the person on the balcony was Prince Khydius himself. He looked up at the prince, who seemed to be staring right through him. The fine hairs upon the nape of his neck stood on end as he countered the prince's intense gaze. Darshima anxiously traced the direction of his stare, and it terminated directly upon his right arm. His markings stood out boldly under the bright light flooding the atrium. The prince's eyes lingered upon it briefly and then searched about the room. A cold sweat broke out upon Darshima's forehead as his mind replayed the unexpected encounter. He turned away from the balcony and nervously hoisted his bag upon his shoulder. As he looked around, a sense of relief came over him. No one seemed to notice their silent exchange.

The prince looked at his guests and flashed a broad smile.

"My apologies for the unintended disturbance," said the prince, his deep voice echoing throughout the atrium. "I look forward to welcoming you all tonight at my reception."

The crowd cheered at the sight of Prince Khydius and broke into a frenzied applause. The prince offered a polite wave, and his smile dissolved as quickly as it had come. He stepped away from the balcony and walked back through the doors. The guests exchanged astonished glances, unsure of what to make of his unanticipated appearance, then resumed their conversations.

Darshima and his family waited at the front of the line for admission to the inner chambers. A uniformed member of the royal staff approached them with her hands extended in a welcoming gesture.

"Greetings Eweryn Family, I hope your journey to The Vilides was enjoyable," she said, her voice ringing with a restrained, but cheerful tone. She was a tall Vilidesian woman with smooth dark skin, bright grey eyes, and a broad smile. Her tightly coiled black hair was fashioned in a crown of elegant braids, woven with chains of gold. She wore a white and blue robe that covered her shoulders and draped over her slender frame. She cast an appraising eye upon Sasha as he reached into his case and handed the invitation to her.

"Whom have you brought with you, Sasha?" She opened the golden vessel and withdrew the scroll. Her delicate hands unfolded the silk fabric, and her gaze moved swiftly between the embroidered script and their faces.

"My father Sovani, my mother Dalia, and my brother Darshima." Sasha gestured toward his family as he spoke. When Sovani heard Darshima's name, he let out a deliberate cough.

"Darshima is only here to serve as Sasha's assistant during the ceremonies." He dismissively waved a hand in Darshima's direction.

"The valets will lead you to your suite. You will find the rest of your luggage awaiting you there." She handed the invitation back to Sasha and pointed toward the interior of the palace. She then snapped her fingers, and one of the porters handed her a grey cloth bag before scuttling away.

"Darshima, here are your uniforms for the week. After you assist your family, please return to the atrium promptly for further instruction. I will direct you to the quarters you will share with the other assistants during the ceremonies." She handed the bag to him. Darshima gulped nervously, and a knot formed in the pit of his stomach as he took it from her. His pulse thudded as a dull, familiar sense of disquiet came over him. He didn't know how he would make it through the week.

A pair of burly, uniformed valets escorted the family up the grand marble staircase. They walked through an opulently furnished corridor, supported by an immense colonnade of veined marble arches, filigreed with gold leaf. The sunlight spilled through rows of hexagonal windows in the vaulted ceiling high above, reflecting warmly upon the gleaming stone floors. Towering marble busts of the dynastic rulers stood on pedestals lining the corridor. Richly painted tableaux depicting sweeping vistas of the four moons and historic battles adorned the walls of the cavernous space.

The valets admitted them to their suite and quietly exited. Larger than their home in Ardavia, it contained several rooms appointed in lavish style. As his family settled in, Darshima walked slowly around the magnificent apartment, taking in the sights and smells. The air held the sweet fragrance of wildflowers and perfume. His fingers glided along the finely crafted furniture, made of dark lustrous woods from Gordanelle's tropical forests. The rich curtains, plush patterned rugs, and crisp woven linens came from Wohiimai's finest looms. He looked at the white plaster walls, glittering with painted rays of gold. Hanging chandeliers, fashioned of rare crystals mined on Iberwight caught the afternoon sunlight and emitted a soft white glow.

Darshima made his way to a wall of tall, rectangular windows framing the room and beheld the intriguing view before him. The impossibly vast Vilidesian cityscape beckoned just beyond the clear panes. From the high vantage point of the palace, the bay and the city spread out, abutting the horizon. He eyed the unending rows of soaring, jagged towers that seemingly floated above the waters. The enormous grey sphere of Benai occupied the eastern sky and the three other moons hung in a line just above the city. Growing up he had heard tales of this place and its importance as the realm's capital. Now he understood why it engendered so much awe. He felt as if he were at the center of the universe.

The click of footsteps upon the stone tile abruptly pulled Darshima from his daydream. He turned around to see his father standing in the center of the apartment. Sovani looked around, a smile spreading across his face.

"I could get used to this." He turned to Dalia, his voice brimming with contentment. "The first reception will begin shortly, so we must prepare."

"I'll be ready soon," said Sasha as he walked over to his quarters. Sovani's cheerful smile faded as he turned toward Darshima.

"Help Sasha with his things and then return downstairs at once. You mustn't be late." He pointed toward the pile of bags just beyond the threshold of the door.

Darshima's excitement dissipated, and the feelings of anxiousness crept back. He avoided Sovani's stare, and collected his bags along with Sasha's items. He followed Sasha to his room and closed the door behind them.

Darshima knelt upon the floor amid the luggage and set to work. He opened the cases and one by one unpacked Sasha's garments.

"We've finally made it." Sasha sauntered to the edge of the large, canopied bed, let out a contented sigh and collapsed atop the downy coverings.

"So we have," whispered Darshima, as he held the garments. He unfolded the fine tunics, trousers, and jackets, meticulously smoothening out their wrinkles as he arranged them in the ample closets. He bit his lip as he worked, trying to stave off the simmering feelings of resentment. Unsure of what awaited him downstairs, his mind replayed the assistant's words back in the grand foyer. He had no idea what his accommodations would be, but he knew they would be a far cry from the luxury of this apartment.

Darshima finished unpacking Sasha's clothes and walked to the opposite end of the large room. He stood before a comfortable sofa along the wall, richly upholstered in lustrous white silk. His gaze drifted down to his wrinkled, damp tunic. Imagining the commotion he would cause were he to rest his weary, sweaty frame upon such a fine furnishing, he took a step back. He shook his head in frustration, sat down on the cool stone floor, and let out a sigh.

Darshima reached for the bag that the staff member had given him and sifted through its contents. He eyed several sets of short-sleeved grey tunics and trousers, similar to the uniforms of the porters. He let out an audible groan and rested his head against the wall.

"What's the matter?" Sasha sat up on the edge of the bed.

“I’m just a bit tired.” Darshima stared at his brother, who was now up and moving about. Sasha rifled through the garments in the closet, tossing several articles onto his bed. Darshima’s eyes narrowed in mild annoyance as Sasha rummaged through the items that he had so carefully organized.

“What are you doing?” Darshima propped himself against the wall, his back aching from fatigue.

“The prince is hosting the welcome reception this evening and I must get ready.” Sasha rushed around the room, trying on various trousers and shirts. “You should get ready too, they’re expecting you downstairs.” Sasha pointed toward the door, then stepped into the bathroom.

“I just need a moment more.” Darshima’s face grew hot with embarrassment as he leaned against the wall. He eyed his shadow as it stretched across the floor, growing longer in the waning sunlight. A yawn escaped his lips, as the combination of the voyage and the faster Ciblaithian days caught up with him. He rose to his feet, slid out of his clothes, and changed into the grey palace uniform. He stashed his old garments in his bag and walked to the mirror. His brow knit in frustration as he examined himself in the loosely fitting uniform. The imperial seal, embroidered in gold thread, gleamed prominently over the right breast.

Darshima imagined himself walking behind Sasha and assisting him for the entire week, wearing this uniform. His mind racing, he drew in a slow breath and tried to calm himself. He walked back to the corner of the room and sat along the wall. The sound of rushing water from the bathroom broke the consuming silence. A warm cloud of steam seeped from underneath the bathroom door, enveloping him in its fragrant scent.

Darshima closed his eyes and fell into a lull amid his racing thoughts. The sounds of the water faded, and as he drifted into a fitful bout of sleep, he felt a hand clasp his shoulder. His eyes snapped open to see his father stooped before him.

"Wake up Darshima. You are late for your meeting in the atrium." Sovani stood back up and glared at him.

Darshima rose to his feet and stretched, attempting to soothe his weary muscles. He looked around him, unsure of how much time had passed. Orange jets of flame rose from gilded torches in the corners of the room, casting a soft glow against the walls. He looked at the windows to see the sun had already set. The innumerable lights of the skyline glittered against the darkness, reflecting upon the waters of the bay.

Darshima pulled his gaze from the window and met the stares of Sovani, Sasha, and Dalia. They were dressed in their best attire for the upcoming reception. Sovani and Sasha wore their hair combed back in an elegant style. They were dressed in tailored black trousers, boots, white tunics, and black embroidered Vilidesian overcoats. Dalia wore a shimmering metallic blue gown and white slippers. Her silky hair was parted and cascaded down her back. Thick gold bracelets graced her wrists, and an intricate necklace of glittering Iberwightian crystal hung about her delicate neck. A fine white and gold silk shawl covered her shoulders, and she clutched a small leather purse. He had never seen them dressed in such finery.

Darshima looked down at his plain servant's tunic, his heart seized by an aching sense of humiliation.

"They are waiting for you, Darshima." Dalia's fingers nervously adjusted the crystals of her necklace. Her eyes glinted with concern as she beheld him.

"You must hurry, or we will all be late." Sovani let out an impatient sigh.

Sasha folded his arms across his chest, his brow knit in frustration as he stared at the ceiling. Darshima's pulse raced as feelings of anger replaced his embarrassment. He had not wanted to come here, but his family had forced him to join them. They had always made his decisions for him, from working at the construction site to making him serve Sasha at the prince's celebration.

Darshima beheld his family in their fine clothing, their stares cutting right through him. Never in his life had he felt more like an outcast, nor had the differences between him and his family felt more apparent. He drew in a deep breath and tried to maintain his composure. Like a lightning bolt, Sydarias' words of defiance charged through his mind. When Darshima had shared his dilemma during their voyage, Sydarias had encouraged him to make his own choice and not serve as Sasha's assistant.

A knot formed at the pit of his stomach, and he pondered the outcome of such a move. He had always honored his family's wishes, but he was no longer at home. He was an adult in this world and could do as he liked. His heart beating boldly, he willed himself to say it aloud.

"I won't do it." Darshima narrowed his eyes and glared at his family. His father's brow wrinkled in disbelief.

"You wouldn't dare," barked Sovani. He stomped toward Darshima, but Dalia swiftly extended her hand and tapped Sovani's chest. He froze in mid-step, looked upon his wife, and then squarely upon Darshima. His nostrils flared as he drew in an angry breath.

"I know that being here is hard for you Darshima, but please help your brother. This is an important week for him." Dalia's lips curled into a frown, her voice wavering.

Darshima felt the corners of his eyes grow damp as he looked at her. He hated to see his mother so upset but to his own surprise, he held firm.

"I don't want to serve as Sasha's assistant. Don't you understand how humiliating this is for me?" Darshima shook his head, his voice filled with anguish.

His eyes narrowed, Sovani stepped past Dalia.

"Stop thinking only about yourself." He seized Darshima by the shoulders. "This is not your decision to make. You will do as I say."

"I am sorry Sasha, but I won't do it." Darshima wrested himself from his father's grasp. He angrily tore off the tunic, threw it upon the ground, and stood bare-chested before his family. Sasha glared at him with a wounded frown upon his lips.

"How dare you disobey me!" Sovani snarled at Darshima and swiftly raised his hand. Just as Sovani was about to strike him, Sasha cried out.

"Father, stop this at once!" Sasha rushed between them and grabbed Sovani's wrist.

"What are you doing?" Sovani's face contorted in a look of utter surprise.

"This is supposed to be a celebration and you're ruining it." Sasha trembled, his voice brimming with frustration. "I don't need an assistant for the ceremonies this week."

"He is your brother and he should be grateful to serve you." Sovani spat the words as he yanked his wrist from Sasha's grasp.

"He is far too old for this role father, and it's embarrassing to him. Why won't you see that?" Sasha threw up his hands in exasperation. "We are nothing like these wealthy Vilidesian families who have servants, and that's fine. We don't need to impress anyone."

Shaken, Sovani stared at Sasha, the color draining from his face. He then turned to Darshima.

"So be it. Get dressed, you cannot stay here." Sovani stepped away from Darshima, his voice trembling with uncharacteristic emotion. "When the week is over, you will find somewhere else to live and to work. You are no longer welcome in my home or at the construction site."

Darshima's stomach sank, and a wave of anguish hit him as he registered his father's words. He hastily pulled off the rest of the uniform and changed back into his old tunic and trousers. As he grabbed his belongings, Dalia let out an angry gasp.

"I will not allow it. He is our son and you will not kick him out of our house." She turned to Darshima. "What has gotten into you?" Her voice wavered.

"I don't mean to cause any trouble, but I just can't do it." Darshima let out an anguished sigh.

"Is this what you want? To make your father angry, to abandon your brother and to hurt me?" Dalia shook her head, a pained frown forming upon her lips.

"I don't want to hurt you, but I have made up my mind." His heart rose into his throat, and his eyes grew damp at her stinging rebuke. Sasha stepped forward and faced him.

"I understand, you're free to go. We will be fine." A wounded smile crossed Sasha's lips as he embraced Darshima.

"I'm sorry, Sasha," stammered Darshima as he returned the hug.

"Don't be." Sasha peered into his eyes for a moment longer and then let him go. Dalia looked on, a drained expression spreading upon her face. She retrieved a handkerchief from her purse, and dabbed the corners of her eyes.

"Where will you stay, Darshima?" she asked, her voice weighted with concern.

"I will find something," he replied hesitantly. Darshima looked down at the floor and avoided her stare. He couldn't bear to see the sadness in her eyes. He grabbed his bag and started for the doorway.

"Darshima, wait." She walked toward him, the rich fabric of her gown trailing behind her. She rifled through her purse and pulled out a small leather envelope, the heavy coins inside clinking against each other. "Please take this." She extended it toward him. "You will need to pay for your for lodging and provisions."

"You don't have to worry mother, I can take care of myself." He pushed the envelope back toward her. He had brought his own money with him to cover his expenses.

"Darshima, please take it, I won't allow you to refuse my help," she pleaded.

"Thank you," he whispered, as he grudgingly took the envelope and shoved it into his bag. She put her hands upon his cheeks and looked at him intently.

"I want you to be careful when you are out there. This world can be dangerous. I will not be around to protect you." Her hands dropped to her sides and a shadow of sadness crossed her features. "I shouldn't have let your father bring you here," she whispered.

Her words took him by surprise. Dalia was always sure in her decisions and rarely expressed such regret.

"I'll be fine, please don't worry about me." Darshima reached over and embraced his mother. She returned the gesture and kissed his forehead. Dalia cleared her throat and then stepped beside her husband.

Sovani glared at him and tapped his foot, the click of his boot echoing loudly throughout the room.

"Stop this spectacle and leave at once!" He pointed toward the door. Darshima turned away from them, stepped out of Sasha's room, and exited the apartment before he could change his mind.

He walked down a grand hallway, his moccasins padding softly against the checkered tile. The chilled air was filled with the melodious harmonies of an orchestra and the excited murmurs of a large crowd. A pair of uniformed valets at the end of the corridor waved to him, their smooth, dark skin glistening under the torchlight.

"You are late for the meeting in the atrium. The other assistants are already at their posts, please come with us." They looked upon him sternly, beckoning him to hurry.

"I won't be joining the others. Can you show me the exit?" asked Darshima.

The pair exchanged confused glances, then nodded solemnly. They accompanied him through a discrete door along the hallway, and down a maze of dimly lit corridors. The valets showed him to a service exit, bade him good evening, and headed back into the palace. A pair of uniformed sentries ushered him through a large iron gate. Darshima jumped as it clanged loudly behind him, echoing in the night. A warm breeze blew through his clothes as he walked away from the palace, down a steep, winding wooded path.

A sense of numbness overwhelmed Darshima as he walked forward. He had never quarreled with his family, nor had he ever seen them so angry. His mother's words reverberated through his head. He wasn't sure what had come over him. His stomach sank as he recalled the sadness upon her face. Her disappointment hurt him more than anything else. He shuddered as the image of Sovani's open hand flashed before his eyes. Only children were disciplined in such a manner back on Gordanelle. His father's threat to strike him for his transgression said far more than his words ever could.

Darshima trudged along the path, trampling over the stones and upturned roots at his feet. His face flushed with a mix of anger and sadness, he cast his gaze upon the ground. For weeks, he had pleaded with his family to excuse him from this trip, but they had ignored him. He had gone against their demands, but he felt that he had been left with no other choice. He nervously shook his head as he mulled the repercussions awaiting him when he returned home. An Ardavian child who acted in a manner contrary to his parents' wishes was looked upon unfavorably. He would be on his own with no family, no place to live, and no job. His heart fluttered with worry as he contemplated his uncertain future.

The terrain grew steeper as he walked along the path toward the city. The image of Sasha standing between him and his father hung before his eyes. Sasha had always defended him, but this was the first time Darshima went against their father. He drew in a deep breath as he pondered Sasha's selfless move. Tears fell from the corners of his eyes, and he stopped in the middle of the trail. His chest felt heavy as the weight of his transgression settled into a new and worrisome reality. He dried his eyes with the back of his hand, then looked over his shoulder. The immense stone towers of the palace stood boldly in the moonlight and loomed over him. His gaze lingered upon the grillwork of the closed gate, veiled in shadow.

Darshima peered up at the night sky and drew in an anguished breath. Starlight, like bright gems, studded the cloudless firmament. He glimpsed the deep emerald sphere of Gordanelle, the white crystalline orb of Iberwight, and the blue-grey crescent of Wohiimai. Amid his worries, he felt a growing sense of relief. It felt as if a burden had been lifted from his shoulders. He had stood up to his father and his family and chose not to be his brother's servant. Somehow, he would find a way to deal with the repercussions of his decision. He dusted himself off and continued along the trail.

Chapter Eleven

Darshima reached the end of the winding path and walked through a series of tall, guarded gates leading to the edge of a busy thoroughfare. He started down the crowded walk, unsure where to go. The streets were filled with noisy, hurried throngs of pedestrians ducking in and out of shops and businesses. The air rippled with the din of aircraft in the sky and the rumble of four-wheeled vehicles on the ground speeding past, their tires kicking up clouds of sand and dust.

With each step, his worries lessened some. For the first time in a very long while, he was unencumbered by any obligations. Much of his time back home was spent working at the construction site or helping his family. A hesitant smile crossed his lips as he contemplated this unexpected situation. He had always wanted to travel beyond Gordanelle and see The Vilides. Circumstances aside, he was finally here and free to do as he liked.

Darshima made his way through the crowds, walking along the tidy boulevards and through the bustling intersections. He craned his neck up and glimpsed the urban scenery before him. Dense, shimmering clusters of glass and metal towers surrounded him, their pinnacles stretching toward the stars. He squinted as he peered through the clear panes, curiously eyeing the silhouettes of people carrying about their lives.

The ghostly form of Benai occupied the eastern sky, floating high above the buildings. Appearing much larger here than back on Gordanelle, its light illuminated the glazed edifices in its soft, celestial glow. The wide bands of planetary rings appeared as if they were slowly grinding themselves into the horizon.

Thick, low-hanging clouds steadily drifted by, obscuring the moons. A lump rose in Darshima's throat as he saw Gordanelle disappear behind the mists. He missed Ardavia more than he would have imagined. Darshima shook his head and tried to ignore the feeling. He would be on Ciblaithia for only a week and wanted to see as much as possible. Darshima's chest tightened anxiously as his thoughts returned to the argument at the palace. Whether he wanted to or not, he would have to return to Gordanelle, and somehow find a way to reconcile with his family.

As Darshima turned down another boulevard, the sky grew noticeably darker. Save for a few hurried stragglers, the crush of people and vehicles crowding the streets earlier that evening had all but disappeared. He stopped in the middle of the pavement, a sense of worry rising within him. He didn't know what to make of the strange calm. Darshima looked upward and saw a lone freight vessel streak across the evening sky, its beacons flickering rhythmically. He imagined it was rare to see the skies over the capital so empty. He walked onward, looking cautiously around him.

The evening breeze stiffened, and Darshima hoisted his bag upon his shoulder as he moved along the abandoned streets. The winds picked up, and the atmosphere around him grew hazy. The skies rapidly filled with a fearsome, blinding cloud of sand and debris. Eyes narrowed, Darshima pushed against the steadily rising gusts. The winds grew stronger, and he struggled to walk forward. He threw his whole weight into the buffeting gusts just to remain standing.

His clothes flapped wildly as the air blew violently through them. Darshima squinted his eyes against the whipping winds until they were nearly closed, the stinging sand striking his cheeks. He folded his arms across his chest and tried to protect his hands, now chafed and bleeding from the particles of golden dust scratching his exposed skin. His chest burned as he choked on the acrid mix of soot, sand, and engine exhaust. Out of desperation and near suffocation, he tore off a bit of cloth from the hem of his tunic. He clutched the tattered rag to his face and drew in a haggard breath. Searing jolts of pain coursed through his bruised hands as the wind-borne grains of gold dug into his raw skin.

The gusts roared past his ears with the deep howling rush of what seemed like a thousand aircraft engines. The wind tore violently at his hair, threatening to snatch it along with his scalp. He had never been in such danger before, save for that evening with the powilix. He pushed the thought aside and staggered forward.

An overwhelming sense of terror coursed through him. There was nowhere to hide. He stumbled against the ferocious gale and tried to stay on his feet, but he was too weak to continue. His heart pounding with fear, he leaned against a doorway, closed his eyes, and shielded his face from the flying fragments. He choked on the dusty air as he breathed, the fierce winds sucking the air from his aching lungs.

Darshima's mind raced with dreadful thoughts of his impending doom. Without warning the door behind him gave way. He let out a yelp as a strong hand clasped his shoulder and pulled him across the threshold. The door slammed closed, and the roar of the wind tempered to a soft moan. He let out an exhausted sigh, then collapsed to the ground.

Chapter Twelve

Sasha

The sun steadily rose above the horizon, and pale slivers of light illuminated the wispy blanket of clouds. Sasha, his parents, and the other guests stood attentively in the balmy morning air. They waited in an immaculately tended garden nestled high amongst the spires of the palace. Hexagonal in design, its cobbled walkways spread out from the center in a radial pattern.

The meticulously kept lawns appeared a stunning shade of green. Trees, hedges, and flowering plants from Gordanelle and Wohiimai offered shade and vivid bursts of color. A stout stone wall covered in a tapestry of leafy vines surrounded the garden. The palace towers loomed high above, casting the inviting space in shadow and light. In the distance, the grandeur of the immense Vilidesian skyline spread before them, glittering in the early morning rays.

This opulent space was Prince Khydius' personal garden, and one of his favorite places of retreat. His guests mingled upon the lavish grounds, anxiously awaiting his arrival. The prince's birthday was today, and the official festivities would begin with a ceremonial greeting shortly after dawn. The ferocious sandstorm that swept in the evening before had dissipated as quickly as it had come, and the skies had mostly cleared. The palace and its grounds were fortunate to avoid the frequent Ciblaithian storms. Its strategic location at the edge of the western peninsula offered fresh ocean air, and protection from the region's occasionally inclement weather. Though at the center of Vilidesian affairs, the palace stood both literally and figuratively as an oasis above the frenzied thrum of the capital.

Sasha moved away from his parents and paced along the paths of the garden, his boots clicking upon the pavement. He fidgeted with the sleeves of his white shirt and adjusted the fabric of his black embroidered overcoat and trousers. Beads of sweat dripped down his temples and he blotted them away with a handkerchief. Though it was early morning, the heat was already stifling. He couldn't imagine how the members of the court wore such elaborate dress in this hot climate.

Sasha's heart fluttered with a sense of unease as he reflected upon the events of the previous night. The argument between Darshima and their parents had hurt him deeply. He knew that Darshima had not wanted to serve as his assistant, but he had been unaware of how much it had bothered his brother until yesterday. After Darshima left, he tried to talk with his mother and father, but they changed the subject. Sasha had been in no mood to attend the prince's reception, but his father pleaded with him to focus on the important days ahead and forget about Darshima. They attended the reception together and his parents reveled in the royal splendor and pageantry, but he remained sullen the entire evening.

Much to his parents' disappointment, Sasha had excused himself early and retired to their suite without them. He had fallen into a restless slumber and awoken in a start from a terrible dream about Darshima. Most of the details had faded, but the dream had left him with a keen sense of disquiet. He couldn't remember the last time he had a nightmare.

Sasha walked along the garden's stone paths, away from the other invitees, his mind still troubled by the fragments of his dream. Out of the corner of his eye, he saw his parents in their formal attire, milling about with the other guests. Sovani looked toward him for a moment and waved, but Sasha avoided his gaze. The way Sovani had treated Darshima upset him, and he couldn't help but see their father differently.

Sasha shook his head in disbelief as he thought of Darshima's bold and unexpected move. Though he wouldn't have the benefit of an assistant during the ceremonies, he didn't mind. He was proud of his brother. Darshima had finally stood up for himself and made a decision on his own. Once they returned home, he vowed to find a way to help their father reconcile with Darshima. Like their mother, Sasha couldn't imagine Darshima living apart from them.

Sasha was nearing the end of a path when the air around him rang with the rapturous sound of a brass fanfare. He reluctantly walked back to the large group and rejoined his parents. They stood among the other finely dressed guests and waited patiently. An ornately carved pair of wooden doors at the garden entrance groaned open.

A large phalanx of uniformed soldiers wearing the prince's colors of blue and white stepped through the doorway. Bearing gleaming silver and gold shields emblazoned with the prince's personal seal, they strutted forward in their leather boots. Horn players and drummers dressed in similar attire marched with them, blasting rousing harmonies and staccato rhythms that echoed against the stone walls of the garden. The soldiers flanked the sides of the walkway and stood at attention.

Prince Khydius glided through the doors, a shimmering gold cloak fluttering behind him. He wore a finely embroidered white shirt, black trousers, and boots. Thick chains of gold wove through his braided hair in complex patterns, catching the rays of the sun in a glittering burst of light. The severe expression gracing his features dissolved into a genuine smile as he recognized several faces in the waiting crowd. He offered a wave and his guests cheered.

Dressed in similar finery, Emperor Aximes emerged after the prince, his golden cape shifting in the light breeze. The emperor wore an elaborate, hexagonal pointed gold crown atop the short locks of his woolen black hair. Worry lines marked the skin of his dark brown face. His leather boots clicked as he walked stiffly along the garden path. A stern gaze filling his cloud-grey eyes, he set his square jaw in a contemplative frown. As a form of acknowledgment, the emperor lifted his golden scepter toward the crowds on either side of him, and they politely bowed their heads.

Empress Keleyra walked beside her husband, the train of her lavish blue robe fluttering with her silver cape. Gripping a filigreed silver scepter in her bejeweled hand, she issued a curt nod to the guests. The dark brown skin of her smooth, oval face glowed warmly in the sun. A gem-studded silver tiara sat upon her tightly curled reddish locks, fashioned in an elegant crown of braids. The empress looked toward the prince, her amber eyes narrowed in the morning light.

“Welcome to our guests." The emperor raised his scepter once more. His deep voice echoed against the walls and was met with rapturous applause.

“We are thankful that you all traveled to join us for this most special occasion." The empress waved, to sustained clapping.

Standing between his parents, Prince Khydius offered a polite nod to the assembled crowd. Sasha eyed him, and he appeared somewhat fatigued. His stance slightly unsteady, the prince pressed his boots into the pavement, as if the breeze would topple him. His guests offered a heartfelt cheer and the prince returned it with a warm smile.

Emperor Aximes, like many of his predecessors, had been a controversial ruler during his nearly eighteen-year reign. Having deposed a distant cousin to ascend the throne, he was unpopular throughout the realm. To contain the realm’s growing deficits, he raised taxes and imposed wide-ranging tariffs, which led to decreased wages and economic stagnation.

Under Vilidesian rule, the realm had enjoyed centuries of peace and stability. As such, the emperor had reduced the overwhelming Vilidesian military presence upon the moons. Framing it as a conciliatory move, he argued that the strife that had once riven the four moons had been caused by armed conflict. Most citizens ignored the emperor's platitudes and saw his decision as a cost-cutting measure. The expense of maintaining such an extensive fighting force had placed a significant financial burden upon the dynasty. Despite many protests, Emperor Aximes scrapped dozens of warships and closed several military installations.

To fall back into favor with the public, the House of Fyrenos placed Prince Khydius at the forefront of the dynasty. The emperor's only child and heir to the throne, the prince was no less pampered than the other members of the court. Nevertheless, the public adored him, as he seemed different from the rest of the family. He bore little physical resemblance to his parents or his cousins. His athletic build and delicate features contrasted with dynasty's characteristic stocky stature.

Beyond his appearance, Prince Khydius differed in other ways from the members of the dynasty. He was charismatic, knowledgable, and showed empathy toward the concerns of his subjects. Well studied in the affairs of the moons, he rarely stayed cloistered amid the rarified atmosphere of the palace. He traveled extensively throughout the realm, visiting places both wealthy and impoverished. The prince often sided with the Vilidesian subjects on popular issues, to the disapproval of the emperor but the praise of the citizens.

The prince's gaze swept steadily over the guests standing before him until it fell directly upon Sasha. His pulse thudding nervously, Sasha looked back at the prince, whose eyes lingered curiously upon him. The corners of the prince's mouth wrinkled in a subtle smile, and then his gaze moved onto the other guests. Sasha exhaled an anxious breath after the unexpected exchange and looked at the ground. As he straightened his attire, his thoughts raced. He wondered what about him had attracted the prince's attention.

The applause quieted and Sasha looked up to see a small contingent of rather tall, pale men and women with narrowed auburn eyes walk through the doorway. Their faces bearing solemn expressions, they approached the prince and stood around him in a close circle. Numbering a dozen in total, these people were Prince Khydius' Omystikai counselors. Clad in stiff blue robes with wide sleeves stopping just above the wrist, they stood out from the other members of the court. They wore heavy chains of glittering sapphires and diamonds about their necks. Elegant white cloth headdresses with long golden tails sat atop their heads, shifting gently in the breeze.

Sasha looked around as a reverent hush fell over the crowd. He had heard of the Omystikai, but like most people, he had never met one. The counselors closed their eyes, extended their hands over the prince, and chanted a series of incantations from ancient texts. Their strong voices rose and fell in sweeping harmonies. From what little Omystikaiyn Sasha had learned during his early years of schooling, he could understand only a few of the phrases. They beseeched the heavens to protect the heir to the throne, ensure his good health, and give him a prosperous reign.

Though virtually all of them lived on Iberwight, the Omystikai had gained a degree of prominence throughout the realm. Their ancient culture and complex traditions were shrouded in mystery and remained an enduring source of interest and speculation. Centuries ago, a small population from the most influential order had migrated from Iberwight and settled in The Vilides at the behest of the dynasty. The house of Fyrenos relied heavily upon their preternatural abilities of divination in conducting imperial affairs. Beyond the palace, they wielded influence in civic and economic domains.

At the end of the incantation, the counselors unfolded a shimmering white silk stole, embellished with rays of golden thread, lines of Omystikaiyn script, and swirls of glittering, multihued gems. An enduring symbol of the Omystikai bond with the heir apparent to the Vilidesian throne, the stole was seen as a representation of the union between the two cultures and had been passed down the Fyrenosian line of succession. The counselors draped the stole over Prince Khydius' shoulders and then closed their eyes. The lead counselor gently rested his hands upon the prince's head and led them all in a final prayer. At the conclusion of the ceremony, a retinue of soldiers escorted the counselors back into the palace.

The royal staff then directed the guests toward the opposite end of the garden and seated them at long rows of banquet tables, draped in crisp white linen. Sasha lingered at the rear of the crowd as he walked toward the tables. The palace attendants shuttled between the seated guests and served a sumptuous breakfast of grilled wild game, grains, loaves of sweetbread, and other delicacies. Several of the invites that Sasha had befriended asked him to join their table, but he politely declined.

Sasha approached a table and saw his father seated at one end with several other guests. In mid-conversation, Sovani looked up at him, offered a hesitant smile, and adjusted the collar of his overcoat. Dalia sat silently at the opposite end of the table, nodding politely as the guests around her chatted. She wore an elegant green robe with chains of gold around her neck, and crystal bracelets upon her wrists. Her brow slightly furrowed, she appeared deep in thought. A small frown crossed Sasha's lips as he beheld her. His mother and father had not yet reconciled after yesterday's argument.

Sasha sat down in the carved wooden chair across from his mother. A pair of attendants placed steaming plates of food before them.

"Good morning, Sasha." Dalia offered a brief nod, picked up a silver fork, and began to eat.

"Good morning, mother." Sasha looked at her and sensed a particular sadness. Despite her calm demeanor, he knew that Darshima's unexpected departure had affected her deeply. Sasha stared down at his plate, lost amid his thoughts when he felt her hand rest gently upon his. He looked up and met her gaze.

"You haven't even touched your breakfast. What is the matter?" She rested her utensil down and narrowed her eyes as if she were trying to read his thoughts.

"I've felt better," he replied flatly. Before he realized it, his feelings came forth in a rush.

"I'm worried about Darshima. We should've done something to convince him to stay." He shook his head in frustration.

"I am worried too." She cast her eyes down at the table and anxiously gripped a cloth napkin beside her plate.

"We should've let him stay at home. Father shouldn't have forced him to come here." His heart sank as a sense of regret filled him. He wished he would have done more to stand up for Darshima.

Sasha stared at the food on his plate. His appetite had all but disappeared.

"What is it about Darshima that makes father treat him so harshly?" He looked up at her. "Why would you say such a thing about your father?" She moved her hand away from his and stared off in the distance.

"You needn't speak to me as if I am a child. I see the difference in the way he treats us." Sasha narrowed his eyes.

"Any distinctions you see are because you both are very different." She straightened the folds of her gown and looked at the guests seated around them.

"You let Sovani kick him out of our home." Sasha's jaw fell agape in disbelief.

"He went against his father. What choice did I have?" Her lips trembled. She leaned forward, her eyes pleading. "We must not speak of this now Sasha. Remember where we are."

Sasha finished his meal in silence, his thoughts churning. For as long as he could remember, he was aware of the differences between him and his brother. Sovani was often critical of Darshima and remained distant. Sasha tried to ignore it but as he grew older, he felt a burden of guilt over being the favored son.

Sasha ruminated over the starkness of their family's circumstances, and his heart sank even further. Darshima slept in an old converted storage room on the ground floor of their home, while the rest of the family slept on the upper level in bright, spacious rooms. He and Dalia were the only ones who celebrated Darshima's birthday, while all of the neighbors, as well as the extended Eweryn family, held a festive party for his. He had long tried to reconcile their father's behavior toward Darshima, but after yesterday evening, he no longer could. He understood that his brother was not as outgoing or skilled as he or Sovani, but he felt there was something more.

"Do you think father will really make him move away?" he asked.

"I will think of something. I won't let him be turned out onto the streets," she said firmly.

"I'll do whatever I can to help him." A worried frown spread upon Sasha's face.

"Though it is hard, try not to worry. You have earned your invitation to be here with the prince. We must celebrate your accomplishment," said Dalia. She tried to strike a cheerful tone, but her voice betrayed a subtle hint of melancholy.

"I'll try as best as I can," he sighed.

"I believe Darshima is more capable than we know." A wistful smile crossed her lips.

Sasha looked up at his mother, his mind drifting back to the harrowing moment when Darshima tried to hunt the pair of powilix. Though he nearly ended up being run over a cliff, he had come closer to killing them than he ever had. Despite his brother's failures, Sasha had faith in him. What Darshima lacked in skill, he made up for with his bravery and determination.

Chapter Thirteen

"He's still breathing!" exclaimed a woman, her voice brimming with surprise. The howl of wind rushing past the door blended with her worried voice. Darshima's ears filled with the din of conversation, the clink of plates and glasses, and the faint strains of music. He let out a sigh as a sense of relief washed over him. His eyes, blinded by the sand fluttered open, and he made out a dim space filled with vague shapes and human figures. He wasn't quite sure where he was, but he was thankful to be sheltered from the storm.

The hands grasping his shoulders picked him up from the ground and ushered him forward. His legs aching, he walked tentatively as he was led further into the space.

"Have a seat." She guided him onto a soft, padded bench. "This might sting a bit, but you'll feel better." Darshima heard the sound of sloshing water in a basin over her light humming. He then saw a hand reach over to him and gently dab his cheeks with a steaming rag, its soothing aroma filling his nostrils.

"That stings." Darshima drew away from her, wincing as a burning sensation spread across his skin.

"It's just a mild astringent to treat your scratches," she chuckled. "At least you don't look nearly as bad as you probably feel."

"I feel pretty terrible." He shook his head at her remark, then grimaced at the ensuing pain.

"You're lucky we found you. You could've died out there." She mopped his forehead with the cloth, stopping periodically to wring it in the basin.

The burning went away, and as his vision came back into focus, he looked around him. He appeared to be in a small, but busy cafeteria. Dim, glowing glass orbs hung over the crowded tables of diners, casting a diffuse, yellow light over the smoky atmosphere. They hunched over as they ate and concentrated on their plates, neither looking up nor down. A small musical ensemble at the front of the hall produced a subdued melody. Their bronze horns glinted in the muted light, issuing notes that seemed to hang in the air.

As Darshima settled upon the bench, his eyes met those of the woman who had helped him. Seated opposite him, she folded the damp cloth, draped it along the rim of the metal basin and placed it upon the glass table between them. She rested her arms upon the cloudy rectangular surface and looked up at Darshima. She wore a dark blue armless smock, and a bright red apron draped loosely over her black trousers. Her smooth skin was a deep bronze, like the setting sun. A cascade of wavy, dark blond hair hung at her shoulders, arranged in a loose braid. Her oval face was marked by a fine brow and piercing, bright grey eyes.

"Are you feeling any better?" she asked, her eyebrows knit in concern.

"I'm okay. Thank you for saving me." He gestured toward the door behind them.

"You're not from around here are you?" A polite smile crossed her lips.

"I'm just visiting," he said, his throat scratching as he answered. Darshima put his hands to his mouth and let out a violent cough, clearing his lungs of the sand.

"You almost sound like an Ardavian." She put a finger to her temple.

"How can you tell?" His eyebrows arched in surprise.

"Your accent is different," she replied. Darshima could barely pay attention to her words. He found her attractive and couldn't help but stare.

"I am Erethalie." She offered a curt nod and extended her hand.

"That's a beautiful name, it suits you." A smile crossed Darshima's lips as he shook her hand. He was a novice at talking to women. Sasha was much better at it than him, and quite popular back home. Despite his brother's suggestions, Darshima tended to make foolish blunders that no amount of advice could fix.

"Despite nearly losing your life, you managed to keep that Ardavian charm." Her voice rippled with dry laughter as she rolled her eyes.

"I'm sorry," he muttered, shrinking back into his seat.

"I didn't mean to tease you, but at least once a month, I have to rescue a foreigner who gets stuck in a sand storm." Her expression softened a bit.

"I didn't mean to put you at risk," said Darshima.

"Don't worry about it, just be careful next time." She waved his words away with a hand. "You didn't tell me your name." The corners of her lips curled into a friendly smile. Her magnetic gaze pulled his eyes toward hers.

"My name is Darshima," he replied.

"Relax Darshima, you're safe here." She patted his hand, her eyes twinkling with a sincere expression.

They started to chat again, this time on more amicable terms. Slowly but surely, Darshima took a liking to her and started to feel at ease.

"Where are you from?" asked Darshima.

"I've lived here in the capital for many years, but I am originally from Wohiimai." She casually pointed to the ceiling above their heads.

"I hear it's a beautiful moon." Intrigued, Darshima leaned forward in his seat. He had never met anyone from there before.

"It's definitely more peaceful than this urban chaos," she sighed.

Her full name was Erethalie Danthe and she had just turned nineteen. A university student on break between semesters, she spent her days working for her father's business. She occasionally picked up night shifts at the cafeteria to earn extra money. She was born and raised on Wohiimai in the coastal city of Pelethedral, a day's journey from the capital, Renefydis. Her mother belonged to a large family of herdsmen and her father was a Vilidesian man descended from a long line of intrepid navigators. His forebears had charted some of the first routes between the moons. Her father ran a small but profitable courier service that shuttled parcels between the cities of the realm.

Her family moved to The Vilides when she was an adolescent, but her memories of the boundless plains and expansive skies of Wohiimai remained vivid. Though she worked in her father's office, she dreamed of traveling to the distant corners of the realm with his navigators. As she was a young woman, her parents had expressly forbidden it, fearing for her safety. Even so, her father had taught her how to fly both air and spacecraft from an early age. Her experience gave her a sense of bearing so keen that she could tell Darshima the names of the streets in his neighborhood.

Darshima gazed upon Erethalie, his pulse thudding with a sense of curiosity as she spoke. He had never met anyone like her before. In the midst of their conversation, she interjected.

"Have you had anything to eat?" She bit her lip in concern. Before Darshima could answer, the sharp hunger pangs he ignored during his ordeal responded with a growl. Erethalie laughed and shook her head as she stood up from the bench. She walked toward the smoky kitchen, her leather boots clicking softly upon the stone floor. Darshima's eyes lingered on her figure as she faded into the dimness. Before long, she reemerged with a tray.

"I hope you don't mind Vilidesian fare, it's our specialty." Erethalie set the aluminum tray down in front of him, heaped with fried meat and starchy roots. She retrieved a metal fork from her smock and handed it to him as she sat back down. Darshima had never tried Vilidesian cuisine before, but he was so hungry, he didn't care. Within minutes, he had consumed every savory, greasy morsel and only a small pile of bones remained.

"Thank you," he mumbled.

"At that rate, I am surprised that you didn't eat the tray." She stared at him, her hands folded upon the tabletop.

"I didn't realize how hungry I was." His face flush with embarrassment, he slid the tray toward the center of the table.

"Oh my, what is that?" She exclaimed as she saw his arm. Her delicate fingers traced the intricate patterns along his right wrist, traveling steadily up his forearm.

His chest tightened as a wave of nervousness came over him. Back home, the markings never garnered even a passing stare. He had been in the Vilides less than a day and they had already twice drawn peoples' attention. She stared intently at his arm, her thin brow knit pensively.

"I've never seen anything quite like them," she whispered to herself as she studied the intricate lines. "I've seen the temporary markings that you Gordanellans get for ceremonies, but these look different." For religious observances, weddings, and funerals, Gordanellan men and women marked themselves with complex designs and symbols in vibrant inks of red and ochre that washed away with water.

She turned his arm over in her hand as if it were some curious object, pouring over every detail. Unable to bear her scrutiny, Darshima pulled his arm away and folded it across his chest, trying to conceal the markings. Erethalie looked up at him, her eyes widening in surprise. She appeared as if she had been snapped out of a trance.

"I didn't mean to upset you, I was only curious." She avoided his gaze and smoothed out the wrinkles in her smock.

"It's nothing," he grumbled.

"What do they mean?" She leaned forward, her eyes drawn back to the markings.

"They don't mean anything." He shook his head in confusion. The markings had always been there, and he had never given them more than a passing thought.

"I am sorry Darshima, I meant no harm with my questions. There's something different about you." She looked up and offered a contrite smile. They sat together and listened to the music from the ensemble, when a woman dressed in a similar uniform approached them.

"Get back to work. You're not being paid to chat with the diners." Her bright grey eyes narrowed in mild disdain, and she shot a stern gaze at Erethalie. The woman stepped closer to the table, her dark brown skin gleaming in the dim light. She muttered a few words and rapped her knuckles upon the tabletop.

"I'm sorry, I'll join you in a moment." Erethalie shook her head and let out a sigh. The woman stared at both of them, then walked away, her braided black hair swaying with each stride. "She's in charge of this place, so I must get going." Erethalie pointed toward the back of the cafeteria where a crew of workers brought out trays and collected dishes.

"I didn't mean to interrupt you." Darshima peered over his shoulder toward the kitchen.

"You didn't disturb me at all. I couldn't leave you out there." She rose from her seat and Darshima stood up with her.

"It was nice to make your acquaintance, Darshima. Come back and say goodbye before you return home." She briefly clasped his hand.

"Thank you Erethalie, you really saved me." His eyes met hers and held them for a moment. She let go of his hand, collected the basin and food tray, and then walked toward the kitchen.

Darshima hoisted his bag upon his shoulder, reached into his pocket, and left a few coins upon the table to pay for his meal. Before leaving the cafeteria, he made a brief stop in a small lavatory. He hastily washed up and changed his clothing, which had been shredded by the sandstorm. Peering at his reflection in the mirror, he noted a few scratches upon his forehead. His hands were bruised, but not as badly as he had feared. He shook the sand from his hair and then splashed some cold water upon his face. He put on a clean set of black trousers and an armless tunic, placing his old, tattered clothes into his bag. He would keep them as proof that he had survived a Ciblaithian sandstorm.

Darshima moved toward the entrance and stepped through the door, the frenzied sounds of traffic greeting his ears. The warm air held a salty dampness that felt good against his skin. Reddish rays from the morning sun streaked across the brightening sky. He let out a yawn and stretched his stiff muscles, still aching from the beating he took during the storm.

He walked along the pavement and looked around to see the streets filled with harried pedestrians and vehicles. Grains of golden sand stirred upon the pavement amid the gentle gusts of wind, crunching under the soles of his moccasins. He started down a large boulevard sloping gently toward the bustling bay in the distance. The shimmering surface teemed with enormous freight ships, their metal, scythe-like hulls carving through the waves. Like a mirage, the opposing pair of peninsulas and their jagged blocks of soaring towers hovered over the calm blue waters.

Darshima looked toward the western peninsula and could just make out the royal palace perched upon its steep edge. His chest tightened with a wave of anxiety, the memories of the argument with his family coming back to him. He tore his gaze away and tried to think of something else. He anxiously bit his lip as he ruminated on the days ahead. He didn't know how he would pass the time. He didn't even know where he would sleep. His return trip to Ardavia was in a week, and his departure date couldn't be changed without a steep fee, which he couldn't afford. Until then, he would have to find someplace to stay.

He moved with the bustling crowds, jostling for space upon the busy sidewalk. Despite the early hour, the city hummed with activity. The narrow, terrestrial boulevards were clogged with lines of wheeled vehicles, their engines growling as they crept forward. He looked up at the dense matrix of overlapping aerial traffic. Thousands of gleaming metal craft glided swiftly overhead, casting their moving shadows upon the streets and buildings below. The collective noise of their engines filtered down in a monotonous, deep drone. Far above the city, the three other moons hung in a line, glimmering against the ghostly form of Benai and its red rings.

Darshima wandered along, his eyes lingering upon the soaring rows of glass and metal towers. He stood still for a moment in the middle of the pavement and craned his neck upward. The crowds of pedestrians parted around him, seemingly unaware of his presence. The height and closeness of the buildings reminded him of a forest, but it was quite different. He looked around in disbelief, realizing that all the lands around him been paved over with streets and structures.

Like all Gordanellans, Darshima revered nature. Though raised in Ardavia, nature was never very far away. He had grown up hiking through the surrounding rainforests and swimming in the meandering rivers. The bounty of Gordanelle's forests and seas were its greatest resource. The moon's unique flora and fauna had long been the source of life-saving medicines and treatments. As such, many citizens of the realm traveled to Gordanelle on retreats, seeking both restoration and rejuvenation.

He walked from one block to the next, startled by the scarcity of plants and wildlife. The parks and gardens at the bases of the buildings were meticulously preened, irrigated, and cultivated to survive in the arid, manmade environment. Lost amid his thoughts, Darshima felt something nudge his side. He spun around to see a boy dressed in rags and torn sandals standing unusually close to him, his small hands deftly unfastening the clasps of his bag.

"What are you doing?" Darshima yanked his bag away and grabbed the child's wrist. Darshima rifled through its inner pockets, relieved to find that nothing was missing. The young child stood frozen, the brown skin of his grimy face contorted into an expression of fear. His piercing grey eyes held a look of sadness that gave Darshima pause.

"I'm hungry, sir," stammered the boy. The locks of his ear length, curly black hair trembled as he shook in fear. Darshima's pulse thudded with surprise, and he released the boy's hand. His heart sank as a sense of pity replaced his anger. Darshima reached into his bag, retrieved a few coins, and offered them to the boy. He accepted them with both hands, staring wide-eyed at the golden pieces. The child looked up, said a hasty thank you and scuttled back into the crowd. Darshima's gaze lingered upon him until he disappeared.

Darshima refastened his bag and continued down the sidewalk, this time much more vigilant of his surroundings. He looked upon the bustling streetscape, his mind racing over what had just happened. During their voyage, Sydarias had warned him that things were different here. He was now beginning to understand what that meant.

Though by far the wealthiest society, Darshima had long heard about the veins of poverty and deprivation that existed amid the ostentatious signs of fortune. There was a startling level inequality in The Vilides that the peoples of the other moons found troubling. While most Vilidesians made a decent living and provided for their families, there was a cadre of prosperous clans with deep ties to the industry and the dynasty. Their immense wealth and power superseded imagination, and the riches of the realm lay at their feet.

There was also an untold number of citizens who possessed little more than the clothes upon their backs. Subsisting in the shadows of these stupendous towers and gilded temples, they largely remained out of view. Amid their misfortune, they eked out a meager existence on the margins of society, surviving on the charity offered by the shrines and almshouses around the city.

His eyes vainly searched the crowd for the impoverished child amid the throngs of people, milling about in their fine garments. The other moons had their share of problems too, but extreme poverty wasn't one of them. Families on Gordanelle and Wohiimai were large and closely-knit. Generations often lived within the same town and took care of each other during difficult times. It was rare for someone facing tough circumstances to be without at least food or shelter.

Darshima thought of the child's circumstances, and a pang of worry jolted through him as he pondered his own. His stomach sank as the tense argument with his family replayed in his mind. The sense of guilt he felt when leaving the palace slowly crept back at the edges of his heart. Despite their disagreements, his family had provided for him. He had abandoned them during an important moment and didn't know if they would ever forgive him.

Darshima had no idea how he would face them when he returned to Gordanelle. His father had kicked him out of the house, and he didn't know where he would live. He stood still for a moment amid the swell of pedestrians and drew in an anxious breath. Thoughts of his mother and brother coming to his defense the night before filtered through his mind. He clung to a sliver of hope that his mother would reason with his father. Darshima prayed that they would let him stay at home until he found a new place to live and work. His heart rising into his throat, he vowed to somehow find a way to settle things with his family. The harried crowds moved around him and he began to walk, pushing his worries aside.

His eyes scanned the streets as he remembered Sydarias' warning about heeding his surroundings. The sunlight grew more intense, and he broke into a sweat as he wandered through the varied districts. Darshima strolled along the manicured boulevards, with no particular destination in mind. He peered into the shop windows and eyed the luxurious clothing and wares.

Darshima walked along the majestic thoroughfares, taking in the famous monuments and the well known urban vistas. As a child, he had read about these places, but he had never imagined seeing them with his own eyes. He stared up at the triumphal arches commemorating ancient battles and hallowed victories. Amid the crowds, he sidled up to ornate pedestals and gazed at the colossal stone statues of Vilidesian royalty, long gone.

A sense of amazement filled him as he took in the varied sights. Ardavia was the only city he knew. Also bustling and cosmopolitan, it had briefly been the capital of the realm. Even so, he felt an unmistakable difference here. The Vilides was so much larger, so much busier, so much more imposing. Whether it was the ordered magnificence of its plan, the frenetic thrum of its traffic, or the sophistication of its citizens in their daily routine, there was an imperial grandeur and a deep sense of elegance that permeated everything.

Darshima ambled along, the late morning heat steadily sapping his energy. Out of the corner of his eye, he spotted an inviting park nestled amongst a cluster of lofty towers and decided to rest. He walked through the gates and approached a row of stone benches. A nearby group of spindly trees with large green, diamond-shaped fronds offered welcome shade. In the middle of the park lay a large, tiled circular pond with an impressive fountain of water spraying up from its center.

Darshima sank onto a bench and let out an audible sigh, thankful for a moment's rest. He had no idea how he would spend the week, but he was glad to have some time to himself. As his mind sketched plans for the coming days, the immediate concern of finding shelter for the evening brought him back to the present. He had yet to find a place to stay. Accommodations were expensive here, and his money would only go so far. He bit his lip nervously as he mulled over potential plans and their probable cost. A stream of pedestrians strolled past him, their fine tunics and headdresses catching his eye. He drew in a breath, and his worries lessened some. The day was still young and somehow, he would manage to find somewhere to sleep for the night.

Darshima closed his eyes against the sunbeams and reclined under the shade. A gentle wind carried a refreshing mist from the fountain onto his flushed skin. The sound of engines far above filtered through the trees and into his ears. Above the din, he heard the delicate flapping of birds' wings as they flew overhead. Over the gurgling waters of the pond, he made out the sharp click of footsteps against the stone walkway. His eyes fluttered open and he looked nervously at the crowds around him, chiding himself for getting too comfortable. He couldn't risk being pickpocketed again.

Darshima peered upward at the sky, crowded out by the blocks of towers surrounding the park. Between them, he spied sinewy bands of aerial traffic wending their way through the open spaces, like streams of glistening particles amid the clouds. His back aching against the stone bench, he sat up and looked around him. The shadows grew shorter as the noon hour neared, and the sun approached its zenith. His stomach rumbled with hunger yet again.

He rose from the bench and walked out of the park in search of something to eat.

Chapter Fourteen

Darshima wandered along the boulevards amid the throngs of pedestrians when an idea came to him. Sydarias had invited him to visit, and Darshima had yet to make any plans. Though he enjoyed what he had seen so far, he knew he couldn't spend the entire week simply walking around. He hoped Sydarias could give him suggestions about reasonable places to stay and perhaps some interesting things to see.

He rummaged through his bag, retrieved the crisp blue metal card, and held it before his eyes. The bright gold lettering glinted in the long rays of the sun, bearing Sydarias' name and address in neat Vilidesian script. He squinted at the letters, unsure of the location, then retrieved the small communicator from his bag. Though he barely used it, he was glad that he had brought it with him.

Darshima tapped the coordinates upon the glass screen and the device instantly rendered an intricate map tracing the route. Sydarias lived on the other side of the city, along the coast of the eastern peninsula. It would take him hours to get there on foot. He would have to hire a coach if he hoped to arrive before dusk.

Darshima walked toward a row of oblong vehicles hovering at the side of the road. The Vilidesian aerial coaches were similar to the ones in Ardavia, but they were noticeably larger and much swifter. People in The Vilides were famous for having an eye for the largest, most luxurious, or the fastest thing that they could or couldn't afford. He approached a vehicle, its silver, angular surface gleaming in the sunlight. The door slid open with a mechanical whine, and a pleasing rush of cool air welcomed him. He greeted the driver and headed for the back of the vehicle. Upon hearing Darshima's accent, the driver invited him to sit in the front of the cabin to get a better view.

Darshima obligingly took the seat on the driver's right side, and settled upon the padded leather bench. A stocky old man with a jolly temperament, the driver had a pleasant laugh that filled the cabin. A fine white stubble covered the dark brown skin of his jaw. He wore a long-sleeved grey tunic, black trousers, and sandals.

"What's your destination, young man?" His bright grey eyes swept appraisingly over Darshima.

"I am traveling here." Darshima handed the card over to him. The driver took the card, held it up to the windshield, and his eyes widened noticeably. Darshima's brow furrowed in curiosity as he noticed the change in the driver's demeanor. The driver pulled his gaze from the card and studied Darshima. He examined it once more and then looked back at Darshima, running a hand through the tight coils of his grey hair.

"Is it too far? I can pay more." Darshima reached into his bag for the envelope of coins. The driver gently shook his head.

"The distance is no problem." He turned his gaze back toward the windshield.

"What is it then?" asked Darshima. The driver let out a soft chuckle.

"You're going to visit a member of the Idawa clan. They're one of the wealthiest families in this city. You must be someone important." A reverent smile crossed the driver's lips as he handed back the card.

"That's not so. I met Sydarias on the journey from Gordanelle," exclaimed Darshima. "We sat together in the standard class section of the ship." His mind raced as his eyes scanned the card. Sydarias had mentioned nothing of his family's fortune during their conversation.

The driver grabbed the circular controls with one hand, then punched a series of icons on the glowing instrument panel with the other. They rocketed upward from the street at a terrifying pace, the ground shrinking rapidly from view. Darshima gripped the armrests of the seat, and his stomach sank. He clenched his jaw and waited for the sensation to pass. His head spinning, Darshima stared at the driver, who didn't even flinch as the craft maneuvered. The engines let out a deep growl and the vessel shuddered under the power of the swift ascent. They merged into a dense band of traffic and hurtled toward the horizon.

They traveled across the city, the tower blocks around them careening past in a blur of shimmering glass and metal. Darshima peered through the window, marveling at the speed of the vehicles around them as they sailed over the parks and spires. They flew across the blue waters of the bay and arrived over the eastern peninsula. The craft then descended back to the ground and landed with a gentle thud, amid the bustling afternoon crowds.

"You will find their buildings at the end of the road." The driver yanked a lever and settled in his seat.

"You mean their apartment?" Darshima turned to him, surprised.

"The family owns the group of towers over there, and they live at the top of the tallest one." He pointed through the windshield, toward an imposing cluster of skyscrapers that soared above several dozen immense towers in their midst.

"Thank you," Darshima grabbed the envelope from his bag and handed several coins to the driver, but he refused them.

"I cannot accept your money. The Idawa clan has a longstanding relationship with our transport company. We accommodate all of their guests." The driver bowed politely.

"There must be some mistake." Darshima's eyes widened in astonishment. He tried again to hand over the coins, but the driver shook his head. Darshima offered his thanks and put his money away. He grabbed his bag and stepped out of the craft, into the afternoon heat. With a great rush of wind, the coach launched itself back into the sky. He craned his neck upward and watched its gleaming form disappear among the stream of vehicles flying overhead.

Darshima pulled his gaze away and walked down the avenue. He looked anxiously at the buildings ahead of him, the driver's words about the Idawa clan echoing in his mind. Many Gordanellan homes were treated as heirlooms and remained in the family. Darshima's parents had inherited their home from Sovani's mother, who had inherited it from her mother. His jaw dropped in astonishment as he contemplated a single family owning an entire building, let alone a block of towers. He couldn't fathom the sort of fortune that would be necessary.

Darshima continued further along the avenue amid the crowds. Tall, stately trees flanked both sides, their long green fronds dancing lazily in the breeze. As he peered around the elegant neighborhood, his heart fluttered nervously.

"I don't belong here," he muttered anxiously. Darshima stopped in the middle of the sidewalk and looked up at the soaring towers, their spires partially obscured by a thin veil of clouds. He wondered if Sydarias or his family would treat him differently when they learned that he did not come from any sort of wealth. As he was about to turn back, worries about the rest of the week came back to him. At a minimum, he needed to find a place to stay for the night. Sydarias could at least point him in the right direction. He let out a nervous sigh and continued toward the buildings.

Darshima stopped in front of a sign at the end of the road that matched the address upon Sydarias' card. His eyes narrowed against the sun, he peered through the gated entrance of a small plaza. The inviting space was paved in geometric designs of red and white stone. Stands of tall, leafy trees flanked the walls. In the center stood a well-manicured garden, its vivid arrays of color managed to look vibrant amid the sweltering heat. At the center of the garden sat a dark granite fountain. Thick jets of clear water rocketed from its top and cascaded down its lower tiers into a large, circular reflecting pool. A small crowd of men, women, and children relaxed upon the surrounding benches, enjoying the cooling mists.

A quartet of immense towers occupied the opposite edge of the plaza, and the sun glinted upon their clear glass facades. Darshima peered up as far as his neck would allow and saw the summit of the tallest one, piercing through the wispy layer of clouds. As he approached, the gates slid open and he crossed the plaza. He walked through the glass doors of the entrance and a welcome, chilly breeze greeted his skin. He stood before a marble desk and met the stern gaze of a uniformed doorman.

"I'm here to see Sydarias Idawa." Darshima carefully held up the card.

"It would be my pleasure, sir." The man's disposition softened considerably as his grey eyes scanned the shimmering object. He led Darshima through the lobby and toward an airy atrium, the tails of his embroidered grey overcoat fluttering behind him. The doorman directed Darshima toward a bank of elevators, offered a salutation, then returned to his post.

Darshima retrieved the communicator from his bag and punched in a sequence of numbers from the card.

"Hello, this is Darshima. We met on the ship from Ardavia. Do you remember me?" Darshima held the device out in front of him and stared into its gleaming array of lenses. The device let out a chime, the screen flickered to life, and a moving image of Sydarias' face appeared upon its glass surface.

"Of course I remember you Darshima, where are you?" asked Sydarias, his voice echoing through the small speakers.

"I'm in the lobby of your building." Darshima angled the device so Sydarias could see behind him.

"Excellent, I'll be there in a moment." As Sydarias waved, his voice crackled and the image faded to black. Darshima stowed the card and the communicator back in his bag and waited. He looked around the atrium, his eyes taking in every detail.

Sunbeams flooded the large glass panes and cast the inviting, oval space in splashes of copper-colored light. The gleaming, pale stone walls were adorned with vivid etchings depicting sweeping vistas of the city. Much to his surprise, Darshima began to wonder about the structural details of the building. His apprenticeship had sparked a budding technical interest in tall structures such as these. A pang of sadness coursed through him when he remembered that he would no longer be working at the construction site. He shook his head and tried to think of something else.

Over the thud of hurried footsteps, Darshima heard the muffled ringing of the device. As he pulled it out of his bag, the screen flickered on and showed Sydarias' grinning face.

"Are you coming down to meet me?" asked Darshima.

"Look over your shoulder," said Sydarias, who stood behind him, stifling a snicker. Darshima turned around to see Sydarias' face less than a nose length away from his. He was dressed in a long white linen tunic open at the collar, trimmed in gold, with the sleeves folded at the bicep. His blue trousers were cuffed at the ankle and he wore black leather boots.

"Well, there you are." Startled, Darshima stepped back, offered a smile, and took his joke in good stride.

"How have you been?" Sydarias gave him a jovial pat on the back and led him through the atrium. His voice echoed throughout the space.

"I'm a bit tired, but otherwise fine." Darshima walked faster to match his bold stride.

"I can see. You look like you've been through a storm." Sydarias reached over and adjusted Darshima's collar.

"Is it that obvious?" A shy smile crossed Darshima's lips as they came to a stop before the bank of elevators.

"I hadn't expected to see you so soon after we parted ways, what with your obligations at the prince's party." His brow wrinkled in curiosity.

"I couldn't follow through with it." Darshima stared at the floor, his voice wavering.

"Wait, you're not at the palace. You decided to leave!" exclaimed Sydarias, his lips curling into a smile.

"It didn't go over well with my family." Darshima's pulse thudded anxiously as images of the previous night flashed before his eyes. He stared at the ground, avoiding Sydarias' gaze.

"I can see you're upset. Whatever happened at the palace, I am sure things will work out. Let's go upstairs and you'll tell me about it." He ushered Darshima into an awaiting carriage, and the transparent doors closed behind them.

Sydarias tapped a button on a panel, and the elevator moved upward with a hushed whir. Darshima narrowed his eyes against the rays of sunlight flooding through the curved glass panes. Sydarias leaned against the wall, his lips pursed in a casual expression. Darshima pressed his nose against the glazed panel and peered out upon the city.

They ascended amid the steep canyons of soaring buildings, and the crowds of people on the streets below shrank into mere ambling dots. The sloping hills of the narrow peninsula and the surrounding blue waters of the bay came into striking view. The carriage continued upward through the dense bands of traffic and thin layers of clouds.

"So what happened?" Sydarias sidled over to Darshima.

"I told my family that I wasn't going to be my brother's servant, and they're upset with me." Darshima pulled his gaze from the window.

"You did what was right for you, and that's what matters." The corner of Sydarias' eyes wrinkled in a sympathetic gaze.

"My father dismissed me from my job and kicked me out of the house. I don't know what to do." Darshima let out a pained sigh.

"We will figure something out, don't worry." Sydarias rested a hand upon his shoulder. Darshima stared at the floor, feeling little comfort from Sydarias' words.

The elevator arrived at the top of the tower with a gentle hush, and the doors parted. Darshima followed Sydarias to the end of a wide, sunlit corridor and they stopped in front a grand set of carved wooden doors.

"Welcome to our home, Darshima." Sydarias placed his hand upon the gilded doorknob. His voice carried a subtle air of cynicism that caught Darshima by surprise.

Sydarias pushed open the doors, and they stepped past the threshold. Darshima looked around him and felt enveloped by a sense of spaciousness and light. The interior had the airy and orderly ambiance of a gallery. Gleaming grey and white marble tiles checkered the floors, and the high, coffered white ceilings were outlined in maroon wood trim. Rays from the sun bathed everything in a golden glow. The outer walls of the apartment were fashioned of tall panes of clear glass. Captivated by the view, Darshima walked over to get a better look.

"You must be the Darshima that Sydarias has been talking about," said a soft-spoken voice.

Darshima spun around to see a woman greet him with a gentle smile. She was of medium stature with intense amber eyes and deep bronze skin. Her silky black hair, slightly grey at the temples was fashioned in a loose bun. She wore an elegant yellow robe, accented with thick chains of gold around her neck, and leather sandals upon her feet. She politely bowed to Darshima in a traditional Vilidesian greeting, and he returned the gesture.

"I am Madame Idawa, Sydarias' mother." She adjusted the folds of her robe.

Her regal disposition and low voice lent her an air of sophistication. The appearance of her features, combined with her Ardavian accent signaled her Gordanellan heritage, and Darshima felt at ease.

"We were just about to serve dinner, won't you join us? She offered a polite smile.

"Thank you very much," he said, his stomach growling softly at the thought of food. He hadn't eaten anything since that morning and wasn't going to turn down a meal. Madame Idawa led him and Sydarias through a spacious, interior hallway. The whitewashed walls were adorned with various paintings and works of art, including portraits of the Idawa lineage.

They walked past a large, luxuriously appointed living room with sofas, tables, and rows of wooden bookcases. She ushered them through a set of glass doors and onto a large outdoor terrace. The balustrade was flanked by a row of green, leafy hedges and fiery orange, spherical flowers that hung like fragrant lanterns. Darshima marveled at the rare blooms, which were typically more at home amid the Gordanellan jungles than upon the ledge of a Vilidesian skyscraper. An oval glass table with gold dinnerware and a set of finely carved wooden chairs sat near the foliage.

"Darshima, why don't you relax and enjoy the view? We are waiting for Mr. Idawa to arrive." She stood at the edge of the table, her bejeweled hand resting upon its gleaming surface. A courteous smile crossed her lips, and the steady breeze gently teased at her black locks. "Will you help me with the food, Sydarias?" She waved to him, her golden bracelets clinking softly. Sydarias stepped away from Darshima and followed her back indoors.

Darshima's eyes lingered on the entrance as they disappeared through the doors. He sauntered across the smooth stone tiles toward the edge of the terrace, and leaned his elbows upon the balustrade. Squinting his eyes against the sunlight, he looked at the vista surrounding him. His gaze wandered over the immense forest of towers, as it gradually faded into the expansive deserts beyond the city limits. The rippling golden dunes stretched toward the horizon and merged with the blue sky in a broad arc. The sun's orange disk blazed overhead and the jagged skyline appeared as a glittering silhouette against the pale forms of Benai and the other moons.

Darshima peered down toward the street, his eyes tracing the shimmering exterior of the building. The glass facade tapered into an elegant column amid the clusters of surrounding towers, piercing the thin veil of clouds and meeting the plaza far below. He made out the sandy, beach-lined coasts of the narrow, densely populated peninsula. As he took in the details, his mind contemplated the feats of Vilidesian engineering that prevented this slender stretch of land and its innumerable skyscrapers from slipping beneath the waves.

Amid his thoughts, he was struck by the sense of peace and quietness that existed above the fray. The only noises that reached his ears were the soft gusts of wind and the hushed drone of the freight and passenger vessels as they plied the skies below. He felt as if he were inhabiting an entirely different city above the clouds. The sound of an opening door, followed by the scraping of a chair broke the tranquil ambiance. Darshima turned around to see Sydarias sitting at the table, his arms folded across his chest. He clenched his jaw and his eyes smoldered. Perplexed, Darshima walked over to the table and sat beside him.

"Is everything okay?" Darshima peered at him.

"My father is back from one of his meetings. As usual, he's in some sort of mood." He shook his head.

Before Sydarias could say anything more, Sydarias' father stepped out onto the terrace. Mr. Idawa was an older man of a stocky build with dark brown skin, who stood slightly taller than his son. His square, dimpled face was marked by bright grey eyes and faint worry lines. A tightly curled, well-coiffed mop of salt and pepper hair sat atop his head. He was neatly dressed in a patterned white linen tunic with the sleeves rolled up, and the collar was undone. Thick chains of gold hung about his neck. His crisp black trousers and polished leather boots contrasted boldly against the sunlit terrace.

"What's going on Sydarias, where are all of the servants?" he asked, his lips curling into an impatient frown. Sydarias rose from his seat and faced him.

"As we do every year, we dismissed them for the afternoon so they could prepare for the prince's birthday celebrations." He glared at his father.

"Well don't just stand there, go back inside and help your mother." Mr. Idawa pointed toward the entrance. Sydarias let out a sigh and walked back through the doors, avoiding Darshima's gaze.

Darshima sat quietly at the table and waited for him to return. His mind raced at the sudden change in Sydarias' demeanor. Arms folded across his chest, Mr. Idawa paced along the balustrade.

"So you must be Darshima." A bold smile crossed his lips.

"Yes, I am." Darshima stood up, his pulse thudded as a wave of nervousness passed through him. Mr. Idawa approached him, extended his hand, and offered Darshima a firm handshake.

"Sydarias tells me that you're from one of the colonies?" he asked.

"I'm from Gordanelle, sir," replied Darshima.

"Please, sit down." Mr. Idawa gestured toward the table and they took their seats. Darshima briefly glanced down and checked his appearance in the reflection. He had never been invited to anyone's home for dinner, let alone such a luxurious one. He tugged at his tunic, wishing he had worn something more suitable.

"How was the voyage from Ardavia?" Mr. Idawa leaned forward in his chair. His eyebrows were knitted in an intense expression.

"It was pleasant," said Darshima.

"Ah, Gordanelle." Mr. Idawa's gaze drifted upward and his eyes filled with a thoughtful glimmer, as if he were searching the sky for some long-faded memory. "A very rugged and stunning place, I might say. It is where my wife was born."

"It is indeed home." A wistful smile crossed Darshima's lips as he caught a glimpse of the moon out of the corner of his eye.

"I am sure it is, but there is no place like The Vilides." Mr. Idawa leaned back in his chair and let out a chuckle. "The possibilities here are limitless."

"I imagine they are." Darshima looked upon the innumerable buildings surrounding them, imagining the myriad ways that people led their lives here.

"The economic output of this city alone is greater than all of the moons combined." Mr. Idawa's eyes narrowed in a sober expression.

Unsure what to say, Darshima shrugged his shoulders. Though he understood only the basic facts about the realm's economy, it was no surprise to him that Vilidesian wealth surpassed all of the other territories. Back home on Gordanelle, nearly all of the manufactured goods and services they used came from Vilidesian businesses. Virtually all of the large public enterprises on the other moons were underwritten by Vilidesian banks. Mr. Idawa went on to discuss the family's companies and how they had grown increasingly profitable under his decisive leadership.

Sydarias and Madame Idawa reemerged onto the terrace, carrying large golden trays, laden with braised meats and stewed grains, glasses, and a decanter of amber-colored, fortified wine. They gently rested the items down and took their seats. As they began to dine, Madame Idawa poured the spirit.

"How was your day?" Madame Idawa turned to her husband, her polite voice showing a slight hint of strain. He remained silent as he tore into his plate, seemingly unaware of her words.

"I apologize, my mind is somewhere else," he muttered between hurried bites.

"You seem preoccupied, is there something the matter?" She glared at him, the corners of her lips wrinkling into a slight frown.

"Everything is fine," said Mr. Idawa, his voice rising with an edge that gave them all pause. He turned toward Darshima. "Sydarias tells me that your brother earned an invitation to the prince's birthday celebration." He set down his utensils and picked up his glass.

"He worked very hard to earn it." Darshima placed a hand upon the table, nervously playing with the cloth napkin beside his plate.

"What a rare honor, especially for someone from the colonies. He must be an exemplary young man," he muttered between gulps.

"He is a good brother." Darshima looked squarely at Mr. Idawa. His heart beat with a pang of remorse, his mind filling with thoughts of Sydarias and their parents at the palace without him. He tried to shrug off the feelings and cleared his throat. It had been his decision to leave, and his regrets wouldn't change anything.

"I have three sons, and none of them have ever succeeded in gaining an invitation." Mr. Idawa rested down his glass with an audible clatter. He picked up his fork and shoveled in another mouthful of food.

"When I was this one's age, I had already attended several royal functions. Young men and women are different these days." He gestured toward Sydarias with a dismissive wave of the hand.

"It's such an exclusive event father, much more than when you were young. It's nearly impossible to get an invitation. It certainly wasn't for my lack of trying." Sydarias narrowed his eyes and stifled a groan.

"That kind of attitude will not get you very far in life. You chose to leave the family business and pursue your studies. You will have to try even harder if you hope to accomplish anything as a professor." Mr. Idawa glared at Sydarias, clearly incensed. "While you sit here dining casually with us, your older brothers are out in the city, working hard to help me with my affairs." Sydarias clenched his jaw and stared back at him. He opened his mouth to speak, but said nothing, and let out a frustrated sigh.

They finished the remainder of their dinner in an uneasy silence. Sydarias' parents bade them good night and then retired to their quarters, leaving the two upon the terrace by themselves. They lingered at the table, taking in the late afternoon views of the city and the sea.

"I'm sorry about dinner. My parents are usually more welcoming." Sydarias drummed his fingers upon the table, a disappointed frown crossing his lips.

"It's okay, I am thankful for the invitation. My parents can sometimes be overbearing as well." Darshima offered a knowing smile, taking some solace in the fact that he wasn't the only one who faced a trying familial circumstance.

"My father and my brothers will be attending several meetings around the city this week, so we won't see much of them." Sydarias leaned back in his chair and his frown eased a bit. As he explained, Mr. Idawa was rarely at home and often traveled throughout the realm to take care of the businesses. Sydarias' brothers looked after their father's affairs on Ciblaithia, and he saw them infrequently.

They picked at the remainder of the food on their plates, and though Sydarias insisted against it, Darshima helped him clear the table. Dishes and utensils in hand, they headed indoors and brought them back into the spacious kitchen. Sydarias then led him through the apartment, up a grand flight of marble stairs and down another airy hallway.

Sydarias threw open a set of double doors at the end of the corridor, and they walked through his room. Darshima caught a glimpse as they passed by, his jaw dropping in astonishment at its opulence. The room occupied two spacious levels, wrapped by windows looking out onto the surrounding cityscape. The pale stone floors, covered in blue woolen rugs, gleamed in the waning sunlight. Elegant wood furnishings stood neatly arranged throughout the space.

They bounded up another flight of stairs and walked onto the upper level. Darshima followed Sydarias through a set of open glass doors and onto a smartly appointed terrace. They settled into a pair of comfortable, dark wooden chairs near the balustrade. The setting sun drifted steadily beyond the horizon, leaving fiery streaks upon the darkening sky. The silhouettes of Benai and the moons glowed brightly. The metal frames of passing ships appeared as glittering fragments amid the fading light. In the distance, the tranquil surface of the bay cast a shimmering, fractured reflection of the vast skyline.

As they looked out over the city, Sydarias turned to Darshima.

"I am glad you decided to visit me," he said softly, the steady breeze carrying his words. The evening light gave his bright grey eyes a striking air.

"Thank you very much for the invitation." Darshima leaned back in his chair.

"I want to apologize again for my father's tone at dinner. He's been under more stress than usual, as of recent." Sydarias stared at the ground, a look of resignation briefly crossing his face.

"You don't have to apologize, my father can be short-tempered too. Is he worried about his businesses?" asked Darshima.

"That's part of it." Sydarias lifted his head and set his gaze upon the sky.

His voice trailed off as if his mind were somewhere else.

Silence fell between them, and the air grew cooler and quieter as the noisy bands of traffic steadily thinned. Darshima turned back to Sydarias, whose eyes were still trained upon the sky. He looked upward and saw nothing but the stars, Benai and the moons above.

Darshima shook his head and sighed. He reminded himself that The Vilides was built upon the ruins of an Omystikai city, and its memories were ever-present. As a child, he remembered hearing that the people here had been influenced by their ancient ways. Though long exiled to Iberwight, Omystikai customs had left an indelible mark on the culture, language, and art of Ciblaithia. Like the Omystikai, the Vilidesians were prone to observing the skies and interpreting the positions and movements of celestial bodies. Darshima curiously eyed Sydarias as he looked toward the stars.

"Are you okay?" asked Darshima. He waited for a response, but Sydarias remained silent. Darshima then reached out and gently nudged his shoulder.

"Is there something wrong?" asked Sydarias in a groggy voice. He peered at Darshima, eyes widened as if he had just been roused from a deep slumber.

"I should ask you the same question." Darshima wrinkled his brow, unsure what to make of Sydarias' unusual behavior.

"Forgive me, I am just a bit tired from the trip back home." Sydarias breathed softly and glanced down at his hands, folded in his lap. Darshima let out an anxious sigh. He had wanted to ask Sydarias for suggestions about where to stay for the night, but he seemed too preoccupied. His chest tightened with a strain of anxiety as he remembered that he had yet to find any sort of lodging.

His visit with Sydarias and his family had taken much longer than he had anticipated.

"Thank you for the dinner, but it's getting late. I must find someplace to stay while I'm here in The Vilides." Darshima rose from his chair.

"What do you mean?" Sydarias shot a puzzled glance at him.

"I was supposed to stay at the palace during the ceremonies, but as you know, I left." Darshima started toward the door. "I still need to find an accommodation for the rest of my time here." Sydarias jumped to his feet and faced Darshima.

"Didn't you plan on staying here with me?" Sydarias shook his head in confusion.

"Thank you, but I could never ask such a thing from you," stammered Darshima, his eyes widening in surprise.

"You'll stay here with me. I won't take no for an answer." Sydarias rested his hand upon Darshima's shoulder.

"I don't want to impose upon you and your family." He shook his head, his mind replaying the tense meal with Sydarias and his parents.

"You wouldn't be an imposition at all. Besides, we won't have any more dinners with my parents." Sydarias let out a soft chuckle.

"Really, dinner was fine. I am thankful for the meal." Darshima nodded politely.

"Be honest, they're be a bit much." Sydarias tilted his head, gesturing toward the apartment. "This environment can be difficult at times." He let out a weary sigh.

"I meant no such thing." Darshima tried to fight off a smirk, but he couldn't help it. Sydarias burst into a laugh.

"But you'll stay?" Sydarias cleared his throat. Darshima bit his lip as he decided. The Vilidesians were famous for their well-intentioned but sometimes overbearing hospitality, and Sydarias was no different. To refuse a Vilidesian's invitation was considered an insult.

"I don't know how to thank you, Sydarias." Darshima gratefully clasped his hand.

"I bet this wasn't the visit you were expecting." Sydarias guided Darshima toward the door.

"You're right about that." Darshima nodded, letting out a soft laugh as he contemplated the unanticipated change in his circumstance.

"I'm sorry for what happened to you at the palace last night, but I promise we'll make up for it this week." Sydarias gave him a friendly slap on the back.

"I appreciate it," said Darshima, taken aback by Sydarias' ready generosity. They walked inside, and Sydarias set to work preparing a place for Darshima to stay

Chapter Fifteen

Darshima tossed and turned as he drifted in and out of restless sleep. He lay atop the large downy bed, its soft sheets pulled loosely over him. He tugged at his linen shirt and trousers and tried to make himself comfortable. A sense of unease had roused him earlier that night, and he couldn't fall back to sleep. After several attempts, he sat up and let out a frustrated sigh.

The sheer curtains fluttered lazily before the open window, casting amorphous shapes in the cool evening breeze. Soft starlight filtered through the clear panes, bathing the large room in a muted, pale glow. Save for the distant drone of traffic, the room was quiet. His fatigue creeping back, he slumped onto the sheets and closed his eyes.

As Darshima drifted into another bout of sleep, the distant sound of footfalls reached his ears and filtered through his thoughts. His eyes fluttered open and he lay still, listening closely. His gaze darted about the dark corners of the room as he searched for the source of the noise. The steps drew nearer until they stopped just behind the door. The sound of soft knocking broke through the tranquility.

Darshima rose from the bed, shuffled across the room, and opened the door to see Sydarias, dressed in a similar set of clothing, staring back at him. He nervously fidgeted with his sleeves as he peered into the room.

"May I come inside?" whispered Sydarias, his voice echoing throughout the large space.

"Of course." Darshima offered a groggy nod and stepped aside. They walked through the shadows, over to a corner of the room, and sat upon the cool stone floor. Sydarias rested his back against the window and faced Darshima.

Beyond the clear panes, Darshima eyed the white flickering lights of passing aerial vessels in the distance. They skillfully navigated the maze of innumerable towers, their facades aglow amid the still blue void of the night. Sydarias cleared his throat and Darshima turned toward him.

"I'm sorry about everything today, Darshima," he said.

"You don't have to apologize for anything." Darshima slowly rubbed the sleep from his eyes. "I owe you a debt of gratitude for letting me stay with you."

"I wouldn't have let you stay anywhere else." Sydarias smiled softly and brushed aside Darshima's words with a wave of his hand.

"You must be confused as to why my parents and I have been acting so strangely," said Sydarias.

"I didn't want to say anything about it." A chuckle escaped Darshima's lips, and he fell silent as he saw Sydarias' expression darken. Sydarias shifted uneasily and stared down at the floor as if he were searching for the right words.

"Is everything okay?" Darshima leaned closer to him.

"All is not well here in The Vilides," said Sydarias. He briefly peered over his shoulder at the evening sky. Starlight flooded through the window and bathed him in a peculiar glow. His icy mood filled the whole room, and even the bustling cityscape seemed to crystallize behind him.

"What do you mean?" asked Darshima.

"Haven't you heard any of the administrative reports?" Sydarias tilted his head to the side, a perplexed frown crossing his face.

"I haven't really paid any attention to them." Darshima shrugged his shoulders.

Sydarias' eyes narrowed in a pointed gaze. He turned around and faced the window.

"Why do you keep staring at the sky like that?" asked Darshima, his voice wavering with a hint of exasperation. Darshima scooted over to Sydarias and gently nudged him aside with his shoulder. As they stared together through the glass, Darshima's eyes wandered amid the patch of heavens that commanded Sydarias' attention. He saw Benai, the moons, and the usual arrays of constellations, but nothing out of the ordinary.

"Why aren't you aware of anything happening here?" Sydarias stared intently at him.

"I guess I don't know." Darshima shook his head. He had heard of some recent turmoil, but nothing more than the usual political gridlock.

"The dynasty has been greedy and the realm is going through a difficult period." Sydarias let out a pained sigh.

"How is that even possible?" Darshima's eyes widened in disbelief. Back home on Gordanelle, Vilidesian influence was everywhere. Trouble in the capital was something he had never contemplated.

"We have been asking the very same question," said Sydarias.

"What's going on?" Darshima's brow furrowed in confusion.

"Beneath the order you see in the streets, there is turmoil." Sydarias lowered his eyes and glared at the floor.

After nearly eleven centuries of peace and prosperity, Vilidesian strength had begun to wane. The dynasty's once absolute rule over the moons had come under increasing scrutiny. The current rulers lacked the vision and leadership of their predecessors. They were more focused on personal enrichment and paid little heed to the hard-earned consensus among their diverse subjects. Several members of the dynasty were implicated in sordid scandals and unsavory arrangements with prominent enterprises and industries throughout the realm.

As their conduct came to light, the dynasty feared the loss of its power. In an attempt to halt the rise of subversive elements, the emperor enacted laws to limit the press. He issued restrictions on trade and travel between the moons. The Vilides, as the capital and crossroads of the realm, derived its power and prosperity from the free movement of goods, capital, and people. Therefore, the Vilidesians suffered the most from these onerous laws.

As the economy stagnated, citizens aired their grievances through general strikes and mass demonstrations. Many businesses struggled, including those held by the Idawa clan. Generations ago, the family established a simple parcel delivery business serving the capital. Over the centuries, it had grown into a leading enterprise with divisions that included freight, passenger travel, and shipbuilding. The restriction of trade had forced their businesses to abandon several lucrative ports of call.

Beyond the sands of Ciblaithia, the other capitals began to subvert the emperor's rule. Renefydis and Gavipristine went as far as issuing their own mandates governing trade between the territories of their moons. The dynasty ultimately forced them to rescind these laws but their actions set a startling precedent for the entire realm. In eras past, this type of rogue action upon the other moons would have brought a strong and forceful response from Vilidesian forces. In the face of popular protests and dissent from the other moons, the emperor was forced to repeal most of the laws restricting commerce and the press.

Despite its vast wealth, omnipresent culture, and unchallenged military might, The Vilides was finding that its hegemony was no longer unassailable. The populations of Gordanelle, Wohiimai, and Iberwight had grown steadily over the centuries and exceeded Ciblaithia's by billions. Ardavia, whose urban population was the Realm's second largest, had long seen itself as a counterweight to Vilidesian influence. Furthermore, the Ardavians did not forget their history albeit brief, as founders of their own realm.

As the evening wore on, they talked about the changes facing their world.

"Come to think of it, there were protests in Ardavia," said Darshima as he remembered the crowds at the palace gates during his voyage to the port.

"We Vilidesians don't care much for the Viceroy of Gordanelle. He is one of the most corrupt members of the dynasty." Sydarias narrowed his eyes and scowled. Darshima remained silent, unsure of what to say. He had never paid much attention to politics on Gordanelle, but he knew things had become more difficult there. People worked harder and earned less, while the Vilidesians continued to accumulate unprecedented levels of wealth.

Sydarias' gaze lingered upon the window as Darshima contemplated his words.

"You're so intrigued by the sky. Is this why you want to study astronomy?" asked Darshima. Sydarias shot him a curious glance as if he had been caught off guard.

"Aren't you familiar with any of the ancient lore of the moons?" he asked.

"I remember learning some of it as a child. The stories are quite interesting," said Darshima, as he tried to think back to the lessons he studied in school.

"The lore is more than just interesting, it is our heritage written upon the sky." Sydarias rose from the floor. "Come with me Darshima, I want to show you something." He shuffled across the room toward the door. His figure vanished and reappeared in the uneven beams of light between the shadows.

Darshima leapt to his feet and followed Sydarias as he opened the door and stepped past the threshold. He did his best to avoid crashing against the furniture veiled in darkness. They walked down a dim hallway and climbed up a narrow stairwell, its crystal treads glowing softly in the shadows. Darshima followed Sydarias onto the landing, through another set of doors and onto a terrace above his room. The cool air sent a chill through Darshima's spine, and their nightclothes fluttered in the steady breeze.

Sydarias stopped in the center of a tiled path and lifted his gaze skyward. He motioned for Darshima to stand beside him.

"Look up at the sky and tell me what you see." He pointed toward the firmament, the spiral pinnacle of the tower looming above their heads.

"I don't see anything." Darshima peered up toward the stars and saw nothing that struck him as unusual.

"Look between the rings, and you'll see what I have been seeing all along." Sydarias made a sweeping gesture in the direction of Benai. Its surface appeared a dark grey, and its rings seemed more vivid than the night before.

Darshima squinted and saw the three other moons gleaming boldly in an arc against the fine bands of debris that composed Benai's rings. Gordanelle shone the emerald hue of its virgin forests, Iberwight gleamed the crystalline color of snow, and Wohiimai glowed the cloudy blue-green color of its vast fields and oceans.

"They seem to be in a different position. Is that what you're talking about?" asked Darshima. Sydarias stood still with his arms at his sides. His eyes were transfixed upon the sky and he spoke softly. Intrigued, Darshima stepped closer and listened to his words.

"On the night of the thousandth solstice, the gilded moon, obstinate in its pride shall stand alone," he whispered. Darshima didn't understand the passage, but Sydarias' somber tone gave him pause. It seemed as if he were reciting some sort of text.

"What is that supposed to mean?" Darshima shook his head, unsure of the significance behind the cryptic words.

"It's just an old Omystikai saying." Sydarias pulled his gaze away from the sky and stared at the ground, his curly locks shrouding his face. He seemed as if he were trying to convince himself of his own words. The evening silence filled the space between them, and Darshima's brow wrinkled in confusion.

"How come you were saying those words?" asked Darshima, his eyes glinting in the evening light. Sydarias looked up at him, a solemn expression spreading upon his face.

"Its nothing, Darshima," said Sydarias, his voice rising above the winds. Darshima closed his eyes briefly and tried to think of a different way to ask his question.

"Why does the position of the moons intrigue you so much?" asked Darshima. "They seem to have you acting rather strangely this evening." Sydarias nervously bit his lip as he listened.

"I don't want to trouble you with old stories. We Vilidesians sometimes get carried away with the old Omystikai lore about the heavens," he replied.

"Those legends are in the past, why let them worry you?" Darshima looked over to Sydarias.

"In ways both large and small, the past informs both the present and the future." Sydarias peered at Darshima, his eyes gleaming in the starlight.

Darshima walked to the edge of the terrace amid the gusts of wind and braced against the balustrade. He folded his arms across his chest and closed his eyes. Darshima let out a sigh, trying to control his frustration, but Sydarias' peculiar behavior unnerved him. One moment he was jocular and outgoing, the next he was secretive and superstitious. Darshima began to wonder whether he should've made other arrangements for his week. He was now a guest of the Idawa family, and it would be extremely rude for him to leave. The welcome coolness of the railing upon his back calmed him some.

Darshima wished Sydarias would say what was troubling him. He couldn't understand how a quote or the position of the moons could affect him so deeply. As a child, Darshima remembered hearing that the Vilidesians were an intelligent, industrious but notoriously complex people. Their inner motives were sometimes hard to discern and often ruled by celestial movements. As he spent time with Sydarias and his family, he was beginning to understand what that meant.

"The winds are picking up. We should go back inside." Sydarias pointed toward the entrance.

"Tell me what those words mean." Darshima stepped closer to him.

"It's just a phrase from an ancient text. Their meaning remains a mystery." Sydarias shrugged his shoulders, approached the wall, and stood beside him.

"Then why is it bothering you so much?" Darshima's lips wrinkled in a quizzical frown.

"The Omystikai once ruled this moon. They knew its past and they know its future. With all the recent turmoil here, things have never been so unclear." Sydarias let out a sigh.

"I am sure things will get better here, they always do." Darshima's gaze lingered upon the brilliant city lights surrounding them.

Sydarias remained silent. The starlight shone brightly upon his face, now drawn into a wary look. He gazed at the sky with his eyes fiercely narrowed, and the light gave them an ethereal appearance. He beheld the celestial sight with an almost adversarial stare, as if it would inflict harm. Darshima cast a curious glance at the astral ballet dancing gracefully upon the black expanse of sky, but saw nothing.

"Let's go back to sleep, it's getting late," whispered Darshima. Even though he didn't understand what was troubling Sydarias, he could sense the depth of his concern. Darshima wished he could somehow put him at ease. He rested his hand upon Sydarias' shoulder and guided him away from the wall, toward the door.

Chapter Sixteen

Darshima narrowed his eyes against the blinding light and looked upward. The sun hung high overhead in the cloudless blue sky, casting the golden sands of the arid landscape in a mesmerizing, metallic glow. The intense rays beat upon his head, sending rivulets of sweat pouring down his temples. He lifted a hand and adjusted the simple cloth of his checkered black and white Ciblaithian headdress. Wrapped around his nose and mouth, its tasseled ends fluttered in the hot, dry breeze. Bits of sand made their way through the fabric, the rough grains scratching against his cheeks. A smile crossed his lips as he thought of how different this place was from Gordanelle. Though it had only been a few days since he had arrived on Ciblaithia, he was growing accustomed to the unique climate.

A steady wind blew through Darshima's white linen trousers and shirt. Damp with sweat, the cool fabric clung to his skin. Sydarias, dressed in an identical outfit, plodded beside him. A brown leather satchel hung loosely over Sydarias' shoulder, rhythmically tapping against his side. Far ahead, they spied small groups of travelers in similar white garments, walking slowly along the road.

Darshima and Sydarias were on their way to visit the ruins of an Omystikai temple just outside of the city, in the small mining village of Pardesp. They had set out just after dawn via aerial coach to the city limit, then continued by wheeled coach through the desert to reach the beginning of the path. An ancient road built by the Omystikai, it had survived through many ages. Too rutted for vehicular traffic, they traveled the path by foot. Sydarias had tried to find an aerial coach to take them directly there, but none were willing to venture beyond the city limits or to such a rural area. Darshima didn't mind and was enjoying the hike.

They walked up the gently sloping, deeply worn black cobblestones, their leather sandals crunching against the fine layer of sand underfoot. Darshima curiously eyed the faded characters etched upon the smooth surfaces. They appeared in unfamiliar and complex geometric forms, dashes and curlicues. Earlier in their trek, Sydarias had eagerly pointed out the writings, recognizing them as an Omystikaiyn prayer for travelers. He even recited several of the verses as they stepped upon the arcane glyphs.

The foreign words echoed in Darshima's ears, sounding unlike anything he had ever heard. Sydarias' knowledge of this ancient language impressed him. Unlike the Ardavians, the Vilidesians learned basic Omystikaiyn script during their formative years. Most could not fluently speak the language as adults, but they could at least read its written form and say a few traditional phrases.

They walked along the road, giant rows of gilded dunes looming on either side of them. Their soaring peaks gently drifted with the winds and seemed to bend against the horizon. Off in the distance, Darshima spied a row of enormous, cone-shaped spirals rising from the sands. Beneath the transparent surface, he could make out a glistening black liquid flowing rapidly, like water.

"What are those structures?" asked Darshima, as he pointed to them. Sydarias paused for a moment, adjusted his headdress, then turned toward the spirals.

"They're fuel wells. That's how we extract fuel from the reservoirs under the dunes." He shielded his eyes with a hand and peered at them.

"So this is where all of the fuel comes from?" Darshima shook his head in wonderment.

"Yes, every drop. There's no other source in the realm. Trade ships couldn't voyage between the moons without this fuel. Your parents couldn't fly their vehicles around Ardavia without the fuel from Ciblaithia." Sydarias pointed with his index finger, tracing the shimmering fluid surging through the spirals. Darshima politely nodded and cast his eyes downward. His family didn't have a vehicle of their own. Personal aircraft were much too expensive for the average Gordanellan family.

They trudged along the road and came to a stop as fatigue crept up on them. The sun rose higher in the sky, its rays growing more intense.

"It's getting brighter out here." Sydarias pulled the fabric from his nose and panted under the heat. He briefly shielded his eyes with both hands and peered at the vast expanse of desert before them. He then reached into his bag and produced a small copper canteen of water.

"Here, take a drink." He passed the canteen to Darshima, who put the cylindrical vessel to his lips and drank heartily of the cool water.

"Thank you," he said between gulps. Darshima handed the canteen back to Sydarias who took a swig, then stowed it back in his bag.

"I forgot that I brought these visors." He reached deeper into the bag, retrieved two small leather cases, and handed one to Darshima. "Put them on and you will be able to see better."

Darshima took the case and ran his fingers along the fine-grain leather. He unfastened the silver clasp and it popped open, revealing the visor. He gently picked it up and held it against the light. Fashioned of a large, curved blue crystal pane, it automatically dimmed under the intense rays of the sun. The frame was made of a finely polished silver metal that fused seamlessly to the crystal.

"It's very impressive." Darshima gently turned over the exquisite object in his hand.

"These visors were handmade in Gavipristine and are the finest available. The crystal is tuned to protect your eyes from the harmful rays," Sydarias looked at him matter-of-factly as he slid the visor over his eyes. He turned back to Darshima. "Go ahead, give it a try."

Darshima put on the visor, the cool metal and crystal sending a refreshing tingle through his temples. His eyes feeling better, he craned his neck and looked around. The dunes and the sky were colored with a pleasing blue tint. In the corners of the visor, he spotted complex readouts superimposed upon his view. There were symbols denoting their coordinates and altitude along with a miniature map. Astonished, he glimpsed at Sydarias who chuckled at his expression.

"This is amazing!" exclaimed Darshima.

"If you like it, you can keep it." Sydarias gestured toward him. Darshima's eyes widened in disbelief. He shook his head and gently pulled off the visor. He handed it back to Sydarias and squinted against the bright sunlight.

"I couldn't accept this, it's far too nice," said Darshima, taken aback by the gesture.

"I have more pairs in different colors than I could possibly ever use. You can keep it." Sydarias waived a hand, brushing off the suggestion.

"Are you sure you won't miss this particular shade of blue?" Darshima rolled his eyes and smirked.

"The color suits you better. After all, you're the one with cobalt eyes." Sydarias stared at Darshima and chuckled.

"You're much too kind, and you've already lent me these clothes for our hike." Darshima looked down at his linen garments. He hadn't brought anything suitable for trekking in the desert, and Sydarias had given him an outfit to wear.

"It's no bother at all." Sydarias gently shook his head.

"I won't need it back home on Gordanelle." Darshima pushed the visor toward Sydarias.

"My mind is made up. It already belongs to you, and I don't want it back." Sydarias grinned as he gently deflected Darshima's hand. "Thank you." Darshima hesitantly put the visor back over his eyes and acclimated to the view.

They walked along the worn cobblestones, gusts of hot wind filling the silence between them. A contemplative frown crossed Darshima's face as he looked at the blue-tinged scenery surrounding him. Visors such as these were an expensive luxury. It would take him several month's pay at his job to afford one, and Sydarias seemingly had no trouble giving them away. As Darshima's week with the family progressed, it became clear to him that the Idawa family did not want for anything material.

Despite the unforgiving heat, Sydarias had chosen this day to visit the temple. The Vilidesian calendar predicted a rare solar eclipse during the afternoon. The Vilidesians, like the Omystikai who preceded them, were fervent observers of the sky. They frequently attended celestial events at their temples and shrines. Notable astronomic phenomena were treated as public celebrations, and most citizens received a holiday from their duties. The fact that this eclipse coincided with the Prince's birthday celebrations made it all the more significant. As a budding astronomer, Sydarias was keen to observe the phenomenon. He had chosen this location beyond the city limits, to get away from the crowds and for a better view. He also wanted to show Darshima a part of Ciblaithia beyond the urban sprawl of the capital.

Though the Omystikai had long been banished to Iberwight, traces of their ancient civilization still existed amid the shifting desert sands of Ciblaithia. It wasn't unusual to hear of Vilidesian archaeologists discovering a previously unknown temple or tomb. The particular site they were visiting was a temple that remained among the best preserved on the moon. Scholars had long ago discovered that it had been dedicated to observing the movements of

Iberwight. A surge of excitement coursed through Darshima as his mind sketched a vision of the ruin. He remembered reading about ancient structures such as these in his schoolbooks, but never imagined he would see one with his own eyes.

The incline grew steeper as they trekked along the road. Darshima looked to his sides and the dunes loomed even larger overhead. Ciblaithia was famous for the immense drifts of gold sand covering much of its surface. To the other moons, gold was highly valued for jewelry, ornamentation, and industry. As the realm's only source of this precious metal, the Vilidesians amassed great wealth from its trade.

The stifling heat getting the better of them, they stopped to catch their breath.

"Is the sand here really made of pure gold?" Darshima panted as he gestured toward the shimmering dunes.

"It's mostly a mix of silica and a crude gold alloy," replied Sydarias in a practical tone.

"So if I fill my pockets, will I be rich?" Darshima knelt down and picked up a handful of the gritty, glittering grains and held it before his eyes. Sydarias laughed heartily.

"It takes money and effort to refine this sand into something useful. Besides, the truly valuable gold is deep beneath our feet." Sydarias pointed a finger toward the ground, laughed again, and let out a sigh. Darshima's gaze darted between Sydarias and the handful of sand. A strong gust of wind blew between them and tore the golden grains from his palm, the pile dissolving into nothingness.

They plodded along the worn path, the sun shining upon them as it traveled across the sky. Fatigue caught up with them again, and they took another break under the intense rays. Darshima looked over his shoulder and beheld the expansive Vilidesian skyline, which seemingly occupied the entire horizon. Though they stood in the middle of the desert, the city seemed ever-present.

The innumerable towers glittered under the blinding sun, rippling in the withering waves of heat. From their perspective, the capital appeared as a mirage, its enormous spires floating just above the sands.

Darshima felt a tug on his sleeve and he turned back around. His eyes met Sydarias' through their visors.

"We're nearly there," he said, his voice rising with excitement.

"I hope so. I don't know how much more of this heat I can take." Darshima drew in a breath of hot air, leaned over and rested his hands upon his knees.

"Once we get there, we'll take a long rest." Sydarias patted Darshima upon his back. Darshima stood up, stretched and adjusted his headdress.

As they walked onward, a pang of sadness crept over him. His time on Ciblaithia was drawing to a close, and he would be returning home to Gordanelle in a few days. A wave of anxiety came over him, and he cast his eyes upon the road. He was uncertain how his family would receive him when they met again. The argument with his father and his sudden departure from the palace had changed everything. He shook his head and looked forward, trying to ignore his growing sense of worry.

Though his tenuous circumstances were never far from his thoughts, Darshima had thoroughly enjoyed his stay. He and Sydarias had moved past their awkward introduction and had become good friends. During their time together, Sydarias had given Darshima an extensive tour of The Vilides. They ambled amid the steep canyons of glass towers and strolled along the fabled shopping boulevards. Sydarias had shown him famed imperial monuments and magnificent parks in the renowned districts of the city. They lounged upon the city's pristine beaches and even swam in the warm waters of the bay. Sydarias had invited him to dine at fine restaurants and attend lavish banquets. They toured historic museums and even attended a lively performance in one of the city's famous theaters.

Darshima was taken aback by Sydarias' kindness. For the entire week, he displayed the typical if not excessive Vilidesian hospitality. Despite Darshima's vigorous protests, Sydarias treated him to everything. He could not remember a time in his life when he had enjoyed himself so much. As the date of his return drew nearer, the feeling of sadness only grew stronger. When he came to The Vilides, he never expected that he would have made a friend. Darshima didn't know when Sydarias would return to Gordanelle but vowed someday to repay the kindness if he came to visit.

Darshima's calves burned as they walked up a particularly steep hill. Sydarias put a reassuring hand upon his shoulder.

"This is the last stretch," said Sydarias, breathlessly as they trudged up the incline. With a final push, they scrambled to the summit. Head drooping, Darshima stopped for a moment and heaved in exhaustion.

"Look, we're almost there!" exclaimed Sydarias, gesturing with his hand. Darshima dusted the sand from his pants, lifted his gaze, and looked ahead. The road ended abruptly at a large, white trapezoidal tunnel that bored straight through the immense dunes. Darshima eyed the structure, his brow wrinkling in curiosity. Its elegant shape and detail were unlike anything he had ever seen.

"What is it?" Darshima turned to Sydarias.

"This is the path that will take us to the site." Sydarias cast a knowing gaze at him.

They walked steadily toward the structure, hewn from radiant white stones that seemingly glowed in the bright sunlight. Its finely carved perimeter was adorned with a series of golden glyphs and abstract symbols, much like those upon the cobblestones of the roadway. A sense of intrigue stirred in Darshima's heart as he thought about the ancient people who built this tunnel so long ago.

He couldn't imagine how it had managed to resist the ages of sandstorms on this moon.

Darshima followed Sydarias through the entrance, and was enveloped in the cool darkness. Further ahead, beams of sunlight illuminated the other end of the tunnel. Darshima blinked his eyes in surprise as his visor automatically adjusted, allowing him to peer through the shadows upon the path. They walked steadily, their footsteps echoing amid the emptiness. As they made their way through, Darshima reached out and touched the walls, his fingertips sliding against the smooth polished surface. The stones fit together so well, that he couldn't even distinguish the gaps between them.

The light grew brighter as they drew closer to the opening and then stepped back into the sunlight. Sydarias stopped and turned to Darshima.

"We've arrived," he said in a reverential tone, making a sweeping gesture toward the landscape before them.

They stood at the edge of an arid valley, hemmed in by rows of golden dunes. At its rim, Darshima counted the entrances of seven other identical tunnels that bored underneath the sands. A roadway passed through each of them and traveled in a gently sloping, straight line to the concave desert floor. His eyes followed the roads toward the center of the valley, where they terminated before a white stone structure of immense proportions.

A vast octagonal podium rose from the golden sands, tapering into a truncated pyramid with a broad, flat top. Each road ended at the chamfered vertices of the structure. Long staircases carved in stone travelled up each steep vertex. Each staircase terminated atop the podium in a pair of enormous cantilevered stone arches that loomed above the structure. The curving arches met in the center and supported a golden oculus that hung high above the structure, giving the appearance of an open-air dome. In the center of the podium below the oculus, lay a deep black circle that seemingly devoured the sunlight.

The sands stirred gently around Darshima as he surveyed the details of the valley. His heart beat with a profound sense of awe as he beheld the exquisite structure, easily larger than the royal palace itself. He felt as if he had been transported to another time and place. He wondered how this ancient building had survived the raging colonial wars, eons of neglect, and the ebb of time.

"I've never seen anything like it before." Darshima turned to Sydarias, his eyes widened in disbelief.

"Well, what are we waiting for?" Sydarias beckoned him. They hiked down the road, stepping carefully upon the black cobblestones, the pyramid looming overhead as they approached. Darshima took in every angle of the imposing edifice and realized that it didn't seem like a ruin at all. It stood perfectly intact and easily rivaled the finest monuments that the Vilidesians or Ardavians had ever built.

"How old is it?" asked Darshima, his eyes transfixed upon the pyramid.

"The historians aren't quite sure, but they estimate that it's several thousand years older than anything the Vilidesians built." Sydarias lifted his gaze toward the structure and shrugged.

The Vilidesians, with their abundant reserves of gold and iron, were known as the metallurgists of the realm. The Ardavians with their domes and steeples were its master stonemasons. This Omystikai structure easily surpassed the grandest stone buildings in Ardavia in terms of its magnificence and craftsmanship. Darshima wondered how the ancient Omystikai could have built such an immense, sophisticated structure without the aid of modern tools, devices, or machinery.

"How did they do it?" asked Darshima.

"No one knows. We Vilidesians understand that greater builders preceded us." Sydarias bowed his head in deference. A spark of recognition flashed through Darshima's mind. As he contemplated Sydarias' observation, the salient words of his history professor came back to him.

The ancient explorers from Benai who voyaged to Ciblaithia had expected to find a barren moon like all of the others, but were astonished to encounter a previously unknown race of people. The Omystikai civilization at the time comprised of several peaceful kingdoms much older and more advanced than the empires on Benai. Records from the era described extraordinary cities with advanced infrastructure and wondrous technology, ruled by a highly intelligent elite class. The ensuing colonial wars waged against the Omystikai engulfed the entire moon, resulting in untold devastation and their near annihilation. Armies from Benai asserted their dominance and systematically destroyed temples, libraries, and universities guarding entire eras of Omystikaiyn history.

With the eventual rise of the Vilidesian Realm, the House of Fyrenos sought an earnest reconciliation with the exiled Omystikai. Recognizing the importance of their culture to the wider realm, they sought to study their traditions. At the behest of the dynasty, scholars excavated and preserved Omystikai ruins all over the moon. Despite their efforts, most Omystikai remained marginalized and isolated on Iberwight.

Darshima and Sydarias walked down the gently sloping road toward the ruin, which seemingly grew larger with each step. The pyramid stood out amid the sands, nearly blotting out the sky. The structure was hewn of the same gleaming white stone as the tunnel that led them there. Darshima's pulse raced as they drew nearer, his sense of anticipation growing.

The golden grains of sand shifted slowly around the base of the pyramid. They came to a stop at one of the immense staircases leading up to the podium and stood for a moment. The smooth stone treads, embellished with carved lines of symbols seemed to rise magically from the dunes. Despite the eons of exposure to the elements, the stones somehow remained polished and unworn.

Darshima lifted the visor from his face and looked up toward the top of the stairway to see the stone arches framing the blue sky beyond. The ruin had an undeniable sense of permanence and seemed as timeless as the sands around it. In the near distance, he spied the small groups of people who had walked ahead of them. They settled upon white blankets amid the sands, protected from the sun by the enormous shadow of the structure.

"Can we climb up to the top?" Darshima pointed to the summit of the structure.

"Lead the way." Sydarias gestured toward the stairs.

Darshima faced the looming staircase, and they began their ascent. His legs burned with fatigue as he marched carefully upon the gleaming stones. The soft whisper of the steady gusts filled his ears as they rose above the desert floor.

Midway up the staircase, they sat down and rested. Darshima took in the sweeping view just above the tops of the dunes, the buildings of the vast skyline glowing in a reflected blaze of light. He sat beside Sydarias amid the whistling winds, marveling at the spectacular sight. Though Darshima admired the capital, he enjoyed the solitude of the desert. Sydarias looked up at the sky and methodically tapped the side of his visor. His lips curled into a frown.

"I just calculated Iberwight's present azimuth, and the eclipse will start soon," he whispered.

"Let's get going then, I would hate to miss it." Darshima rose from the steps. Sydarias let out a sigh and lifted himself to his feet.

"I bet when we first met, you didn't expect you'd be spending a day with me in the desert," exclaimed Sydarias.

“I never would’ve imagined it.” Darshima panted as they resumed their climb.

“Are you sure that you’re not missing anything at the palace with your family?” He turned to Darshima.

“I’d rather be here fatigued and sweating in the desert sun with you than miserable at the palace.” An earnest smile crossed Darshima’s lips.

“Well, it’s not too late to change your mind, the palace is just over there.” Sydarias gestured broadly toward the skyline behind them, the spires of the royal palace hovering faintly upon the horizon. Darshima rolled his eyes and let out a loud laugh as they continued their ascent.

With a final push, they clambered up the remainder of the stairs and reached the summit. Darshima’s eyes widened in disbelief as they passed under the soaring pair of arches. Fashioned from enormous stones, its cantilevered piers were wider than the oldest tree trunks in the forests back home on Gordanelle. His eyes traced the eight pairs of stone arches as they crisscrossed the open air, meeting above the center of the podium. They held themselves aloft and supported the oculus with no internal supports. The degree of engineering and exactitude that the ancient builders employed left him speechless.

The winds calmed down as they moved toward the center, and the air grew noticeably still. Darshima couldn’t quite identify how, but he sensed that this was a deeply sacred space. He walked across the vast platform with Sydarias and took in the details of the structure. The smooth white stones shimmered in a subtle shade of blue, reflecting the sky above. An intricate, inlaid design of arcing gold lines traversed the gleaming surface and met at the center of the platform, framing the large black circle in the center.

They walked together upon the octagonal surface, making their way along one of the golden arcs toward the circle. Darshima peered over his shoulder, surprised to see that they were the only two there.

"How come there's no one else up here?" He turned to Sydarias.

"Don't you remember what a trek it was to get to this place? It's not for the faint of heart." Sydarias shook his head and chuckled. "We Vilidesians are a pampered lot. Most folks stay close to home and feast for the eclipses."

Darshima's pulse thudded as they approached the black circle. The surrounding rim of gold gleamed boldly in the sunlight, appearing like the oculus hanging high above them.

They lifted their visors and peered downward. Darshima felt as if he were at the edge of a foreboding well, plunging into the unknown abyss. The circle was the deepest shade of black he had ever seen. It appeared as if a patch of the nighttime void had been painted upon the white stone. Darshima peered closer, and his eyes caught the reflection of countless flecks of gold embedded within the black surface. To his surprise, their positions shifted with a subtle fluidness, reminiscent of the stars in the evening sky. He stood still, transfixed by the ethereal sight.

Darshima cautiously stepped onto the surface and Sydarias followed. Though it felt like stone, it absorbed the sound of their footsteps. The points of glowing gold dissipated around his feet, swiftly traveling in swirls and eddies amid the blackness. His heart fluttered with a mixture of fright and wonder at the spectacle.

"What magic is this?" asked Darshima in hushed awe.

"It's a rare kind of stone that the Omystikai used for their altars. No one has ever found the quarry where they mined it. Only a few temples have them." Sydarias shrugged.

"And no one ever tried to loot this stone?" Darshima tapped his foot against the surface, his ears straining to hear the faint sound. Sydarias shook his head vigorously.

"Ages ago vandals tried, but none succeeded. Our archeologists tell us that these stones are among the heaviest materials ever discovered. No modern machinery can remove them." Sydarias pointed toward the stone. "Besides it might bring misfortune to anyone who attempted."

"Are you serious?" Darshima looked up at him, intrigued.

"There is so much we don't know about the ancient Omystikai. It's better to preserve their ruins than to destroy them," replied Sydarias.

Before Darshima could ask any more questions, Sydarias shouted.

"Look at that!" He pointed a finger toward the sky. Darshima lifted his gaze from the stone and looked upward. They pulled their visors back over their eyes, which darkened as they stared directly at the blazing sun. The fiery disk steadily diminished into the shape of a crescent as Gordanelle, Wohiimai and then Iberwight transited before it. The air around them stood still, and an enveloping silence permeated the temple. Darshima's heart thudded in excitement as he beheld the moving celestial bodies. He had never witnessed anything like it before.

"There hasn't been a total solar eclipse with Iberwight in generations." Sydarias adjusted the visor upon his face.

"It's beautiful," said Darshima, his eyes transfixed upon the sky.

The sun's disk steadily shrank as the final moon made its transit. The sky grew darker and the stars revealed themselves. Darshima glimpsed downward at the black surface, the points of gold forming into distinct constellations that mirrored the stars above.

"How is this possible?" Darshima's chest tightened anxiously, and his mind raced as he tried to make sense of the strange phenomenon.

"Vilidesian mineralogists have never been able to figure out the true properties of this stone." Sydarias cast a knowing gaze at him, then looked toward the heavens.

The air around them grew noticeably colder. Before long, the transiting moons blotted out the entire sun, save for its thin, glowing corona. The sky darkened to a deep shade of blue, and the vast field of stars glowed brightly. On Iberwight's surface, Darshima spied the city lights of Gavipristine, glowing like scattered embers.

As the moons continued their transit, the temperature unexpectedly plummeted. Confused, Darshima looked around the temple, rubbing the back of his arms for warmth. To his astonishment, a thin, glistening coat of frost appeared upon the ground at their feet. Branching patterns of ice crystals blossomed from the center of the black stone, steadily expanding outward. They drew their thin garments against their shivering frames. Darshima exchanged a perplexed glance with Sydarias.

"What's happening?" exclaimed Darshima, his breath coming out in icy puffs.

His sense of anticipation dissolved into a nascent fear. A deep and aching chill steadily sank into the marrow of his bones. Never having experienced such coldness in his life, a feeling of disbelief came over him. Moments ago, the air was thick with unbearable heat and now, he stood shivering in frost on the realm's hottest moon. The light from the corona cast the arches above them in peculiar shades of wavering shadow and light.

"I am not sure." replied Sydarias, his teeth chattering. They looked up toward the sky as Iberwight and the other moons completed their eclipse. The sky grew brighter and the stars faded as the sun reemerged. The frost upon the ground evaporated as the heat rapidly returned, giving off a subtle cloud of steam.

Darshima removed his visor and gazed upon the black stone at his feet. The flecks of gold stood frozen in a similar formation as the stars above, just before the eclipse. He then turned to Sydarias.

"I could've sworn those specks were moving." Darshima shook his head in disbelief. Sydarias' brow wrinkled in confusion at Darshima's words.

"I didn't even notice. I told you this place was special." Sydarias shrugged his shoulders and offered a grin.

"Thank you for bringing me here." Darshima put the visor back on and looked around them. He briefly placed his palms upon his brow and drew in a breath. His head throbbed with a vague, vice-like tightness. Fatigued and flushed, Darshima hesitantly stepped away from the stone. His heart pounded against his chest and he drew in a deep breath.

"It was no trouble at all." Sydarias paced slowly along the perimeter of the circle, staring curiously at the stone. Darshima stood amid the gentle winds, contemplating the mystery of this place. Despite the return of the heat, his muscles shivered as the sensation of coldness clung to him.

"The sun will be setting soon, and we should return to the city before nightfall. It gets quite dark out here." Sydarias tapped the side of his visor, adjusting its tint. He motioned with a hand toward the stairway leading back to the desert floor.

They crossed the platform, climbed down the stairs, and stepped onto the weather beaten roadway. Darshima looked over his shoulder at the looming temple, his mind replaying the preceding moments. Images of the moons' eclipse and the mysterious black stone hung before his eyes. He then turned toward Sydarias, who walked a few steps ahead upon the cobbled path. Though he couldn't explain it, Darshima felt as if something had shifted within him, much like the golden particles embedded in that stone. The sands swirling around them, they passed through the tunnel and toward the shimmering towers of the capital.

Chapter Seventeen

Sasha

Sasha sat amid the opulence of the grand hall and took in the splendid scene. Thick ribbons of woven gold hung from the cavernous rotunda in a web of gleaming catenaries. Chains of multicolored Iberwightian gems dangled from the tiles of the vaulted ceilings. The large crystals glittered in the warm torchlight from gold candelabras lining the frescoed walls. Exotic plants and colorful blooms from the Gordanellan rainforests festooned the massive stone pillars supporting the rotunda. An intoxicatingly sweet, floral fragrance hung in the air. Ornate, silver fountains near the banquet tables spewed jets of vintage wines from Wohiimai's most exclusive vineyards into a grand, shimmering cascade.

The harmonious tones of an orchestra filled the room, melding imperceptibly with the low din of the chattering guests. Performers in elaborate costumes of silver and gold danced about the center of the chamber in choreographed routines, to the graceful, syncopated beat. Three gilded, jewel-encrusted thrones sat upon a carved wooden dais under the rotunda, at the center of the checkered stone floor. A row of exquisite banquet tables sat before the thrones, abounding with roasted wild game and fine delicacies from the sea.

The prince's guests mingled with each other at a group of rectangular wooden tables before the dais, and their parents sat at tables further back in the large chamber, looking on proudly. Rows of uniformed valets, servants, and siblings serving as assistants lined the walls. They stood patiently in the shadows, ready to offer aid at a moment's notice. Other palace staff milled about the room, refilling glasses with wine, and carrying trays of food.

Sasha sat amongst a large group of boisterous young men and women dressed in formal attire, and indulged in the decadent feast.

Like them, he wore black trousers, polished boots, a white collared shirt, and an embroidered black overcoat in the formal Vilidesian style. Though he had only made their acquaintance during the week, they had already become friends.

As Sasha lifted his fork, he heard someone call his name. He looked up to see a young Wohiimaian man named Naathius staring at him. Fair-skinned with long reddish-blond hair that hung over his shoulders, bright green eyes, and a square jaw, he cut a strapping figure in his formal wear. He was an admiral in the Vilidesian aerial corps and had received several commendations for his training efforts in the villages around Pelethedral.

"I understand you are very skilled at hunting the powilix, everyone's been talking about it. How do you succeed in killing such a deadly animal?" he asked between bites of his meal.

"It takes practice, like anything." Sasha leaned back in his chair, the memories of the last hunt fresh in his mind. The Gordanellan hunting tradition was unique and many people had asked him questions about it during the week.

An image of Darshima at the cliff edge facing the powilix materialized before Sasha's eyes, and his heart sank. He had wanted so badly for Darshima to succeed at the hunt. If his life hadn't been at risk, Sasha knew that Darshima would have somehow killed them. Sasha had participated in the hunt year after year, and though he was pleased with his success, it didn't mean as much to him anymore.

"I imagine that you have keen eyesight." Naathius firmly rested a hand upon the table. "If you ever tire of chasing beasts through the jungle, you must consider joining the aerial corps. Our realm needs people like you."

"It's much more complicated than running through the forest. It requires a great deal of skill." Sasha shook his head, a mild frown forming upon his lips. “I imagine you're talented in your own right, commanding such large ships.”

“It also requires skill, but we have nothing like the powilix on Wohiimai. I can't imagine what it would be like to challenge one with merely a bow and arrow, ” said Naathius, his eyebrows arched in amazement. “Though our traditions are different, they are both important to the realm.” he deftly speared a strip of grilled meat with his fork.

“They certainly are.” Sasha offered a polite nod and turned back to his plate.

At the other end of the room, Sasha spied his mother and father sitting together, looking elegant in their formal attire. He flashed a brief smile, and they waved to him. They still had yet to work out their differences since Darshima's abrupt departure. For the sake of the celebration, they decided to put their argument aside until they all returned home.

Despite his brother's absence, Sasha and his parents had enjoyed themselves during their stay. The week had gone by in what had seemed like an instant. They attended several sumptuous feasts and lavish ceremonies. Along with the other invitees, he had witnessed some of the ancient dynastic rituals. Performed by the Omystikai advisors, these rituals were legendary in their secrecy and elaborateness. In addition to the week of festivities, these traditions formally marked the prince's entry into adulthood and confirmed his future role as the Emperor of The Vilides.

Sasha had nearly finished his plate when the orchestra broke out into a loud and brassy fanfare. He set down his utensils and looked toward the rotunda to see Prince Khydius and his parents, the emperor and the empress make their entrance. Sasha and the others rose to their feet as the imperial court filed through. The prince wore a fine, white high-collared shirt embroidered in silver, a black waistcoat, black trousers, and black leather boots. Gleaming chains of gold and diamonds hung about his neck, and a shimmering blue and gold cape draped over his shoulders. His black hair, woven with chains of gold and crystal, was fashioned in two elaborate braids that fell over his shoulders.

Wearing elaborate court vestments, along with their capes and crowns, the emperor and empress accompanied the prince. Following them were his cousins, Aris, the Defender of Wohiimai, and Loren, the Defendress of Gordanelle. They wore folded cloth headdresses atop their braided black locks and golden sashes over their formal attire. A retinue of uniformed servants followed closely behind the procession.

The prince looked around and surveyed the large, attentive crowd, his cape trailing behind him. Sasha and the other guests greeted him with a standing ovation and a rousing cheer, but it didn't seem to soften the serious expression upon his face. The prince raised his hand, the applause quieted, and Sasha and other the guests resumed their seats. He stepped upon the dais and stood before the throne, looking upon the beaming crowd.

"I would like to thank you for attending my celebration," he said. His mellow voice resonated throughout the hall, commanding everyone's attention. "As you know, tonight marks the occasion of my seventeenth birthday. Whether you've traveled from near or far, I am thankful that you are here to celebrate with me." He flashed a thoughtful smile and the crowd responded with thunderous peals of applause.

Despite the controversy surrounding him, the prince was still very much loved by the people of the Realm. There were murmurings that he was exigent and often disagreed with the emperor and the empress. Nevertheless, tonight was a special occasion and all grievances were temporarily forgiven. He paced along the dais and continued his speech.

"Each of you seated before me has shown intelligence and character beyond that of your peers. This celebration is as much for you as it is for me." He gestured toward the invitees and they applauded loudly. "Your leadership and strength give me hope for the future of our realm."

The prince then recounted several stories of their impressive accomplishments. Sasha looked upon him, surprised as he recited the accounts from memory. Many of the young men and women served in the realm's military, others took care of the sick and needy in the cities. Other were aspiring teachers, scholars, and artists who made impressive contributions to their communities and beyond. He finished his speech and thanked them for their efforts. The guests cheered the prince and he waved heartily to them.

Prince Khydius stepped down from the dais, and much to his guests' amazement he mingled with them. As heir to the realm, he was expected to sit upon the dais during official functions, but the prince was never one to follow convention. The emperor and the empress sat upon their thrones and looked upon him with stern expressions. The prince's seat, however, remained empty as he engaged the eager crowd.

As Sasha chatted with the other guests at his table, he spotted a flash of motion from the corner of his eye. He turned to see Prince Khydius make his way toward them, and his heart leapt in surprise. The prince's servants cleared a space for him and set down a high backed, gilded chair directly across from Sasha. The prince dismissed them with a wave of his hand and they scuttled away.

The guests seated beside the prince fell silent, waiting attentively he settled in his chair.

"Please continue your discourse, don't let me interrupt." He nodded toward them.

Sasha and the other guests spoke cautiously, and he listened. The prince rested his arms upon the crisp, white tablecloth and folded his well-manicured hands together, his gold and jewel rings glittering in the soft torchlight.

His pulse racing with a mixture of awe and anxiety, Sasha hesitantly looked toward the prince, whose piercing eyes countered his stare.

"How are you, Sasha?" asked Prince Khydius in a low voice, as if he intended the conversation to be only between them.

"I am well, Your Highness. My parents and I thank you very much for this invitation." Sasha's chest tightened in surprise as he realized that the prince knew his name.

"I am glad to have you at my celebration. You have shown great leadership in your community by training the young men in the ways of your traditional hunt. My aides tell me that you are among the most skilled hunters on all of Gordanelle." He leaned back in his chair, beaming at Sasha.

"Thank you, Your Highness." Sasha humbly bowed his head and then shared some of the harrowing details of his recent hunt, much to the prince's delight. Hunting was not a tradition familiar to the Vilidesians. The custom of pursuing wild animals in the forest was truly a foreign idea to most people beyond Gordanelle.

"May I ask you something?" whispered the prince. A fine sweat broke out upon Sasha's brow as he registered the prince's words. His thoughts raced as he contemplated what the heir to the throne would want to ask him. Sasha nodded nervously, unable to find his voice.

"I remember seeing you and your parents on the day of your arrival. Who was that fellow carrying your bags?" The prince leaned forward, staring intently at Sasha.

"That was only my brother Darshima, Your Highness," said Sasha. "Did he offend you?" A concerned frown crossed Sasha's lips as he mulled over the details of that day. He tried to recall anything they did that might have gone against royal protocol.

"He certainly did not offend me in any way, but there was something about him that caught my attention." The prince knit his brow in mild frustration and put a hand up to his temple in thought. "Please forgive me, but I cannot recall what it was." He smiled politely.

"I understand, Your Highness," replied Sasha, breathing a sigh of relief that his family had not offended the prince.

"I must meet the other guests, but thank you for being here, Sasha." The prince firmly shook Sasha's hand. With a nod of his head, he signaled his aides who rushed to his side and offered their assistance. The prince rose from his seat and moved about the room, his servants in tow.

It was just after the prince moved away that Sasha's heartbeat finally slowed to a normal pace. Never in his wildest dreams had he expected to speak directly with the Prince of The Vilides. Sasha's gaze lingered upon him as he moved about the room. The Prince chatted with the other invitees, but he didn't sit down at any of the other tables. Sasha half-listened to the conversation of those around him, but he could not focus. The prince's question about Darshima lingered upon his mind.

Chapter Eighteen

His thoughts wandering, Darshima drifted in and out of a fitful bout of sleep. The linens covering him grew heavy and felt unbearably warm. His nightclothes were drenched with sweat and clung to his skin. With a swipe of his arm, he threw the covers aside. He lifted his head from the downy pillow and looked around. His damp locks hung before his face, blocking his vision. He clumsily swept them back with his hands. Intense beams of sunlight stung his eyes, filling them with tears. The muscles of his neck burned with fatigue as he struggled to keep his head upright. With great effort, he moved his arms and flipped over the pillow, then collapsed back onto the bed in a heap, overcome by exhaustion.

Darshima clenched his jaw as a dull, hazy ache resonated through his skull. As he tossed and turned, a sharp bolt of pain shot through his back and radiated along his arms. He pushed his face deep into the pillow, muffling his cries as the sensation faded away. A haggard sigh escaped his lips, and he forced himself to sit upon the edge of the bed.

His illness was inexplicable. He had felt relatively fine yesterday after returning from the desert, but as the evening wore on, the aching chill in his bones had persisted. Sydarias had shivered beside him, but his symptoms had subsided before they left the desert. Darshima had retired to bed early that night and bundled himself under the covers, only to break out in unbearable sweats, then shaking chills. Today was the day before his return to Gordanelle, and he felt terrible. He tried to blame his symptoms on the stress of returning to Ardavia and the argument with his family, but it felt like something more serious.

Darshima slowly pushed himself up from the bed and struggled to his feet. He felt as if he were weightless, like the breeze from the open window would carry him away. His vision came in and out of focus, and the forms of the furniture blurred with the bright sunlight. Everything seemed to spin around him. He carefully moved one foot in front of the other, trying to stay upright.

He didn't know where he was going, but he was restless and felt the urge to leave the room. The cool floor tingled against the bare soles of his feet with every step, and his knees trembled with weakness. He shuffled forward until he felt something hit his ankle. The room spun violently around him, and he felt himself fall sideways. A sharp pain surged through his back and shoulders as he felt himself colliding with the hard stone tile. A moan escaped his lips as an agonizing spasm coursed through his entire body. Too exhausted to get up, he lay still and closed his eyes.

Darshima couldn't remember a time when he had felt so ill, and he was much too exhausted to care. The pain lingered as he lay there amid his mental fog, drowsily contemplating how to get up from the floor. Just as he drifted off to sleep, he heard the distant click of a door opening. The muffled sounds of Sydarias' worried voice filtered through the ringing in his ears. Thudding footsteps echoed louder and then softer as he faded in and out of consciousness. He felt a strong force lift him and carry him back to the bed. His head hummed with the chattering of muffled voices, their conversation unintelligible to him.

The bright sensation of a thin beam of light scanning the depths of his eyes brought him out of his haze. As he tried to flinch, the deep voice of a man called out to him.

"Please do not move," said the voice of a person who seemed to be looming over him.

Darshima obediently lay still as his vision and hearing came back into focus. The man held a glowing white, cylindrical crystal in his hand.

After examining Darshima's eyes, he placed the object into a leather case beside him and sat upon the edge of the bed. He had a kind face marked by dark leathery skin, large grey eyes, a prominent nose, and a crown of grey, woolen hair. Muted sunlight filtered through the drawn curtains, and gave him a subtle radiance. He wore a buttoned, long black tunic and black trousers. A white, fabric cloak embroidered in elegant gold Vilidesian script hung upon his shoulders, signifying his status as a physician.

"How do you feel?" he asked, his brow wrinkling with a genuine air of concern.

Darshima hoisted himself up, sat at the edge of the bed, and drew in a breath. He carefully rose to his feet and tentatively walked around. The feelings of weakness had disappeared, and he could support himself without trouble. His vision had returned to normal and his ears no longer rang. The dull headache had subsided, and the pain in his back and arms had diminished to an almost imperceptible tingling.

"I feel fine." Darshima's eyes widened in astonishment. He could neither believe nor explain what had happened. A moment ago, he felt so ill that he could barely open his eyes, and now he felt completely fine. He walked around the room, expecting the dizziness to return, but it didn't. Dumbfounded, he made his way back to the edge of the bed and plopped down upon the soft covers.

"Are you sure?" A deep frown spread across the physician's lips.

"I'm sure," replied Darshima. The physician looked him over once again and placed a hand upon his forehead.

"Honestly, I have never seen anything quite like it." He rested his hands upon his bag. "I am not sure why you were feeling ill. Perhaps it was the exhaustion from your long journey to the desert. People from the other moons oftentimes struggle with our arid climate."

With his case in hand, the physician rose from the bed and started for the door, his leather boots scraping softly upon the tile. "There are some self-limited afflictions that people catch from the desert sand, I presume it was one of those," he said over his shoulder. As he reached for the door, he abruptly turned back around. "Forgive me, I meant to examine your arms. You mentioned that they were still bothering you."

The physician walked toward Darshima and sat down beside him. Darshima rolled up the sleeves of his shirt and extended his arms. The markings on his right forearm stood out vividly against his skin, a deep shade of bronze after his day in the desert. Eyes narrowed, the physician held his arm and examined it closely. He let out a knowing sigh as his fingers traced the markings, then let go of Darshima.

"It looks to me as if you've had your arm marked recently. Perhaps the ink made you sick." His eyebrows furrowed in curiosity. "I have never seen markings quite like these. It looks to be indelible." The physician curiously pinched his skin. Darshima's pulse raced nervously and he remained silent, not wanting to draw any more attention to himself. "You must've had it marked at one of your ceremonies or rituals back home on Gordanelle." His eyes glimmered, and he appeared deep in thought.

"I didn't have it marked anywhere," stammered Darshima. A puzzled frown crossed the physician's lips.

"How can that be?" he asked as he pointed toward the markings.

"I've had them for as long as I can remember." Darshima turned away and tried to avoid his piercing stare.

"How can that possibly be true?" The physician's expression of puzzlement dissolved into a look of disbelief as he pondered Darshima's words. He was about to question further, but stopped when he saw the seriousness in Darshima's eyes. He summarily grabbed his case, rose from the bed, and walked to the door. He shot a peculiar stare back at Darshima. "Whatever afflicts you, I have no power to cure." He lowered his gaze and then left the room, firmly closing the door behind him.

Darshima remained seated upon the bed and stared blankly forward. A chill coursed through him as he contemplated the physician's unusual words. He didn't know what to make of his strange reaction or his abrupt departure. Before Darshima could think further, he was interrupted by a soft knocking at the door.

"Is everything okay, Darshima?" asked Sydarias, his voice muffled behind the door. Darshima jumped to his feet, opened the door, and greeted him. Wearing an embroidered white tunic, black trousers, and sandals, he shifted his weight as he stood in the doorframe. A concerned expression crossed his features as he stared at Darshima.

"I'm much better now, I didn't mean to worry you." Darshima stepped aside and let Sydarias through.

"You collapsed onto the floor and I had to pick you up. I'm very worried." Sydarias folded his arms across his chest.

"I didn't even realize it. Everything is still hazy, but I'm feeling better now." Darshima rested a hand upon Sydarias' shoulder.

"Are you sure?" Sydarias' expression softened a bit. "I hope you don't go back to Gordanelle and tell everyone that a Vilidesian forced you into the desert, and you fell ill."

"I would never say that." Darshima shook his head and chuckled as the image of them in the sweltering desert came back to him. They stood in the doorway and Sydarias stared at him, a slight frown spreading upon his lips.

"Come with me, we have dinner ready for you. You haven't eaten anything all day." Sydarias gestured toward the door.

"Is it already afternoon?" exclaimed Darshima.

"You've been ill since last night. Let's get you out of this room for a spell." Sydarias ushered him past the threshold.

"You don't have to worry so much about me," said Darshima, as his stomach let out an aching growl.

"You're not the only one who hears that. I believe I do have to worry about you." Sydarias playfully rolled his eyes as he pointed to Darshima's abdomen. Darshima shook his head and tried to suppress the bashful smile spreading across his face.

They walked through the hallway, down the staircase and onto the terrace where they were greeted by Madame Idawa, who sat patiently at the dining table. She wore a vivid yellow robe that covered her shoulders, and her silky hair blew gently in the wind. Thick chains of gold and diamonds hung about her neck, gleaming in the late afternoon sun. The forest of towers and spires behind her gleamed a warm shade of copper in the rays of light, framing her in a striking portrait. A flurry of servants in grey trousers, tunics and smocks moved around her, setting out plates of food.

"Things move so much more smoothly when the servants are here." Sydarias let out a contented sigh as he watched them at work. Sydarias and Darshima offered their greetings to her as they sat down at the table. Madame Idawa acknowledged them with a polite smile.

"How are you feeling, Darshima?" Her eyebrows knit into a look of worry.

"I'm feeling well, madame," said Darshima. She surveyed him intently, an air of maternal concern crossing her features.

"Moments ago you were frightfully ill. I am glad that you've recovered." She unfolded a white cloth napkin and placed it upon her lap.

The servants set plates of sizzling meat and grilled roots before them and scuttled away. She motioned for the two young men to eat and they eagerly tucked into their meal. She looked on, her brow furrowed in a pensive expression.

“Did the physician find anything wrong?” She held her fork and tentatively picked at the food.

“He didn’t find anything.” Darshima shook his head in between hasty bites, his hunger getting the better of him.

“Aren't you going to have any dinner?” asked Sydarias as he pointed toward her plate.

“Perhaps I’ll save it for later. I don’t have much of an appetite.” She gently set down her fork, a forced smile crossing her lips.

They finished their meal and rose from the table. A team of servants rushed after them to clear their plates.

Madame Idawa led them across the terrace toward a set of wooden chairs and a small glass table alongside the balustrade. They took their seats and she sat facing them, her back against the skyline. Another pair of servants brought platters of chilled beverages and rested them upon the table. Darshima sat amid the tranquil ambiance and gazed upon the urban vista surrounding them. A thin blanket of clouds had moved in with the arid breeze, partially obscuring the view. Rays of sunlight streaked across the sky, and the pale forms of Benai and the moons steadily regained their color.

As Darshima sat with Sydarias and Madame Idawa, his heart beat with a keen sense of sadness. It was his last evening in The Vilides, and he would be returning home in the morning. He looked at the horizon and tried to take in every detail, not wanting to forget any of it. He had finally visited Ciblaithia, and its grandeur had left him with a profound sense of awe. Whether it was the majestic avenues crowded with shops or the dense bands of traffic gliding among the forests of towers, he had enjoyed every moment. Their pilgrimage to the ruins amid the golden dunes was perhaps his most cherished memory.

Darshima sat lost in thought, his eyes lingering upon the clouds moving below. He felt a strong connection to this place that he hadn't expected. Though Gordanelle was home, he had never experienced a similar feeling there. He would miss The Vilides and promised himself that he would return someday.

The sound of his name being called roused him from his thoughts. Darshima turned toward Sydarias and his mother, who looked at him with concerned stares.

"I'm sorry, I wasn't paying attention," said Darshima, a timid smile crossing his lips.

"Why don't you stay with us for a few more days. The rest would be good for you," said Madame Idawa.

"Thank you, but I feel fine now." Darshima reclined in his chair and tried to conceal his disbelief. He was as surprised as they were that his health had recovered so rapidly.

"Well Darshima, it is your last night with us. It was a pleasure having you as our guest. Sydarias should make more friends like you." The corners of her eyes wrinkled as she stared at him. "I must say that you came into our lives quite unexpectedly."

"Darshima is more than enough. How many more friends must I make?" Sydarias playfully rolled his eyes at her pronouncement and laughed.

"Thank you again for everything. I'll always be grateful." Darshima bowed his head politely.

The three sat on the terrace as the sun drifted closer to the horizon, sharing happy memories of their week together. Darshima felt at ease in their presence and he relished the moment. He didn't want it to end.

"As it's your last evening here, what would you like to do?" asked Sydarias.

"I am fine with anything." Darshima looked out upon the city, wondering what more Sydarias could possibly find for them to do. Sydarias rubbed his chin in thought.

"Perhaps we should go and view the procession for the prince's birthday," An eager smile crossed his lips.

"I would love to see it." Darshima's eyes lit up at the suggestion. He had never witnessed an imperial parade.

"We should leave now. It will be crowded." Sydarias rose from his seat and Darshima followed him.

"Please be careful out there with those revelers, it will be mayhem," said Madame Idawa, her lips curling into a worried frown. "Why don't you both stay in for the night? Darshima is still recovering, and traveling so far might be too much for him." Her gaze lingered upon them as they moved away from the balustrade.

"Don't worry mother, we will be fine." Sydarias reached out and placed a reassuring hand upon her shoulder. She let out a sigh as she looked up at Sydarias, and gently patted his hand. They bid her farewell, then headed indoors to get ready for their evening.

Chapter Nineteen

Darshima stood in the sun-drenched foyer and waited patiently for Sydarias. Dressed in a white linen shirt folded at the sleeves, black trousers, and leather boots, he smoothed out the threadbare wrinkles in his outfit. Sydarias had offered him a set of clothing to borrow, but Darshima had politely turned it down. Sydarias had already lent him garments for their trek through the desert and insisted he keep the crystal visor. Darshima truly appreciated Sydarias' seemingly limitless generosity during their week together, but he knew that he needed to rely on himself as well.

Sydarias entered the room and casually waved at Darshima. He wore a crisp blue shirt, embroidered with fine rays of gold, black tailored trousers, and polished leather boots.

"There you are." his eyes brightened as he saw Darshima.

"I've been waiting for you. Aren't we going to be late?" Darshima started toward him.

"There is no way we will make it there on foot. The streets are far too crowded." Sydarias folded his arms across his chest.

"Should we hire a coach then?" A puzzled expression crossed Darshima's face.

"They are probably all taken by now, but I have a faster way of getting there. Come with me." Sydarias' lips curled into a knowing smile as he beckoned him. Darshima followed Sydarias back through the house and up the staircase to his room.

As Darshima walked up the treads, his heart fluttered. A wave of unsteadiness came over him, much like he had felt that morning. He grabbed the banister and drew in a breath as a fine sweat broke upon his brow. He took a moment to gather his strength, and the sensation lessened some. Darshima resumed his march up the stairs, moving faster to catch up with Sydarias. He tried to ignore the lingering sense of dizziness, wanting to enjoy his last evening in the capital.

When he arrived at the top of the stairs, Sydarias stood waiting. "Hurry up, Darshima." He smiled, playfully tapping his foot against the tile. Darshima shook his head in exhaustion as he approached Sydarias. He had often wondered what it would be like to live in a spacious home such as this, but he now saw the drawbacks.

They passed through a set of glass doors and stepped onto the terrace. The sky glowed a brilliant orange as the sun drifted toward the horizon. The air had grown noticeably cooler since dinnertime. Sydarias stood in front of a gleaming black vehicle, its long angular frame hovering effortlessly above the ground. Its metal fuselage tapered into a pair of large engine pods at the rear. A triplet of headlights from its nose cone cast intense white rays onto the balustrade.

"This is how we're going to get to the procession. Trust me, it will be much faster." Sydarias stepped toward the craft, and a compartment under the seat automatically opened with a whir. He retrieved two leather gilets and threw one over to Darshima. "Put this on, it will be chilly."

"Thank you." Darshima pulled his arms through the vest and fastened the buttons in front. As the compartment closed, Sydarias put on his gilet and hopped aboard the craft. He leaned forward, gripped the pair of semi-circular controls, and slid his feet into the toeholds. With the press of a button, its engines let out a low growl, emitting a jet of glowing red exhaust from their rear vents. The craft rose higher and he guided it around the terrace, its reflection moving against the polished stone tile. He approached Darshima and lowered the vehicle.

"What are you waiting for?" he beckoned with a hand. Darshima eagerly climbed aboard and sat behind Sydarias upon the black leather seat. They hovered upward and drifted forward until they were beyond the railing of the terrace. A steady gust of wind howling in his ears, Darshima peered down at the city below. His heart thudded in fright when he realized that there was nothing between them and the ground. His eyes swept over the swift bands of noisy traffic and the geometric patterns of lighted streets between the glowing edifices.

"Do you have these types of vehicles in Ardavia?" Sydarias glanced over his shoulder.

"Yes, of course, we're not as quaint as you Vilidesians like to think!" said Darshima, his voice barely audible over the roar of the engines. Sydarias laughed and then turned back around.

Darshima tried not to show his surprise, but it was difficult. Most people their age back home could only admire such an expensive craft, perhaps dream to ride upon one, but never dare think of owning one.

Sydarias reached into a compartment behind the controls and retrieved two black helmets with tinted crystal visors. He put one on and handed the other to Darshima. As Darshima slid the helmet on, the visor's tint gradually brightened and he was able to see the late afternoon sky. Arrays of glowing symbols flickered at the edges of the crystal.

"Hold on tightly, we are going to be traveling rather swiftly. I don't want you to fall!" shouted Sydarias, as he glimpsed over his shoulder.

"Okay, but don't go too fast." Darshima wrapped his arms around Sydarias' waist and braced himself.

"Are you ready?" He tapped lightly upon the throttle with his foot, and the engines issued a deep roar, sending them higher above the ground.

Just as Sydarias was about to press the throttle again, the terrace door flew open and Madame Idawa stepped out, her silken robe swirling around her like the veil of clouds below. She walked up to the balustrade and looked toward them. A worried frown crossed her lips.

"Please be careful while you are out there," she said in a stern voice. "You must keep your wits about you." She turned to Sydarias, her lips parted as if searching for the right words. She put a hand to her bejeweled neck, the expression of concern upon her face growing more intense.

"What's wrong, mother?" asked Sydarias, his voice rising with nervousness.

"Must you go?" Her eyes widened in concern.

"We will be fine, don't worry so much about everything," said Sydarias, his voice audible just above the engines.

"Just heed my words. Please take care of yourself." She stretched her hand over the railing and tried to reach Sydarias, but the craft hovered just beyond her grasp.

Her hand fell to her side, and she turned toward Darshima. A shiver coursed through him as he encountered her piercing stare. Her lips quivered ever so slightly as she glared at him. It was as if she wanted to say something, but couldn't bring herself to pronounce the words. Madame Idawa then looked up to the sky, her gaze lingering for a moment amid the stars. She turned toward Sydarias once more, walked back inside, and closed the door behind her. She stood still, peering at them through the glass pane.

"I don't understand what's the matter with her," exclaimed Sydarias. "She has been acting strangely this whole week." He leaned forward in his seat and tapped his fingers against the glowing instrument panel in the center console.

The change in Madame Idawa's disposition hadn't gone unnoticed by Darshima. Toward the end of his stay, she had become more anxious around him. She would stare at him intently when he wasn't paying attention. As soon as he caught her eye, she would turn away. He didn't know what to make of it.

The loud rumbling of the engines behind him broke through Darshima's thoughts. "Here we go!" Sydarias looked over his shoulder, his voice blending with the noise. Before Darshima could respond, Sydarias slammed his foot down upon the throttle and they shot forward. The wind howled fiercely past their visors, tearing violently at their clothes. Darshima grabbed onto Sydarias and struggled to stay aboard the moving craft. They dashed across the sky, passing through the large shadows of the lofty towers, blazing radiantly in the long rays of the sun.

Sydarias stepped harder upon the throttle, and the nimble craft surged forward. The buildings moved swiftly by until they became a blurred barrier of gleaming glass and metal. They cruised straight ahead until he aimed the craft downward, toward a wide snaking band of traffic below them.

"What are you doing?" exclaimed Darshima, his shouts torn away by the wind. They descended at a steep angle, the onrushing air pressing their visors firmly against their faces. The engines growled deeply as they hurtled toward the ground. Darshima clenched his jaw against the disorienting, weightless sensation as they plummeted, fighting the queasiness rising in his stomach.

The line of traffic grew larger as they approached. Sydarias slowed the craft down and skillfully merged into the dense layer of swiftly moving vehicles. Off in the approaching horizon, Darshima saw the glass and stone towers of the royal palace pierce through the clouds. Bold arrays of triangular banners fluttered atop its gleaming spires. Sydarias guided them toward the palace amid the heavy traffic, until they unexpectedly ground to a halt. They sat amid the motionless sea of vehicles, waiting to move. Darshima peered at the glowing lights of the surrounding craft, and the dense clusters of towers rising above the clouds.

"At this rate, we'll miss the procession," shouted Sydarias. Frustrated, he slammed his fists against the controls.

"It's no big deal if we miss part of it." Darshima rested his hand upon Sydarias' shoulder. "It isn't anything to get upset about." Sydarias sat up straight, the muscles in his neck tightening.

"I just hate sitting still." He rested his hands back on the controls and leaned forward. "Hold on, we're going to take a shortcut," he called out over his shoulder. Before Darshima could protest, Sydarias pressed upon the throttle and they jolted forward.

Sydarias darted below the line of motionless vehicles and raced downward, weaving between several different planes of traffic. They flew skillfully past various types of vehicles, the pulsating roar of their engines rising and falling as they rushed by. He aimed toward a large opening in a lane at the other end of the vast expanse of sky. As they approached the space, a fleet containing dozens of enormous vessels descended ahead of them. Darshima held on tightly as the ships sent a turbulent rush of wind in their direction.

The late afternoon sunlight glinted brightly off the metal panels of their long, angular fuselages. Sydarias guided the craft toward the rear of the fleet, their visors dimming against the brilliant red jets of exhaust spewing from their paired engine pods. Darshima leaned forward to get a closer look at the massive vessels. He narrowed his eyes and tried to make out the bold markings imprinted prominently upon the stern of each craft. They drew nearer, and he read the name aloud.

"Idawa...those vessels bear your name Sydarias!" exclaimed Darshima. His pulse quickened as a feeling of surprise came over him. The name was one that he recalled seeing on some of the large ships crowding the skies over Ardavia. He didn't know why it hadn't come to him sooner.

"What other name did you expect to see?" Sydarias looked over to Darshima and let out an incredulous laugh. From Mr. Idawa's description, the family and their enterprises were prominent, but Darshima had no idea they were so important.

"They're one of the fleets from our passenger lines," Sydarias pointed a finger toward the vessels. "At this hour, they must be returning from Renefydis." A shiver coursed through Darshima as he contemplated that a single family could possess soaring tower blocks and entire fleets of ships.

Darshima eyed the enormous vessels, his chest tightening with worry as they drew closer. The warm exhaust gently buffeted the craft as they trailed behind the fleet. Darshima's apprehension manifested itself as a vice-like grip around Sydarias' waist. Sydarias looked over his shoulder.

"Don't worry, we won't get hurt. We are just going to bypass them," he shouted.

"What do you mean?" Darshima shook his head in confusion.

"We can get past this fleet, just look at those large gaps between the ships!" Sydarias leaned against the controls.

"You must be crazy." Darshima bit his lip and let out a nervous laugh.

"The procession will be starting soon, and we'll miss it if we don't hurry." Sydarias tapped a row of symbols on the instrument panel before him.

"It seems dangerous. I think we should wait." Darshima narrowed his eyes at the formation of ships and saw barely any space between them.

"The bands of traffic above and below are at a standstill. The only way that we can get through, is to go forward. That is unless you can think of a better way." Sydarias shrugged his shoulders.

Darshima looked all around them and saw lines of vehicles floating in the sky, waiting behind the fleet. He looked toward the ships ahead, and they seemed to have moved even closer together. Before he could think of a suggestion, Sydarias stepped upon the throttle, and he hung on tightly as they accelerated. They dashed forward and flew through the nearest row of passenger ships, the glazed panels in their sterns giving off a soft white glow. Darshima eyed the passengers milling about on the dozens of glass-enclosed, cantilevered decks of the vessels.

Sydarias guided the craft through the brightly lit, windowed fissures between two adjacent vessels. The fleet had just reentered the thick Ciblaithian atmosphere, and Darshima began to sweat under the intense heat radiating from the gleaming metal fuselages. They sped past the windows, the passengers on the opposite side of the glass leaping back in surprise.

"See, it's not so bad," shouted Sydarias.

"If you say so," yelled Darshima, shaking his head in disbelief.

They darted between the vessels, the hot winds blowing through their clothes and against their visors. They cleared the first few rows of vessels with no difficulty. Sydarias stepped harder on the throttle, and they moved faster. At one point, they were moving so swiftly through the rows that it seemed as if they were traveling through intense blasts of white light.

Sydarias guided them through much of the fleet, when the vessels surrounding them abruptly drifted downward. Darshima's stomach sank as a wave of fear seized him. Sydarias steered the craft in the same direction with the enormous ships, narrowly avoided their scorching airframes. Darshima's heart pounded in fright as the giant, floating structures moved within a handbreadth of them. He cowered in his seat, waiting to be pulverized, when the ships ahead unexpectedly parted, creating a gap large enough for them to pass. Sydarias maneuvered the craft through the widening crevice as the vessels diverged.

"I think we're free!" Sydarias sped toward the opening.

"Not yet!" Darshima pointed a finger at the changing scene ahead.

Instead of emerging into the open sky, they had unexpectedly entered an enormous gap between the fleet. Darshima's ears hummed as the space reverberated with the low drone of their engines. Slivers of the darkening sky shone through the fissures between the shadowy vessels surrounding them, giving the space a peculiar feeling. They made a circuit around the enclosed hollow between the airframes, seeking a gap or a clearing, but found none.

"What do we do now?" Sydarias let go of the handles and threw his hands up in frustration.

"We'll just have to wait for an opening." Darshima peered over Sydarias' shoulder. They moved slowly along with the fleet, searching for an exit, but the ships held steady. Sydarias let out an annoyed groan.

"I'm sorry about the delay, I thought I could find a faster route," he huffed, his voice blending with the mechanical din.

"Save your apology, I see something." Darshima pointed toward a ship below them, moving from its place in the formation. "Do you think you can make it through?"

"I'll try!" Sydarias grabbed the controls and nosed the craft downward, his foot jamming hard upon the throttle. They raced forward, and just as they were almost clear, the ships abruptly repositioned themselves. Gusts of wind buffeted violently against the craft as they hurtled forward. The vehicle's frame shuddered under the velocity as Sydarias pressed the engines past their limit.

Their surroundings blended into a bluish-white blur of metal, glass, and light as they raced onward. The shrinking gap desperately beckoned as the fleet of vessels closed in around them. With a roar and a violent rush of wind, they dashed through the narrow space. They emerged into the open air and sped away from the fleet. His pulse racing with both excitement and terror, Darshima let out a rowdy cheer. He was astonished at Sydarias' incredible skill.

"Where did you learn to fly like that?" he yelled over the gusts.

"Those were just some basic maneuvers." Sydarias looked over his shoulder and laughed heartily. "No more shortcuts, I promise."

He eased up on the throttle and they glided beneath the clouds, toward the towers of the palace.

Chapter Twenty

Amid the fading sunlight, they descended over the waters of the bay and approached the coast of the western peninsula. Sydarias parked the craft upon an inviting grassy lawn, situated at the edge of a rocky bluff. They stowed their gear and walked toward an open space among the crowds. Sydarias led them toward a patch of vacant grass, with a clear view of the royal palace and its vast hexagonal plaza. The building stood majestically amid the surrounding clusters of towers, its stone spires and turrets hearkening back to a bygone era. Darshima reclined beside Sydarias upon the lawn and observed the lively scenes in the streets below. The syncopated beats of heavy drums and the shrill, frenetic notes of tambourines filled the humid air.

Darshima eyed the flurry of activity around the palace gates. Thousands of revelers dressed in flowing costumes of gold, blue and white, readied themselves for the royal parade and the entire evening of revelry to follow. He had never witnessed a procession of such grandeur. Celebrations for members of the dynasty were regular events on all of the moons, but they were not nearly as large or ostentatious as the fabled ones here in The Vilides.

"Are you ready to go back to Gordanelle?" Sydarias turned to Darshima.

"I wish I could stay, but I must return home." Darshima leaned back upon his elbows and cast his eyes skyward in thought.

He had enjoyed himself during his stay with Sydarias and couldn't recall a time when he had been treated so kindly or felt so welcome. Though he would miss Sydarias, Darshima was concerned about his family, and what awaited him back home. His pulse thudded anxiously as the memory of the argument with his father floated before his mind. As his time on Ciblaithia drew to a close, worries about his next steps preoccupied him. He had yet to figure out where he would live or work back home in Ardavia.

He shook his head and tried to ignore the troubling thoughts rising within him. This was his last night in the capital and he wanted to enjoy it. Somehow he would make things right when he saw his family again.

"Thank you for an amazing visit, but I must resume my old life." A wistful smile crossed Darshima's face.

"If I haven't convinced you to move to The Vilides, then I've failed as a host." Sydarias raised his eyebrows in a mildly alarmed expression. After a moment, they both burst into laughter.

"I never thought that I would have seen or done so much. I could never repay you for your kindness," said Darshima.

"Honestly, it was my pleasure. If you hadn't been here, I would have sat idly at home this week." The corners of Sydarias' eyes wrinkled wistfully as he spoke.

"I don't believe that for a moment." Darshima shook his head and chuckled. "You're from a wealthy family and can do whatever you like."

"It isn't all that it's made out to be." Sydarias' lips curled into a slight frown, and a shadow of sadness briefly crossed his face.

Before Darshima could say anything, Sydarias continued. "I will be traveling to Ardavia soon. We should meet again." His frown disappeared, and he flashed an eager smile.

"I would enjoy that very much." Darshima rested his hand upon Sydarias' shoulder.

As his mind sketched plans for Sydarias' trip to Ardavia, Darshima's heart sank. He would never be able to treat Sydarias to a similar, lavish visit. He couldn't offer him a place to stay, or even a family to welcome him. As the worries of his circumstances crept back into his mind, he drew in a pained breath and looked at the scenes around them. He tried his best to enjoy the evening, and avoid thinking too much about the days ahead.

They lounged amid the groups of spectators, soaking up the lively atmosphere. Darshima saw the crowds around them thinning out as people left the park. Lines of spectators walked toward the avenues below, seeking a closer view of the procession. His thoughts drifted from the activity surrounding them to concerns about his brother. Darshima hadn't seen Sasha for the week, and he missed him. Though they didn't always get along, Sasha was a good brother. A pang of regret filled him as he stared at the palace, memories of their last moments together filtering back to him. He bit his lip and tried to forget the feeling. He would find a way to make his absence up to Sasha.

Amid his thoughts, Darshima glimpsed a small flash of white over Sydarias' shoulder. His gaze darted toward the source, and he saw a man standing in the distance. He leaned forward to get a better look, his eyes narrowing in curiosity as he observed the man's features. Darshima had never seen anyone like him before. Tall and athletic in stature, his pale skin was the color of unblemished snow beneath the fading sunlight. A fine brow, prominent cheekbones, and a chiseled chin graced his youthful face. His narrowed eyes were a brilliant shade of sapphire that had a peculiar, subtle luminescence to them. His lips were drawn into a contemplative frown.

His long, silky black hair was fashioned in a tail that blew wildly in the wind. He wore black trousers fastened at the waist with a thick golden cord, a wide-sleeved black shirt with buttoned flaps at the neck, and split-toed leather boots. A series of inked characters began upon his right ear and trailed down the side of his neck. He stood with his arms folded across his chest and gazed directly at Darshima.

Darshima's heart pounded as a wave of anxiety coursed through him. The man's stare gave him an unfamiliar and rising sense of foreboding. He almost appeared as if he were from a different time and place. Passersby walked around him, seemingly unaware of his presence. Darshima peered at the man and pointed him out to Sydarias, who looked over his shoulder, his eyes widening in surprise.

"I wonder why he is here," whispered Sydarias, the disbelief evident in his voice.

"Is he someone important?" Darshima's brow wrinkled in confusion.

"I am not sure, but he is an Omystikai. They rarely appear in public." Sydarias turned around to get a better look.

"How come?" asked Darshima, shaking his head.

"Very few of them reside here in the capital, and they all belong to the imperial court." Sydarias narrowed his eyes in a perplexed look. "I have to say, I've never seen one like him before."

Darshima stared at the man, who now paced along the edge of the bluff. He had a distinct presence about him, and a serious bearing that Darshima could almost feel. He remembered reading about the Omystikai and their tragic history, but never in his life had he seen one. Darshima leaned toward Sydarias,

"Are the legends about them true?" he whispered, referring to their purported abilities of divination.

"They certainly are true. People have exploited their talents for generations." Sydarias bowed his head, his voice striking a somber tone as he spoke of the misdeed. Darshima nodded at Sydarias' words, reflecting upon what he had learned about their ancestors' exile to Iberwight and subsequent centuries of struggle. He looked up to steal another glimpse, but the man was nowhere to be found.

"Where did he go?" Darshima blinked his eyes in surprise.

"I have no idea. Perhaps he went down to the parade." Sydarias looked around them and shrugged his shoulders.

The sun sank below the horizon, the slivers of its burning disk casting the last of its radiance upon the rippling waters of the bay. Benai's silhouette grew brighter and its vivid grey hue shone boldly against the dark sky. The red and white planetary rings blotted out the other moons, appearing almost as a stain upon the deep blue, star-washed sky.

In the distance, Darshima saw the masses of costumed revelers moving about in a frenzy to the syncopated drumbeats. As the hour for the parade drew near, they formed neat lines facing the wrought iron palace gates. The music grew louder and the crowds grew more fervent, boisterously singing and chanting the prince's name. An eager smile crossed Darshima's lips as he took in the sight, his pulse bounding as he felt the liveliness in the streets.

The music faded and as the air grew silent, the crowds started to clap, the sound of thousands of hands echoing like soft rainfall. The deep clear peal of a lone bell broke through the noise and the revelers erupted in joyful cheers. They were soon drowned out by the clangorous harmony of thousands of bells and chimes from temples and shrines throughout the city. The use of bells was a Vilidesian tradition, borrowed from the ancient Omystikai. The sound symbolized strength and clarity and was used exclusively during royal ceremonies and religious festivals.

"I think that this will be the finest parade that the House of Fyrenos has ever hosted," shouted Sydarias, his voice lost amid the thunderous notes.

Darshima looked on the crowds, his heart beating with excitement amid the celebratory displays. Under the chiming of the bells, he heard a faint rumble that differed from the applauding hands. He turned his gaze away from the crowds, pointed an ear to the sky, and listened. A sound, much like the thunder of an approaching storm, or the faint drone of a faraway engine filtered down to his ears. He tried to dismiss it but the noise was persistent and seemed to grow louder.

"Do you hear that noise?" Darshima turned to Sydarias, who closed his eyes and listened.

"Yes, but I don't know what it is." He shook his head, clearly puzzled.

They rose to their feet and walked to the edge of the bluff to see if they could identify the source. Traffic over the city had been rerouted to accommodate the celebration, which would include a fly-over of the prince's aerial fleet at the conclusion of the parade. The sound steadily amplified, drowning out the chime of the ringing bells. Darshima's eyes darted about, searching the city and the skies above.

He craned his neck upward and spotted what appeared to be countless dark, dashed lines on the horizon, rapidly coming into view. His heart seized with a wave of confusion, he pointed out the unusual formation to Sydarias. The dashed lines grew in size until they revealed themselves as an enormous fleet of airborne ships, much larger than anything he had ever seen. The oblong vessels approached the city center, crashing indiscriminately through the bands of traffic before them.

Darshima's stomach sank to his knees, and his limbs felt heavy with dread as he witnessed the chaos unfolding above them. Hoards of revelers stood in the streets, their faces turned toward the heavens. The once clear evening skies had been taken over by hundreds of these strange craft. Their engines issued a deep, sonorous growl that shook the air with a deafening sound. The immense ships steadily moved into formation, grazing against the buildings and raining debris upon the streets below.

Chapter Twenty One

Darshima and Sydarias stood together upon the bluff and beheld the terrifying scene rapidly evolving around them. From the armada of ships blanketing the skies, swarms of smaller vehicles emerged. The craft descended upon the city like a merciless cloud, screeching through the urban canyons. They fired volleys of missiles, indiscriminately destroying buildings both old and new, sacred and secular.

The once orderly bands of aerial traffic devolved into a tangled, nebulous swarm as they tried to escape the foreign craft. They struck violently against buildings in their haste, sending cascades of sparks and shards of glass down upon the frantic citizens below. The Vilidesian aerial corps chased the invaders throughout the city, zipping back and forth across the expanse of sky in a pitched battle. They exchanged rapid fire with the enemy vessels, sending a torrent of mortar shells and debris onto the streets below. Errant artillery from the fierce exchanges pulverized entire city blocks, incinerated parks, and leveled buildings.

Darshima stood paralyzed, his chest heavy with fear as his eyes scanned the carnage in the streets below them. The celebratory mood of the evening had all but evaporated as people fled down the once-grand boulevards, now littered with rubble, broken stones, and charred bones. They trampled over the mangled bodies of their fellow revelers, the thud of pounding feet drowning out their dying screams.

The battle intensified as hundreds more of the smaller ships emerged from the larger craft. They fanned out over the districts and descended upon on the streets amidst the fleeing crowds. Darshima looked on in fear as platoons of foreign soldiers dressed in black helmets and green fatigues disembarked from the vehicles. Pistols in hand, they moved aggressively to subdue and capture the fleeing crowds. Those who resisted were immediately seized or brutally shot.

Darshima spotted fleets of the foreign craft as they raced toward the palace, then descended upon the plaza. Hundreds of soldiers disembarked, mowed down the gates and stormed the entrance. Intense explosions set the windows aglow and shook the building's ramparts.

"My family!" Darshima gasped in terror as he witnessed the siege. His heart rose into his throat as he imagined them fighting for their lives within those walls. He needed to do something. As he started to scramble down toward the street, he felt Sydarias grab his shoulder.

"Don't go!" Sydarias pulled Darshima back and glared at him, his eyes filled with fear. "You will die down there."

"But I must save them." Darshima looked helplessly up at the sky, his pulse racing. Bright searchlights atop the tallest towers of the city swept across the night sky, their powerful white beams probing the darkness like ghostly fingers.

"It's too dangerous. You will be killed!" shouted Sydarias, his voice lost amid the scream of sirens and the echo of bomb blasts. Darshima lifted his hands to his ears, shielding them against the deafening noise.

"What's happening?" Darshima looked around disoriented, his eyes widening in fear.

"I don't know, but we have to flee." Sydarias yanked his arm and pulled him away from the bluff.

Darshima ran frantically behind Sydarias upon the grassy terrain. They jumped onto his craft, put on their helmets, and fled as the first towers fell. Terrified revelers ran alongside them as they pulled away from the lawn. Several others mounted their vehicles and sped past them. Others looked on as they ascended, desperately lunging toward them, trying to hitch a ride to safety. Their cries tore painfully at Darshima, but he knew they could not save anyone else without risking their own lives. They climbed upward through the suffocating skies, filled with thick, stinging smoke and hot ash.

Sydarias navigated through the frenzied swarms of vehicles, nearly colliding with a squadron of the invading craft. They darted through the once majestic canyons of skyscrapers, weaving through the chaotic layers of traffic. As they raced forward, the rows of towers loomed over them as a treacherous, smoky forest of warped steel, shattered stone, and broken glass. Sydarias banked sharply to the right and zipped down a narrow street.

The screeching sirens, growling engines, and roaring fires filled Darshima's ears in a disorienting cacophony. He frantically shook his head, trying to find a moment of clarity amid the maelstrom. Darting just above the street, they flew past the charred ruins of buildings and dodged the objects raining upon them. To his acute horror, many of those falling objects were people jumping from the buildings above. They leapt in a desperate attempt to avoid the smoke and flames that threatened to consume them.

Darshima's eyes widened in terror as he spied the silhouette of a large family standing at the ledge of a broken window in one of the burning towers just ahead of them. The curtains billowed wildly around them as the air rushed into their apartment. Bright tongues of flame surrounded them, illuminating their faces. They held each other's hands, exchanged stoic glances, and without warning, leapt together into the open air. Their bodies, large and small fell rapidly, tumbling headlong into the burning streets below. Darshima felt his heart descend with them. He bowed his head and closed his eyes as they flew by, his tears falling as he heard the distant but unmistakable, sickening thud.

Sydarias veered sharply to the left, and zipped down another broad avenue toward the direction of his home. They darted between the flaming wreckage and falling debris, charting a wild course. The skies grew more treacherous as the artillery fire whizzing past them grew in intensity. He abruptly abandoned the route home and guided them toward the dunes, their dark, undulating forms barely visible amid the plumes of smoke. Like many of those fleeing, they didn't know where to go. The entire city seemed to be under siege, and every district had either been captured or appeared vulnerable to attack.

They flew above the ruined streets, trying to avoid the foreign craft strafing the ground below with mortar shells. Darshima looked around, his pulse beating against a rising sense of fear. Everywhere he turned was aglow with flame.

"We have to leave or else we will die here!" Darshima pointed frantically toward the burning streets. Sydarias slowed the craft, made a broad turn away from the dunes, and again headed back toward the city. They flew above the destroyed avenues, weaving between the columns of smoke.

"Why are we going back?" A cold sweat broke out upon Darshima's brow as they passed over the familiar scenery.

"We must go back home, my father will know what to do. We have a compound far away from the city where we can hide." Sydarias glimpsed over his shoulder, his voice muffled by the visor. His eyes caught Darshima's for an instant. Darshima's pulse quickened as he sensed Sydarias' desperation.

"We will die trying to get there." Darshima's eyes widened in fear.

"Everything is under attack and I don't know where else to go." Sydarias punched the air with a desperate fist. "This craft won't be able to make the journey. Heading back is our best hope for survival. We can then all leave the city together."

"What if they're not home?" shouted Darshima, his voice drowned out by the artillery fire.

"I don't know." Sydarias' shoulders slumped as he turned back around and gripped the controls. Darshima eyed the squadrons of foreign craft darting across the skies. His heart thudded with terror as images of the seized palace flooded his mind. His family might still be in there, and he feared them either dead or captured. He briefly closed his eyes as an aching sense of helplessness seized him.

They darted through the frantic swarms of traffic and falling wreckage. As they approached Sydarias' building, Darshima saw the bright lights of dozens of vehicles departing their private terraces. The vessels fanned out over the city, disappearing as they raced beyond the dunes at the horizon. Sydarias guided the craft upward around the gleaming edifice, and landed on the terrace just outside his room. Their helmets in hand, they hastily dismounted and ran inside.

Darshima followed Sydarias as he charged down the staircase. They threw open doors and searched the rooms of the apartment, but found no sign of Sydarias' family. As they rushed through a spacious parlor, Darshima froze before a large window and stared at the burning city beyond. What was once a sweeping view, had been transformed into a sea of fire. Many of the towers billowed with oily smoke and breathed tongues of flames from their broken facades. Muted wails of sirens and mortar fire filtered through the thick panes of glass.

Darshima stood paralyzed, a keen feeling of dread taking hold of him. He tried to comprehend what he was seeing, but he could not. The firm grip of Sydarias' hand upon his shoulder caught his attention.

"They're not here," stammered Sydarias, his voice filled with fear.

"Where could they have gone?" Darshima turned toward him.

"Their vehicles aren't here either. They must've fled with my brothers." Sydarias shook his head in disbelief.

"Did your father leave a message?" asked Darshima.

"There's nothing." Sydarias threw his hands up frantically. "I don't know what happened to them." His voice trembled, and he let out a worried sigh.

"What do we do now?" Darshima's throat tightened with a rising sense of fear. They had risked everything to return here and escape with Sydarias' family, but they were nowhere to be found.

As Sydarias turned to him, the building shuddered violently and the air rumbled with the deep sound of an explosion. The building swayed like a pendulum against the forceful impact, and they instinctively shielded their heads with their arms. Darshima peered around them as the sounds of crashing glass, and the groan of stressed metal filled the air.

"We must leave." Sydarias grabbed Darshima's arm and they ran through the apartment, jumping over the strewn furniture. They bounded up the stairs to Sydarias' room, trying to maintain their balance upon the trembling floors. Darshima followed Sydarias back out onto the balcony, littered with burning wreckage. They scrambled over the buckled tiles, boarded the craft, and ascended into the frenzied skies.

They sped away from the shuddering building amid the smoke. Hot debris raining upon them, Darshima and Sydarias frantically put on their helmets. Darshima glimpsed over his shoulder and saw billowing plumes of smoke rise from the base of the building, shrouding its facade. Sydarias guided the craft down one boulevard after another, plying through crowds of escaping vehicles. They traveled along a main arterial leading toward the dunes, the silhouettes of their wavy peaks looming in the darkness.

Darshima peered fearfully through the chaos when the deep, concussive staccato of several explosions shattered the air around them. The sharp, earsplitting whine of grinding metal and the crunch of breaking glass punctuated the low rumble. The vehicles around them rapidly gained speed, accelerating like minute particles caught in a fierce gale. Sydarias stepped upon the throttle, and Darshima felt the craft jolt under them as they lurched forward.

They raced through the burning winds, bits of debris scratching painfully at their skin. Darshima glanced over his shoulder to see what had caused such a stir. His heart froze in terror as he spied a series of crumbling towers, crashing swiftly downward from the sky above them. The immense forms hurtled through the smoke and darkness, rapidly encompassing his view.

"Sydarias, watch out!" shouted Darshima, his words torn away by the gusts. Sydarias glimpsed over his shoulder to see the enormous line of buildings tumbling toward them.

"I don't believe it," he murmured as he jammed his foot on the throttle, racing past the vehicles around them.

As they cleared the group, an intense blast rocked the craft, nearly dashing them from their seats. Darshima looked back to see that the towers had struck the ground below them. The impact sent forth a fiery, rapidly advancing cloud of dust and ash. Sydarias jammed the throttle down as far as it would go, and they raced forward.

"Fly lower!" Darshima gripped Sydarias even tighter. Sydarias aimed the craft downward to escape the encroaching dust. As they flew, Darshima eyed stands of trees flanking the avenue far below, their burning fronds waving wildly in the smoky gusts. His heart beat with a jolt of recognition when he realized that they had strolled along that same avenue only a few days ago.

They careened above the road, past other fleeing craft, when a hail of debris suddenly pelted them. A searing hot fragment struck Darshima between his shoulder blades. He shuddered as a sharp wave of pain surged through his back, knocking the wind right out of him. As the ache subsided, he crouched down into his seat, and tried to maintain his balance as they dashed through the skies.

Sydarias turned abruptly to the left and darted toward a large, hexagonal glass building topped by a golden, pyramidal dome. Out of the corner of his eye, Darshima spied a fragment the size of a tree trunk hurtle toward them. Before he could react, the object forcefully struck the side of the vehicle.

"What was that?" Darshima gripped his seat as it shook violently against the impact. His head spinning, he looked fearfully around them. His stomach sank as they drifted toward the edge of the building's facade.

We've been hit, and we're going to lose power," shouted Sydarias, his voice barely audible amid the blasts. He shot a glance over his shoulder at the engines behind them. Even through his dusty visor, Darshima could see the fear written in Sydarias' eyes. The engines let out a shudder, then a mournful groan and sputtered into silence as the craft teetered in mid-air.

Sydarias turned back to the instrument panel. He feverishly flipped the control switches and jabbed his finger at the display screen, but the engines remained quiet.

"What do we do now?" Darshima frantically shook his head.

"We will have to bail." Sydarias angrily punched his fist against the glowing screen. The craft lurched forward and then abruptly powered off. Darshima's stomach rose into his throat as he felt the terrifying pull of gravity. They plummeted downward like a stone, rapidly gaining speed. Sydarias tried his best to avoid the flying pieces of debris around them. He skillfully threw his weight to maneuver the damaged vehicle, now not much more than a piece of debris itself.

The features of the devastated landscape below grew rapidly before their eyes as they hurtled toward the ground. They drifted over a small pond in an adjacent park, the wind howling past Darshima's ears.

"Jump!" shouted Sydarias. He let go of the controls and launched himself from the craft. Looking on in terror, Darshima drew in a deep breath and leapt from his seat. They tumbled together in the open air amid the violent winds, bracing themselves for the impact.

With a loud splash, Sydarias and then Darshima plunged into the pond. They sank below the greasy, fuel stained surface, littered with burning debris. The impact dashed Darshima's helmet away from his head and knocked the wind from his lungs. His body aching, he felt himself floating amid the cold darkness, his foggy mind repeating the moments before their plunge. Arms flailing, he struggled amid the murky waters. His face breached the surface, and he desperately sucked in a breath. He spotted Sydarias just ahead of him.

"Are you okay?" Darshima panted as he reached out to him.

"I'm okay." Sydarias tore off his helmet and hastily wiped the foul water from his face.

They swam past the sinking wreckage of Sydarias' vehicle to the nearby shore and clambered out of the water, onto a grassy bank. They sat amid the chaos, the acrid stench of smoke and burning fuel stinging their throats. The air above them rumbled with the drone of low flying craft. Darshima craned his neck upward and looked at the strange, rounded vehicles racing above them.

"We must run before they see us." Sydarias pulled Darshima's sleeve. They moved from the water's edge and dashed into the shadows toward the base of the hexagonal tower. Darshima followed Sydarias through the warped and shattered entrance, shards of glass crunching underfoot as they stepped into the enveloping darkness.

Darshima walked behind him as they made their way through a maze of damaged corridors, broken arches, and splintered doors. Darshima's pulse thudded in fear as they walked through a dark hallway, past rows of fractured wooden beams that appeared as menacing teeth. They snuck up a grand marble staircase and stumbled into a cavernous chamber imbued with the staid air of a library.

Their footsteps echoed as they walked upon the cracked stone tiles. Moving in the shadows, Sydarias furtively led Darshima along a dimly lit, torch-lined path between several rows of wooden desks. Darshima looked to the perimeter of the room and saw a row of large, arched windows spanning from the floor to the ceiling. Yellow flames from the raging fires outside licked at their fractured panes. Faint rays of starlight filtered through the room, casting it in a spectral glow.

They made their way toward a low bank of desks beside the wall of windows and crouched together underneath one of them. Exhausted from their flight, they sat still amid the bone-rattling explosions, rapid-fire artillery exchanges, and the intermittent heavy shelling beyond the walls.

"Is it safe in here?" whispered Darshima.

"I think so," stammered Sydarias, his voice echoing throughout the chamber.

"What is this place?" Darshima peered around them.

"It's a library for astronomers. I used to study here sometimes." Sydarias' eyes surveyed the destruction, his voice wavering.

A strong series of blasts rocked the space, and they cowered as the floor shook beneath them. They huddled together and stared at the windows, now aglow with fiery jets of red and blue flame. The walls trembled violently, sending heavy tomes onto the floor with a thud. A thunderous sound of fracturing wood echoed throughout the cavernous space, filling their ears. Darshima shuddered at the deafening noise, clenching his jaw in fright. He stole a glance at the entrance to see an enormous pile of destroyed shelves and scattered books blocking the path. The splintered wood and shredded volumes cast an ominous shadow before them. He rested his head against his knees and let out an anxious sigh. The touch of Sydarias' hand upon his shoulder did little to calm him.

"Are you hurt?" whispered Sydarias. Darshima looked up and shook his head.

"I don't think so," said Darshima, barely able to find the words to respond.

"This was once a beautiful place." Sydarias gestured toward the shadows. Darshima looked around as his eyes adjusted to the darkness. The flickering torches lining the pathway partially revealed the rich celestial mosaics adorning the vaulted ceilings high above them.

Darshima sat in silence amid the steady bomb blasts, his mind frantically sifting through the events occurring around them.

"What's happening?" He looked toward the ceiling, his voice cracking. A particularly powerful explosion rocked the building and they huddled closer together. They crouched deeper under the desk as the floors shook, and a shower of debris fell. Darshima's eye caught the glimmering shards of mosaic tile, glass, and gold leaf, raining down upon them like falling stars.

"We are under attack," whispered Sydarias, choking on the words.

"Who would do such a thing?" asked Darshima.

"I don't know." Sydarias shook his head, eyes closed in disbelief.

The thought of an attack on The Vilides seemed so foreign, and wholly unfathomable. Darshima couldn't conceive what would have provoked an assault against the capital. The Vilides had been the unquestioned seat of economic and military power for nearly eleven centuries. Despite their disputes, the four moons enjoyed a relatively stable and enduring peace. He had never heard of any resistance against Vilidesian rule. Even if forces on Gordanelle, Iberwight, Wohiimai banded together to stage a rebellion, they could never challenge Vilidesian might.

"They seemed like foreign craft." Darshima's eyes narrowed as he tried to recall their features.

"But where would they come from? There are no living worlds beyond our own." Sydarias shot a perplexed glance at him.

Darshima stared at the ground, shaking his head as a wave of confusion came over him. Sydarias' words were what Darshima and every citizen of the realm had grown up believing. There were no other inhabited worlds beyond the four moons of Benai. The ancient disaster that destroyed the planet, had annihilated everything in known existence, except the moons of the realm. This unanticipated attack shattered that belief in every sense. From the devastation he had witnessed, Darshima sensed that a battle of this scale could not have come from within the realm. The force was sophisticated and overwhelming, and the fleets were distinctly foreign.

"Those ships must have come from a place beyond our skies," whispered Darshima.

"Why would you say such a thing? It can't be." Sydarias vigorously shook his head. Darshima and Sydarias sat shivering in their damp clothes. The shadows around them grew bolder amid the faint beams of early morning light filtering through the windows. The wail of distant sirens and the growl of engines broke through the steady clatter of explosions. They remained under the desk, too scared to move and unsure where to go. If they dared to move, they would be in full view of the windows and vulnerable to the unknown dangers lurking outside. They huddled together, waiting for some sort of pause in the cataclysm unfolding beyond the walls of the library.

As they sat beside each other, their shadows grew bolder in the approaching dawn. The blasts increased in force and frequency, rattling the windows enclosing the room.

The loud clicking sound of stressed metal filled Darshima's ears. A deep vibration coursed through the building, and the floor shuddered beneath them.

"I don't know how much longer we can stay here." Sydarias trembled as he looked around them.

"If we go out there, we will die." Darshima glared at Sydarias, his eyes widening in terror as he contemplated fleeing.

"If we stay here, we will also die." A hesitant frown crossed Sydarias' lips as he turned to the window. The building shook violently, and the desk jolted upward. A row of large tiles buckled in front of them, sending plumes of debris into the air. They crouched even lower, holding onto each other as the floor lurched forward. The sound of crumbling stone and shattering glass filled their ears. Darshima's eyes darted into the shadows as the room quaked around them. He knew it wouldn't be long before the building was either seized or destroyed.

"We cannot escape, the doors are blocked." Darshima gestured toward the pile of destroyed bookshelves blocking the entrance. Sydarias pointed to a door at the opposite end of the room.

"There is an exit at the other side of the room, but we have to move past the windows," he whispered.

"What if we don't make it?" asked Darshima.

"It is our only chance. There might be someplace else we can hide," replied Sydarias.

Sydarias devised a plan to sneak past the windows toward the exit. They would stay hidden while trying to catch a glimpse outside to find a different, possibly safer location. When it was clear, they would sprint toward the door and flee the building.

Their chests pressed tightly against the floor, Sydarias, then Darshima crawled slowly out from under the desk toward a wide gap in the center row. As Sydarias was poised to move in full view of the window, Darshima reached out and grabbed his leg.

"Be careful, we don't know what's out there," whispered Darshima.

"I'll try my best." Sydarias briefly looked toward him and nodded. They crept forward together, moving slowly amid the shadows.

Darshima followed Sydarias behind another desk and peered around its square frame, catching a glimpse through the window. Dawn had arrived, and the skies broke under the faint sunlight. His eyes adjusted to the dusty rays filtering through, but he could neither recognize nor comprehend what he was seeing. Beyond the window lay a vast, fiery wasteland of twisted and glowing wreckage. Most of the towers of the city remained standing but many had fallen. Those that remained upright were badly burned. The once-grand edifices were pocked with gaping holes that shot columns of bright flame and belched thick plumes of smoke.

Through the fog, beams of sunlight glinted off the immense fleet of foreign vessels. They blanketed the skies in broad rows that seemed to stretch beyond the horizon, and had remained in the same position since the beginning of the attack. Below the ships, Darshima eyed hundreds of smaller craft on patrol throughout the city, zipping about rapidly and firing indiscriminately upon the buildings. Darshima stole a glimpse at Sydarias, whose face was contorted in an expression of both fear and rage. A tear rolled down his cheek, and he dashed it away with the back of his hand.

Darshima stared fearfully through the window, trying to make sense of what was happening when a brilliant red light abruptly shone through the fractured pane. They scurried behind a row of desks, the jarring sounds of engine noise and mechanical chatter filling the room. A throbbing, high-pitched whine rose above the roar and grew in intensity. Darshima frantically covered his ears but he couldn't block out the sound. His eardrums ached as the noise grew louder. The deafening crack of shattering glass echoed through the room. Without warning, the wall of windows burst into a hail of glittering shards that scattered all over the floor.

Violent winds howled through the breached room, whipping up papers and books, and tearing at their clothes.

"We have to run!" Sydarias yanked at Darshima's sleeve. They crawled away from the desks, desperately trying to avoid being seen. The deafening wake of engines rattled the room, filling the air with the oily odor of exhaust. Out of the corner of his eye, Darshima spied what appeared to be the dark form of a small, unmanned aircraft patrolling the opposite side of the room. It glided past the broken wall of windows, its shiny rounded shape appearing as a mere distortion of the morning light.

Darshima cowered in terror. His instincts told him to flee, but a feeling of dread had numbed his legs. Sydarias trembled beside him. Darshima wanted to reach out and reassure him but feared any movement would be detected. The craft surveyed the room, issuing intense, thin beams of red light from its nose cone. He eyed the vehicle as it traveled the length and breadth of the space, kicking up a flurry of dust and debris. The vehicle then floated back through the shattered panes, leaving the room in an uneasy silence.

Darshima lay against the stone floor, unsure of what to do. His heart pounding with fear, he pressed himself harder against the surface. His arms felt heavy, and he carefully moved them, attempting to relieve the numbness.

"I think they've left for good," whispered Darshima.

"Let's make a run for it. This is our chance." Sydarias motioned with an arm toward the door.

They rose to their feet and carefully started toward the exit, when a fleet of oblong craft burst through the broken windows. Soldiers wearing black helmets, silver visors, and green fatigues sat atop the machines and hovered above the floor. They raced through the room, whipping up a turbulent cloud of dust and debris. The vehicles activated their bright red headlamps and swarmed around Darshima.

Sydarias pulled Darshima's arm and desperately dragged him toward the door, when three of the craft rushed past them and blocked the exit. Darshima tried to turn back, but he and Sydarias were chased into a corner. Backs pressed against the wall, they stared fearfully at the group of vehicles.

Their red lamps grew more intense and flashed in a rapid and complex sequence. Darshima threw his hands up and tried to shield his eyes from the blinding lights, but soon felt his senses overwhelmed. His stomach churned as a strong wave of nausea came over him. A dense fog clouded his racing thoughts, and the jarring sounds around him faded into a suffocating quietness. Darshima heard a dull thud, followed by an echo and struggled to move his head, which felt unusually heavy.

He turned his body, but felt as if he were submerged underwater. His eyes drifted down to see Sydarias sprawled upon the floor, unconscious. Panicked, Darshima reached down to grab him but lost his footing. After a fall that seemed to last several seconds, Darshima's knees connected forcefully with the floor. His back ached with a sharp spasm of pain as he collapsed beside Sydarias.

Darshima lay dazed upon the floor, paralyzed by a deep sense of exhaustion. He helplessly eyed the flurry of activity around them. The soldiers dismounted from their craft and loomed over him. They spoke in an unusual language of guttural whispers and consonants that had never before graced his ears. His vision dimmed as he felt a pair of hands hoist him up to his feet.

A heavy cloth hood with the sickening aroma of burning ash fell over his head. The smell filled his mouth and nostrils with a bitter taste that twisted his stomach in a queasy knot. He tried to clear his stinging throat, but the pain only worsened. He felt a cold metal collar encircle his neck and coughed desperately as it pressed against his throat. The soldiers forced his hands in front of him, and he felt the cold, metal weight of manacles and chains encircling his wrists and ankles. They clinked with every movement, echoing harshly in his ears.

Darshima felt a pair of hands push him forward across the floor. He could just make out pinpoints of light through the rough fabric hood draped over his head. As he struggled against the cumbersome shackles, his legs buckled beneath him and he tumbled to the ground. Darshima scrambled to regain his footing, when suddenly, a powerful yank at his collar pulled him upright. He rose with such a force that his legs briefly lifted off the floor. The muscles of his neck throbbed painfully and he gasped desperately for air. His hands shot up toward his neck, but he couldn't break free of the chains binding his wrists. He wheezed loudly and clenched his jaw to stifle the pain. A pair of hands gripped his arms and forced them back down in front of him.

As he was shoved forward, the pulsating roar of engines filled his ears. He shuffled along and felt the crunch of broken glass underfoot. Gusts of wind and engine exhaust blew through his torn clothes as he was forced to walk up an incline. His boots clicked against what sounded like a metal plank. He stepped hesitantly, unsure where to place his feet. The pair of hands pushed him into the dark interior of what sounded like an aircraft.

Darshima felt several people encroach upon him, his ears straining to understand their hushed murmurs. They chained his arms to a bar over his head and his ankles to the floor below. The sickly odor of the hood and the engine exhaust overwhelmed him, blurring his vision. He coughed and gagged violently as the waves of nausea grew worse. An acute sense of dread rose within him as his mental fog subsided, and he realized what was happening.

Darshima shuddered as he listened to the desperate moans and screams of what sounded like dozens of men and women around him. He thought he heard Sydarias' faint voice, muffled by the cloth covering his head. Darshima wanted to say something, anything to make sure it was him. He coughed forcefully as he tried to speak. His throat burning and his body aching, Darshima vigorously shook his head as he tried to form the words.

The loud whine of a motor broke through the drone of the engines. The clang of a metal door slamming reverberated through the cabin and sent a chill through Darshima's spine. He shuddered as the floor rocked forcefully beneath him. The ship lurched upward, and he felt a dull thud against his side as he collided with another warm, shackled body.

As he drifted back into his foggy stupor, Darshima heard the rattling of chains and then felt something nudge his side.

"Are you there, Darshima?" asked Sydarias, who stood chained beside him. His weak voice was barely audible amid the commotion. A flood of relief came over Darshima as he heard Sydarias' voice, but it was tempered by a sense of horror. His heart sank as he realized Sydarias had also been captured.

"I'm here," said Darshima, barely recognizing his own garbled words. Sydarias let out a stifled sob that pierced right through Darshima. His eyes grew damp and a sharp lump formed in his throat. The ship rudely jostled him about, the manacles tugging at his aching wrists. The suffocating odor of the hood seemed to grow stronger, and he found himself slipping in and out of consciousness. He mustered what was left of his energy, and nudged Sydarias with his hip. Fear, pain and exhaustion having taken his words, Darshima simply wanted Sydarias to know that he too had been captured, and was right there with him.

Chapter Twenty Two

The forceful blast of icy water upon Darshima's bare skin jolted him awake. He shivered, and his teeth chattered as a deep sense of cold permeated through him, sinking into his bones. His eyes fluttered open under the bright white light flooding the room, and he narrowed them against the stinging intensity. The room seemed all the brighter as the walls, floors, and ceiling appeared to be made of a lustrous white metal. Darshima looked around the oval space, blinking as torrents of water poured from the ceiling, thoroughly soaking him. He pursed his lips but could still taste the cold, bitter droplets.

Darshima reached for his neck which ached terribly, but couldn't move his arms. He looked down and saw that he was completely naked, and his arms and legs were shackled to the wall. Through the cold mists, he saw dozens of men and women around him, chained to the walls of the room, in a similar undressed and stuporous state. Some shouted at the top of their lungs, desperately crying out the names of loved ones. Others stood silently, their heads slumped drowsily against their chests.

Darshima's pulse thudded with a deep sense of terror at his strange surroundings. His mind, though still foggy, sifted through the events before this moment. He remembered fleeing the bluff with Sydarias and then crashing into the pond. He recalled hiding in the library and being captured, but not much else. His veins bulged, and he grunted as he struggled against the shackles holding his arms and legs, but they wouldn't give.

Darshima peered around, desperately searching for Sydarias amid the crowd. He looked to his right and saw Sydarias chained beside him. His head drooped downward, and he snored softly.

"Sydarias!" Darshima shouted between coughs, retching as a spray of foul-tasting water filled his mouth. He shut his eyes and waited for the dreadful moment to pass. He looked over again and saw Sydarias stir briefly, then fall back into a stupor. His mind raced fearfully as he wondered what was happening to them.

The torrent ceased and the room fell silent, save for the echo of dripping water. A pair of metal doors at the opposite end of the room slid open. A large team of soldiers wearing loose-fitting, impervious green suits, boots, hoods, and thick silver-tinted visors marched toward them and then divided into groups. Darshima saw pairs of them stop momentarily in front of each captive. His ears bristled as the air crackled with the sound of a mechanical whine and the pop of an electrical discharge, followed by cries of pain and stifled sobs.

Through the mist, Darshima stared wide-eyed as a pair of soldiers approached him. One soldier held an ovoid metal tablet and tapped his gloved fingers methodically against its glowing screen. The other soldier withdrew a black pistol from the holster on his hip. Darshima fearfully eyed the glowing tip as it pulsed with intense red light. The soldier turned a series of dials and then stepped closer. Darshima drew in a startled breath as he felt the soldier jab the pointed tip against his left flank. A flash of intense, fiery pain coursed through his rib, and he let out a shout as the sensation filled him. The stench of burning flesh wafted toward his nostrils, sending his stomach into a queasy knot. The soldier pulled the pistol away, and the pair moved over to Sydarias. Darshima's blood surged as Sydarias screamed in agony, his shouts blending with the sounds of the whirring device.

Darshima grit his teeth and stifled his sobs as the burning subsided. He glimpsed downward and saw a small line of unfamiliar, triangular symbols neatly etched in red upon the skin below his left rib. Darshima turned to Sydarias and saw an identical line of symbols upon his flank. His chest tightened, and a sense of despair filled him as he beheld the strange mark.

Darshima lifted his head to see another pair of soldiers approaching. They unshackled him and Sydarias from the wall, chained them together, and forced them to march with the other captives. Darshima turned to Sydarias who was now awake. He stared at the floor and shuffled forward.

"Sydarias, what's happening?" Darshima called out, struggling as he tried to get closer to him. Sydarias lifted his head and offered a vacant stare.

"I don't know," he mumbled.

The soldiers ushered them into a drafty, adjacent room whose walls were lined with rows of dull metal shelves. Shivering as he waited, Darshima stared at the people around him. Some were still lethargic, others were awake and struggling against the heavy restraints. The soldiers forcefully yanked at their chains, dragging them back into line. His eyes widened in disbelief when he saw they also had been branded with similar lines of strange script.

The soldiers pulled out stacks of clothing and issued each of them a set of black boots, loose-fitting grey trousers, and vests, featuring an unfamiliar triangular blazon on the right breast. They briefly unchained the captives and allowed them to dress. A few of the men struggled to break away and flee but were swiftly subdued by the soldiers, metal truncheons in hand. Bruised and bloodied, the soldiers forced the captives to put on their uniforms and placed them back in their chains.

Trembling and soaked, Darshima felt the shackles release from his wrists. He cautiously took the uniform and the pair of stiff fabric boots the soldiers handed him. He struggled to pull the rough, thin garments over his damp skin. When he finished dressing, the soldiers grabbed his arms and placed the restraints back upon him. He winced as the cold metal dug sharply into his skin.

Darshima peered out of the corner of his eye and spotted Sydarias standing beside him. His head hung down and he grimaced in pain. Sydarias shivered in the chilly room as he struggled to put on the uniform. "Sydarias, we have to get out of here!" yelled Darshima as he fought against the chains and tried to reach out to him. As Sydarias lifted his head toward him, a soldier forcefully yanked Darshima back. He grit his teeth as a jolt of pain coursed through his arms. The soldier shouted a harsh string of unintelligible words in Darshima's ear, and his heart bounded in fear. He cringed as the damp heat of the man's breath filled his ear. He then turned toward the soldier and beheld his angry frown. Darshima's eyes swept over the soldier's silver visor, his pulse racing as he glimpsed his terrified, distorted reflection.

After Sydarias had dressed, the soldiers reached toward him to put back on his shackles. Sydarias deftly stepped away, avoiding their grasp. They let out angry shouts and started toward him. As Sydarias pivoted to run, one of the soldiers tripped him, sending him onto the cold metal floor with a thud. Sydarias scrambled up to his knees and one of the soldiers landed a powerful kick to his side. Sydarias crumpled to the dull metal floor, stifling his shouts as he writhed in pain.

Darshima's heart bounded with rage as he witnessed Sydarias suffer.

"Leave him alone!" shouted Darshima as he tried to break free. The pair of soldiers beside Darshima brutally forced him the ground. As he struggled to breathe, he felt the dull, weighty pressure of a knee digging right between his shoulder blades. His chest pressed against the floor, Darshima lifted his head and saw Sydarias back upon his knees. Sydarias' eyes smoldered in an expression of suppressed rage as he stared forward. He received another forceful kick from the soldier, then fell facedown upon the floor, where he lay still. Darshima lay in anguish as he witnessed the scene, realizing he could do nothing to help.

A team of soldiers hovered over Sydarias, cautiously studying his motionless form. The nearest one rudely nudged him with his boot, when Sydarias' hands unexpectedly sprang out from under him. Sydarias seized the soldier's foot and forcefully twisted it at an unnatural angle, causing the bone to snap loudly. The soldier shrieked in hysterical pain and tumbled to the ground.

The others tried to subdue him, but Sydarias swiftly jumped to his feet and raised his fists in a fighting stance. Several more uniformed men rushed over to restrain him, but retreated as one of the soldiers withdrew a small silver tube from his utility belt and aimed it at Sydarias' chest. He flicked his wrist as if trying to activate the weapon. Sydarias reacted instantly and leaped into the air. He spun around once, landing a swift, crushing kick to the man's arm. The device flew from his hand and crashed against a wall, shattering into a cascade of brilliant sparks and glowing metal fragments.

The soldier cowered in a corner, writhing in pain as he cradled his broken, bloodied limb. Sydarias landed back upon his feet and awaited the man's next move. Darshima looked on in stunned silence at what Sydarias had just done. Many Vilidesian men and women learned martial combat in their youth but rarely used it. He had no idea that Sydarias could fight so well.

Within moments, a team of soldiers rushed Sydarias. His fists flew in a coordinated fury, striking one of them squarely in the face. The soldier's visor cracked under the force of Sydarias' blow. The man's hands shot up to his face as a stream of blood ran down his cheek. Sydarias issued another forceful kick, striking another soldier in the flank, sending him reeling against the wall. The room erupted in howls and cheers as the captives witnessed Sydarias fight the group of soldiers.

Before he could land another blow, a larger team of soldiers burst into the room and tackled him. They pressed Sydarias against the wall and clasped a pair of shackles around his wrists. Darshima, still pinned upon the floor, looked at him in awe. Sydarias exchanged a brief but defiant stare with Darshima as the soldiers dragged him away.

Chapter Twenty Three

Darshima crouched alone, shivering in the dim light of the small chamber. He drew a thin blanket over his shoulders, but it offered no warmth. A haggard sigh escaped his lips in a puff of steam. He rested his head against the cold wall, his weary eyes lingering upon his surroundings. The lights in the ceiling above cast a faint greenish glow over the dank space, its dull metallic walls curving around him in a semicircle. A small faucet and basin sat at one end, and a latrine in the other.

A metal sliding door with a rectangular slot beneath it stood in the middle of the opposite wall. Darshima glared at the door, his jaw set in frustration. His eyes scanned its dented and scratched surface. It was him who had made those marks in his initial bouts of despair. He didn't know if he had been in that cell for hours, days, or weeks. There were no windows or natural light to help him acclimate. Time seemed as if it had come to a halt. His recollection of the events before his capture felt as if they were slipping away.

Darshima's chest tightened as a wave of anxiety came over him. Being trapped in the confines of the small space weighed upon him, and he was desperate to leave. His face grew hot, and a rising sense of anger filled him as he stared at his bleak confines. With his remaining strength, he jumped to his feet and launched himself against the door. His shoulder collided against the square plank, sending an explosive thud throughout the cell.

Darshima clenched his teeth in pain as the forceful impact radiated through his shoulder. The door didn't budge at all. His pulse pounded in fury as he glared at the immovable object. He let out a blood-curdling shout at the top of his lungs, his voice ringing loudly in his ears. He banged his closed fists furiously against the hard surface, the broken skin of his knuckles smearing the metal with bright red streaks of blood. Like the times before, there was nothing he could do to move that door. He braced against it and let out an anguished cry. His aching, bloody hands fell to his sides and he slumped over. He dragged himself back to the opposite wall and curled up on the chilly metal floor as a deep sense of despair overwhelmed him.

Darshima rubbed his bruised knuckles, now throbbing in pain and tried to console himself. He didn't remember how many times he had tried to escape, and had stopped counting after the first dozen attempts. The cool, humid air was still, except for the occasional sharp sounds of clanging metal and the unnerving cries of other captives echoing through the walls. He covered his ears against the mournful voices, their disembodied wails sending a shiver through him.

Darshima sighed as his exhaustion got the better of him, and he drifted in and out of a fitful daze. His mind aimlessly filtered through his disconnected memories, from the small stiff bed in his room back home, to the way that the late afternoon sunlight shimmered on his mother's hair. His eyes grew damp as the images of his family came to him. He tossed upon the hard floor in a fit of worry, shuddering at the thought of them being beaten and suffering somewhere far from home. He hoped that they had somehow managed to escape such a miserable fate. Hot tears fell from his eyes, and he stared blankly at the ceiling.

During his first moments in the cell, Darshima had been seized by overwhelming feelings of fear. He tried to reckon the turn of events that led him and the others here. He understood that there had been a war, and he was one of many prisoners. He didn't know why he been captured, or what these people wanted with him. His heart thudded in his chest as the memories of the invasion flooded his mind. The dead and damaged bodies piled in the streets, the burned and twisted buildings amid the flames, and the searing explosions hung before his waking eyes. He shook his head and vigorously rubbed his face, trying to dash away the harrowing images.

Darshima's thoughts drifted to Sydarias. His memories of him, though recent, were beginning to fade, like a well-worn photograph. Though in vain, he tried not to think too much about Sydarias, the mere thought sending him into inconsolable fits of worry. He hadn't seen Sydarias since he had been dragged away by the soldiers after the brawl. A small smile crept across Darshima's lips as he thought about Sydarias and his bravery. At least Sydarias had shown their captors that someone among them had the will to fight back.

The enveloping drone of rising engines filled his ears and shook the floor beneath him, rattling against his ribs. Thoughts of his present circumstance flooded his mind, chasing his errant thoughts away. His eyes darted nervously around the cell, and he envisioned the vessel hurtling through the abyss. His pulse raced as he mulled over a myriad of terrifying fates awaiting him at the other end of the unknown journey.

The sound of scraping metal emanating from the door pricked his ears. The tiny slot snapped opened at the bottom of the doorway, and he shielded his eyes against the stark beams of greenish white light. A flat, metallic tray shot through the opening, careening against the floor with a loud screech. His ears prickled as the object came to rest at his feet. The slot slammed shut with a thud that echoed through the cell.

Darshima hunched over the rectangular tray and examined the steaming, gelatinous contents and the cylindrical pitcher of water. He gingerly lifted the tray to his nose, then placed it back down. To stave off his gnawing hunger, he stuck a finger into the quivering, greenish pile and shoveled the slimy contents into his mouth. A wave of nausea seized his stomach, and he doubled over. He gagged and then let out a violent cough as he tried to clear his throat of the sulfurous taste.

Darshima had lost count of how many trays had slid into his cell since he had been there, and how many he had pushed back. Faced with ever-present hunger pangs, he had forced himself to eat the strange food, but it often made him sick. His thirst getting the better of him, he grabbed the pitcher and gulped the bitter-tasting water. He pushed the tray away with a foot, then threw the metal cylinder aside, which landed with a loud clatter. He slumped back against the wall, his gaze lingering upon the door.

He began to drift into another daze, when a sharp clanging noise from the door jolted him awake. Darshima crouched further against the wall as the large panel slid open. His eyes narrowed against the light, he saw the silhouettes of two soldiers and one captive between them. They uttered something in their language, threw the captive to the floor, then slammed the door behind them. Darshima rose to his feet and slowly approached the captive, who wearily pushed himself off the ground.

"Where am I?" he mumbled groggily as he sat up. At first, Darshima couldn't believe whose voice he was hearing, but his suspicions were confirmed by the angular lines of Sydarias' face.

"Sydarias, it is you!" whispered Darshima. "I thought you were dead." He knelt beside Sydarias and wrapped his arms around him in a tight embrace. His pulse slowed as a flood of relief came over him. Through the dim light, Darshima could sense something different about Sydarias, his already lean frame appearing thinner.

Before he had a chance to properly settle, Darshima peppered him with questions.

"What happened to you after the fight? Who are these people that captured us?" he asked, desperate to know what Sydarias had experienced. Sydarias slowly raised a hand and Darshima fell silent.

"They kept me in a different part of the ship." Sydarias briefly closed his eyes, his voice wavering. "I was alone, and I can't remember much else." His head drooped and he fell silent.

"Why did they let you go? How did you find me?" Darshima jostled his shoulder.

"I don't know." Sydarias shook his head. "I think they are keeping us in pairs or groups." He raised his vest and dragged his finger across the line of symbols etched under his left rib. Darshima lifted his uniform and eyed the markings upon his own rib, which were identical.

"Do you have any idea where we are?" Darshima moved closer to him, his voice trembling under the weight of the question. Sydarias let out a pained sigh.

"It doesn't matter. We are trapped and have no chance of getting out of here." He stared blankly at Darshima.

Darshima's heart pounded as he felt the despair in Sydarias' voice. He had never heard him speak in such a tone. His eyes lingered upon the ceiling, until Sydarias' voice broke the tense silence.

"There was nothing." Sydarias let out a tortured sigh and leaned backward. His head landed with a thud against the wall behind them.

"What do you mean, nothing?" Darshima sat up and glared at him. Sydarias slowly turned toward Darshima, the shadows of the room shifting over his face, forming dark bands across his features.

"As they moved me to this cell, I caught a glimpse out of a window." His damp eyes glittered angrily in the dim light.

"What did you see?" Darshima leaned closer.

"I saw..." Sydarias opened his mouth, but fell into an incoherent stutter and then silence.

"Sydarias, say something." Darshima grabbed him by the shoulder, but he said nothing. He weakly pulled himself from Darshima's grasp, and stared blankly ahead.

Darshima's heart sank to the pit of his stomach as he looked at Sydarias slumped against the wall.

"I didn't mean to be hard on you," whispered Darshima. He sidled next to Sydarias and caught a glimpse of his face in the light. The brightness in his grey eyes had dimmed, and he seemed like a shell of his former self. Sydarias closed his eyes, and his chest shook as he stifled a sob. He rested his head upon Darshima's shoulder.

Darshima put an arm around Sydarias and drew him nearer, trying to comfort him as he drifted into a fitful sleep. A wave of sadness roiled Darshima as he held his friend. Whatever Sydarias had been through had clearly shaken him. Sydarias' soft breathing echoed against the walls of the cell, blending in with the drone of the engines.

As they sat there, Darshima again felt himself losing track of time. He couldn't remember whether it had been minutes or hours since Sydarias had last spoken. His mind raced as he contemplated what might have happened to Sydarias during their separation. He could only imagine how harshly the soldiers had treated Sydarias. The fierce streak of independence that he admired was no longer there.

Darshima's thoughts were disrupted again by the loud creak of the opening door. His pulse quickened, and he sat up straight against the wall. He stared nervously ahead, narrowing his gaze against the light. Darshima shook Sydarias' shoulder, and he awoke from his slumber, rubbing the sleep from his eyes. A group of soldiers entered the cell and loomed over them. The silver visors covering their faces hid much of their expressions, but their frowns were visible. Darshima, then Sydarias warily rose to their feet. The soldiers stood in front of them and grabbed them by the arms. They put manacles upon their wrists, then chained them together.

The soldiers then forced Darshima and Sydarias out of the cell and led them down a long hall, bathed in stark white light.

Darshima looked around him and saw the other cell doors slide open. Men and women in chains like him were dragged out into the corridor by teams of soldiers. A lump formed in his throat as he saw the fear and exhaustion written upon their worn faces. They forced the captives to march through a dizzying labyrinth of chilly corridors, with no clear direction. Darshima panted as they trudged on, his boots thudding against the dull metal floors. The soldiers chatted with each other, shouting and laughing raucously as they prodded the captives along. Darshima clenched his jaw as he listened. Though he couldn't understand them, their laughter amid such misery angered him.

Sydarias, weakened and starved, grimaced with every step. His head drooped and his eyes were half-open.

"Keep walking Sydarias, lean on my shoulder," whispered Darshima. Sydarias lifted his head, then rested upon Darshima's shoulder as they moved along. Darshima's legs ached as he supported them both. He gazed ahead and saw what looked hundreds more in shackles, trudging along, the crowd growing larger as they were forced from their cells. The sheer number of captives stunned him. He wondered if there was anyone left in The Vilides.

They moved through a convoluted and disorienting path of narrow hallways veiled in shadow. He shook his head as the jarring thud of footsteps, and the sharp rustling of chains filled his ears. The growl of the engines grew louder and the cold air around him stirred into a stiff breeze. The collective sound of their marching echoed around them as they entered a dimly lit room of immense proportions.

Darshima stole a glimpse off to his side and saw a large bank of cantilevered, circular windows. As they moved closer, his palms grew sweaty and his chest tightened with a wave of apprehension. Having seen no daylight nor the outside world since his capture, he ached for some hint of their location. They slowly filed past the row of glass portals, and he shivered as a frigid gale blew against his skin. Too nervous to look outside, he closed his eyes tightly and drew in a deep breath.

With what force he could muster, he slowly exhaled, willed his eyelids open, and stared at the vista beyond the windows. As he registered the scenery before him, his blood turned cold and he lost all feeling. There were neither stars, nor worlds, nor even a glimmer of light to greet his anxious eyes. There was but complete void. Nothing but a desolate blackness of the coldest kind met his gaze. An icy numbness stirred in his chest and flowed outward with every heartbeat, suffocating the nascent traces of hope left within him. He now understood why Sydarias had been rendered speechless back in their cell. The all-encompassing emptiness surrounding them could not be conveyed by words or emotions, but only by the very silence and desolation it conjured.

Chapter Twenty Four

Darshima narrowed his eyes against the bright sky. A cold, misty wind whipped violently around him and through his clothes. The pavement beneath his feet swayed noticeably with every stiff gust, and he struggled to maintain his balance. His legs, feeble from his stay in the prison cell, could barely support his weight. He looked around the oval-shaped amphitheater, trying to gain a sense of where they were. Sydarias stood silently next to him, his head bowed. Their arms and legs were bound in chains and they were shackled together at the waist. They stood in a long line of chained pairs. Darshima looked furtively around him and glimpsed groups of soldiers dressed in green fatigues and black, knee-high boots. Pistols holstered at their sides, they surveilled him and the other captives.

Darshima and Sydarias waited with the others in the middle of an expansive plaza. Throngs of spectators sat upon on a semi-circular array of metal bleachers at one end of the space. The immense freight vessels that had transported them stood parked at the opposite end of the amphitheater. Trails of steam rose from their bulbous green airframes, still warm from their entry through the atmosphere.

Darshima breathed in the cold damp air and stole a glance toward the heavens. His eyes widened in disbelief as he beheld the unfamiliar sky. The misty, pale blue atmosphere appeared like a frosted pane of crystal, barely veiling the void of space just beyond. Thin wisps of white clouds punctuated its vast emptiness. Linear trails of vapor spanned the sky as fleets of airborne vessels traversed the seemingly infinite expanse.

In the distance, he heard the low roar of crashing waves. Darshima tried to glimpse his surroundings, but the view was obscured by hundreds of men and women like him, bound in chains.

They looked weary and disheveled from what had undoubtedly been the longest voyage of their lives. Many of the captives stood tentatively upon the unsteady ground, putting on brave faces. Others grew nauseous, retching and vomiting with every tremor. Some openly grieved, their wails rising above the winds. Others, particularly the very young, nestled against their parents, stifling sobs in their garments. His heart pounded in disbelief as he beheld the tableau of despair before him.

Darshima turned his gaze to the crowds seated in the stands. They appeared very different from the people from back home. There were men, women, and children, dressed in heavy, dark colored overcoats and white underclothes. They wore narrow-brimmed black hats upon their heads to protect against the cold mist, and their pallid skin had a ruddy appearance. The men wore beards, and the women kept their light brown hair unshorn, letting it drape over their shoulders. The spectators sat rigidly in their seats and gazed toward the plaza. Hushed murmurs rose from crowds as they pointed at the rows of captives in chains. Darshima looked at their muted expressions, seeking some hint of familiarity, but he found none.

The booming voice of a man rose above the chatter of the crowds. He stood on a raised metal platform in front of a podium positioned between the spectators and the captives. He was short-statured, and his small features accentuated the roundness of his face. A wide-brimmed black hat sat atop his head, and a long grey coat with silver buttons draped over his loose dark clothing.

The man spoke in a commanding tone, his severe gaze alternating between the rows of captives behind him and the crowds seated in the bleachers before him. With one hand, the speaker gestured toward the captives and in the other, he held an iron gavel. As he shouted commands, the soldiers responded with a loud chant that echoed throughout the amphitheater. They moved into position behind the captives, forcing the shackled pairs onto the stage before him.

Darshima eyed the people in the orderly crowds as they raised their hands, showing the speaker a variety of unfamiliar signals and gestures. With a pound of the gavel, he pointed toward the soldiers, who then dragged the captives from the stage and toward the awaiting spectators. Some groups were auctioned in lots of several dozen, but others were split apart. Soldiers wrested screaming children from their parents, husbands from their wives, and brothers from their sisters.

The spectators took charge of their new slaves, dragging them by their chains, toward rows of smaller, oblong vessels parked behind the bleachers. Darshima broke out in a cold sweat, his pulse thudding in his ears as he witnessed the unspeakable horror. His gaze darted between the desperate captives being ushered to the stage and the crowds in the stands. Their stolid faces remained unyielding to the heartrending spectacle unfolding before them.

As they crept closer to the stage, Darshima's chest tightened like a vice, and a wave of fear overwhelmed him. He struggled to lift his feet as he climbed the steps, the heavy chains clinking sharply together. He and Sydarias stood at the center of the dull metal platform with two dozen other young men and women. Darshima felt a pair of hands forcefully turn him toward the spectators. He looked to his sides, his heart rising into his throat as the soldiers positioned them in a line.

From his vantage point upon the stage, Darshima spotted a gap in the bleachers and glimpsed what lay beyond the throngs of people. An ocean of violently churning green water stretched to the distant horizon. The vast body of water sent up massive waves that crashed against each other, forming treacherous whirlpools and swirls of icy mist. He drew in an anguished breath as his gaze swept over the alien vista.

Darshima turned to Sydarias, whose eyes were fixed in space. The muscles of his jaw rippled methodically as he stifled the expression of sadness spreading across his face. Darshima frantically turned back to the crowds, which grew increasingly restless. Dozens of hands shot up in the air, jockeying for the speaker's attention. Darshima stared at the hundreds of pairs of indifferent eyes, his stomach sinking as he saw the spectators signal the speaker with a myriad of gestures.

The sharp pounding of the gavel echoed through the air. Darshima snapped to attention as the piercing sound resonated within him. A deep ache settled in his chest, and an acute feeling of despair seized him. His heart felt as if it had been cleaved in half.

"No..." he stammered, his voice breaking. Darshima shook his head vigorously, as the gravity of the transaction that had just taken place sank to the depths of his being. He felt Sydarias nudge his side.

"The Vilides will not let this stand," whispered Sydarias, his voice wavering.

"It cannot be true." Darshima turned to Sydarias, his eyes welling up with hot tears. He felt the abrupt tug of the chains as the soldiers ushered them together off the stage, toward an awaiting vessel and an unknown future.

Chapter Twenty Five

His shoulders aching, Darshima reached down toward the ground. He plunged his fingers into the damp, greenish soil and yanked at a stubborn weed growing between his feet. The toes of his fabric boots and the cuffs of his thin grey trousers were caked in the sticky mud. He wrapped his fingers around the thorny stem, and it pricked sharply against his palm. His back glistened with sweat as he worked, the burning rays of afternoon light searing his bare skin. Darshima's frame cast a long shadow upon Sydarias, who toiled beside him, his boots and trousers coated in mud. The muscles of Sydarias' back rippled as he methodically pulled the tenacious weeds from the ground.

Darshima lifted his head, gazed at the sky, and drew in a haggard breath. He cupped his hands against his face and shaded his eyes against the triplet of white blazing suns radiating down upon him. He had beheld this unusual celestial formation every day as he worked in these fields, but the alien sight still sent a shiver through him. He had marked the sunrises and sunsets since the first time they had been marched into the fields and had lost count at seventy. His neck aching, he let his head droop back down toward the soil. He had long given up hope of finding any trace of familiarity in this strange place.

The humid air clung to Darshima's skin with no hint of a breeze to offer relief. Apart from a short break at midday, he and the others had been out in the fields since dawn, pulling weeds and tending to the crops. Darshima stared at the diaphanous, green leaves of the waist-high plants. The sunlight filtered through them and cast the soil below in stippled light and shadow. Clusters of glistening, orange-colored buds drooped beneath the leaves, oozing a clear sap. The viscous fluid gave off a sickly sweet aroma that hung in the air, clinging to the back of his throat. He reached for a clump of weeds near a trunk, deftly seizing them at the stems to avoid snapping their roots.

Darshima tried to think about anything else but the fields around him as he worked. He struggled to adjust to his disquieting reality, but with every new day that dawned, it sank in a little deeper. His old life back home in Ardavia seemed like a distant and foreign concept. He let out an anguished sigh as he looked around, his chest tightening with a mixture of fear and bitterness. Memories of the violent chain of events that brought him to this strange land flashed before his mind. He froze for a moment, his heart thudding in a bout of panic. As the familiar sensation passed, he resumed the tedious work before him.

Darshima and the others had never heard of their captors. They had never known of this foreign place. To him and the others, it was inconceivable that a world beyond their own existed. In addition to the peculiar triplet of suns, the days here seemed to stretch on interminably. He couldn't tell if time here was even the same. The only certainty he grasped was that he was one of many who had been captured from his world to toil in bondage on the hostile fields of another.

Darshima stood up, stretched the stiff muscles of his aching back, and looked around. He drew in a breath and tried to shake the heavy thoughts. Hundreds of men and women toiled all around him in the heat. Like him, the men were bare-chested and wore grey cloth trousers and boots made of thin fabric. The women wore grey armless fabric robes and boots similar to the men. They yanked at weeds, pruned the wayward stalks, and cleared the desiccated leaves. The triplet of suns moved across the sky in synchrony, casting their stark white rays across the captives' gaunt forms. His eyes graced the lines of symbols stamped upon their sinewy flanks. Their expressions bore a mixture of blankness and resignation as they worked.

Darshima shook his head in disbelief as he looked upon his fellow captives. They were the children of a mighty realm that spanned four moons, the descendants of emperors and empresses. He couldn't fathom how they had been reduced to mere slaves. A shudder coursed through him as his mind conjured images of his mother, father, and brother toiling in a field just like this one. He imagined their gaunt faces and their worn, grimy hands plowing through the soil. He closed his eyes and dashed away a tear with a mud-stained palm. A lump formed in his throat as the sadness washed over him. A haggard sigh escaped his lips, and he resumed the task.

The trio of suns drifted toward the horizon and Darshima tugged at the weeds around him, his vision blurred by the sweat pouring from his brow. The heat and the hunger steadily sapped his energy as he toiled amid the plants. He gripped a particularly tenacious weed with his right hand. As he yanked, it snapped at the stalk, and a thorn lanced the tip of his index finger. He winced as a stinging jolt of pain coursed through his digit. He brought his hand to his face and eyed a small gash oozing blood. The dark red droplets ran down his arm and dripped into the soil.

He lifted his finger to his mouth to stanch the bleeding, the salty metallic taste of his blood sending a wave of nausea through him. He looked again at his throbbing fingertip, and the bleeding had slowed some. Clenching his teeth in frustration, he faced the row of plants and went back to work. He peeked furtively between the rows of plants as he pulled the weeds, his gaze trained upon a row of immense cone-shaped towers looming upon the horizon. The shiny metal structures gleamed in the sun, appearing as a line of unflinching sentinels. Teams of soldiers stood watch at the top of each one. They surveyed the fields with telescopes, whose giant lenses glinted in the sunlight.

Further afield, Darshima spied a small squadron of soldiers darting across the sky. They patrolled upon a fleet of metallic, oblong vehicles, soaring high over the fields in the formation of an arrow. A droning wake of dust and exhaust trailed them, and the plant stalks swayed beneath the turbulent gusts. They swarmed over a particular patch and then descended beyond his view, their engines falling silent.

The air shook with a chorus of aggressive shouts and fearful screams, then the sharp ping of artillery fire. The sound of several blood-curdling yelps, followed by an ominous silence sent a cold shiver through Darshima. He closed his eyes and trembled as a bolt of fear gripped him. He didn't want to imagine the fate of the poor captives who had somehow managed to rouse the soldiers' ire. Their engines reignited, and he looked on as they vaulted over the fields toward the row of towers in the distance.

Darshima and the others had learned early on that they were under near-constant surveillance. During their first few weeks, several of the slower workers had been taken away and severely beaten. Some returned to the fields, but others disappeared. Out of fear, Darshima and the other captives worked harder and saw less of the soldiers. Even so, he knew they were not safe from them.

As he had done back in his old life during difficult times, Darshima focused his thoughts inward. Though he tried, the misery around him flooded his senses at every turn. The persistent threat of violence or worse, settled in his chest with a sick and unrelenting heaviness. He closed his eyes and drew in a deep breath, trying to concentrate on the weeds at his feet. As much as he wanted to mourn his old life back home, he knew he needed to save his energy to survive the present. He forced his eyes open and plunged his hands into the soil. He furiously yanked at the stiff weeds around his feet, bits of soil flying everywhere.

The shadows grew longer, and the light faded as the suns dipped below the horizon. As he reached for another weed, the sound of a shrill whistle punctuated the air. Darshima felt a hand rest upon his shoulder, and he stood up. His eyes met Sydarias' stare.

"We're done for the day, let's go back inside." Sydarias' chest heaved as he panted from exhaustion. His hair was matted, and sweat poured down the sides of his neck. He wiped his damp brow with the back of his wrist, streaking mud upon his forehead.

Darshima followed Sydarias through the dirt rows of plants, the soil clinging to the soles of their boots. The last rays of light retreated against the growing ebb of the darkening sky. He trudged amid the lengthening shadows, toward the low, rectangular rows of metal barracks arranged beside the footpath. Amid the lengthening shadows, he saw the haggard silhouettes of hundreds of other slaves like him, returning to their dwellings.

Another day's labor had exhausted him beyond measure. He shuffled along the rusty porch, willing himself to remain upright. A frown crossed his sullen face as Sydarias pushed open the door, and they stepped across the threshold of the rudimentary building. Darshima peered around the dimly lit room, his gaze lingering upon the rows of neatly arranged metal cots spread before him. An anguished sigh escaped his lips, and he closed his weary eyes. The thought of a night's rest gave him no respite. Tomorrow would be the same.

Chapter Twenty Six

Darshima's eyes scanned the clusters of glistening, palm-sized bulbs dangling from the branch before him. Rays of stark afternoon light reflected off the thick opalescent skin, setting the rainbow flecks of color ablaze. The green, tubular plant stalks drooped under their weight. He leaned forward and drew in a breath, the sweet floral aroma filling his nostrils. His stomach growled and his mouth watered as the scent lingered. He wrapped his gloved fingers around the ripe bulb and gauged its firmness. He twisted it upon the woody branch, and it gave way with a soft snap. He gently placed the bulb with several others, nestled in a fiber sack draped over his shoulder.

During the past several days, he and the other captives had been out in the fields collecting the ripening fruits. Teams of farmers, dressed in the same green fatigues as the soldiers had shown them how to harvest these delicate items. From what he understood, they were a valuable part of the plant and would rot if damaged. As they harvested, groups of soldiers made frequent trips through the fields to ensure that the captives were not being rough with the produce. Some of the captives succumbed to their hunger and ate the strange fruit. Those who had been caught were severely beaten, then forced to work in chained pairs.

Darshima wasted no time and walked over to the next cluster, the pangs in his stomach growing sharper. Sydarias sidled up to the plant beside him and performed the same repetitive task. Hundreds of men and women worked around them in long green rows for as far as he could see. Remaining mostly hidden by the shoulder-high plants, they silently picked the fruit under the withering sunlight.

Darshima moved on to the next plant, examining it to see if the fruit had ripened. As he reached for a bulb, the grating drone of engines shook the air around him. He glimpsed over his shoulder to see teams of soldiers flying upon their aerial vehicles, just above the fields. He covered his ears as the diamond-shaped formation of craft roared overhead, kicking up a cloud of dust. Sharp bits of dirt and debris struck the bare skin of his back, stinging him. His pulse thudded nervously as they vaulted past. The sound of the engines dissipated and he resumed his task, not even taking the time to dust himself off.

The labor was tedious and the fruit was heavy. As Darshima worked, he struggled under the weight of the sack, the rough fiber strap chaffing the skin upon his shoulder. His vision grew blurry as the heat wore him down. His throat dry with thirst, he gripped the metal canteen strapped to his hip and gently shook it, but it was empty. He clenched his jaw in frustration. Like the others, he had worked relentlessly since dawn and didn't know how much longer he could continue. He trudged weakly over to the next plant in the row, hoisting the bag upon his shoulder.

Darshima looked to his side and caught a glimpse of Sydarias who steadily worked, gently placing the fruit in his sack. Sydarias frowned softly, his gaze trained upon the row before him.

"Do you have any water?" Darshima pointed toward Sydarias' canteen. Sydarias lifted his head, the restrained look in eyes softening as he stared at Darshima.

"There's still some left." Sydarias unhooked the canteen from his trousers and handed it to him. Darshima unfastened the metal cap and drank mouthfuls of the cool water, ignoring the slightly bitter taste at the back of his throat.

"Thank you," muttered Darshima. He took another sip, his thirst still unquenched.

"It's hot out here. We must save some for later." Sydarias reached for the canteen and Darshima handed it back. Sydarias fastened the vessel back onto his belt and resumed his task, his gloved hands carefully collecting the fruit.

Darshima's gaze lingered upon Sydarias for a moment. He then turned back to the plants in front of him and worked to collect the produce from his row. He winced in pain as he struggled to carry the heavy sack, filled with fruit. He moved steadily along the row, his muscles stiffened from the repetitive motion. His pulse thudded nervously as he plucked the ripe bulbs, the waxing and waning drone of the patrolling aircraft grating his ears.

By mid-afternoon, he and Sydarias had finished collecting the produce from their row. With their sacks laden, they stepped away from the plants and joined a line of men and women on their way to discharge their harvest. They walked toward a large, oval metal receptacle at the head of the row to offload the bulbs. Darshima trudged along, hoisting the sack upon his shoulder, trying to keep his footing upon the muddy path. He looked up at the soldiers seated upon their craft, hovering just above their heads. Silver visors glinting in the sunlight, the soldiers surveyed the line, remaining expressionless as the captives filed past.

Darshima and Sydarias arrived at the front of the line and removed the sacks from their shoulders. Pairs of soldiers stood beside the container, surveying them as they unloaded the fruit onto a vertical array of metal pallets. The soldiers turned each sack inside out and made sure they were not hiding any produce. Their empty sacks in hand, Darshima and Sydarias started back toward their row.

They shuffled wearily along the path as they followed a group of captives.

"How much longer do we have? I don't think I can carry on like this." Sydarias turned to Darshima, his voice heavy with exhaustion.

"Today will soon be over, then we can rest." Darshima put an arm around his shoulder. Sydarias bowed his head as a somber expression crossed his face. His lips parted slightly as if to speak, but he then fell silent.

"We will feel better when we return to the barracks." Darshima gently nudged him.

Just ahead of them, a group of three young women stumbled along, their loose grey uniforms shifting upon their gaunt frames. Their silky, reddish-blond hair fell in long tails upon the tan skin of their necks. The woman in the middle was pregnant, and she struggled along the uneven path. She draped her arms upon the shoulders of the women at her sides, who obligingly carried her.

Darshima didn't know much about them but had heard they were sisters from a family of shepherds in Pelethedral. They had managed to remain together during their capture and worked beside each other in the fields. The pregnant woman had been separated from her husband after the invasion, and his fate was unknown. Her pregnancy had shown itself early on, but she stayed with her sisters. Darshima always saw them toiling together, easing each other's burden however best they could.

"When do you think she will give birth?" Sydarias pointed toward the woman.

"I don't know, but she shouldn't be here working in this heat." Darshima bit his lip and shook his head. He could only imagine how fatigued, and how thirsty she must be.

The woman struggled to maintain her footing upon the damp soil. Her sisters did their best to carry her, but they also struggled to remain steady. She unexpectedly stepped into a deep, muddy rut that caught her boot. With a yelp, she stumbled to her knees, her threadbare robe crumpling around her. Her sisters knelt beside her, supporting her back and shoulders to comfort her. They tried to help her up, but she refused and began to weep.

One of the sisters whispered something desperately in her ear, but the pregnant woman shook her head. They gently rested her down upon the soil. Her sisters removed their empty sacks from their shoulders and used them as pillows, placing them gently under her head. One of them looked up at Darshima and Sydarias, her bright green eyes wide with fear.

"Do either of you have any water? She's very weak," she pleaded. Sydarias dashed ahead and Darshima followed closely behind him.

Sydarias knelt beside the woman. A small crowd of captives formed around the sisters. Her eyes were closed and her hands rested upon her round abdomen. A grimace crossed her young face as she winced in pain. Beads of sweat glistened upon the flushed skin of her forehead, and she drew in labored breaths. Sydarias uncapped his canteen and put it to her lips. She took a few sips, but coughed violently and pushed it away. Sydarias looked upon her, his eyes wide with concern.

"You must drink, or you'll die of thirst." He offered his canteen again but she panted, too weak to reply.

"Are you about to give birth?" Darshima moved closer and knelt beside her, his chest tightening with worry.

"I don't know," she whispered, her fragile voice barely audible. A lump formed in Darshima's throat as he beheld her in her vulnerability. He turned to Sydarias.

"It is much too hot out here for her." Darshima reached for his pant leg and tore off a patch of the fibrous cloth. He outstretched his hand toward Sydarias who poured a bit of water from his canteen and doused the fabric. Darshima gently placed it upon her forehead. She lifted her hand and held the cool rag to her head. Her sisters massaged her shoulders and legs as she rested.

Darshima's heart pounded as a sense of fear rose within him. He knew she was ill, but he didn't know what else he could do to help. She needed proper rest, but the soldiers did not care. Forbidden to leave the fields before sundown, the captives often fainted in the sweltering heat from hunger and exhaustion. When others tried to care for those who fell ill, the soldiers intervened and beat them all. The most they could do is find a secluded area for the unwell to take a bit of rest.

The woman stirred as she regained some of her strength. Her eyes fluttered open and she peered anxiously at the crowd surrounding her.

"Are you feeling okay?" asked Darshima. She nodded weakly. Before she could speak, the rising drone of engines filled their ears. Darshima turned around to see a fleet approaching them. Terrified, the crowd dispersed and fanned out through the fields. They took cover between the plant stalks and shallow irrigation ditches along the rows, fearful that they had been seen. Darshima and Sydarias remained beside the sisters.

Darshima stared at the advancing group of craft, his pulse racing in fear. The shouts of the soldiers rose above the engine noise. They arrived in a flurry of dust and hovered in front of them, pointing their fingers at the sisters, who cowered fearfully upon the ground. The leader signaled his men with a wave, and they floated closer. A rising sense of helplessness filled Darshima as they encroached upon them. He did not know what they intended to do the sick woman, but he imagined the worst. She had been forced to work in the fields with no regard to her condition. Darshima had not seen any other pregnant women since he had been in this world, and he feared what would become of her.

Darshima looked over to the women, his eyes growing damp with tears as he saw them tending to their ill sister. He imagined that they were good people who led humble and honest lives back on Wohiimai. He imagined they belonged to a family who missed them dearly. Here, they had been reduced to slaves and would likely be forced to work until their very last breath.

The soldiers hovered in front of them, the headlights of their craft casting beams of red light upon Darshima and the others. Without warning, they drew long-barreled rifles from their holsters and aimed them squarely at the sisters. A wave of anger coursed through Darshima as he eyed the metal devices, which discharged a painful electromagnetic jolt that could stun a man for days. He couldn't imagine what such a weapon would do to a pregnant woman and her unborn child.

The leader let out a terrifying shout, and Darshima's heart seized in fright as the soldiers fired their rifles. The atmosphere crackled as a searing, white bolt of electricity surged across the field, striking one of the sisters. She let out a blood-curdling scream and slumped forward. Stunned, she drew in several shallow breaths, then collapsed onto the ground.

Eyes widened in terror, Darshima looked upon the soldiers as they pointed their weapons toward the pregnant woman. He leapt to his feet and stood before their vehicles, raising his arms to defend her. Sydarias jumped up from the ground and joined Darshima, a fearful look upon his face as he stared at the soldiers.

"She is sick," shouted Darshima. The leader remained expressionless as he trained his weapon upon her. He motioned to pull the trigger, and Darshima's stomach sank to his knees.

"Leave her be!" he yelled at the top of his lungs.

A sense of rage, like none he had never felt before roiled within him. His pulse raced and he clenched his shaking fists. Time seemed to slow down as he saw the soldiers steady their aim. His eyes locked upon the leader, whose finger slowly depressed the trigger.

Without warning, the ground beneath them shuddered violently. The atmosphere rumbled with a profound, sonorous vibration that sounded like the roar of ten thousand engines. The deafening rumble of stressed metal and breaking glass filled the air. The rows of plants trembled back and forth, the sharp rustling of their leaves rising from the fields. Sydarias and the other captives fell to their knees, covered their heads, and shouted in terror. Others held onto each other and cowered as the soil quaked. Darshima stood firm, unmoved by the temblor.

The soldiers floated aboard their craft, unperturbed as the ground shook beneath them. They seized their triangular steering controls and rose higher into the air. Mouths agape in surprise, they scanned the fields around them, trying to determine the source of the disturbance. The shaking ceased and the cacophony diminished.

In the distance, the low wail of sirens screeched above the receding rumble. Columns of oily black smoke loomed above the horizon, climbing toward the sky. The soldiers hovered in front of Darshima, their intense gazes just visible through their visors. Their leader pointed toward the rising smoke and then barked at his soldiers. They secured their weapons, then flew off in a flurry of dust to investigate the damage. Darshima watched them as they departed.

"Let's get them out of here!" shouted Sydarias. Darshima turned to see him pointing at the captives surrounding them. They ran to the sisters and helped the pregnant woman to her feet. The wounded sister had received a glancing blow but still lay dazed. A pair of women hoisted her up and supported her on their shoulders. They led the sisters to a secluded spot amid the fields that offered some shade. Sydarias started toward Darshima, a look of incredulity upon his face.

"What just happened?" he glared at Darshima, eyes widened in disbelief.

"I don't know." Darshima shook his head in confusion. The ground had never shaken so violently before, and he didn't know what to make of it. He was grateful that they had not been injured.

"At least she's safe," said Darshima.

"She's safe for now." Sydarias knit his brow in a pensive expression.

Darshima cast his eyes downward, a sense of despair filling him as he contemplated Sydarias' words. Safety was not guaranteed in this world. At any moment, their bodies or lives could be taken. He shuddered as he replayed the images of the sisters facing down the soldiers.

"We must get back to work before we are seen again." Sydarias rested his hand upon Darshima's shoulder. They walked down the rutted path toward their row, amid the fallen stalks and crushed fruit.

Chapter Twenty Seven

Darshima lay still amid the darkness, the humid evening air weighing upon him like a shroud. The soft sounds of snoring permeated the tranquil barracks. His gaze lingered upon the corrugated metal ceiling, bathed in faint starlight filtering through the dusty panes of glass. The skin of his back chafed against the thin fiber mattress upon his cot. An open window beside him issued a soft breeze that offered little relief against the stifling heat.

Though the hour was late, exhaustion left his mind numb and sleep eluded him. The days working in the fields had become too numerous to count. The plants had grown taller and now loomed over him. He and the others had spent hours pruning the leaves and pulling weeds in preparation for the next round of harvests. He drew in a deep breath, the sweet aroma of the bulb sap filling his nostrils. After what had been a long and tiring day of cultivating the plants, he had bathed in the communal basin behind the barracks, but the scent still clung to his skin.

Darshima closed his eyes amid his swirling thoughts. Earlier that evening, he and his fellow captives had a rousing conversation after returning from the fields. Over a sparse meal of boiled roots, morels, and leaves, they shared bittersweet memories of their homes and their former lives. Several of them were students at universities in Ardavia and The Vilides. Others were farmers and herdsman on Wohiimai, some were gold miners on Ciblaithia. Naturally, the Vilidesians boasted the most, to the playful derision of the others. They were all children of the realm, and each thought that his or her home was the best.

Others spoke with tears in their eyes as they shared stories and legends about their towns and villages. They spoke of the richness of their culture, the strength and kindness of their people, and the beauty of their lands. To sustain each other, they shared happy memories but kept the sad ones mostly to themselves. They had all survived a scale of devastation and violence that no words could fully describe. In the still of the night, amid the solitude of their thoughts, Darshima and the others quietly grieved for their homelands. They mourned their families, whose fates either remained unknown or had been cruelly sealed.

A stifled cry from one of his fellow captives rose amid the silence. The sound pricked Darshima's ears, sending an anguished shiver through him. He rolled onto his side and tried to ignore the mournful voice. Darshima and the others did their best to comfort each other from the physically demanding work and the emotional toll of their struggle. They shared their meager possessions, scraps of food, and clothing to ease each other's burden. As time stretched on, Darshima tried to maintain a sense of hope, but it was dwindling. Despite the misery surrounding him, he held onto the belief that someday, somehow they would find their way home.

He tossed upon the mattress and tried to chase the heavy thoughts from his mind. The day would soon begin and he needed to rest. The jarring sound of a thud beside his cot awoke him from his daze. A hand firmly clasped his shoulder, and his heart leapt in surprise. He shuddered as a blast of hot, humid breath entered his ear.

"Wake up Darshima, we are getting out of here," whispered the voice, brimming with a clear sense of urgency.

Darshima jolted upright, and his eyes met the intense gaze of Sydarias. The lines of his face were drawn up in a resolute expression. Dressed in the grey trousers and vest of his work uniform, he knelt beside Darshima.

"What do you mean?" Darshima shook his head in disbelief. Sydarias slept upon the cot beside his, and Darshima hadn't noticed him stirring at all during the night.

"Get up, we have to leave now." Sydarias extended his hand.

"If we are caught, they will punish us." Darshima vigorously shook his head.

"We must try, or else we will die here," whispered Sydarias, his voice cracking with desperation.

Darshima's heart bounded fearfully in his chest as he contemplated Sydarias' risky proposal. From the glint in his eye, Darshima knew Sydarias wouldn't change his mind. Darshima gulped nervously as his thoughts raced. He couldn't let Sydarias face this risk alone. He gripped Sydarias' hand and pulled himself up from the mattress. Darshima grabbed his uniform from underneath his cot, put it on, and followed Sydarias through the door.

They emerged into the humid night and moved away from the barracks, the low roofline veiled in shadow. Further ahead, Darshima eyed a group of a dozen young men and women. They skulked quietly through the rows of plants, remaining hidden amid the leaves. The harsh drone of engines rumbled in the distance, punctuating the stillness of the night. Darshima lifted his head toward the sound and spotted several hovering points of white light sweeping the fields. A bolt of fear coursed through him as he recognized the familiar craft.

"There are soldiers are everywhere, we will surely be caught," whispered Darshima, his voice trembling.

"We must follow the group." Sydarias briefly glanced over his shoulder toward Darshima. They approached the other captives, exchanged brief nods of acknowledgment, and crept with them amid the plants.

"How are we going to escape?" asked Darshima as they moved through the shadows between the rows. He drew in a nervous breath as the feelings of doubt rose within him.

"They think there's a way out just beyond the fields." Sydarias pointed in the distance as they trudged over the rutted ground.

"What if we don't make it?" stammered Darshima. Sydarias spun around and faced him, his damp eyes glittering in the starlight.

"Whatever fate awaits us out there is better than what we endure here," sighed Sydarias. His anguished voice rose above the rustling leaves. "We're going to make it, but we must hurry." He hastily wiped his eyes with the back of his hand.

"I believe you." Darshima nodded, a lump forming in his throat. He wanted to trust Sydarias, but he feared this plan. Captives who stoked the ire of the soldiers were routinely beaten or simply disappeared. His pulse quickened as he recalled the sisters from Pelethedral who had been fired upon for merely taking a much needed rest.

Darshima followed Sydarias and the others through the vast, starlit fields, venturing out further than he ever had before. The night air was broken by their muted footfalls over the dirt paths. The fields gave way to tall stands of wild grass and a dense line of looming trees. He shivered as the temperature grew noticeably colder.

Darshima drew a nervous breath and followed Sydarias into the shadowy woods. A thick, tangled mass of underbrush and prickly weeds enveloped them, tearing at their clothes. As they walked deeper into the forest, a cluster of faint lights shimmered through the tree branches.

"Let's walk toward the lights, maybe we can find an escape route," whispered one of the men.

"How do we know that it's safe? It could be another group of soldiers," replied one of the women, her hushed voice filled with worry.

"This is the only path I see," he replied. Several others chimed in, voicing their agreement.

"What if it is a trap?" she asked.

"What other choice do we have?" he blurted desperately. Her bright grey eyes darted between the cluster of strange lights and the group. An anguished frown spread across her lips.

"I cannot do this." She trembled as she backed away from them.

"Please don't go, we must stay together!" He clutched her arm and drew her nearer.

"I cannot take the risk." She wrested her arm from him, then ran from the group.

"Wait!" He desperately called out to her as she sprinted away, her footfalls thudding softly against the soil. He started after her, but several other captives held him back.

"We must continue without her," one of them whispered. His eyes brimming with tears, the man shook his head as the group pulled him back toward them.

Darshima's gaze lingered upon the woman as her form disappeared into the thicket of trees. His stomach sank as the noise faded, the doubts he felt about their plan of escape only growing stronger.

"Maybe she's right, we should turn back." He looked to Sydarias.

"I won't force you to continue. Do as you will, but I must try." Sydarias' eyes pleaded with Darshima, his voice wavering. Wracked with anguish, Darshima's heart rose into in his throat. Despite the unknown danger they faced, he couldn't bring himself to leave Sydarias.

"I'll stay with you." He stepped closer to Sydarias. He shook his head and tried to forget the image of the woman running away.

They crept through the brush beneath the canopy of trees, and to Darshima's surprise, the ground gave way to a metal grating that stretched along the boundary of the forest. The cluster of lights appeared in full view, and the group burst into a sprint, their footsteps thudding against the hard surface. His eyes trained upon the fixed array of light, Darshima ran behind Sydarias until the people ahead of them unexpectedly stopped. He stumbled to a halt and stared at the captives ahead, his pulse racing nervously. A woman and a man stood with their backs to the group and faced the lights.

"Why have we stopped?" asked Sydarias, panting as he tried to catch his breath.

"We cannot continue," she said, frantically waving at the clear space in front of them. "We're surrounded by some sort of clear wall. It's impassable."

"How is that even possible?" Sydarias walked to the front of the group, while Darshima stayed back.

Darshima's eyes widened in incredulity as he looked around him. The night sky appeared distorted, and the points of light appeared in repeating patterns. What he had once thought was a sky full of stars was an image refracted in triplicate. It was as if he were staring through a prism. Darshima walked forward and joined the crowd before the wall. He hesitantly stuck his hand out in front of him, striking it against the cold, hard surface. Heart pounding anxiously, he put both hands up to the clear barrier and examined it. They indeed were trapped behind a wall of smooth glass. Darshima looked to his left and right, and craned his neck up, gazing in disbelief at the warped starlight all around him. Sydarias stood beside Darshima and inspected the wall with his hands.

"We've been trapped like caged animals," exclaimed Darshima, his voice brimming with anger.

"We mustn't waste time, let's look for an opening," whispered Sydarias.

"We don't even know what is out there," said Darshima, pointing toward the darkness.

"We've made it this far. We must find out." Sydarias ran his hands along the dimly lit glass, feeling for any nuance in the smooth surface. He stepped away from Darshima and pushed against the barrier.

"I think I found a door," Sydarias excitedly waved for the others to join him. Several captives hurried over and helped him pry it open.

"What happens if we're captured?" whispered Darshima.

"I don't know, but we must try," Sydarias grunted as he pressed his shoulder against the wall. With a great big heave, he and the other captives pushed the door, and it opened with a low groan. A stiff gale of cold, damp wind rushed past them, and they scrambled through the entrance.

Darshima hesitantly stepped beyond the glass and joined them. The air was thick with a fine mist that soaked through his clothes. He inhaled the cold atmosphere, the pungent odor of engine exhaust and volatile chemicals filling his lungs. He stepped away from the door, his boots clicking against a hard, metallic surface that glistened in the dim light. The terrain sloped downward toward a perimeter flanked by a low retaining wall that seemed to stretch for as far as he could see.

Darshima looked up at the night sky, awash in complex and unfamiliar constellations, the intense points of starlight burning through the mists. His mind raced as he thought of the interminable days before this moment. He had not seen much starlight since coming to this world, and realized that the glass enclosing them must have somehow diminished it.

He turned his gaze toward the horizon to see the same peculiar cluster of bright lights, now undistorted in the open air.

He burst into a sprint toward the wall behind Sydarias and the others, their feet slipping upon the smooth, wet ground. Darshima was mere steps away, when the group of captives came to an abrupt halt. He lurched to a stop, nearly crashing into Sydarias who froze a few paces ahead of him. Darshima pushed desperately past, his heart thudding as he eyed the barrier that seemingly separated them from freedom. He lunged at the wall but multiple pairs of hands grabbed him by the arms and waist, holding him back.

"Don't go!" shouted several of the captives. Darshima struggled against them, but he could not move. He let out a haggard sigh and relented. He desperately wanted to leave behind the wretched fields and reclaim some shred of his former life.

"The wall is impassable. You must be careful!" whispered one of the captives, as they let him go.

Darshima stepped toward the edge of the wall and hesitantly looked ahead. At first, he thought his eyes were deceiving him. He frantically rubbed them, but the vista remained unchanged. There was no land beyond the wall. He peered down through the mists and saw turbulent whirlpools and eddies churning upon the surface of the dark expanse of water below. Off to the side, he spied an immense shadow looming upon the turbulent waves, forming a fixed black circle upon the starlit surface of the ocean. Further afield, he spotted the peculiar clusters of light that had led them to this place. They appeared as giant, glowing glass ampules floating above the sparse clouds, casting vast circular shadows upon the water. Through their thick, lighted domes, he could just make out dense canopies of trees.

The group stood beside Darshima and looked out in incredulity upon the peculiar vista. His thoughts raced as he realized they were not in fact on any sort of land as he had previously thought. They appeared to be upon one of many vast, floating vessels, hanging motionlessly above an ocean. He shook his head, then turned to the captives beside him. His eyes met their stunned expressions, and he recognized their disbelief, mirrored in his own.

"How are we going to escape?" he asked aloud. He was met by silence and fearful stares. There would be no easy way to flee. They were far too high to jump into the treacherous ocean. Even if they made it to the water's surface alive, there was no land in sight where they might take refuge.

The rising wail of an alarm abruptly pierced the steady rush of wind. A flood of stark white light from somewhere high above illuminated the ground, casting Darshima and the other captives in a spectral glow. They spun around and looked toward the door behind them, a mixture of fear and terror upon their faces. They had been caught. Darshima's stomach sank to his knees as an acute sense of fear seized him.

The captives disbanded and scattered off in multiple directions. Sydarias grabbed Darshima by the arm and they ran, trailing a small group of five men along the edge of the wall. Darshima pushed himself to keep up with Sydarias, his feet slipping upon the wet ground.

Darshima sprinted along the wall, the path ahead obscured by the enveloping mists. His lungs filled with the acrid air and burned with fatigue. He ran even harder, trying to maintain his balance upon the sloping surface. Over the stiff gusts of wind, the angry shouts of the soldiers reached Darshima's ears, sending a chill down his spine. He glanced over his shoulder and met the gaze of a team rapidly advancing upon him.

"They're right behind us!" he shouted. Darshima ran as fast as his legs would carry him, the blood surging through his arteries.

He charged down a straightaway when a pair of soldiers suddenly burst out of the darkness and tackled him, seizing him tightly around his waist. His heart pounded in fright and his feet slipped out from underneath him. Limbs swinging, he struggled to free himself, but the soldiers were much stronger than him. Darshima let out a shout as the men slammed him against the ground. His body aching, they wrenched his arms behind his back and pressed his face against the cold, wet surface. He felt a hand grip his hair and forcefully yank his head upward. He shuddered as his ears filled with the angry, guttural shouts of the soldiers. Darshima gritted his teeth as a searing jolt of pain coursed down his neck.

Darshima's pulse raced in terror as he realized that he had been caught. The soldiers shackled his wrists and ankles, and he stifled his shouts as the cold metal dug sharply into his skin. The soldiers forced him to his feet and propped him up by the arms. They pushed him forward, and he struggled to move under the weight of the chains. Darshima looked around, his heart numb with despair as he saw that the other men and women had also been captured.

The soldiers maneuvered him into a line with the other captives and made them face the wall. Darshima stood frozen in fear, his eyes sweeping over the vast ocean, churning violently beyond the perimeter. The sky opened and a torrent of rain fell, thoroughly drenching him. The wind whipped through the night air and Darshima stole a glimpse at the others. The stark floodlights illuminated the hopelessness and misery etched upon their gaunt faces. A tide of despair overwhelmed him as he contemplated the dreadful fate that awaited them all.

The soldiers stood at attention beside the captives, listening intently to the words of their leader standing before them. A tall and brawny man, his ruddy features and square jaw were contorted into a restrained frown. He wore a long grey overcoat, black brimmed hat, grey trousers, and knee-high leather boots. The leader pulled his gaze from the soldiers, then slowly filed past the captured men and women. Crimson eyes glinting, he looked at each of them and muttered a string of words. He shook a gloved fist and then spat at the ground before them. Darshima clenched his jaw and his pulsed quickened at the man's sudden, terrifying gesture.

He turned to his soldiers and spoke forcefully, in what sounded to Darshima like a string of commands, but they stood still. The leader marched toward them, the puddles of water splashing around his boots. He stopped in front of the two soldiers restraining Sydarias and loomed over them, his nostrils flaring. The leader grabbed the soldiers by the collars of their grey fatigues and pulled them closer. He muttered the same string of commands at them, their crimson eyes widening in fear. The leader let them go, and marched back to his position. He folded his arms across his chest and tapped his boot against the metal ground, the sharp click piercing through the thrum of the rain.

The soldiers exchanged a resolute nod, then dragged Sydarias toward the wall, his chains scraping loudly against the ground. Darshima looked on helplessly as they pulled Sydarias closer to the edge.

"What are you doing?" yelled Darshima, his voice lost amid the howling winds. A deep sense of dread came over him as he realized what was happening. A flood of emotions stirred within him as his memories of Sydarias rushed forth. Images of that day, when they first met in Ardavia aboard the ship flashed before his eyes. Darshima's mind reeled through the moments they had shared, from their first week together in The Vilides, to the harrowing nightmare of their capture during the capital's invasion, and now the unending horror of their enslavement in this foreign world. He clenched his jaw and stifled a sob amid the driving rain as he beheld Sydarias, cornered, and bound in chains. Weak with fear, Darshima felt his knees buckle. The soldiers beside him yanked his shackles and dragged him back up to his feet.

The soldiers forced Sydarias to stand with his back against the wall. His chains rattling, he cowered before them in fright. He trembled as the winds tore through his soaked, tattered uniform. One soldier grabbed him under the arms, and the other grabbed his legs, hoisting him onto their shoulders as if he were a mere piece of furniture. The misty skies darkened, and the torrents of rain fell harder. Brilliant veins of lightning darted across the night sky in vivid flashes of blue and white. The subsequent peals of thunder shook Darshima to his core. Through the bursts of light, Darshima glimpsed the haggard, distant stare on Sydarias' face. His drenched clothes hung from his gaunt frame, his matted hair clung to his forehead, and rivulets of water poured down his cheeks.

Sydarias' eyes caught Darshima's for an instant, and they shared a solemn gaze. Sydarias closed his eyes tightly, clenched his jaw, and awaited his fate. Darshima's heart froze. He held his breath and felt a cold numbness flow through him. In one swift motion, the soldiers heaved Sydarias' shackled body over the wall toward the churning sea far below.

"No!" shouted Darshima. A deafening cry erupted from deep within his spirit, hidden in a place unknown to him. The weakness that encumbered him abruptly vanished. He felt an intensely powerful jolt of energy surge within every fiber of his being. It seemed as if the lightning above were flowing directly through him. His mind shifted into a singular state of focus as he saw Sydarias' body move upward in a long arc over the wall. Darshima forcefully yanked his arms from behind his back. He heard the sharp, metallic snap of the chains binding his hands, followed by the sudden cries of the soldiers restraining him.

The broken chains hanging at his wrists, he desperately reached toward Sydarias. His heart thudded as the unfamiliar, overwhelming sense of power flowed through him. He caught a glimpse of the soldiers standing at the wall, and they looked upon him, their mouths agape in fear. As they threw their hands up to shield their faces, they were knocked forcefully to the ground by a powerful gale.

Sydarias' body reached the top of its trajectory and fell downward just beyond the edge of the wall. Darshima, arms outstretched, looked on helplessly. The energy surging within him grew more intense. His heart pounded so forcefully that he felt as if it would leap out of his chest. He fixed his gaze upon Sydarias, and his skin tingled with a sharp and unusual sensation of electricity.

To Darshima's complete and utter disbelief, Sydarias stopped falling. His body came to a halt in mid-air, its silhouette illuminated by brilliant bolts of lightning that seemed to flash all around him. Sydarias hung motionlessly for several seconds, then drifted back upward over the wall in a broad arc. He floated over the heads of the soldiers and the captives, toward Darshima. Sydarias briefly lingered in the air, then tumbled at Darshima's feet with a clatter as his shackles struck the ground.

Darshima's chains rustled as he knelt down and reached for Sydarias.

"Have I died?" Sydarias stared at Darshima, his eyes wide with terror.

"You are alive, Sydarias." Darshima desperately wrapped him in an embrace, trying to protect him.

"But...how?" he stammered.

Darshima could not comprehend what had just happened, but he knew it was nothing short of a miracle. He could feel his strength fading and his grip on Sydarias slipping. Before Darshima could say anything more, he collapsed to the ground and his vision blurred. The sharp thud of pounding footsteps and the shouts of the soldiers filled his ears as he fell into a stupor.

Chapter Twenty Eight

Darshima marched slowly through the fields in a line with the other captives. The triplet image of the sun radiated its piercing beams down upon him. The stifling air was rank with the pungent aroma of damp soil and decaying vegetation. Rivulets of sweat poured down his neck and bare chest. With his hands bound in front of him and his feet shackled, he struggled to move against the manacles. Sydarias marched ahead of him, and Darshima felt the tug of the dull metal links at his waist as they moved in tandem. He eyed the dark brown skin of Sydarias' sinewy back as it glistened under the sun, his muscles rippling as he bore the weight of his chains.

After their failed escape attempt, the soldiers brought them back inside the colony and detained them in one of the surveillance towers beyond the fields. They had been stripped to their undergarments, placed in shackles, and sequestered in dark and musty cells. They had received neither food nor water. At dawn, they were forced out of the cells, chained together in a line, and made to march. Dozens of soldiers dressed in green fatigues walked beside them, monitoring their every move.

Darshima's heart rose with a sense of relief as he looked upon Sydarias. His memory of what happened the night before was hazy and dreamlike, but he knew that he had almost lost Sydarias forever. He shivered as the memories of the unbelievable energy surging through him flashed before his eyes. His mind replayed the soldiers throwing Sydarias over the barrier and into the ocean. He couldn't understand how Sydarias had managed to survive.

Darshima didn't know what this strange power was or what it meant. He wasn't even sure how such a force could channel itself through him, or through anyone for that matter. Nonetheless, he sensed that it was the reason that Sydarias was still alive. Darshima eyed the cylindrical restraints upon his wrists and attempted to pull them apart. He let out a grunt as he struggled against them, trying to summon the same peculiar energy that he felt the previous night. Despite his attempt, the metal cuffs refused to budge. His frustration growing, he relented and let his hands go limp. He shook his head as he trudged onward, trying to rid himself of the unusual thoughts circling through his mind. Sydarias was alive, and that was the only thing that mattered to him.

Darshima marched in the middle of the single-file line, his chains rattling in rhythm with the other captives. He looked around, unsure where they were being led. He clenched his jaw as the growing fear gnawed at him. Out of the corner of his eye, he saw the other captives hard at work, tending to the rows of plants. Some glimpsed furtively over their shoulders as the line passed, offering a solemn nod in solidarity. Others kept their backs to them and toiled feverishly, trying to avoid the ire of the soldiers.

Darshima trudged through the dirt rows, the shackles at his feet growing heavier with each step. His parched throat aching, he drew in a deep breath of the stifling air. Despite the physical torment of the march, Darshima felt different. He didn't know what it was, but something had changed within him. In times past, the fatigue would have been too much to bear. Despite everything that had happened to him, today he somehow felt stronger.

The chain of captives wended their way through the fields until they reached a clearing with a low metal platform. A small crowd of slaves with shackles upon their wrists and ankles, gathered around the platform to witness the spectacle. Low murmurs rose from the group as they beheld Darshima and the others, their drawn faces bearing expressions of both fear and resignation.

The soldiers led Darshima and the other captives up onto the stage, where they arranged them in a line facing the crowd. Darshima felt a pair of hands unshackle him from the rest of the group and restrain him tightly so that he could not move. A deep voice permeated the din of the crowd. Darshima turned toward the voice, his chest tightening anxiously as he recognized the face of the leader who captured them the previous night.

Dressed in stiff grey fatigues and black boots, the leader stood before the line of young men and women, and folded his arms behind his back. He leered at them from under the brim of his black hat. Beads of perspiration shimmered on the ruddy pink skin of his cheeks, and his crimson eyes glistened with a veiled hint of disdain. He turned away from the captives and then marched toward a group of soldiers, who stood at the edge of the platform. In a low voice, he issued orders to them, his forceful gesticulations telegraphing calculated anger. He then stepped off the stage, crossed his arms against his chest, and glared at them.

Darshima's pulse raced as he watched the interaction between the leader and his soldiers. He didn't know what was happening to them. The sound of boots clicking against metal pricked his ears. Darshima looked on as a pair of soldiers dragged a captive from the end of the line, and led him toward the front of the stage. He was young, barely an adult, and he had the bronze skin, black unshorn hair, and amber eyes of a Gordanellan. The soldiers stepped away from the young man and stood off to the side of the stage. The chained captive cowered in front of the crowd, his thin frame shuddering spasmodically as he stifled his sobs.

Another pair of soldiers stepped directly behind the captive and stood in tense silence. The leader made a gesture with his hand and they retrieved long, thin whips of braided silver fastened to their belts. The soldier on the left nodded to his partner on the right, and with an exaggerated arcing motion, they simultaneously lashed the young man's back.

They struck him mercilessly, and he let out a chilling cry that pierced right through Darshima. The flesh of his shoulders flayed open with each blow. Rivulets of blood ran down the small of his back and stained the fabric of his pants. Darshima shivered with fright. He wanted to close his eyes, but the horror of the event paralyzed him. His pulse bounded in his temples and he felt faint as he witnessed the brutal act. After ten blows, the young man collapsed into a bloody heap upon the stage. The soldiers dragged his limp, moaning body off into the field. Mouths agape, the shackled spectators stared ahead in muted terror at the harrowing scene unfolding before them.

A young Ciblaithian woman was subsequently dragged to the front of the stage. She struggled against the soldiers, but they soon overpowered her. They forcefully tore open her robe and exposed her back, its smooth, deep-brown skin glistening in the stark sunlight. Her long black braids hung before her expressionless, oval face. Drawing their whips, the soldiers flailed her without delay. Tears streamed from her bright grey eyes as she endured the lashes. Her screams pierced the air, visibly shaking the spectators. She withstood fifteen lashes before succumbing to the trauma and then collapsing. The soldiers ushered more of the captives to the stage, meting out their cruel punishment, then dragging their bloodied, bruised bodies off the stage.

Darshima felt the soldiers push him toward the middle of the platform. He stole a glance to his side and saw Sydarias, who stared numbly ahead, his eyes glittering with tears. Sydarias peered at Darshima, slowly shaking his head as a resigned frown crossed his lips. Darshima's nostrils flared, and his chest heaved as he breathed in the humid air, thick with the stench of blood and sweat.

Darshima stood at the center of the stage, in front of the other captives. The soldiers' footsteps echoed in his ears as they walked away. His heart thudding uncontrollably, Darshima set his jaw and stood still. He stared at the hushed crowd and heard the rhythmic footfalls of the second pair of soldiers moving behind him. He listened as they reached for their belts and shivered as he heard the sharp click of the slack whiptails hitting the platform. His muscles tensed in dreaded anticipation of the first strike.

The explosive crack of an object moving through the air at high speed stunned his eardrums. The sharp sting of the whiptail jolted him as it sliced open the bare skin of his back. A burst of vivid color momentarily blurred his vision. Darshima opened his mouth to scream, but no sound came forth. Overwhelmed by the searing pain, he winced and drew in a halting breath. A sharp crack, and then another sting of pain flooded his senses. His remaining strength soon withered under the lashings. He gritted his teeth in agony and stifled the guttural shouts rising from his chest. He locked his knees and stiffened the muscles of his legs, willing himself to stand. Without warning, a flurry of forceful lashes pelted his shoulders. He closed his eyes as the pain seemingly coursed through every fiber within him.

Darshima's heart thudded in his chest, and he panted as he felt the warm trickle of blood stream down the small of his back. The weakness overwhelmed him, and his vision dimmed. His legs burned with fatigue, and he fell to his knees. A sharp bolt of pain coursed up his thighs as he struck the platform. His back felt as if it were aflame.

The leader barked a command, and the lashings stopped. Darshima felt the grip of the soldiers upon his arms as they tried to pull him up, but he pushed them away and rose to his feet under his own strength. The soldiers then grabbed him forcefully by his chains and dragged him off the stage. Darshima limped as they led him away, the muscles of his back seizing as he tried to suppress the unbearable pain.

With what energy he could summon, he looked back over his shoulder at Sydarias, who was being pushed toward the center of the stage. Darshima caught his gaze and offered a weak nod.

Sydarias stared at him, his lips parted in awe. He turned away from Darshima and faced the crowd, a look of smoldering defiance glinting in his eyes. His chest heaving, he drew in a deep breath and awaited his punishment.

Chapter Twenty Nine

Metal trowel in hand, Darshima knelt upon the soft soil. The leaves of the surrounding plants offered scant shade against the refracted sun, its intense rays beaming in triplicate upon the raw skin of his back. He adjusted the fabric satchel resting upon his hip, the heavy crystals inside rustling with every motion. He sidled up to one of the plants and plunged the trowel tip into the damp soil. He dug a small circular trench around the woody, green trunk until the topmost roots were just visible, coursing a sinuous, white web through the dirt. He then reached into the sack and grabbed a handful of the clear crystals, sprinkling them in a circular motion around the plant. His eyes lingered upon the cascade of gleaming gems as they spilled from his palm and into the trench, their facets catching the light as they tumbled into the dark soil.

With both hands, Darshima gently buried the crystals with a mound of dirt and then moved along the row. He winced in pain as he crawled upon the soil, the skin of his back still tender from the lashings. He drew in a breath of humid air, then settled before another large plant. Darshima paused for a moment and looked behind him, catching a glimpse of Sydarias. Also upon his hands and knees, Sydarias performed the same tedious task upon the adjacent row of plants.

Darshima and the other captives had been in the fields since dawn, tending to the plants and preparing the depleted soils with the mineral crystals. From what little Vilidesian the farmers spoke, they instructed Darshima and the other captives how to sow these crystals. The plants needed the nutrients to bear fruit during the next round of harvests.

Darshima clambered along the row and repeated the painstaking chore, plant by plant. His mind drifted as he dug through the soil. He had counted twelve days since their escape attempt. After their punishment, he and the others were thrown back into the cells for the night, then marched back into the fields the following morning to perform this onerous work. As time dragged on, the physical pain lessened, but a gnawing sense of despair settled in the pit of his stomach. The escape attempt had nearly cost them their lives and put their desperate situation in stark relief. He was one of many people imprisoned upon a floating colony above a roiling ocean, far from home.

As his fingers kneaded the soil, Darshima's mind sifted through memories of that harrowing night. His hands abruptly froze as the image of Sydarias tumbling toward the ocean came back to him. His recollection of the following moments was hazy, but he remembered Sydarias miraculously floating back upward over the ledge and landing at his feet. He couldn't understand how it had happened, but he knew it had something to do with the burst of unnatural energy that coursed through him.

His heart pounding, Darshima blinked his eyes and tried to forget the terrifying image. None of it made sense, but as he thought of this seemingly impossible event, his despair somehow lessened. His mind sifted through the details of that night, trying to conceive of an explanation for what had happened, but he was left feeling more confused. His hands trembling, he shook his head, looked at the plant before him, and dug faster.

The ache in his back growing worse, Darshima pushed himself up to his knees. He wiped his sweaty brow with the back of his hand, then stretched his tense muscles. He took a breath, then hunched back down. As he started to dig a trench around another plant, he heard the clink of metal and a grunt of impatience. He looked over to see Sydarias jab at the soil, then toss his trowel aside.

"What happened?" Darshima's eyes drifted toward the cluster of plants beside Sydarias.

"I keep hitting the irrigation pipes, the soil is too shallow here." He pointed at the ground and let out an angry sigh. Darshima moved next to him and stared at the gleaming silver conduits coursing amid the roots, beads of cold condensation shimmering upon their cylindrical surfaces.

"Do your best and move onto the next plant before they see us." As Darshima turned back to his row, he glimpsed an anguished frown spread upon Sydarias' face. Drenched in sweat and covered in grime, Sydarias folded his arms across his bare chest and shot a hostile glare at the plants and the surrounding soil.

"What does it matter if I continue or not? We are going to spend the rest of our lives in these fields as slaves." He looked up desperately the sky, his eyes filling with tears.

"We must have hope. We won't survive any other way." Darshima's heart rose into his throat as he looked at Sydarias, overcome with despair.

"We will die amid these plants, and it will go completely unnoticed." Sydarias' shoulders slumped, and he sank back upon the ground. Darshima stared at him, unsure what to say. He was also struggling with their circumstance, but a small part of him refused to accept this horrible colony as their final resting place. Darshima couldn't explain why, but he felt that they would somehow find their way home. Sydarias' attempt at escape had been too soon, and he had sensed it all along.

"I'm here beside you, suffering with you." Darshima set his tool aside. He then crawled next to Sydarias and picked up his trowel.

"These people have stolen us from our homelands, but we cannot let them destroy us. We must continue." He handed the trowel over to Sydarias, but he refused to take it.

"Why should we continue and labor for these people? I would have been better off dying when they threw me off the ledge." Sydarias threw up his hands in exasperation.

"But you are here, living and breathing." Darshima rested the trowel upon the soil. Sydarias tore his eyes from the sky and shot a piercing stare at Darshima, his frown dissolving into a contemplative expression.

"My memory is hazy from that night. I should have died, but for some reason, I survived. I don't understand." Sydarias cast his gaze upon the soil, then toward Darshima, his brow furrowed in a look of confusion.

"I don't understand either," whispered Darshima, his heart beating nervously. He looked in Sydarias' eyes for some hint of recognition about what happened that night, but he saw none.

"We have managed to survive despite all of this misery, so we must continue. We owe it to those who have died." Darshima held Sydarias' gaze.

"Neither our lives nor theirs even matter to these people. Hopefully, the dead have found more peace than we have." Sydarias' eyes narrowed in a mournful stare.

"A death here would not bring our souls any peace, but just a different type of misery." Darshima's eyes grew damp as he looked between the stalks at the other captives, hunched over and laboring. He imagined those who had died here continued their toil in the afterlife.

"We cannot do much, but each breath must be our act of defiance," said Darshima. Sydarias bowed his head, briefly closing his eyes as he contemplated Darshima's words.

Darshima moved closer to him. "They cannot make us forget our history or our heritage. They have taken almost everything from us, but they cannot take who we are."

"I hope you're right." Sydarias' head hung solemnly.

"The Vilidesians haven't forgotten us. We must have hope that our realm will rescue us someday." Darshima put an arm around Sydarias and drew him closer.

"Please don't let me die here, Darshima." Sydarias stifled a sob and rested his head upon Darshima's shoulder.

"This place will not be our end. We must pray for deliverance from this misery." Darshima held Sydarias as he shuddered.

He reached over, grabbed Sydarias' trowel, and handed it to him.

"We must get back to work before they see us." Darshima gestured beyond the surrounding plants, toward the watchtowers in the distance. Sydarias sat up, cleared his throat, and dried his eyes with a muddy hand.

"I have nothing left to give but my faith. I believe you, Darshima." He grasped the tool, his eyes softening in an earnest look. Darshima nodded firmly, turned back to his row of plants, and grabbed his trowel. He scooped up a shovelful of dirt and dug around the next plant, filling the circular trench with a handful of gleaming crystals.

Chapter Thirty

Darshima leaned against the doorframe and stared at the setting sun, wincing at the smoldering ache in his back. The pain had mostly subsided, but it still lingered. He had lost track of how much time had passed since their attempted escape and subsequent punishment, but recalled seeing more than fifty sunsets. He shifted his weight from side to side and gazed toward the horizon. His eyes warily traced the soldiers upon their craft as they zipped over the fields, trails of dust billowing behind them. Earlier that evening, he had finished a simple supper of boiled roots with Sydarias and the others in the humid barracks. Needing a respite from the heat, he stepped out onto the porch.

Over supper, Darshima and the other captives comforted each other and for a moment, tried to forget their suffering amid the fields. They were all children of the realm and missed home deeply. Many spoke with tears in their eyes about their towns and villages among the moons. They feared that everything had been destroyed by the invasion, and that they would never see home again.

He listened to their vivid accounts of roving armies and piles of bodies in the streets. They spoke of dark ships raining fire from the skies and cities bombarded to oblivion. Their stories overwhelmed him. The belief that he would one day return to Gordanelle was the only thing that gave him strength. He couldn't bear to imagine that his home lay in ruins, but he feared that it had shared the same dismal fate as so many other places.

Darshima stood amid the steady breeze, the humid air offering little comfort. The triplet of white suns hung just above the horizon, marking the end of another day since he had been torn away from home. The weeks and months blended together as the drudgery of cultivating the plants wore at him. Like so many days before, the work began at dawn and finished at dusk. At times, he found himself struggling to remember what life was like before he was captured.

The vast fields spread out before him in all directions. His gaze lingered over the tall plants as they swayed rhythmically in the winds, their branches laden with the spherical bulbs, ready for the next harvest. He and the others had worked hard to prepare the plants for what would be several days of backbreaking work, collecting and hauling the produce. It seemed as if only yesterday that those fields were empty, and now they were brimming with life. Like the other captives, Darshima had expended his last quantum of effort, turning the damp soil, sowing the seeds, pruning the plants, pulling the weeds, and harvesting the fruit. A sigh escaped his lips, and his chest grew numb with sorrow. He imagined repeating these exhausting tasks over and over until he drew his last breath.

The trio of burning disks slipped beneath the horizon, and darkness encroached. The distant click of gears grinding, and the low hum of machines rose above the wind. As his ears filled with the familiar, droning sound, an unexpected smile crossed his lips. He listened to the discordant symphony, and let out a sigh. The jarring notes almost reminded him of the night creatures that flitted about on diaphanous wings, hovering around his mother's garden back in Ardavia. Darshima closed his eyes and let the sound envelop him, the memory of home offering a brief respite from his day of toil in the fields.

The hushed sound of footsteps, followed by the snap of a twig broke through the din. Startled, Darshima opened his eyes and looked around, the empty fields greeting his weary gaze. A gentle rustling, like the sound of wings in flight, filled his ears and a brilliant burst of light caught the corner of his eye. His heart thudding in surprise, he turned his head toward the fading glow but saw nothing. A tingling sensation ran through him, and the fine hairs upon the nape of his neck stood on end. He rubbed the back of his arms as a cold shiver ran through him. For an instant, he forgot the oppressive heat enveloping him. His eyes darted all around, searching for the source of the light, but he saw nothing.

"I must be seeing things." He shook his head, rubbed his eyes, and let himself slip back into the din.

The soft drone began to lull him into another daydream, when the plodding sound of footsteps from behind startled him. As he opened his eyes, Darshima felt a hand upon his shoulder and turned around to see Sydarias.

"How are you, Darshima? You left so soon." Sydarias' eyebrows wrinkled in concern.

"I'm just tired, that's all." Darshima's shoulders slumped wearily.

"Do you mind if I join you?" Sydarias yawned, stretching his arms over his head.

"I'd like that," said Darshima.

"Let's sit in the shade." Sydarias pointed toward a nearby tree, and they stepped off the porch. They walked along the rutted path, clumps of dirt clinging to the hems of their trousers

Darshima sat down beside Sydarias upon a patch of cool grass beneath the drooping, leafy boughs. They stared out pensively at the fields, the soft drone filling the silence between them. Darshima swept a hand through his wavy hair, which now hung just above his shoulders. He faced the ground, plucked a blade of grass, and twisted it between his fingers.

"I don't know how much more of this I can bear. Every day brings the same misery." Darshima threw the grass aside and let out an anguished sigh. Sydarias' eyes narrowed in worry as he saw the change in Darshima's countenance.

"You told me to remain hopeful, and we must. We will make it home someday." Sydarias leaned over and clasped Darshima's shoulder, his voice wavering. "I cannot do this alone. I must be strong for you, and you for me."

"Forgive me, but it's been a difficult few days." Darshima lifted his head and looked at Sydarias with an earnest gaze. Though Darshima sensed Sydarias' doubt, his words meant a lot to him. They needed each other if they had any hope of surviving.

They sat together amid the fading light, when Sydarias turned to Darshima.

"You know, I never would have guessed that you were so strong." Sydarias' gaze lingered upon the ground and he ran his hands through the carpet of grass. A contemplative frown crept across his lips.

"What do you mean?" Darshima looked at him with a puzzled expression.

"You were able to withstand all of those lashings during our punishment." Sydarias' eyes widened in astonishment.

"What are you talking about?" grumbled Darshima, his tone harsher than he intended. "I suffered just like everyone else."

"You received twice as many lashes as the rest of us, and you didn't even pass out. You were the only one to stand up and walk away afterward. Your scars have almost healed." Sydarias ran an appraising hand along Darshima's back, his skin tingling under Sydarias' fingertips.

"It doesn't matter, it still hurts." Darshima looked upon the fields, the shadows of the plants growing longer.

"I only received a few, but I'm still healing." Sydarias swept aside his curly locks, which had grown just past his shoulders, and pointed to a pair of linear scars upon the smooth dark skin of his shoulders. Darshima rested his hand on Sydarias' back. He shuddered as his fingers ran over the thin, uneven mounds of flesh, the memory of that day flooding his mind.

"Darshima, I wanted to talk to you about the night that we tried to escape." Sydarias faced him.

"What's the point?" Darshima's pulse thudded nervously.

"At first I didn't remember anything, but it all finally came back to me. You saved my life." His eyes flickered with an intensity that caught Darshima by surprise.

Darshima turned away and avoided his gaze, reluctant to think about that night. He trembled as memories of Sydarias being pitched over the ledge resurfaced. His chest tightened with a sense of both incredulity and fear as he recalled the intense surge of power that flowed through him. Every part of him wanted to deny it, but he knew that the burst of energy came from within him.

"Don't you remember what happened?" Sydarias grasped Darshima's shoulder.

"It doesn't matter Sydarias, nothing has changed. We are still here." Darshima folded his arms across his chest.

"I want to tell you what I saw." As Sydarias drew in a breath to gather his thoughts, Darshima pulled away from Sydarias' grip, and scooted away upon the grass.

"Please, I don't want to relive it..." Darshima started to stand up, but Sydarias grabbed his wrist and drew him closer.

"I remember looking at you as the soldiers threw me over the wall. There was a brilliant aura of light enveloping you. I heard you shout. I saw you break the chains around your wrists. You pushed away the soldiers restraining you, and they hit the ground hard." Sydarias waved his hands excitedly as he spoke.

"I don't know what you mean." Darshima turned away as Sydarias continued.

"You stretched your hands out toward me. There was a flash of lightning, then a gust of wind. When they tossed me, I felt myself flying upwards, slowing to a stop and then tumbling toward the water. All of a sudden, I felt an overwhelming force lift me, and then

I stopped falling." Sydarias' eyes glittered with tears. "I floated back over the ledge and landed at your feet." An expression of disbelief spreading upon his face, he shook his head slowly. "I should have died, but you saved my life."

"It must have been something else. The wind was so strong, and the lightning cast a strange glow over everything that night," said Darshima, gaining a shaky confidence in his reasoning as he spoke.

"I have no doubt that you saved me." Sydarias shook his head, displeased with Darshima's explanation.

"I don't want to hear anymore," said Darshima, his voice wavering with exhaustion. "You're still alive. That's all the matters." He rested his hand upon Sydarias' arm.

They fell into silence as the last rays of daylight faded. Darshima mulled over Sydarias' account of that evening. Everything about the events of that fateful night defied any sense of rationality. He didn't know what force within him could have possibly saved Sydarias from certain death, but somehow it had happened. Sydarias would not accept any other explanation, and nor could he.

"Let's go inside and get some rest. A new day awaits and we will need all of our strength." Sydarias tapped Darshima's shoulder, and they rose from the ground and dusted themselves off.

They trudged back to the barracks under the warped points of starlight. Sydarias put his arm around Darshima's shoulder and drew him closer. Darshima briefly lifted his head and offered him a weary smile. Darshima's eyes lingered upon the ground as they walked along the muddy trail. Like Sydarias, he somehow needed to find the strength to continue. They owed this much to each other. Darshima followed Sydarias onto the porch and across the threshold of the humid building. Fatigued from another day's toil, they settled upon their cots and drifted off to sleep.

Chapter Thirty One

Darshima laid upon the stiff sheets, dwelling amid the languid fog of his thoughts. No matter how hard he tried, sleep came in fits and starts. The soft snoring of dozens of men and women around him filled his ears. The sharp sound of a creaking door broke through the murmurs, and he stirred in his cot. His eyes fluttered open to see a thin blade of light piercing through the gap. He drowsily shook his head at the disturbance and blamed it on a gust of wind.

Darshima turned upon his side and clutched his pillow, burying his forehead in its threadbare fabric. A pleasant, almost floral fragrance wafted through the room. His nose wrinkled as he breathed it in, but before he could identify it, the scent disappeared. As he drifted off again, he felt a hand gently shake his shoulder.

"Darshima, you must wake up," whispered an unfamiliar voice. Its deep resonance roused him from his stupor. Darshima cast the pillow aside and let out a groggy sigh. His eyes fluttered open, and a pair of vivid, glowing sapphire eyes greeted him. Startled, Darshima sat straight up and looked around the room. His pulse raced in fright as he stared at the figure kneeling before him, veiled in shadow. The voice and the eyes belonged to a man whom Darshima had never met.

"Who are you?" Terrified, Darshima pulled his shoulder away from the stranger. He moved to the edge of the cot and reflexively clenched his fists.

"Please do not fear me, I am here to save you," he whispered in an almost impeccable Vilidesian accent.

"I don't understand." Darshima's chest tightened as a wave of anxiety came over him.

"I promise to explain everything, but you must come with me." He leaned forward, his voice heavy with a sense of urgency.

"Where are you taking me?" Darshima sat still, too afraid to move.

"I am taking you back home, but we must leave now." The stranger stood up and gently tugged at Darshima's arm.

"But how? Why have you come here?" Darshima peered at him through the darkness, trembling in disbelief as he registered the man's words.

"You are the reason I am here," said the stranger.

"This must be some sort of dream." Darshima vigorously shook his head, trying to rid himself of the last traces of sleep.

"This is no dream. Please come with me, we are running out of time." The stranger pulled his arm again. Dressed in only his underclothes, Darshima rose from the cot and hastily put on his uniform. He then moved toward Sydarias to wake him.

"Where are you going?" whispered the stranger.

"I must wake my friend." Darshima approached Sydarias' cot.

"Darshima, we have no time." The stranger followed him.

"I cannot leave without him. We have traveled very far together." Darshima turned around and faced the stranger.

"Bring him if you must, but we have to hurry." The stranger let out a sigh and walked toward the door, the inky shadows obscuring his identity.

Feeling the stranger's intense gaze upon him, Darshima knelt beside Sydarias.

"Wake up, we are leaving." Darshima shook him by the shoulder.

"What are you talking about?" mumbled Sydarias, his voice heavy with sleep.

"Please hurry, someone has come to rescue us." Darshima grabbed him by the arm. Sydarias' eyes fluttered open, and he sat up at the edge of his cot. He followed Darshima's gaze to the corner of the room and stared at the stranger's silhouette. Sydarias nervously stood up and pulled on his uniform, his brow furrowed in a look of confusion.

Huddled closely together, they cautiously approached the pair of glowing eyes awaiting them at the door.

"What about the others?" Darshima gestured toward the dozens of people asleep around them.

"I hope that one day they will be free, but for now we must leave." The stranger placed his hand upon the doorknob.

Darshima looked upon his fellow captives, a lump forming in his throat. They had all grown very close during their struggle in the fields. Their stories were no different than his. Their fears and hopes were all the same. He couldn't imagine fleeing without them.

"I can't leave them here," he whispered, his voice breaking with anguish.

"we must leave them for now ,Though it is hard." The stranger rested a hand upon his shoulder.

"Why me and not them?" Darshima looked up at him.

"You will understand in due time." He peered at Darshima. "If you stay here, we will all perish together. If you come with me, they might be saved one day."

"I don't understand." Darshima's brow wrinkled in confusion at the stranger's cryptic words.

"Please trust me." He stepped toward the entrance.

"I want to," whispered Darshima, unsure what else to do. He would do anything to save his fellow captives, even if it meant leaving them behind for now.

"We should follow him. What other choice do we have?" Sydarias gripped Darshima's shoulder. Darshima turned to the stranger, who waited at the door.

"We will go with you," said Darshima, as he and Sydarias hesitantly walked toward him. Darshima's heart fluttered with a pang of doubt as they stepped through the shadows. He had never met this man in his life and remained unsure of his intentions, or his ability to rescue them. Memories of their prior escape attempt flooded his mind. The haunting images of Sydarias falling toward the crashing waves sent a shiver through him. Despite his misgivings, Darshima felt an unfamiliar, yet persistent urge to trust him. The stranger opened the door and ushered them out into the humid night.

Darshima and Sydarias walked closely beside the man, the dim starlight shining upon him as they moved. Darshima's heart leapt in surprise as his features came into view. A striking man of Omystikaiyn heritage, he stood a handbreadth taller than them. His glowing, narrowed sapphire eyes were almond-shaped and his face was marked by high cheekbones, a small nose, and a square jaw. His skin was smooth and pale like porcelain. His unshorn hair, a deep silky black, was fashioned in a tail that fell at his shoulders.

He wore an unfamiliar uniform of black cloth trousers and a shirt with wide sleeves that ended at the forearm. His shirt was cinched at the waist with a pair of crisscrossing black and gold cloth belts. He wore black leather boots, split at the toes, and carried a black fabric bag strapped upon his back. His serious bearing lent him an air of wisdom that belied his youthful features.

The three moved away from the rows of barracks, down a long dirt path leading into the surrounding lands. The stranger marched assuredly, his steps barely making any noise. They stepped upon the wet blades of grass, and through the rows of cultivated plants as they ventured deeper into the fields. They tread carefully in the shadows along a rutted, overgrown trail between the stalks that Darshima had never seen before.

They followed him amid the rows, and Darshima's stomach knotted in fear. He drew in a measured breath and tried to push aside the dreadful memories of their previous escape attempt. His eyes darted about, searching for any signs of the soldiers. As they moved, he turned to his right and caught a furtive glimpse of the stranger. His strides were bold and he held his head high. The features of his face were drawn into a contemplative frown. To Darshima's astonishment, the stranger's eyes remained firmly closed as he walked.

They reached a clearing between the fields and the edge of the forest, when the stranger stopped unexpectedly.

"There is a vehicle hangar just ahead." He faced the stand of trees. "It is heavily guarded, and we must be careful."

They moved into the woods, treading cautiously along a narrow route, and the stranger stopped again. He turned to Darshima, then Sydarias, and pointed toward the path before them.

"If we are to survive this encounter, you must do as I do." Standing in between them, he reached out and grabbed their hands. "You must run with me, you must not speak and you must not let go of me." Darshima and Sydarias shifted nervously as they stared at him.

Hand in hand, they walked around a bend in the path. Darshima eyed a tall, imposing tower whose gates were patrolled by a group of armed soldiers dressed in grey fatigues. Further afield, he spotted the low, oval form of the vehicle hangar, the metal plates of its roof glinting in the starlight.

"Now, we must run." The stranger squeezed their hands, and they burst into a sprint toward the building.

The humid air rushed across Darshima's face as they fled. He glanced at the stranger, whose eyes remained closed. His lips moved in what seemed to be a silent prayer as they darted forward, his words torn away by the wind. Darshima looked ahead, astonished to see that the soldiers had not yet noticed them. As the trio ran past, the armed men let out a shout. Darshima's stomach sank as he felt the tug of the stranger's hand pulling him forward.

Dozens of troops emerged from the gates of the tower and sprinted toward them. Darshima's pulse drummed in his ears, and time seemed to slow down. His legs felt as if they were weighted by lead. The stranger ran even harder, pulling Darshima and Sydarias along with him. Tears welled up in Darshima's eyes as the men approached. He clenched his jaw, vowing to fight them with all he had. He would rather die than be captured again.

Darshima and Sydarias ran with the stranger as the team advanced, their thundering footsteps shaking the ground beneath him. As they were about to collide, Darshima raised his free arm to defend himself, but to his complete disbelief, the contingent ran around them. As the soldiers darted past, they stared right through him, as if he weren't even there. Darshima shot a glance at the stranger, whose eyes remained firmly closed. The soldiers' shouts filled the night air as they stormed down a muddy trail leading into the fields.

Darshima, Sydarias, and the stranger slowed their pace down to a brisk walk, passed through the gates of the hangar, and stalked between the parked vehicles. The stranger led them toward the back of the building, and they approached the rear of a small, oblong craft. They followed him up a short metal gangway and into the cockpit. He stowed his bag off to the side, secured himself in the pilot's chair and gestured toward the adjacent seats.

Darshima and Sydarias sat down on either side of him and pulled the safety harnesses over their shoulders. The stranger's eyes fluttered open, and his gaze scanned over the windshield and the instrument panel before him. His fingers methodically tapped several rows of unfamiliar, glowing triangular symbols on its array of screens. The rear hatch closed with a deep thud, and the engines rumbled to life.

The craft lifted off the ground and jolted forward. The stranger firmly gripped the triangular steering controls in the console, and they sped through the dark hangar. He skillfully wove through the metal arched columns supporting the structure, appearing like the bones of a giant carcass amid the shadows. Darshima sank in his seat as they flew past the arched gates and the looming watchtower. The craft nosed upward at a sharp angle, and the terrain below shrank rapidly as they ascended.

They flew high overhead, the darkness of the sky yielding to the pale blue light of dawn. Darshima peered through the curved windshield and beheld the green patchwork of fields, scattered buildings, and dense ring of forests that had all but encompassed his life. The stranger guided the craft beyond the line of trees, along the perimeter of the colony. The vehicle's distorted, ovoid reflection shimmered in triplicate against the clear glass of the immense dome as they sailed past. Through the panes, he saw faint traces of sunlight gleaming upon the ocean.

The stranger angled the craft upward and they spiraled along the top of the transparent canopy. They hurtled toward a dark, circular aperture that appeared to be a large vent. He guided the vessel into the opening, and they were enveloped by the blackness. The stranger piloted through the winding tunnels, without so much as grazing against the sides.

Darshima stole a furtive glance at the stranger and noticed that his eyes were again closed. He held onto the controls and manipulated them accordingly, following the winding course of the tunnel. Darshima gazed intently, riveted as the stranger performed this unbelievable feat. He couldn't understand how someone could steer a craft without seeing. Even before he could ask, the stranger lifted a hand from the controls and raised it toward Darshima.

"You will understand soon enough," he whispered. Sydarias leaned forward and exchanged a look of bewilderment with Darshima.

Darshima leaned back in his seat amid the rushing sound of wind and the roar of the engines. A beam of light pierced the darkness and illuminated the rapidly approaching end of the tunnel. With a great rush, the craft emerged into the open air. Darshima looked around at the expanse of sky before them, a sense of awe filling him.

"Freedom?" he whispered cautiously, his heart fluttering as the word crossed his lips. "I don't know how to thank you." Darshima's eyes widened in incredulity as he looked out upon the unbound horizon.

"Thank you for saving us, sir," said Sydarias as a tear ran down his cheek. He buried his face in his hands, let out a sigh of relief, and stifled a sob.

"We are not yet free. We must still escape this world." The stranger trained his gaze upon the vista beyond the windshield. Darshima squinted his eyes against the hazy white sun as it rose above the horizon. He shook his head in disbelief as he beheld the burning disk, astonished that it no longer appeared in triplicate. They climbed higher into the sky, the top of the dome falling away from view.

Darshima looked down upon the open waters and saw dozens of identical floating colonies, the sunlight glinting upon their rounded glass canopies. They stretched toward the horizon in long lines, like the links of a chain. A chill ran through him as he beheld the arresting sight. He imagined the countless men and women like him who were still trapped, toiling away in the fields. His heart thudded as a deep sense of guilt welled up within him. He was free, yet they were not. He couldn't understand why.

"Where are we?" Darshima turned to the stranger.

"This world is called Navervyne." He leaned forward and scanned the horizon, maneuvering the craft even higher.

"Navervyne," whispered Darshima, his tongue tripping upon the foreign syllables.

As they raced over the ocean, the disturbing sight of the colonies floating over the turbulent waters stayed with him. So many people were still left behind. He didn't know how he could go on while they suffered.

"I will come back for them," he said, his voice wavering with sadness. The touch of a hand upon his shoulder interrupted his thoughts and he turned to meet the gaze of the stranger, whose vivid eyes bore a look of sincerity.

"One day you will return for them, Darshima. I believe it," he said. Darshima replied with a solemn nod as he looked toward the ocean. The stranger guided the craft into the horizon, and the image of the floating colonies faded from his mind, settling somewhere deep within him. Though he had physically left the fields, his toil there had wounded parts of his soul that he could not yet name. Darshima knew he would have to fight hard to rescue the people who remained enslaved. He would have to fight even harder to recover the pieces of himself left behind.

Chapter Thirty Two

Darshima peered through the windshield of the craft as they veered toward the city. They had flown over the vast ocean for what felt like hours, and he had seen not a single trace of land.

"We are approaching Stebbenhour, the capital of this world." The stranger trained his eyes upon the vista ahead. Darshima stared in awe as they approached, having never seen anything like it before. A vast, vertical metropolis situated on several immeasurably large, open-air platforms, the city floated high above the boundless ocean. It appeared as an aerial fortress of inhabited clouds, looming above the misty waters.

The stranger guided the craft into a wide band of airborne vehicles heading toward a dense cluster of lofty, angular metal spires near its center. They traveled through the narrow canyons of soaring towers, gliding downward between levels of traffic as they entered the airspace above the city. It felt as if they were speeding through the fissures of a cut crystal.

Darshima shielded his eyes against the stark sunbeams reflecting against the glittering edifices, their surface marked by grids of clear, circular windows. The stranger slowed the craft, then traveled downward into one of the gleaming canyons. The long spindly shadows from the towers above blocked out much of the light. They descended through a layer of smog toward the surface and arrived just above street level, merging into a slow-moving band of traffic.

"We are nearly there." His eyes narrowed as he scanned the vehicles ahead.

"Where are you taking us?" asked Sydarias, his voice betraying a hint of worry. Darshima also felt a twinge of hesitation. They had entrusted their lives to a stranger whose motivations and intentions were yet unknown to them.

“We are going somewhere safe to rest for a few hours.” He steered the craft down an alleyway and through the entrance of a low-lying garage. They hovered through the dark interior, the curved metal fuselages of the neatly arranged vehicles glinting under the dim lights in the ceiling. He piloted the craft toward a far corner of the building and brought it to rest with a gentle thud.

“Do not worry, everything will soon be clear to you.” He beckoned them as he unfastened his harness. He slung his bag over his shoulder, stepped out of the cockpit, and moved toward the rear of the craft. Darshima and Sydarias released their harnesses, rose from their seats, and followed him. Darshima emerged from the hatch after Sydarias and nervously eyed the entrance of the garage.

“Stay close to me, and do not utter a word. This city is dangerous for our kind.” The stranger’s hushed voice echoed throughout the cavernous building.

Darshima and Sydarias followed him out into the open, their thin boots clicking against the rough steel road. A cold, damp wind swirled through the empty street, stirring up a fine veil of mist. Darshima looked warily upon the foreign cityscape, shivering as an uneasy chill ran through him. Clusters of enormous towers loomed overhead, casting the street in a shadowy atmosphere of perennial twilight. High above, in the interstices between the buildings, he could just make out slivers of the pale blue sky.

As they walked down the narrow alley, a thin carpet of fog settled amid the shadows, teasing the corners of Darshima’s eyes. His chest tightened as a wave of nervousness coursed through him. He trained his gaze forward and walked beside the stranger. Despite the cold breeze blowing through his tattered uniform, Darshima kept reminding himself that he was not dreaming and that he had indeed escaped the fields.

The sudden thump of a hand against his chest roused him from his racing thoughts.

"Look out Darshima, Sydarias." The stranger held out his arm.

Darshima looked ahead and met the cold stare of a sentry standing watch upon the street corner. He was a stocky man with a round, pallid face and a black-billed hat upon his head. His lips curled into an indifferent frown as he glared at them. Droplets of fine mist soaked the dark grey trench coat of his uniform, beading upon the glistening row of silver buttons along its front.

The sentry approached them, his black boots clicking upon the damp metal pavement. He stopped directly in front of them and rested a hand on a silver, holstered pistol hanging from his belt. His crimson eyes narrowed, he looked at the stranger and spoke in the same string of hushed whispers and consonants that Darshima couldn't yet understand. Standing a head taller than him, the stranger cast an appraising stare upon the sentry. The stranger responded in the same language, gesturing toward Darshima and Sydarias.

The sentry's gaze softened into a look of understanding as he listened. He peered intently at Sydarias and then Darshima, taking in the details of their faces. Darshima's heart thudded in his chest and he drew in an anxious breath. The sentry lingered in front of them, then backed away. He offered a curt nod to the stranger and then stepped into the shadows.

"I was not expecting him to approach us." The stranger turned toward Darshima, his pale face slightly flushed.

They continued in silence along the desolate streets. Darshima's stomach twisted in an uneasy knot as he pondered their close encounter with the sentry. He closed his eyes for a moment as memories of their struggle in the colony flashed before him. His pulse bounded as he realized that they had nearly been caught. As he drew in a nervous breath, he felt the stranger's hand rest upon his shoulder.

"Do not worry, I am here to protect you." He cast a reassuring gaze at Darshima.

Darshima bit his lip as he struggled to comprehend what was happening around them. He did not understand this world or its people, but he could see that the stranger did. Darshima looked at him, his feelings of apprehension lessening a bit. They moved further down the street, toward a metal doorway veiled in shadow.

Chapter Thirty Three

Darshima and Sydarias sat beside each other upon the cold steel floor of the square apartment, and faced a large circular window. The stranger sat directly in front of them, his back to the dusty pane. A steady rain thrummed against the glass, the sound echoing throughout the room. Dull shafts of afternoon light filtered through and reflected off the stark walls, enveloping him in a faint aura. Cool, balmy air tinged with the acrid scent of volatile chemicals and engine exhaust wafted through rectangular vents in the floor. Streaks of grease and mold blemished the white, peeling paint coating the metallic walls.

The space had an air of transience, as if many souls had passed through, leaving their mark in some way. Beyond the window, the vast city of Stebbenhour spread before them. The misty grey skies were crowded by what seemed like hundreds of lofty, silver spires. In the distance, long filamentous bridges spanned the open air, linking the immense aerial platforms of the city.

The three of them were finishing a small meal of cured, starchy roots that the stranger had brought with him. Despite the unfamiliar, savory flavor, it was satisfying and quieted Darshima's stomach.

"Who are you, and why are you here?" asked Darshima.

"My name is Tenrai Nax, and I am here to rescue you." He cleared his throat, his deep voice resonating throughout the room.

"What is this place?" Sydarias stared through the window toward the city, his eyes narrowing as he examined its details.

"This world is very different from our own." Tenrai glimpsed over his shoulder, then turned back to them.

"It is so dim during the daytime here, yet the sunlight is so stark." Darshima looked at Tenrai. "I don't understand."

"The star that this planet orbits is fading. They use sophisticated arrays of prismatic glass atop their buildings to amplify and distort the light."

"Like the glass dome covering the colony," said Darshima, as he recalled the images of the sun burning in triplicate over the fields. "How far are we from home?" Darshima peered toward the foreign cityscape.

"Very far," he replied. "I have been here only a few days, but I will tell you what I have learned." They leaned in closer as Tenrai shared what he knew.

They had been captured and taken as slaves to the distant world of Navervyne. A lone planet orbiting a dying star, its entire surface was covered in a deep and turbid ocean. Long ago, the planet was home to several fiefdoms scattered among its many islands. Riven by conflict, they engaged in frequent warfare to gain control of scarce resources. As time passed, Navervyne's ocean unexpectedly rose, steadily flooding their territories. Faced with their very extinction, they sought a means to confront the threat of the encroaching seas. The warring fiefdoms banded together and reorganized as a federation of states, known as the Navervyne Republic.

They launched a concerted effort to modernize their insular societies and adapt to the growing environmental threat. They sent legions of their citizens to nearby, more advanced worlds to gain the technical skills to ensure their survival. The Navervynish excelled in the physical sciences and became experts at building spacefaring vessels, propulsion systems, and industrial machinery. From its deep ocean, Navervyne extracted a surfeit of raw metals and minerals for its factories. Its manufactured goods were renowned among its trading partners. The Navervyne Republic gained extraordinary wealth, and within five centuries, its industrial output surpassed its allies.

Despite its growing power, Navervyne remained helpless against the rising waters. Faced with its inevitable inundation, the republic leveraged its technologic expertise to re-establish itself in the misty upper reaches of the planet's atmosphere. Their engineers fashioned immense, sophisticated floating platforms, upon which they built aerial cities and colonies. Stebbenhour, the largest, most advanced city, served as the capital of the newly airborne republic.

"So their territory is gone?" Darshima's jaw fell agape in surprise.

"Every speck of it lies beneath the waves." Tenrai pointed toward the window behind him.

"How can they survive with no land?" asked Sydarias.

"Their struggle is largely what brought them to our world." A somber frown crossed Tenrai's lips.

Within two centuries, Navervyne completed its transformation into an advanced, airborne civilization. The republic wielded hegemonic influence and surpassed its neighbors in most measures. Though modernity had rescued it from the brink of extinction, the migration to the skies created new challenges. Its ocean and atmosphere had been fouled with ages of industrial pollution. Millions of citizens crowded into Stebbenhour and the other floating cities, competing fiercely over shrinking quantities of essential resources.

Using their most sophisticated farming methods, the republic sustained the agricultural yields of its disappearing lands for a century longer. The ocean continued to rise, and Navervyne stood helpless as the last tracts of land slipped beneath the toxic, turbulent waves. Despite facing ecologic ruination, its industries drew ever-increasing quantities of raw materials from the ocean, further polluting the planet's skies and waters.

"They became wealthier, but how did they feed themselves?" asked Darshima.

"The Navervynish imported everything," replied Tenrai.

With no land left, the republic procured significant amounts of food, fiber, and fuels from its neighbors. Though it was expensive and inefficient to transport these goods over long distances, Navervyne was left with no other choice. This costly practice continued for generations, depleting its wealth.

Fearing the starvation of their own citizens, Navervyne's allies restricted their agricultural exports. The loss of wealth, coupled with the growing scarcity of food led to domestic strife on Navervyne.

Seeking a resolution to this grave situation, Navervyne commissioned several dozen floating colonies in the warmer skies above the equator. The republic imported vast quantities of soil and seed, in an attempt to revive the abandoned discipline of agriculture. Built at an enormous cost, Navervyne could little afford either the machinery or the laborers to run these sophisticated colonies. The republic's private enterprises sought to recruit workers from neighboring worlds, but the harsh, polluted climate deterred them.

Facing the growing dissatisfaction of its citizens, Navervyne devised a plan to procure the labor and raw materials that it desperately needed elsewhere. Under the guise of establishing new markets for its enterprises, the republic organized an expedition to the distant, and little known worlds orbiting the dormant planet of Benai. With their advanced instruments, Navervyne's astronomers had long ago probed the skies, discovering the worlds of the Vilidesian Realm from afar. Despite their discovery, Stebbenhour had expressed little interest in establishing contact with them, until now.

"How were they able to see us, yet we couldn't see them?" asked Sydarias.

"Their telescopes were far stronger," replied Tenrai.

Its fortunes depleted, Navervyne persuaded its less powerful allies to help finance an expedition to these new worlds. Under the auspices of the rulers in Stebbenhour, Navervyne's largest industrial and military enterprises covertly amassed an army of epic proportions. Within two years, the republic had organized hundreds of divisions of conscripted soldiers and built an immense fleet of warships, numbering in the thousands. With this formidable fighting force under its control, Navervyne subsequently launched the invasion of The Vilides.

Darshima sat stunned, a cold numbness stirring in his chest. He didn't want to believe Tenrai's account, but the evidence of its truth surrounded him. His eyes narrowed as the memories of the invasion's searing explosions flashed before him. Trying to forget the haunting images, he forced himself to look through the window. His gaze lingered upon the strange buildings and steely skies. He and Sydarias were fugitive slaves in a world that until their capture, they never knew existed.

"Where are you from? Why are you here?" Darshima turned to Tenrai.

"I am from Tiriyuud, and I have traveled very far to find you." Tenrai moved closer to him.

As his features suggested, Tenrai Nax was an Omystikai. Born and raised in the Kingdom of Tiriyuud, he lived amid the frozen hinterlands on the northern hemisphere of Iberwight. It was one of the most remote and unforgiving locations in the realm. The younger of two brothers, Tenrai belonged to an extended family of skilled carpenters. They lived a day's voyage from the capital, but like most other rural Tiriyuusian families, they rarely traveled far from home.

His family prospered for generations in the tranquility and isolation of their village. Tenrai spent his days studying and his nights working alongside his father. From early on, he demonstrated powerful abilities of divination. He was keenly aware of the thoughts and emotions of those around him. His mother, a skilled diviner in her own right recognized his abilities and trained him.

Tenrai's intelligence and abilities gained the attention of the elders of his village. As he grew older, he received formal instruction to hone his skills. When he reached adulthood, he studied in the kingdom's capital and joined a class of elite warrior-diplomats, known as the Guardians. He had earned the rank of knight and served on behalf of his order.

Darshima's pulse thudded in his ears as Tenrai spoke, his fingers fidgeting with the shredded hem of his pant leg. His thoughts racing, he tried to focus on Tenrai's words. Worries about what might happen to them, here in this strange city, eclipsed his relief of escaping the fields. Darshima's mind reeled through the improbable events since their capture, when Tenrai's voice abruptly fell silent. Darshima lifted his head and gulped nervously as he encountered Tenrai's piercing stare.

"Darshima, I understand your fears and your frustration. You both have suffered a terrible ordeal," he said softly.

"I'm sorry." Darshima shook his head as he tried to pay attention.

"I will share my plan with you, but if you are to trust me, you must know who I am." He rested a hand upon Darshima's shoulder.

"Listen to him, he is doing a great deal to help us." Sydarias gently nudged Darshima's rib.

"You both deserve to know what has happened since the invasion." Tenrai's eyes glinted with startling seriousness. "Our home has suffered a disastrous fate."

"What do you mean?" asked Sydarias, his voice wavering.

"The Vilidesian Realm has fallen and is no more." Tenrai solemnly lowered his gaze.

"That cannot be." Darshima vigorously shook his head.

"I don't believe it." Sydarias pressed his hands against his temples and shut his eyes.

"There is no other truth." Tenrai let out a somber sigh.

Tenrai recounted the brutal details of Navervyne's surprise attack, and Darshima's stomach sank with a sense of dread as he listened. The Vilides waged a valiant but ultimately doomed battle against the invaders. The realm's overextended military proved no match, and Ciblaithia was conquered within weeks. In a matter of months, Gordanelle, Iberwight, and finally Wohiimai succumbed to the overwhelming firepower and decisive skill of the Navervynish.

The peoples of the four moons suffered greatly under the heavy-handed rule of the invaders. The emperor and empress had been summarily executed upon their capture. The other members of the dynasty had been killed, captured, or fled to fates unknown. Navervyne assumed direct control of every city and village among the moons. Tens of thousands of citizens had died during the invasion and its aftermath. Thousands more had been captured and sent to the planet to work as slaves in its factories and farm colonies.

The first months after the invasion were marked by turbulence and revolt in the conquered realm. The republic maintained a significant military presence upon all of the moons, administering their forces from the former capitals. Their rule was marked by brutality and indifference to centuries of Vilidesian culture. They imposed their laws and crushed any forms of dissent. Citizens deemed as subversive to their authority were sent to jail, and others simply vanished without a trace.

As Tenrai concluded his account, Sydarias dried his tears with his palms.

"How could this happen?" he wondered aloud. "Vilidesian strength fended off threats for ages. We had peace and stability for more than a thousand years."

"They were unfortunately caught unaware." Tenrai gestured to the vast city beyond the window.

"We grew up believing that the Vilidesians knew everything." Darshima shook his head in disbelief.

"The Vilidesians didn't know that other worlds existed beyond their realm, but the Navervynish knew of us," said Tenrai.

"What about Ardavia?" Darshima clenched his jaw, trying to stifle a growing sense of fear. A chill ran through him as images of his home overrun by merciless, invading armies floated before his eyes.

"The Ardavians have suffered just as much as the Vilidesians. The city has been seized and many people on Gordanelle have been captured." Tenrai bowed his head.

"Is there anything left?" Darshima's stomach sank as he processed Tenrai's words. During his toil in the fields, he had held out hope that life back home was somehow better, but it was not.

"This is our darkest moment, but it shall not last forever." Tenrai turned to Darshima. "I have come here to rescue you, Darshima, so that you might help us." A stark silence fell between them as Darshima processed the words.

"I don't understand." Darshima searched Tenrai's eyes for a hint of meaning but only saw an unflinching seriousness.

"You might be able to save us from this misery," said Tenrai.

"What do you mean? I couldn't even save myself." Darshima's pulse raced as feelings of confusion gripped him. "You must have the wrong person."

"I am not mistaken. You are the one whom I seek." Tenrai folded his arms across his chest.

"Who sent you?" asked Darshima.

"I am here on behalf of my kingdom," he replied.

"How am I to believe this Omystikai man and his tales?" Darshima turned to Sydarias.

"Please show him respect," pleaded Sydarias, gently grabbing his arm. "He has risked his life to save ours."

"What do you intend to do with us?" Darshima pulled away from Sydarias and looked suspiciously at Tenrai, who countered with an equally serious stare.

"Haven't you ever wondered where those markings came from?" Tenrai pointed to the intricate patterns on Darshima's right arm, his eyes wrinkling slightly at the corners.

"They don't mean anything," blurted Darshima. He folded his arms across his chest, attempting to hide them.

"Haven't you ever wondered why you only feel at ease when you are alone, staring up at the night sky?" Tenrai edged closer and caught Darshima's gaze.

Darshima drew in a sharp breath as Tenrai's probing question struck him. Back on Gordanelle, he had often spent his nights alone upon the bluffs behind his parents' home. Peace came to him as he sat along the roaring river, casting his thoughts amid the swirls of stars in the night sky.

"You often feel as if you do not belong," whispered Tenrai.

"How do you know these things?" asked Darshima, his voice wavering as Tenrai read his deepest thoughts.

"I mean no harm, you can trust me." Tenrai's eyes searched Darshima's. "We must leave this place. When we return home, I will explain everything to you."

Tenrai rose from the floor and walked to a cabinet at the far end of the room. He retrieved several articles of black clothing and boots similar to his own, and returned to the young men.

"You both must change into something less conspicuous." Tenrai cast an appraising eye over Darshima's tattered uniform, caked in mud and grime. He then turned to Sydarias. "You may borrow a set of my clothing. You are about my size and they will fit." He handed the garments over to them, then walked toward the window.

Darshima shed his old clothing and put on the pair of trousers, long-sleeved, hooded shirt, and split-toed leather boots. He couldn't remember the last time he had worn new clothing, and the stiff, clean fabric felt refreshing against his skin. He cast the old, tattered uniform in a pile upon the floor. Sydarias changed in a corner of the room and slipped on a similar pair of black trousers, shirt and boots.

Newly dressed, Darshima and Sydarias joined Tenrai at the window and looked out upon the urban landscape before them. Rays of dim sunlight broke through the parting mists. The long, spindly shadows of the cityscape steadily grew as the sun sank toward the horizon. He looked upon the glass facades of the surrounding towers, glittering like shards of a broken crystal.

Below their high perch, Darshima eyed a swiftly moving band of aerial traffic flowing beneath them. The fleets of aircraft were too numerous to count as they whizzed by, their metallic frames appearing as gleaming droplets in a raging river. As they stood in front of the window, Tenrai's calm voice broke through the silence.

"The voyage home will be difficult," he said. They faced him as he detailed his plan.

As evident from the flying vessels below, they stood above a major shipping terminal. One of the largest structures in Stebbenhour, the port handled aerial traffic from the many far-flung colonies and states of the republic. All outbound ships heading to the moons of the former realm stopped at this station. At sunset, a freight vessel destined for Ciblaithia would berth at the port to receive cargo, then continue its journey to The Vilides.

While the vessel was docked, they would jump onto one of the cantilevered decks at the rear. They would then make their way to a safe, secluded location and stow away to avoid detection.

"Where will we go afterward?" asked Darshima.

"We must focus our efforts on traveling safely to The Vilides," he replied.

Darshima offered a hesitant nod as he mulled over the details of the plan. His heart fluttered as a sense of worry came over him, thoughts of his family filling his mind. He needed to know if they had survived the invasion and perhaps made it back to Gordanelle. He had no choice but to wait until they reached Ciblaithia to find an answer.

They stood together and gazed upon the forbidding cityscape. Tenrai's arms hung at his sides and he remained silent. The room brightened as the mists passed, casting him in a faint aura. The sounds of his deep, rhythmic breaths were barely audible above the hum of the traffic. Darshima felt his pulse slow noticeably. The feelings of fear and uncertainty coursing through him were replaced by a profound, unmistakable sense of serenity. Dumbfounded, he turned to Tenrai, who stood with his eyes closed. Tenrai then stepped away from the window, and the sensation dissipated as he moved about the room. Darshima shot a glance at Sydarias who lingered beside him, an anxious expression spreading upon his face. He wondered if Sydarias had experienced a similar, unusual feeling.

Tenrai slung his bag over his shoulder, gathered their tattered old uniforms, and disposed of them down the hatch of an incinerator chute in the corner of the room.

"All traces of our presence must be destroyed. No one can know that we were here," he whispered.

"What if they find us?" asked Sydarias.

"I will protect you." He placed his hands upon their shoulders and guided them away from the window.

"Now we must leave this place." Tenrai ushered them toward the door. Darshima caught a glimpse of the window over his shoulder, the looming towers of the city sending a shiver down his spine.

Tenrai's reassurances echoed in his mind, but his pulse bounded as the sense of fear returned. Tenrai opened the door, and they followed him into the shadows of the hallway.

Chapter Thirty Four

Darshima looked out upon the horizon and drew his garments tightly against his shivering frame. The setting sun appeared against the darkening turquoise sky as a flattened, dull pink disk. The glowing orb slowly dipped behind the towers on the horizon, setting their sharp angles ablaze amid the faint mists. Darshima, Sydarias, and Tenrai crouched in the shadows upon a long narrow metal platform, hanging from the top of the vaulted roof of the cavernous station. The tunnel-like space stood beneath a large, arched aerial span high above the city, connecting two immense towers in the middle. At the opposite end of the station, the platform jutted beyond the paired edifices and out into the open air.

From Darshima's vantage, the city appeared as a frenetic, glowing web of intersecting rays and circles. In the distance, the crowded towers of the city sprawled from one giant platform onto another. The perimeters between the immense, polygonal floating decks appeared as jagged palisades of glass and metal, giving way to the churning ocean far below. He looked out upon the alien vista, his clothes fluttering in the intermittent gusts of wind.

Below them, Darshima eyed a small crowd of uniformed people milling about the large concourse. The grey metal tiles, scuffed by ages of foot traffic reflected the long rays of sunlight. He crouched further into the shadows when he realized that the uniforms were the same kind worn by the soldiers from the farm colony.

"They cannot see us. We are safe up here," Tenrai placed a reassuring hand upon his shoulder.

Darshima's eyes scanned the traffic on the horizon, searching for the vessel that might carry them home. He tried to focus on the perilous moments ahead, but his thoughts kept drifting. His chest tightened with a sense of anticipation as he looked at the stream of vehicles hurtling into the distance. Only a day ago, he and Sydarias were toiling in those merciless fields, and now they were on the verge of escaping. He had waited so long for this very moment, but Tenrai's reassurances did little to assuage his fear that they would somehow be caught.

The sound of Tenrai's hushed voice broke through the cacophony of Darshima's thoughts.

"There it is." Tenrai pointed at the darkening horizon. Darshima glimpsed a massive, fusiform vessel sailing rapidly toward them. The reflection of the starlit sky shone brilliantly on its gleaming metal hull. Darshima's ears filled with the deep roar of the engines, his teeth rattling as the waves of sound buffeted him. The ship drew closer, and their clothes flapped wildly in the turbulent gusts.

With a rush of cold wind and a pulsating roar, the vessel applied its airbrakes and steadily slowed. Tenrai motioned for the two young men to follow him toward the edge of the hanging platform.

"Sydarias, you will not able to make this jump, it is much too far." Tenrai rested his hands upon Sydarias' shoulders.

"But it doesn't seem so." Sydarias pointed toward the approaching ship.

"I will carry you, please trust me." Tenrai handed his bag to Sydarias and then stooped down, motioning for Sydarias to jump on his back. Sydarias hastily slung the bag over his shoulders and then hopped onto Tenrai's back, placing his arms around Tenrai's broad shoulders. As he secured himself, Tenrai wrapped his arms around Sydarias' legs, then stood back up with his living payload.

Darshima wrinkled his brow in confusion as he looked at them. He didn't understand why Tenrai presumed Sydarias couldn't make the jump, yet he could.

"What about me? How am I going to make it onto the ship?" Darshima pointed to the approaching vehicle, his voice wavering.

Tenrai stepped toward him, seemingly unencumbered by Sydarias' weight.

"Darshima you are capable, just do as I do." Tenrai motioned with his head toward the end of the platform, and Darshima followed them.

The ship maneuvered its immense frame in line with the station, displacing the surrounding traffic. It steadily approached the building, whipping up the misty air as it sailed closer. Tenrai, with Sydarias upon his back, drew nearer to the edge of the platform and Darshima walked with them.

"As soon as the ship comes to a stop, we will leap directly onto the uppermost deck." Tenrai pointed as he spoke, his voice barely audible over the roar of the engines.

"I don't know if I can do this." Darshima's eyes widened in fear as the ship hurtled toward them.

"Just concentrate as you jump, and you will succeed." Tenrai turned to Darshima and gazed intently at him, his eyes casting a soft glow.

"If you say so." Darshima drew his clothes against his trembling frame. He dreaded the moments ahead, fearing that he would fall to his death.

As the ship drew closer, the pulsating boom of the brakes ceased, and the craft regained speed. The expression on Tenrai's face changed from confidence to puzzlement, and then to worry. The ship rushed forward as it entered the station, sending up violent gusts of wind in its wake.

"I have made a miscalculation." Tenrai glared at the ship, his brow knit in concern. He had told them the ship would stop to receive cargo but unexpectedly, it was continuing on its way. Tenrai tugged at Darshima's arm and shouted.

"Come on, we must run for it." His eyes bore a look of uncompromising determination. They stepped back from the edge of the platform and readied themselves for a running start. The ship sailed through, and half its length had already emerged through the other end of the station. "Hold on, Sydarias!" shouted Tenrai, his voice barely audible above the winds. Sydarias tightened his grip and Tenrai burst into a sprint. His long legs strode effortlessly as he traveled the length of the platform. Sydarias held on for dear life, his weight seemingly having no effect upon Tenrai.

Eyes narrowed against the wind, Darshima stared ahead, his heart pounding uncontrollably. He burst into a sprint behind Tenrai, the platform clanging and shaking under his gallop. Just ahead of him, Tenrai charged forward at an incredible speed. He reached the edge, and his powerful legs launched him and Sydarias into the abyss.

Darshima's pulse beat faster than ever as he ran. He tried his best to imitate Tenrai's stride but as he was about to leap, his legs froze and he came to a halt. His knees buckled, and he collapsed at the edge of the platform. He drew in a sharp breath as his eyes met the vast, misty void before him. The pit of his stomach twisted into a heavy knot as he stared at the city below.

Shuddering in fear, Darshima eyed the craft as it steadily cruised forward. His gaze desperately honed upon Tenrai and Sydarias aboard the vessel far below, standing at the edge of a cantilevered deck. They jumped up and down, waving at him frantically. Darshima crouched down upon the platform, his fingers clinging desperately to the cold metal grating. Fine beads of sweat broke out upon his brow, and his legs were weighted by a paralyzing dread. He looked on helplessly, his heart sinking as the rear of the ship slid away from the station.

Out of seemingly nowhere, Darshima heard Tenrai's calm voice echo in his ears. His eyes widening in incredulity, he spun around and searched for the source. He trembled in disbelief as he saw Tenrai still standing beside Sydarias upon the deck of the moving vessel, their silhouettes steadily shrinking. The voice was so clear that it seemed as if it were resonating within his skull.

“Do not be afraid. Just leap and you will make it,” said Tenrai. The ship traveled further and cleared the station, its massive frame drifting well away from the building. Darshima’s chest tightened as the thought of being left behind overwhelmed him. He held onto the platform, shivering as both the fear and the cold consumed him.

"I won’t survive this jump, it is too far." He frantically shook his head.

“Darshima, you are more than capable of this. Please hurry, our chance at freedom is slipping away,” said Tenrai. That word, freedom, rang clearly within him like the peal of an ancient bell. For so long, he had pined for freedom, and here it was, vanishing right before his eyes. He would rather die trying to regain his freedom than to be captured, and lose it forever.

“I don’t know how,” said Darshima, his voice wavering.

“Let your spirit see what your eyes will not. Let your mind execute what your body cannot,” whispered Tenrai, his voice fading into the wind.

Darshima’s heart pounded as the words echoed in his head. He could only accomplish this seemingly impossible leap by his faith alone. An unexpected sense of calm filled him as he loosened his grip on the metal grating. He rose to his feet and steadily walked backward until he was at the mid-point of the platform. The lingering doubts dissipated as he looked upon the departing vessel, steadily accelerating toward the horizon. He drew in a deep breath and set his thoughts upon the task ahead.

“I can do this,” he said aloud, trying to convince himself. His skin tingled as an unfamiliar sense of confidence rose within him.

Darshima closed his eyes and let out an anxious sigh. Before he realized it, he was running along the platform. He burst into a sprint, his legs moving more swiftly than they ever had. An intense, yet familiar energy surged through him, growing stronger with each step. The stiff metal grating trembled and swayed under his gallop, his feet remaining steady as he charged forward. He didn't know how, but he sensed the end of the platform as he approached it. Darshima lengthened his stride as he arrived at the edge, and with a powerful leap, he launched himself upward.

His eyes fluttered open as he vaulted into the open air, the platform falling away beneath him. Arms outstretched, he somersaulted through the starlit sky. He narrowed his eyes against the winds and spied the bands of traffic below him, appearing as glowing rivulets amid the steep canyons of buildings. He felt no fear, but a distinct sense of control as he flew through the darkness. Over the howling gusts, he heard his pulse thudding in his ears.

As he reached the top of his arc, time itself seemed to stand still. He hung motionless for an instant, then felt the pull of gravity tug him downward. The wind whipped angrily around him, threatening to strip the clothes from his body. He sailed toward the immense vessel, and it rapidly encompassed his field of vision. Amid the dozens of cantilevered decks, he spied the backlit silhouettes of Sydarias and Tenrai standing at the ledge of the uppermost one, awaiting him with open arms.

He approached the ship feet first and shifted his weight to land near them. His velocity increasing, he stiffened his legs when he realized how swiftly he was falling. With an explosive thud, his feet hit the metal plates of the deck. The thunderous impact coursed up his legs, and through his spine, rattling his jaw. He stumbled and then collapsed to his hands and knees. Every sinew and muscle within him ached. His ears rang, and his head throbbed from the force of the landing. His chest heaved as he drew in deep lungfuls of air.

Tenrai and Sydarias ran to Darshima, grabbed him by his arms, and helped him to his feet.

"You did well." Tenrai beamed at him. Darshima caught his breath and walked unsteadily, holding onto Sydarias as he tried to keep his balance upon the swaying deck.

"Darshima, you soared through the sky!" exclaimed Sydarias, his eyes widened in awe. Between gasps of air, Darshima glimpsed over his shoulder, astonished to see that the vessel had traveled much further than he had imagined. The station stood out among the other glowing towers in the distance, rapidly vanishing as the ship sailed onward.

"We must hurry before we are seen." Tenrai pointed toward the ship's interior.

Darshima eyed the immense, brightly lit deck spreading before them. Hundreds of large cube-shaped, metal containers stood neatly arranged upon the steel floors. They peered around them, seeing no signs of any other people.

"Please, follow me." Tenrai guided them down a path between the containers, toward a doorway leading to the interior of the ship. As they walked, Darshima felt Tenrai's firm hand hold him back.

"We must wait." He seized both of their shoulders and they pressed their backs against a row of containers.

"What's happening?" Sydarias frantically looked around them.

"Stay silent," whispered Tenrai.

The sharp clicking sound of footsteps rose over the drone of the engines and the howling winds. Darshima's heart leapt in fright as he saw a pair of soldiers emerge from behind a row of containers. His stomach sank as he recognized the familiar green uniforms and black brimmed hats. The soldiers' footsteps grew louder as they approached, echoing throughout the cavernous space. Darshima clenched his fists as he stared at them, vowing either to fight or flee. He would not be caught again.

Darshima felt Tenrai's grip on his shoulder tighten. His jaw set, Tenrai's eyes glowed with an incandescence like starlight. He trained his gaze upon the men, and the three pressed themselves tightly against the wall of containers. The soldiers walked toward Darshima, Tenrai, and Sydarias in lockstep, their boots clicking upon the metal floor. The uniformed men glared ahead, completely unaware of them as they marched by. Darshima shivered as he saw the glint in their crimson eyes and breathed in their musky scent. The soldiers moved toward another row of containers and disappeared around the corner.

Darshima let out a sigh of relief, and his eyes widened in incredulity at what had just happened. Tenrai had again managed to hide them from danger while they stood in plain sight. He couldn't understand how it was possible.

"These freight ships have only a small crew, but we must be careful to avoid them," whispered Tenrai, the intense glow in his eyes fading some. Darshima and Sydarias followed him down a path between the rows of containers as he looked ahead. "There is a safe place below deck where we may hide." He motioned toward a doorway veiled in shadow. They stepped past the threshold, entered a dark, humid corridor, and descended a narrow stairway.

Chapter Thirty Five

Darshima rested beside the oval window, his arms folded across his chest. Tenrai sat opposite him, his legs folded and his hands upon his knees. The silence between them hummed with the low rumble of the engines, and the metal floorboards vibrated softly under their thrust. Sydarias sat behind them, perched upon a stack of steel containers.

The ship had crossed the distance back home in roughly twelve Ciblaithian days, which according to Tenrai, was nearly half the time of their first voyage. Exhausted from their escape, Darshima and Sydarias had slept through much of the journey. Tenrai had kept guard while they remained hidden and undisturbed. They had stowed away in a large storage room full of containers on the lowest deck of the ship. Equipped with a small window and a lavatory, it was modest and offered at least some comfort. Along with water from a nearby spigot, they subsisted on the supply of dried provisions that Tenrai had brought from his homeland.

Darshima rested his head against the cold pane of glass and drew in a measured breath. He gazed into the abyss, and his faint reflection stared disconnectedly back. His sullen expression was half-veiled in shadow, half illuminated by the reflected light from Ciblaithia. The golden orb sat boldly in the center of the window, its brilliance driving away the enveloping blackness of space.

Out of the corner of his eye, he saw the serpentine traces of dunes glittering in the morning sun. Cities, like broken shards of glass, spread out upon the moon's arid surface, refracting the rays of the sun into a burst of color. Darshima pried his gaze from the window and turned to Tenrai.

"I don't understand why we can't go to Ardavia. I need to know if my family survived," said Darshima. His voice brimmed with frustration, worries about their fate gnawing at him.

"There is unrest on Gordanelle. I cannot guarantee our safety if we travel there." Tenrai looked over his shoulder at Sydarias. "We will escort Sydarias home, then continue to Iberwight."

"Is it any safer on Ciblaithia or Iberwight? Aren't they also conquered territories?" Sydarias bit his lip, an expression of concern spreading across his face.

"Like Ciblaithia, all of the other moons have fallen to the Navervynish. Tiriyuud however, remains unconquered by the invaders," said Tenrai.

"How is that even possible?" Darshima cast a puzzled look at him.

"Tiriyuud has always remained protected," he replied.

"Not even the Vilidesians could vanquish them." Sydarias pushed himself off the stack of containers and scooted closer to them.

"I thought The Vilides conquered the four moons more than a thousand years ago," murmured Darshima. As a child, he had only heard whispers and speculation about Tiriyuud.

"They conquered everyone but the Tiriyuusians. That is why they are the only independent kingdom within the realm." Sydarias turned to Tenrai.

"This is true. Despite our differences, we learned to exist in peace with the Vilidesians." Tenrai trained his gaze upon the moon beyond the window.

Tenrai belonged to a small sect, or order of Omystikai who called Tiriyuud home. Their order, known as the Order of the Gilded Moon, was named after the Omystikai's original home of Ciblaithia. An ancient and hermetic island kingdom within the realm, it was unlike the Omystikai dominions of Iberwight, which all were ruled indirectly by The Vilides. The true account of this anomalous arrangement had been lost to time, but Tiriyuud had succeeded in achieving an enduring armistice with the Vilidesians.

The Tiriyuusians distinguished themselves by adhering to the ancient Omystikai traditions, practicing them as their ancestors did on Ciblaithia in the eras before their exile.

Tiriyuud's centuries of orthodoxy had estranged it from the other Omystikai orders, which had largely assimilated into the wider realm. Some of the orders even exploited their abilities of divination for political power and material wealth. The kingdom persisted in its isolation, maintaining restricted foreign engagements for purposes of trade, education, and diplomacy.

"With the fall of the realm, I fear for our future." A solemn expression spread upon Tenrai's face.

"I am sorry about your kingdom's misfortune." Darshima's eyes lingered upon the floor and a frown crossed his lips. "Why must I go to Iberwight if people everywhere are suffering?"

"Darshima, we need you." Tenrai rested his hand upon Darshima's shoulder.

"My family needs me more, and I must find them." Darshima shook his head, his voice heavy with worry. Thoughts of their tense final moments together at the prince's celebration flooded his mind. A cold shudder coursed through him as he contemplated whether they had even survived the invasion. He didn't even know where to begin looking for them, but starting at home on Gordanelle made the most sense to him.

"The Vilides and Ardavia are no longer the places that you and Sydarias remember. There is a great deal of strife and suffering," said Tenrai. "Darshima, I believe that you can change this."

"Why do you keep insisting that I can change things? I was captured and enslaved like so many others." Darshima let out an exasperated sigh and pulled his shoulder from Tenrai's grasp.

"You cannot deny what is true," he replied.

"Tenrai is right." Sydarias nodded in agreement. "There's something different about you Darshima, and I've sensed it for some time." Darshima glared at the ground, trying to avoid their stares.

"I don't want to hear any more," he stammered.

"Darshima, you must," said Tenrai, in a measured tone. Darshima scooted away from both of them, toward the containers.

"You broke free from your chains when they captured us, and you saved my life when the soldiers threw me over the colony," said Sydarias as he moved closer to Darshima. "You made that impossible jump onto this ship, and..."

"Will you stop talking about it, Sydarias?" blurted Darshima, interrupting him.

"Darshima, you have an ability that can shake the world." Tenrai reached out and firmly gripped his shoulder. Darshima shuddered as Tenrai's words struck him. His mind flashed to the image of that terrifying moment in the fields on Navervyne, with the sisters from Pelethedral. He remembered confronting the soldiers who threatened them as the ground trembled beneath their feet.

"Was that really me?" he whispered to himself, shaking his head in disbelief. His heart thudded in his chest as he pondered the seemingly impossible coincidence.

"You saved those sisters, Darshima." Tenrai gazed intently at him.

"How is any of this possible?" Darshima's eyes widened in disbelief, wondering how Tenrai could have known what happened. "Why me?" he stammered.

"We may never know why or how, but we must embrace our strengths and accept our weaknesses."

Darshima sat stunned, unsure of how to process Tenrai's declaration. An Omystikai man sat before him, proclaiming that he held the unnatural power to change the very world around him. He didn't want to believe his words, but the evidence was unavoidable.

It was him who had rescued those sisters in the fields. It was him who had saved Sydarias' life. It was him who made the death-defying leap onto the departing ship.

Darshima lifted his head and peered through the window toward Ciblaithia. His chest tightened as a sense of anger rose within him. Tenrai came from a people who claimed the power of divination, yet here they were, fugitive slaves, fleeing for their lives.

"If your people can see into the future, why didn't you stop this invasion?" Darshima leapt to his feet and glared at Tenrai, who remained seated. Sydarias' eyes widened in disbelief, and he rose beside Darshima.

"Darshima, you must show respect for this man. He has risked his life for us." He put his arm around Darshima's shoulder.

"Let him speak, Sydarias." A look of sadness settled in Tenrai's eyes.

"Why couldn't your people save us?" Overcome with emotion, Darshima wiped the tears from his eyes with the back of his hand.

"We tried," said Tenrai, his voice weighted with anguish. "We beseeched the other Omystikai orders to heed this danger and even sought a meeting with the Vilidesians. We were ignored by everyone." He cast his gaze downward and cleared his throat. "Our kingdom was openly ridiculed for suggesting the possibility of living worlds beyond the realm. We were viewed as heretics for believing there was another civilization in existence that could threaten our own." He looked up at Darshima and Sydarias. "We couldn't convince the Vilidesians to investigate these foreign people or their designs of conquest, so we sought our own means of survival."

Before the invasion, the Tiriyuusians searched for some way to avoid the impending disaster. The kingdom's clerics submitted themselves to lengthy sessions of meditation and divination. They came to the startling conclusion that the events leading to Navervyne's invasion were predestined. Their predictions revealed that war and strife were inevitable, and that Tiriyuud's very existence was under threat.

Despite this grim revelation, the key to the kingdom's survival revealed itself to Tenrai in the form of a dream. His vision compelled him to journey to a small settlement beyond the limits of The Vilides, where he discovered the ruins of an Omystikai temple amid the sands. The structure dated back to antiquity, in the era when the Omystikai ruled unchallenged over Ciblaithia. A previously unknown Omystikai seer by the name of Oemiri had engraved several prophecies on a stone tablet. Tenrai had found the remains of this precious relic and brought it back to Tiriyuud, where it was deciphered by the kingdom's most learned scholars.

Oemiri foreshadowed the ancient battle between Fidaxis and Jevidan for control of Ciblaithia. She predicted the persecution of the Omystikai and their exile to Iberwight. She saw the asteroids that wrought destruction upon Benai and its moons. Oemiri divined the turbulent struggle of ages on the four remaining moons and the eventual rise of The Vilides. She predicted the expansion of its realm and its prosperous, millenary reign. Oemiri saw the violent conquest of the Vilidesian Realm by the Navervyne Republic and the brutal subjugation of its people.

Despite the darkness and suffering, Oemiri foretold of a time when Benai's moons would be reborn from the ruins. She foresaw a time when they would rise up against their conquerors in a great struggle for freedom. Oemiri saw the awakening of an order that would seek to restore that which had been destroyed. She predicted that this new era would be ushered in by a talented warrior who would emerge from obscurity.

They sat in stunned silence as Tenrai recounted the prophecy. Darshima looked at him, his mind racing. Never in his life had he spoken with an Omystikai. They were keen observers of celestial movements and forecasters of future events, and it unnerved him.

"Why are you telling me this?" Darshima moved away from Tenrai, his voice brimming with exasperation. Sydarias, jaw agape, turned to Tenrai and then to Darshima.

"Don't you see? This why Tenrai found you," he said emphatically. Darshima glared at Sydarias, as the meaning of Tenrai's words took hold.

"I cannot be the one you're looking for." Darshima tore his gaze away and stared at the floor.

"You are the one that Oemiri predicted," said Tenrai.

"Do you expect me to believe that I am some sort of savior?" exclaimed Darshima. "I am just a boy from Gordanelle." He shook his head in disbelief.

"Only you know who you truly are, but I believe that you are so much more." Tenrai pointed toward Darshima's heart. "Oemiri predicted our plight and foretold of your talents and your strength. Our struggle against the invaders cannot begin without you."

"None of this makes sense." Darshima shifted uneasily as he pondered Tenrai's assertion.

"It will in time." An earnest expression spread across Tenrai's face.

"I don't even know how to begin." Darshima's heart thudded as a wave of apprehension came over him.

"I am here to guide you," replied Tenrai.

An uneasy silence settled among them as Darshima contemplated Tenrai's words.

"If we must travel to your kingdom after The Vilides, I will go with you." Darshima stared at Tenrai. "But, you must help me find out what happened to my family."

"You have my word," said Tenrai. He then turned to the window and pointed toward the moon.

"We will be arriving in The Vilides shortly. As soon as the ship lands, we will make our way out of here."

"Whatever you say, Tenrai," said Darshima, his voice blending with the rising sound of the engines.

Tenrai's incredible pronouncement swirled around his mind. Every fiber within him wanted to resist the words, but it was futile. He could no longer ignore the improbable events that had happened to him and Sydarias since their capture. Deep down, he had felt that it had been more than mere circumstance that had sustained them and ensured their survival. Tenrai's miraculous rescue only confirmed his suspicions. For as long as he remembered, he had sensed something unknown within him, something which set him apart from others. Tenrai's words uncovered these feelings and along with them, a deep sense of confusion.

Darshima turned toward the window and gazed at the glittering dunes upon Ciblaithia's surface. Just beyond its curvature, he caught a glimpse of Gordanelle's verdant crescent, and his heart rose into his throat. The worries about his family rushed back to him. He wanted desperately to find them, but it would have to wait. Tenrai had rescued him and Sydarias, and he had kept them safe during their perilous journey. Darshima knew he needed to follow through and trust him. He turned away from the window and let out an anxious sigh, the ship jostling him as they descended through the atmosphere.

Chapter Thirty Six

Darshima, Sydarias, and Tenrai walked with the crowds along the wide boulevard. They had arrived in The Vilides just after dawn. The cargo vessel had landed at an auxiliary freight terminal at the edge of the bay. They disembarked and made an undetected exit out into the city. A steady wind shifted golden grains of sand over the pavement, its surface pocked with craters and debris. Sunlight filtered through the dusty morning skies, casting the streets in stark light and shadow.

The atmosphere was hazy with a slightly acrid odor that scratched Darshima's throat, making him wonder whether they had just missed a sandstorm. Memories from the raging tempest during his first visit flashed before him, and he shook his head as he tried to focus. He looked around, his pulse slowing with a sense of relief as he saw that much of the skyline remained intact. His eyes swept over the glass and metal edifices, many of them with broken panes and scorched stone. Others had borne the brunt of the invasion and stood completely gutted. Sydarias walked closely beside him, surveying the devastation.

"How long have we been gone?" asked Darshima. His pulse thudded anxiously as he grasped for a sense of how much time they had lost in captivity.

"It has been more than a year since the invasion," replied Tenrai.

"It seems as if it were only yesterday," whispered Sydarias as a shiver coursed through him. Darshima shook his head in disbelief as he thought of the months that had passed by. While he and Sydarias had toiled on Navervyne, those who had remained here had also suffered.

They traversed the scarred surface of a strafed intersection, and Darshima looked toward the sky. Billowing clouds floated above the wide bay, drifting between the peninsulas of the city. His heart leapt into his throat as he saw a fleet of Navervynish vessels sailing overhead. The enormous, grey fusiform ships cast a row of immense shadows upon the waters and cityscape below. Darshima pried his eyes away and looked down at the street, his stomach sinking as the reality of their circumstances became clear. There was no escape from Navervyne and the reach of is newfound empire.

They followed Tenrai through the streets until they came upon an outdoor market. Darshima took in the subdued scene, the communal chatter of bartering voices and clanging metal wares filling his ears. Mostly dressed in worn tunics and robes, the citizens moved steadily around the dusty space. He couldn't help but noticed their resigned expressions as they conducted their business. They used an unfamiliar, greenish metallic coin to purchase the sparse wares and meager provisions.

Scurrying through the crowds, Darshima spotted groups of children shouting and screaming as they chased each other. Faces dirty and dressed in tattered rags, they yanked at the worn hems and threadbare sleeves of the shoppers, begging for scraps of food or coins.

Darshima's heart sank at the troubling scene before him, and he wondered how many of those children were orphaned. Never in his life would he have imagined seeing such destitution in what was once the wealthiest city in the realm. Darshima could sense a collective and profound weariness among the citizens that he understood all too well. Nevertheless, a trace of hope rose within him as he watched them conduct their routines. In the face of such adversity and amid so much devastation, they were somehow eking out an existence.

As they made their way through the crowds, Darshima's ears filled with the foreign but familiar sounds of spoken Navervynish. He listened intently as the guttural murmurs rose amidst the Vilidesian-speaking throngs. Darshima eyed groups of foreign soldiers roving through the streets on foot and in enclosed, metal six-wheeled vehicles. Dressed in uniforms of black boots, loose-fitting grey pants, and coats, they moved brusquely through the crowds. The soldiers peered out from under the bills of their black hats, their narrowed crimson eyes surveying the pedestrians, and their ruddy foreheads flushed with sweat. They wore holstered black pistols upon their hips, their hands never drifting too far from them.

Darshima's stomach sank as the troops moved amid the crowds of people.

"Do not worry, you are safe. They cannot capture you here." Tenrai rested a hand upon his shoulder.

"How can you be so sure?" Darshima trembled in fear as he looked at the uniformed men and women patrolling the streets. He turned to Tenrai, seeking some sort of explanation.

"Trust me," said Tenrai as he nodded calmly. Darshima trained his gaze upon the busy avenue ahead, cold beads of sweat dampening his brow. The fear of being recaptured faded only somewhat with Tenrai's reassurance.

They walked through a large imperial park nestled amid a cluster of soaring towers, their boots crunching upon fragments of crushed stone. The plaza was famous for its circular colonnade of monumental pedestals bearing the statues of the dynastic rulers in their full regalia. Darshima's gaze swept over the familiar place, a lump forming in his throat as he beheld the destruction of the once immaculate space, now littered with debris. Every one of the polished white stone pedestals had collapsed, and only the plinths remained upright. The statues had been torn down and lay broken in large fragments. The expressionless stone faces stared up at the sky, their exquisitely carved features shrouded by the moving shadows cast by the enemy vessels.

As Darshima beheld the toppled statues amid their crushed scepters and shattered crowns, the gravity of what had happened here struck him deeply. Though an Ardavian, he was born a Vilidesian subject like everyone else. The image of the destroyed statues staring into the blue void, whose depths had conjured their doom, seared itself into his soul. He drew in a halting breath and struggled to suppress the waves of disbelief roiling within him. The realm had indeed fallen.

Darshima gripped Sydarias' arm as he looked over the destruction. Sydarias clenched his jaw and fought back his tears as he beheld the ruins.

"How did this happen?" he uttered, barely able to speak.

"I don't know." Darshima shook his head, unsure what else to say. The Vilidesians were a fiercely proud people whose ancestors had united the four moons under a realm that endured for nearly eleven centuries. The ever-present signs of destruction and foreign conquest in the capital was undoubtedly a profound and painful blow to them.

The sun hung directly overhead by the time they arrived at the entrance of Sydarias' home. The once meticulously kept plaza at the foot of the building had been left untended. The foliage had overgrown into a tangled mass, and the once majestic fountain had been reduced to rubble. Though the glass windows were cracked and damaged by smoke, the building stood intact.

Sydarias stared at the ground as Darshima and Tenrai stood beside him.

"I don't even know if they've survived," he whispered to himself.

"We must find out." Darshima placed a reassuring hand upon Sydarias' shoulder.

"We will see you home, then we must be on our way," said Tenrai. They entered the lobby under the watchful glare of a doorman, dressed in a simple grey tunic and trousers. Sydarias stepped tentatively toward thc desk.

"My name is Sydarias Idawa and I live here. Is my family upstairs?" He stared anxiously at the doorman.

"Wait just a moment." The doorman squinted his grey eyes as he leafed through a leather-bound book.

"Do you know if they are here?" asked Sydarias, his voice wavering with emotion.

"I am not allowed to deny or confirm, but I see your name on the register. You may enter," he said as his finger stopped at an entry.

"Thank you," muttered Sydarias. He led Darshima and Tenrai toward the opposite end of the lobby, the large windows casting the airy atrium in a muted light. They boarded the elevator and he pushed a series of buttons. Darshima braced himself as the carriage jolted to life. The shadows shifted along the glass walls as they vaulted upwards, rhythmically veiling their faces. The city shrank as they ascended through the thin layers of clouds and meandering, diminished bands of traffic.

Eyes closed, Sydarias pressed his back to the wall. He held his breath as the elevator slowed to a stop and the doors opened. He opened his eyes, let out a nervous sigh, then escorted them toward the end of the hall. They stood before the large set of doors and Sydarias knocked softly, his fist trembling.

"I pray they are here." He clenched his jaw as they waited.

"We must be hopeful," whispered Tenrai.

The tense atmosphere broke with the sound of approaching footsteps behind the door, then the sharp click of a lock disengaging. The doors swung open, and two young men emerged. Standing barefoot, their bright grey eyes widened in disbelief as they peered into the hallway. Their heads were shaven, and the rough fabric of their blue short-sleeved tunics and trousers clung to their smooth, dark brown skin.

"Is that you, Sydarias?" The slightly taller one exclaimed. They both grabbed Sydarias by the shoulders and pulled him into a tight embrace.

"Elias, Ander my brothers...you're alive," stammered Sydarias as he beheld them.

"I cannot believe it!" said Ander, his voice wavering with emotion. He let go of Sydarias and ran back into the apartment, letting out a shout of joy.

"You have lost so much weight!" Elias cast an appraising look upon Sydarias.

"I have been through so much since we last saw each other." Sydarias' eyes grew damp.

"You must tell me everything." A concerned frown crossed his lips. His eyes lingered over Sydarias' shoulder to Tenrai and Darshima, who stood a few paces from the doorway. "Whom have you brought with you?"

"I would like you to meet Darshima and Tenrai. They saved my life." Sydarias turned around, and they stepped forward. Elias extended his hand to Tenrai, then Darshima.

"Thank you for rescuing him, we thought he had died." He bowed his head.

"We saved each other," replied Darshima. He drew in an anxious breath as images of their toil together on Navervyne flashed before his eyes.

The sound of footsteps interrupted them, and Sydarias' parents emerged with Ander. Mr. Idawa wore a white shirt, black trousers, and leather boots. His closely cropped hair had turned grey, and his face was marked with lines of worry. Madame Idawa wore her greying hair in a long braid. A simple green robe hung from her frame, which had grown thinner. She shuffled to the entryway in leather sandals, her eyes widening in disbelief as she saw Sydarias standing at the door.

"My Sydarias is home?" she said, her voice wavering in shock. She rushed past the threshold and embraced him. "I cannot believe it." A pained gasp escaped her lips, and tears rolled down her cheeks. Mr. Idawa followed closely behind her and hugged them both.

"I never thought I would see you again," said Mr. Idawa, his voice hushed in disbelief. He cleared his throat, regained his composure and turned to Tenrai and Darshima.

"Ander tells us that you both rescued our son." He stepped closer to them and clasped their hands. "I cannot imagine how, but I give you my gratitude."

"We did what we could to help him," replied Tenrai.

"I am glad to see you again, Darshima and I am pleased to meet you, Tenrai." Madame Idawa looked upon them and offered a grateful smile. "Please join us inside." She beckoned them past the entrance.

Tenrai and Darshima followed the Idawa family into their apartment. With a snap of her finger, Madame Idawa signaled a pair of servants clad in grey uniforms standing at attention. They closed the doors and then rushed into the kitchen. The clanging sound of pots and pans filled the air as they set to work. Darshima and Tenrai followed Sydarias and his family through a spacious hallway, toward the back of the home. Though still adequately appointed, Darshima noted that many of the furnishings and paintings were no longer there.

Madame Idawa ushered them into a large dining room bathed in sunlight, and they took their seats around a rectangular glass table. Through the windows, Darshima glimpsed the wounded cityscape, the skies above teaming with Navervynish vessels. His pulse thudded anxiously as he saw their rounded shadows meandering through the canyons of towers. Though he had seen the ships several times already, he didn't know if he would ever grow accustomed to the jarring sight.

The servants reemerged with plates of stewed meat and roots, glasses, and a carafe of dark wine. They set them promptly upon the table, then quietly left.

"I apologize for the simplicity of the meal. It has become so difficult to procure our usual foodstuffs." Madame Idawa frowned.

"We thank you for your generosity during these difficult times." Tenrai nodded politely.

"As you have surely noticed, things are different here," said Mr. Idawa, his voice barely above a contrite whisper.

As they ate, Mr. Idawa recounted their struggles since the invasion. After the Navervynish invaded the city, their soldiers broke through the palace gates, killed the sentries, and stormed the prince's celebration. By the end of the raid, many of the guests had been either captured, killed, or had fled. The soldiers seized the prince and then brutally executed the emperor and empress before the members of the imperial court.

Elias and Ander had been attending to their father's affairs in the city and rushed home as the first enemy ships landed. As they learned of the attack on the palace, the Idawa family and their servants gathered what possessions they could, and fled The Vilides in their personal fleet of craft. They went into hiding at their secluded estate in Raimyd, the ancestral hamlet of the Idawa clan. Located amid the dunes on the opposite side of the moon, it had been largely overlooked by the Navervynish armies, and they had remained safe there.

"We hid at the estate until the situation here stabilized." Madame Idawa gingerly picked at the limp vegetables upon her plate. "We spent our days wondering whether we would survive. We were worried sick about you." She reached over and clutched Sydarias' hand, her voice heavy with sadness.

"I'm glad that you were safe." Sydarias gently squeezed her hand, his eyes growing damp.

Mr. Idawa stared at Sydarias for a moment, then cleared his throat.

"We were also worried about the businesses. Our supply and transport lines have been severely disrupted." Mr. Idawa folded his arms across his chest. "These invaders and their ghastly war have made a terrible mess of things for us all."

Sydarias and his brothers sat attentively as their parents spoke. Darshima listened, but thoughts of his own family consumed his attention. They were neither wealthy nor did they have a private estate where they could hide. Nonetheless, he held onto a glimmer of hope that they might have somehow survived the tumult.

As the conversation lulled, Darshima interjected.

"Why did you return home? Aren't you worried about being captured?" He looked at Mr. Idawa.

"The Vilides formally surrendered to the Navervyne Republic after they agreed to several conditions." Mr. Idawa pushed his plate aside.

"What conditions are those?" Darshima's eyebrows arched in curiosity.

"They may no longer capture our people and take them back to their world," he replied.

"How were they able to stop them?" exclaimed Sydarias.

As Mr. Idawa explained, Navervyne's invasion unleashed a tide of violence and destruction upon the four moons without precedent. Their armies burned homes and seized businesses, plundering untold amounts of treasure and wealth. Their soldiers captured entire villages and towns, enslaving the citizens and taking them back to Navervyne. The invasion had resulted in the fall of the Fyrenosian dynasty and the dissolution of most of the realm's civil administration. Those who remained, along with the Omystikai counselors served as the de facto representatives before the Navervynish.

Facing unspeakable carnage around them, people did what they could to survive and to resist. Ordinary Vilidesians organized mass protests against the invaders. Encouraged by their example, the citizens of the other moons did the same. They flooded the streets, performed work stoppages, and refused to comply with the demands of the soldiers. They traveled in large groups to try and protect each other against capture.

The Navervynish fought viciously against the protesters, killing and enslaving many thousands. Despite the mounting threats of violence and death, the protests increased in force and scope. Within months, the economies of the moons had ground to a virtual standstill. Unable to reliably obtain the labor or raw materials needed for its industries, the Navervynish sought to break the impasse with the Vilidesians and their former subjects throughout the moons.

At the height of the protests, the leaders in Stebbenhour issued edicts prohibiting the capture, sale, and transport of the peoples from the former realm to Navervyne. They eased restrictions on trade and travel between the moons and introduced their currency to exert control over the economy. Much to the protesters' dismay, the Navervynish refused to repatriate the citizens whom they had already captured. Facing severe shortages of food and materials caused by the work stoppages, the citizens of the realm grudgingly accepted Navervyne's terms and relented in their protest.

Despite these new conditions, people still found themselves involuntarily sent to Navervyne. The jails were routinely emptied, and prisoners were transported to the republic as slave labor. Citizens who committed the slightest infraction against the republic's oppressive rules were often arrested, convicted without a trial, and sent to the flooded planet. Rumors abounded of people disappearing from towns and villages, never to be heard from again.

Amid the chaos, the Idawa family maintained their seclusion in Raimyd, hoping they would stay safe. They had only returned to The Vilides after the edicts banning the capture and enslavement of citizens had been issued. It had been difficult to resume a normal life amid the chaos of invasion and foreign rule. Like other Vilidesians, they managed as best they could under the difficult circumstances.

"Iberwight has suffered too," said Tenrai between bites of food.

"How so?" Mr. Idawa tilted his head curiously to the side.

"The dominions have been invaded, and the Navervynish are building bases there." Tenrai folded his hands in his lap.

"Sounds like the same misery here." Mr. Idawa stared grimly Tenrai. "You're an Omystikai, but you don't look like any of the ones I've seen before."

"I doubt you have ever met one like me." Tenrai sat back in his chair.

"Where are you from?" Mr. Idawa leaned forward.

"I am from Tiriyuud," replied Tenrai.

"A most isolated place." Mr. Idawa's eyes sparkled with curiosity. "Where have you traveled from?"

We have just returned from Navervyne." Tenrai gestured toward Darshima and Sydarias.

"How is that possible?" Mr. Idawa shook his head in disbelief.

"I was attending to an important matter on behalf of my kingdom," replied Tenrai.

"Where are you headed?" he asked.

"Darshima and I are traveling to back to Iberwight," said Tenrai.

"What will you do there?" Mr. Idawa rubbed his chin, a quizzical expression crossing his features.

"I won't trouble you with further details, Mr. Idawa." Tenrai folded his arms across his chest. His voice held a firm note that invited no further questions.

"So be it." Mr. Idawa shrugged his shoulders, the curious glitter in his eye fading. "I wish you a safe journey."

The table fell into an uneasy silence, and Sydarias grew visibly upset. His lips curled into a brooding frown, and a turbulent storm brewed behind his smoky eyes.

"Please father, enough about Tenrai and his travels. Why didn't you wait for me after the ships came? Why did you leave without us?" Sydarias gestured toward himself and Darshima, his voice quavering with pent up rage.

"Let us discuss this later, we have company." Madame Idawa gently rested her hand upon his shoulder. Sydarias' brothers avoided his stare and looked down at the table.

"We feared that you were dead." Mr. Idawa glared at him. "I don't know what more I could have done." His expression grew darker at Sydarias' harsh words.

"You didn't even wait," said Sydarias, his voice tinged with sadness.

"We had to flee the city immediately. We would have all died had we waited for you both to return. I had your mother, your elder brothers, and the businesses to take care of." Mr. Idawa clenched his fists as he trembled. "What more could I have done?"

"What could you have done..." An incredulous expression spread upon Sydarias' face, his voice trailing off as he repeated his father's words.

"Don't be so harsh toward him," whispered Darshima as he rested his hand upon Sydarias' tense shoulder. Eyes glittering with tears, he briefly turned to Darshima, then shook his head.

"Father, you don't even care what happened to me. I have been gone since the invasion and I miraculously appear before you today. You haven't even asked where I have been." Sydarias glared at him.

"Sydarias, I promise we will discuss it later," he replied.

"Let us discuss it now. They will not mind." Sydarias pointed toward Darshima and Tenrai.

"This is neither the time nor the place," huffed Mr. Idawa.

"Ask me, father!" Sydarias slammed his fists upon the table, rattling the plates and cups.

"Son, please calm down," said Mr. Idawa. His jaw fell agape in disbelief at Sydarias' anger.

"Didn't you even wonder why I would've been traveling with them from Navervyne?" Sydarias trembled as he spoke.

"Must you carry on like this?" Mr. Idawa glared at him, arms folded across his chest.

"I was a slave, father," he whispered between clenched teeth. Mr. Idawa closed his eyes and let out a pained sigh. His shoulders slumped and he shook his head.

"I cannot believe it." Madame Idawa gasped and put a hand to her mouth.

"I was captured and sold. I worked in the fields of Navervyne alongside Darshima. If it weren't for him and Tenrai, I would have died there," said Sydarias, his voice cracking with pent up emotion. He looked around and met the deferred gazes of his parents and brothers. "I can see that my absence hasn't affected you all very much."

"Sydarias, we have missed you dearly and have worried about you every day since your absence." Madame Idawa sniffled softly and dried her tears with a handkerchief. "I felt such trepidation that night when you left for the prince's celebration. Now I understand why." She closed her eyes and let out a mournful sigh.

"What more could I have done? I did everything in my power to find you!" Mr. Idawa threw up his hands in exasperation.

"Father, you are one of the wealthiest men in The Vilides. Your trade ships ply the skies of every moon. You could have at least tried to find out what happened to me." Sydarias shook his head in frustration.

"You're being impossible." Mr. Idawa pounded his fist on the table, rattling his glass. "These barbarians killed the emperor and empress and captured Prince Khydius. If the prince hasn't returned, how did you expect that I would ever find you?" He stared up at the ceiling and drew in a deep breath as he tried to regain his composure.

"Why couldn't you have waited just a moment longer? We made our way back here after the warships came, and you had all left." Sydarias shuddered in his seat. "If I had waited, we would have all ended up slaves like you." He gestured toward his wife and sons. "Is that what you would have wanted? Your mother, brothers, and I toiling in chains like you and Darshima?"

"I would never want you to suffer as we did." Sydarias wiped away a tear as it streamed down his cheek. "If we could have fled with you, maybe things would have been different." Sydarias sank back into his seat, a solemn frown crossing his lips.

"I would wish for the same thing, but we cannot change the past," whispered Mr. Idawa, his voice heavy with sadness.

Tenrai cleared his throat as he looked around the tense room.

"Sydarias, you and your family have been through a terrible ordeal. You will all need time to heal. You must be patient with each other." He politely rose from the table and signaled Darshima. "Mr. and Madame Idawa, we have returned your son to you. He is safe and unharmed. Darshima and I must be on our way." He bowed deeply and started toward the entrance.

A lump formed in Darshima's throat as he stood up. Though Tenrai explained his plan to deliver Sydarias to his family before continuing to Iberwight, Darshima had desperately avoided thinking about it. They had grown so close during their struggle, and Sydarias had become like a brother to him. They would be parting ways for good and he didn't know how he would move on. A feeling of numbness rose in Darshima's chest as he imagined his life without Sydarias. He vigorously shook his head, realizing that Sydarias belonged here at home with his family. Darshima didn't know what journey he and Tenrai would be undertaking, but he could least take solace in the fact that Sydarias was safe and sound.

Sydarias and his family rose from the table.

"Thank you again Tenrai, Darshima for rescuing our son. We are so very grateful," said Madame Idawa.

"You have my utmost gratitude." Mr. Idawa shook Tenrai's hand.

The family walked with them from the dining room to the entrance of the apartment, where they stood facing each other.

"Sydarias, please accompany Tenrai and Darshima on their way out." Madame Idawa politely gestured toward the doorway.

As Sydarias lingered beside his family, a contemplative frown spread upon his face. He turned from them and then stepped away.

"I cannot continue my life here as it was." He hesitantly shook his head and moved next to Darshima and Tenrai.

"What are you saying?" Mr. Idawa's brow furrowed in confusion.

"Your farewell must include me too. I am leaving with Tenrai and Darshima." Sydarias stared at his parents.

"Whatever do you mean?" Madame Idawa glared at him, her eyes widening in disbelief.

"I am going with them to Iberwight," said Sydarias.

"Sydarias, you belong here with your family." Tenrai turned abruptly to him, his brow furrowed in a serious expression. "Our journey is fraught with perils, and I have brought you this far."

Mr. Idawa shot an angry gaze at Sydarias. "You have only just come home, and are not going anywhere. You are needed here," he said firmly, his voice echoing throughout the room.

"I'm needed here?" Sydarias' eyes widened, his voice barely hiding his incredulity. "You've always made every decision for me, for all of us." He pointed to his brothers and mother. "It ends today."

"Stop at once with this foolishness." Mr. Idawa shook his head.

"You have never trusted me with your affairs like you've trusted my brothers," said Sydarias. "There is nothing here for me anymore. I have made my decision and I am going with them."

Tenrai firmly gripped Sydarias' shoulders and glared at him, his eyes glowing intently. "Sydarias, you haven't the slightest idea of what we face. For your own good, I ask you to stay here and get on with your life."

"I beg you, please let me come with you," replied Sydarias. "I will do whatever it takes to help you both. I want to serve Darshima on his journey."

"What do you mean?" Tenrai's eyebrows wrinkled in a look of confusion.

"I know I can help Darshima. I would have died without him," said Sydarias. Darshima's pulse thudded as he contemplated Sydarias' words. It was clear that Sydarias didn't want to part ways with him either. Tenrai's lips curled into a contemplative frown and a sigh escaped his lips.

"This is your choice to make, Darshima." Tenrai turned to Darshima, let go of Sydarias, and stepped aside.

Darshima looked back at Tenrai, his eyes widened in astonishment. Tenrai's decisiveness had saved them all during their narrow escape from Navervyne, and now he was asking him to make this crucial decision. Darshima would miss Sydarias more than he could ever say. Sydarias was finally at home with his family, and Darshima couldn't bear to be the reason for their separation anew.

"Sydarias, you're safe now. I couldn't ask you to risk your life any further." Darshima felt his heart rise into his throat as a wave of sadness came over him.

"I owe my very life to you. Please let me help you." Sydarias gazed at him, his voice trembling. "We have been through so much together, and I won't leave you now." Darshima drew in a nervous breath as he contemplated the risk Sydarias was willing to take for him. His heart pounded in his chest as he sensed Sydarias' unwavering devotion. Humbled, he turned to Tenrai.

"You must make this decision. Let your intuition guide you," said Tenrai. Even before Darshima thought further, he felt an overwhelming urge from somewhere deep within to accept Sydarias' offer.

"Sydarias shall join us." Darshima put his arm around Sydarias' shoulder and drew him closer.

"What are you doing, Sydarias?" asked Madame Idawa, her voice shaking with worry. She stepped toward him and seized his hand.

"Mother, I am free to make my own decisions. I choose to go with them." Sydarias stared directly at her, his voice thick with emotion.

"You belong here at home, with your family. You shall have not part in whatever trouble these two are searching for." She tried to pull him behind her to protect him, but he stood firm.

"This is no longer home for me or you. It has been conquered and pillaged by foreign soldiers. We have been rendered powerless as they occupy our lands, steal our treasure, and enslave our people. I cannot stand by. I must do something," he said.

A subtle frown of resignation crossed her lips as she contemplated his words. Her eyes grew misty and her grip steadily loosened.

"What about our family? You are still a part of it, aren't you?" She shook her head in disbelief.

"I've seen and experienced too much suffering to stay here." He gently pried his hand away from hers. "I must go out there and help. I cannot change the past, but maybe I can do something about the future."

"How will you survive out there amid this chaos? They cannot guarantee your safety." She put her hands upon her hips, a look of acute concern spreading upon her face.

"They will protect me, and I will protect them." Sydarias gestured toward Darshima and Tenrai.

"You have always been stubborn with your father and me. Nothing I say or do will change your mind once it is set on something." Her lips curled into a bitter frown.

"I'm sorry, but it's true." Sydarias nodded slowly.

"You've only just come back, and now you're giving us no choice but to let you go. It is too much bear." She bowed her head and cried softly.

"I will always be a part of this family, but there is no other choice for me." He embraced her. "You must let me go."

"I pray that I might see you again someday, but I know it is not guaranteed," she said between sobs. He whispered something into her ear, which did little to comfort her.

Sydarias' brothers stepped toward him, and threw their arms around him.

"Please take care of yourself," pleaded Ander. Elias stood beside him, visibly distraught. His lips moved, but he said no words.

Mr. Idawa glared at him, his arms folded across his chest. Sydarias then turned to Tenrai and opened his mouth to speak, but Tenrai responded before he could even utter a word.

"You will have no need for any of your old belongings." Tenrai shook his head. Sydarias cast his eyes downward, his frown dissolving into a look of acceptance.

Just before the trio walked away, Mr. Idawa called out to his son.

"Sydarias, please wait." He reached out and approached him. "I can see that you've suffered greatly this past year, and the experience has made you different," said Mr. Idawa, his voice heavy with remorse.

"I am still your son, but the invasion, our struggle on Navervyne, it all has changed me." Sydarias dashed a tear from his eye.

"I am sorry that I could not do more to protect you." Mr. Idawa sighed and his lips curled into an expression of grief. "I will never understand why you would want to leave us. Do what you must with these two, but never forget that you are a Vilidesian and an Idawa." He embraced Sydarias, then rejoined his wife.

"I won't forget, father." Sydarias slowly stepped away from his family.

He rejoined Darshima and Tenrai at the door, and they departed. As Tenrai led them down the hallway, Darshima put his arm around Sydarias' shoulder.

"Thank you, Sydarias." Darshima drew him nearer. "You will see them again. I give you my word."

His eyes misty with tears, Sydarias looked up at him briefly and nodded. He glared at the floor as they boarded the elevator and traveled down through the clouds. His expression grew more somber as they descended, as if the weight of his decision had finally begun to settle. He had given up his chance to stay in relative safety and comfort with his family, and had chosen to travel to an unfamiliar moon with them. Sydarias' unflinching loyalty left Darshima speechless.

Though Darshima knew their experience on Navervyne had changed them, he was only beginning to understand the profound ways in which it had. He looked upon Sydarias, who waited silently as the elevator jostled them, feelings of gratitude welling up within him. Darshima knew that the journey ahead of them was largely unknown, and would be difficult in ways he could not yet imagine. He felt immeasurably better knowing that Sydarias would be there beside him. The elevator came to a stop at the lobby, rousing Sydarias, who stood quietly amid his thoughts. They left the building and stepped out into the balmy afternoon air.

Chapter Thirty Seven

The trio walked upon the streets, which stood largely empty in the afternoon light. Groups of patrolling soldiers in grey fatigues roved about in their wheeled metal vehicles, kicking up clouds of sand in their wake. Darshima, Tenrai, and Sydarias were on their way to an aerial freighter port near the bay, along the edge of the eastern peninsula. Tenrai had devised a plan for them to stow away on a vessel leaving for Gavipristine that evening, a voyage that would last several days. From there, they would make the journey to Tiriyuud.

Darshima looked around, bewildered at the desolation. During his first visit, he remembered The Vilides as bustling with people, jostling for a modicum of space upon the pavement. The palpable sense of loneliness troubled him.

"Where is everyone?" he asked.

"People are trying to go home before the curfew," said Tenrai.

"There's a curfew?" Sydarias turned to him, his mouth agape.

"They issued it after the riots." Tenrai scanned the horizon as he led them toward the port.

"What happened?" asked Darshima.

"Several months ago, when the protests became violent here, the Navervynish soldiers assaulted and killed thousands of people. Those who weren't maimed, were captured and taken back to Navervyne."

"Even after the invasion, they killed people so wantonly?" asked Darshima. His chest felt heavy with a sense of sadness, as he pictured the violence that likely occurred on the streets surrounding them.

"The soldiers continue to do so," said Tenrai, a somber frown crossing his lips as they moved along the pavement. "After the republic issued the edicts, the protests abated." He gestured toward the emptying streets. "They instituted a curfew that goes into effect every evening at sundown."

"This is terrible." Sydarias shook his head. "We are prisoners in our own city."

"Anyone found in public after dark is at risk of being detained." Tenrai looked up at the late afternoon sky, his hand shielding his eyes against the lengthening rays. "Let us hurry."

They walked down the steep, sloping street and Darshima caught a glimpse of the port at the edge of the bay. Fleets of Navervynish ships hovered over the vast area, their long greenish frames glinting in the sunlight. Above the bands of traffic, the moons hung in a faded trio. Darshima's heart leapt as he beheld the verdant disc of Gordanelle, his desire to return home rushing back. He had so many questions about the fate of his parents and his brother, Sasha. Even if they hadn't made it back to Ardavia, maybe he could try and find answers, or at least find some closure there. His eyes wandered over to the blue-grey disc of Wohiimai and then to Iberwight, its white crescent gleaming like a shard of opalescent crystal against the clear sky.

A feeling of uncertainty welled up within him as Tenrai's revelation echoed in his ears. He looked warily at Iberwight, unsure of what awaited him on that foreign and mysterious moon. Tenrai had revealed little about his plan or their objectives, and Darshima didn't even know how long they would be there. Tenrai saw him as a leader, but Darshima couldn't understand how. He was merely one among countless many, whose life had been torn apart by the invasion.

"We are almost there." Tenrai pointed toward an alley in the distance, between two soaring tower blocks. "There is a side door that leads to an underground tunnel. We will sneak into the port unnoticed."

As they approached, the echo of frightened voices pierced the air. Tenrai exchanged a startled glance with them, and they ran toward the source of the commotion. Darshima rushed with them into the alley and stumbled to a stop. He looked up and saw a uniformed Navervynish soldier with a metal truncheon in hand, viciously beating a boy who appeared to be about ten years old. Dressed in a worn, brown armless tunic, trousers, and leather sandals, he was deep tan and his unshorn, dark blond hair hung about his ears. Strewn bolts of bright, shimmering fabric and scattered metal toys lay upon the pavement around them. The boy struggled to get away, but the soldier gripped him by the collar and lifted him off the ground.

A young woman dressed in black trousers, boots, and an armless red vest motioned frantically behind them. The sunlight reflected off her bronze skin as she jumped and stomped, yelling at the top of her lungs. Her smoky grey eyes grew wide with fear as she witnessed the boy being assaulted. She tore angrily at the soldier's coat, but could not pull him away.

"Wait here." Tenrai looked over his shoulder at Darshima and Sydarias, then hurried toward the commotion. The woman spotted Tenrai as he stalked forward, her mouth agape in surprise.

The soldier threw the boy to the ground, and he landed upon his side with a painful thud. The boy then scrambled to his feet and tried to run away, but the soldier chased him until he was cornered. His back against a wall, the boy stared at the soldier, his emerald eyes widened in terror. The soldier delivered several forceful blows with the weapon, striking his ribs. The boy yelped in pain, his cries echoing throughout the alley.

His eyes narrowed, Tenrai stepped behind the soldier, who remained unaware of his presence. He extended his fingertips toward the back of the soldier's head, closed his eyes, and whispered a string of unintelligible phrases. Without warning, the soldier froze.

His hand hung motionlessly in the air and the truncheon fell to the pavement with a sharp clatter. His crimson eyes rolled into his head, and he fell backward. The soldier collapsed onto the ground with a thud, like a plank of wood, and stared blankly at the sky.

The boy, weakened from the beating stood unsteadily on his feet. He turned his bruised face toward Tenrai, his eyes widened in fear. His lips, cut from the blows parted to speak, but he said no words. He lowered his gaze, gripped his sides, and grimaced. His slight frame shuddering, he let out a pained cough and spat a clot of blood onto the ground. Staggering forward, he reached for Tenrai, then fainted. Tenrai ran to his side and caught him before he hit the pavement. He gently rested the boy against the wall and knelt before him.

"Stay with me, child." Tenrai put a hand upon his cheek. The woman ran to the boy and crouched beside him. She frantically looked him over and placed a hand upon his shoulder. His eyes fluttered open, and he drew in labored breaths. He gripped his side and gritted his blood-stained teeth in pain. She let out a stifled sob and turned to Tenrai.

"He's my brother, Shonan. He did nothing wrong!" she yelled through her tears. Tenrai put an arm around her shoulder and drew her closer.

"I believe you, it is not his fault," he said. Darshima, and then Sydarias stepped forward to help. Darshima caught a glimpse of the woman's face, and his heart skipped a beat. It was Erethalie, the worker from the cafeteria who had saved him from the sandstorm those many months ago.

"Erethalie?" Darshima moved toward her. She looked up at him, and her bright eyes narrowed, then widened in recognition.

"Darshima, is that you?" She exclaimed, dashing away a tear with the back of her hand. She rose to her feet and faced him.

"What are you doing here?" She anxiously ran her fingers through her wavy, dark blond hair. Before he could reply, Tenrai interjected.

"The boy is weak. We must take him somewhere safe." He gathered Shonan in his arms and stood up with him, his brow furrowed in a worried expression.

"We live nearby, and he can rest there." She bit her lip nervously as she looked at her injured brother. "Follow me." She pointed toward the base of a tower at the opposite end of the alley, and led them forward. As he walked, Darshima turned briefly around to see the soldier still lying on the pavement, his chest slowly rising and falling with each breath.

"What will happen to the soldier?" asked Darshima, his heart thudding in disbelief at Tenrai's seemingly miraculous ability to incapacitate with a mere gesture of his hand.

"He is awake, but stunned. He will regain his faculties long after we are gone." Tenrai briefly glanced over his shoulder. "We must hurry, the ship will depart just after nightfall."

They walked through a fractured glass doorway, amid the shadows of a deserted lobby. Erethalie ushered them into the dark cabin of an elevator and pressed several lighted buttons. A pair of metal doors slid closed behind them, and they jolted upward at a rapid clip. The elevator shuddered to a stop near the middle of the tower, and they exited.

They followed her down a narrow, dimly lit hallway, and a wedge of light glimmered across the middle of the tiled path. As they walked by, Darshima turned toward its source and noticed a slightly open door. He caught a glimpse beyond the threshold, and saw that the apartment was empty.

The spacious confines of the dwelling bore no trace of the previous inhabitants. The smooth stone floors were covered in a fine layer of dust. Long beams of sunlight filtered through the grimy, cracked windows and pierced the emptiness, chasing the darkness to the corners of the room. Darshima shuddered, his heart filling with sadness as he tried to imagine the family that had once lived there. Perhaps it was a family like his. He wondered if they had even survived.

They made their way down the path and stopped in front of a door at the end of the hallway.

“Please come inside.” Erethalie tapped a code upon a smudged screen, its clicking sound echoing through the hallway. The lock disengaged with a thud, she pushed open the door and ushered them past the threshold. Enclosed by tall glass windows, the large apartment was almost bare, save for a wooden table and a set of chairs in the corner. The doors to the other rooms were closed, their scuffed wooden panels veiled in shadow. Erethalie ran to a near-by closet, grabbed a pile of blankets, and arranged them upon the floor.

Darshima glanced through the windows at the city surrounding them. The burning sun hung low in the late afternoon sky, its reddish rays reflecting starkly off the warped and shattered facades of the Vilidesian skyline. In the distance beyond the city limit, the dunes shimmered in hues of burnt gold, slowly shifting in the winds. Formations of Navervynish ships hung high above the towers in dark, dashed rows, their silhouettes stretching onto the dunes.

"He can lie down here,” she said. Darshima tore his gaze from the window to see Tenrai kneel down and gently rest the child upon the downy coverings. His eyes remained closed and the color had drained from his face. There were scratches upon his cheeks, and his bruised lips oozed a trickle of blood.

Erethalie went to the kitchen and returned with a metal basin filled with steaming water and a small towel. She knelt beside him, soaked the cloth, and dabbed his cheeks. A worried expression crossed her face as she cleaned him. He flinched as the water touched his skin.

"Everything's okay now, Shonan. We're home," she whispered. Tenrai narrowed his eyes as he surveyed the child. Darshima sat down upon the floor beside Tenrai, unsure how to help. Sydarias sat beside Erethalie, his eyebrows knit in concern as he peered at the injured boy. Shonan moaned softly and lay still. He drew in shallow breaths, and his eyes fluttered open.

"What happened?" he asked, his soft voice wavering. As he tried to sit up, he let out a yelp and grimaced in pain. He clutched his side, clenched his teeth, and fell silent as the tears streamed down his cheeks. Erethalie helped him lay back down, his body shuddering as he tried to stifle the ache.

"You're going to be fine, Shonan." Erethalie rubbed his hand and pressed it against her cheek. Her eyes growing damp, she let out an anguished sigh.

"Close your eyes and rest, child." Tenrai drew closer to him and gently placed his hands upon Shonan's bruised forehead.

Darshima looked on curiously as he attended to the boy. Tenrai closed his eyes and whispered a melodic string of words in a language that Darshima had never heard before. Shonan's breathing grew noticeably slower and deeper. The grimace on his face lessened, and he stopped gritting his teeth. The tenseness that seized his muscles dissipated, and he seemed to relax. His tears stopped flowing and the color slowly returned to his face.

"What is he doing?" asked Darshima, his heart bounding in amazement as he watched Tenrai at work.

"It is an old Omystikai healing technique," whispered Sydarias, his gaze shifting between Tenrai and Shonan. Growing up, Darshima had heard murmurings of the rare abilities of some Omystikai tribes who healed the sick and injured. He had thought it was a legend but looked on in incredulity as the boy seemingly returned to health under Tenrai's hand.

Tenrai's voice grew quieter, and his words were barely audible. His lips stopped moving and a profound sense of calm filled the room. Shonan drew in a loud gasp and jolted upright.

"What happened?" He looked around wide-eyed as he drew in deep breaths.

"Shonan, are you okay?" Erethalie gently grabbed his shoulders.

"I feel fine." He turned toward her and shrugged.

"Does it hurt anywhere?" She looked him over as he vigorously shook his head. He glimpsed up at Tenrai and offered a toothy grin. Erethalie wrapped her arms around Shonan and embraced him tightly. She then turned to Tenrai.

"Thank you for saving my brother. I don't even know your name, but I am so grateful." A tear streamed down her cheek, and she wiped it away with her palm.

"My name is Tenrai Nax, and I am glad to offer my help." He politely bowed his head.

"Why did the soldier strike him?" Darshima turned to Erethalie.

"We were trying to sell some of our belongings, but we were stopped." She shook her head and let out an angry sigh.

"I understand things are bad here, but the soldiers are beating children?" Sydarias' jaw fell agape, his expression revealing both his surprise and disgust.

"We are trying our best to survive, but the soldiers harass us all the time." A frustrated frown crossed her lips.

As Erethalie explained, she and her brother had been on their way to a nearby market. They were planning to trade some of their remaining possessions for a few day's worth of rations, when they were stopped by a Navervynish soldier. He noticed the quality of their items and accused them of stealing. Erethalie denied the accusations, but the soldier refused to listen. Shonan came to her defense and shouted at the soldier, who then proceeded to beat him.

"You came just in time Tenrai, he would've lasted much longer," said Erethalie, her voice breaking with sadness. Shonan sidled next to her and rested his head upon her shoulder.

"I don't know how much longer we can survive here." Her gaze drifted toward the window as she recounted their struggle in the occupied capital.

Erethalie's family, like countless others, had suffered greatly during the invasion. Her parents, older brother, and sister had been invitees of the prince's fateful birthday celebration. She and Shonan had borne witness to the invasion and its fiery carnage from the windows of their apartment. In the days that followed, she received word from a family friend that their parents had been killed during the siege, and their siblings had been captured.

"Why didn't you leave after the invasion? My family ended up fleeing to our estate in Raimyd," said Sydarias.

"This is our only home and we had nowhere else to go," she replied flatly. "Nearly every town and city has been captured." Her eyes widened incredulously as she registered Sydarias' suggestion. "People are being beaten, detained, or simply disappearing without a trace."

"My apologies, but I didn't realize." A contrite frown crossed Sydarias' lips, and he wrung his hands.

"Some people have fled the Vilides, but they're finding the same misery on the other moons." Erethalie shook her head as she stared through the dusty pane, her smooth face lit by the afternoon sunlight. "We were close to leaving, but the Navervynish and their chaos seem to be everywhere."

"Tenrai told us the same thing." Darshima nervously drummed his fingers upon the floor.

"After the invasion, I had planned to take us to Wohiimai so that we could stay with our mother's family, but I have heard nothing from them," she sighed. "There is no refuge anywhere."

Erethalie described the city's descent into turmoil after the invasion. Public services such as sanitation and transportation had become unreliable. Some days, there was no running water in their faucets. Their lives had become a daily struggle, but they persisted. Erethalie and her brother remained in the apartment, fearing the rising rates of crime and violence beyond its walls. They kept current with the events in The Vilides and on the other moons with the once-daily televised broadcast that the Navervynish permitted.

Erethalie did her best to stay strong for the sake of her brother. She made sure that he was healthy and well-fed. She tutored him as best as she could so that he could keep up with his lessons, but they had sold most of their books. They only left their home to obtain rations and other necessities.

Darshima sat silently as he contemplated her words. Sydarias' family had told them how difficult things were, but Erethalie's predicament brought the struggle here into heartbreaking relief. He couldn't help but think about his own family in Ardavia. His chest tightened in fear as he imagined them struggling to survive, much like Erethalie and Shonan.

"You are right Erethalie, there is indeed suffering far beyond Ciblaithia," said Tenrai.

"How can it be possibly worse than here?" A quizzical look crossed her features.

"We traveled from Navervyne and is as bad as one can imagine," he sighed.

"What compelled you to travel all the way to Navervyne?" Her jaw dropped in disbelief. "Where the three of you captured and sent there?" Her vivid gaze darted between them.

"Sydarias and I were slaves on Navervyne, and Tenrai rescued us." Darshima turned toward her, the ever-present memories of his toil there rushing back to him. A solemn expression spread upon his face as he tried to hold back the flood of emotion.

"I am sorry. I cannot imagine the horror of what you both endured." Her eyes grew damp as she looked at them.

"We're simply thankful to be alive," said Sydarias, his voice wavering. "Tenrai, you succeeded in rescuing Darshima and Sydarias?" Her eyes widened in disbelief. "Were any others rescued?"

"I was only able to rescue Darshima and Sydarias. In time, I hope everyone will be rescued." An earnest expression spread upon Tenrai's face.

"What do you mean?" Her eyebrows arched in curiosity.

"I cannot reveal much to you, but one day I hope that you will be reunited with your brother and sister." He leaned toward the window and cast his gaze upon the horizon.

"Do you know if they are still alive?" she stammered nervously. Tenrai turned to Erethalie and Shonan.

"I have never met them, so it is difficult for me to say." He looked at them intently. "Take my hands, and set your thoughts on your siblings."

They grasped his hands and bowed their heads in concentration. Tenrai closed his eyes, his breathing slowed and he grew noticeably paler. Sydarias and Darshima exchanged curious glances as Tenrai, Erethalie, and Shonan sat meditating in silence.

"Your brother and sister appear to be very close in age," whispered Tenrai as his eyes fluttered open.

"They are twins. You can see them?" asked Shonan, his voice rising with astonishment.

"Hush, Shonan." Erethalie shot a stern look at him. He timidly pursed his lips and stayed quiet. As Tenrai fell silent, Erethalie and Shonan exchanged an anxious glance, awaiting his words.

"The brother is named Kelen, he is tall, with curly blond hair and grey eyes. The sister is named Jan, she is smaller, with wavy brown hair and green eyes." Tenrai's brow furrowed in concentration.

"Yes!" They exclaimed in unison, their voices betraying feelings of awe.

"I do not know exactly where they are. They are working together in a factory on Navervyne and appear tired, but healthy. This is all that I can see," whispered Tenrai.

"At least they're together." A tear rolled down Erethalie's cheek. "Can you let them know that we are alright?"

"Think to yourself the words you want to say, and I will communicate them." He gently squeezed their hands. The trio fell back into a contemplative silence. Tenrai narrowed his eyes and whispered a string of cryptic phrases.

"It is done. They have received your message." He gazed at them and let go of their hands.

"I don't know how to thank you, Tenrai." Erethalie turned to him, her voice thick with emotion.

"It is my duty to help however I can." Tenrai bowed his head.

Darshima's pulse raced as he witnessed Tenrai's miraculous feat. He drew in an anxious breath, as images of his parents and Sasha came to him. Perhaps Tenrai could at least tell him if they had survived.

"Tenrai, can you tell me what happened to my family?" asked Darshima, his voice wavering.

"The sun will be setting soon. We must continue to the port." Tenrai rose to his feet, and Darshima's heart sank with disappointment.

"Please Tenrai, I won't take much of your time." Darshima jumped up and faced him. Sydarias rose beside him.

"It is not as simple as it seems. We need strength and clarity, so we must first travel to Tiriyuud." A somber expression crossed his face.

"I don't understand." Darshima shook his head, feelings of sadness welling up within him.

"In time, you will." Tenrai turned toward the entrance. Darshima frowned as he listened. He had no choice but to wait.

"You're leaving so soon?" Erethalie turned from Shonan, toward Tenrai.

"There is a ship departing for Iberwight that we must catch." Tenrai started for the door.

"Why must you travel so far?" she asked.

"We are up against a people that seek nothing short of our complete subjugation. We must fight for our freedom." Tenrai clenched his jaw, then relaxed as his eyes met Shonan's. "Please take care, young one."

"I've heard that Navervyne's armies didn't destroy Iberwight like they did the other moons. Is it safer there?" she asked cautiously.

"There is a degree of peace in Tiriyuud, but trouble still lingers beyond the shores of our kingdom," replied Tenrai.

"There must be some way I can help you." She put a finger to her temple, her brow wrinkled in thought.

"The journey we are embarking on is very dangerous. Shonan needs you," said Tenrai. Erethalie cast her gaze toward the floor and bit her lip. Darshima glared at Tenrai as they walked toward the door. Erethalie's willingness to help them left him humbled. He had hoped that Tenrai would at least listen to her, but he understood that they had little time remaining before the ship departed.

Tenrai opened the door and gestured to Darshima and Sydarias, who offered their goodbyes to Erethalie and Shonan. She remained seated upon the floor beside her brother, a surprised expression spreading upon her face at their abrupt departure. As Tenrai was about to close the door, she sprang to her feet, ran toward them, and held it open.

"Wait, I know how I can help you," she said excitedly. Shonan jumped up and followed her.

"Erethalie, for your own sake, please heed my words," said Tenrai.

"You need transportation," she replied confidently. "You say that you have matters to take care of, but do you have dependable transportation?"

"We will make our passage on a freight ship to Gavipristine this evening. We will then find our way to Tiriyuud. I can reveal no more," said Tenrai, his voice wavering with a hint of uncertainty.

"How reliable is your transport? Are you sure that you will make it there?" She folded her arms across her chest.

"We traveled safely from Navervyne. I expect no less on this journey." Tenrai narrowed his eyes in a subtly defensive expression.

"Tenrai, I am an experienced pilot. Let me help." Her brow furrowed in a matter-of-fact expression.

"Erethalie, we will manage," he replied.

"Our father's ship remains in good condition. The fuel tanks are nearly full and there are adequate stocks of food and water. I still have access to it." She pointed up toward the ceiling.

"You have access to a ship?" Tenrai's eyebrows rose with interest.

"It can easily travel the distance from here to Iberwight and back," she said.

"How was it not seized during the invasion?" Tenrai rubbed his chin as he pondered her words.

"The Navervynish tried to seize personal property, including ships. They relented after the first wave of protests and allowed each family to keep their craft," said Erethalie.

"My parents were able to keep their vehicles as well," added Sydarias.

"My ship can accommodate all of us, but it is small enough to land in almost any field. We won't have to travel through any of the ports, which are heavily policed by the Navervynish." She stepped closer to Tenrai, and Shonan stayed behind her.

"So you could take us directly to Tiriyuud. That sounds much safer than traveling to Gavipristine." Darshima turned to Tenrai, his pulse thudding with anticipation.

Tenrai shook his head. "I appreciate your generosity Erethalie, but it is too risky. I cannot guarantee your or Shonan's safety. We may very well perish."

"And we may very well meet our end here in The Vilides." A resigned expression crossed her face. "Tenrai, let me help you get safely back to your home. The broadcasts say that ships leaving for Gavipristine and the Omystikai dominions are infrequent at best. There is no guarantee that you can easily find a ship headed to your kingdom."

"I have already arranged a sound plan," he said firmly.

"With the infrequent transport between the moons, your plan may not work. Let me help you," she replied.

Darshima's mind echoed with her words from their first meeting. She came from a long line of explorers who had charted some of the first routes between the moons. Although her parents forbid her from flying professionally, her father ran the family's courier business and had taught her how to pilot vessels and navigate routes. If anyone could guide them safely on their voyage, he was sure it would be Erethalie.

Tenrai crossed his arms and looked upon her with an appraising glance.

"What do you think?" he sighed and turned to Darshima.

"You wouldn't have to worry about me or Shonan. We would take care of ourselves." Erethalie looked anxiously at Darshima.

He knew their journey would be dangerous and mulled over the risks they would face, especially with a child. Nonetheless, something deep within compelled him to accept her offer.

"We could use an experienced pilot with her own reliable craft. It would make our journey much safer," said Darshima, memories of their harrowing flight from Navervyne as stowaways coming back to him. "Erethalie, we would be grateful for your service."

"I will get you all to Iberwight safely, you have my word." She grasped Darshima's hand.

Shonan scowled at the group and turned toward his sister.

"If our brother and sister come back, who will meet them?" His lips curled into a frown and he stepped away from her.

"There is nothing left for us here, and we cannot survive like this for much longer." She peered into his eyes. "I don't know if they will come back, but we might find them on our journey."

"So we are going to rescue them?" Shonan's eyes sparkled inquisitively. A tender smile spread across her face, and she held his cheeks with her hands.

"We are going to rescue them, and all of the brothers and sisters, mothers and fathers. Please come, Shonan." She let go of him, and his frown softened. He hesitantly moved toward Erethalie and grabbed her hand.

"We will gather our things and take you to the ship." She turned to Tenrai.

"Please hurry Erethalie, we must leave soon." Tenrai gestured toward the door. He put his hand to his forehead and let out a sigh.

Darshima read the frustration in Tenrai's expression, and his chest tightened with a pang of nervousness. Despite Tenrai's clear misgivings, Darshima felt that he had made the right decision. Erethalie and Shonan hurried into an interior room of the apartment and returned with leather bags slung over their shoulders.

"Follow me." She walked past Darshima, Tenrai, and Sydarias. With Shonan in tow, she stepped through the open door and beckoned them.

Chapter Thirty Eight

The group stepped off the elevator, walked down a dark hallway, and came to a stop before a metal door.

"We are almost there." With a grunt, Erethalie pushed the heavy door open with her shoulder. A cool, steady wind swirled around them as they walked through the secluded, rock-strewn field upon the roof of her building. They made their way under the waning sky, the click of their footsteps just audible above the din of the city. Darshima looked upon the vast skyline surrounding them, the scarred edifices reflecting the last traces of sunlight against the approaching darkness.

Erethalie and Shonan led the group through a patch of overgrown, knee-high weeds until they reached a large hangar at the opposite end of the field. Covered in dried brush and tangled vines, it was barely discernible from the surrounding piles of debris, abandoned craft, and scrapped machinery. Its facade marked by a dozen doors, Erethalie came to a stop in front of the last one.

She pressed her palm upon a glowing keypad and waited patiently. The giant doors issued a restless groan and parted vertically, revealing a large vehicle within. Appearing in good condition, the gleaming blue craft loomed above them and stood upon conical landing struts. Its angular facets gleamed in the fading light. Sleek lines of trapezoidal windows ran from the cone-shaped nose, down the length of the smooth, deltoid fuselage, which terminated seamlessly into the exhaust vents of twin pairs of engines at the rear. As they approached the craft, Darshima noticed a fine layer of dust coating its surface.

"This was father's fastest ship," whispered Shonan. Erethalie put her hand around his shoulder and drew him nearer.

They stood in silence together for a moment, and she stepped toward the rear hatch. As Erethalie approached, a series of white lights in the underbelly of the craft blinked rhythmically. The hatch opened with a soft whir and a long metal plank extended toward the ground, resting with a gentle thud.

"It hasn't been used since the invasion, but it should still fly," muttered Erethalie, as she stepped onto the gangway.

"It's one of the most advanced vessels out there," exclaimed Sydarias, his eyes sweeping over the graceful, geometric lines of the airframe.

No ordinary craft, the model was built by one of the most renowned Vilidesian shipbuilders. Despite its modest size, it was known for its speed, range, and agility. Darshima's mind raced, taking in every detail as they approached the gangway. His heart beat with a sense of confidence, grateful that he accepted Erethalie's offer.

"Our father cherished this ship. It blessed him with many safe voyages." Erethalie beckoned them onto the gangway.

"May it continue to do so," whispered Tenrai.

"How were you able to preserve it so well?" Darshima walked tentatively onto the plank with the others.

"Father always kept this ship close to home in case he needed it. We were fortunate that the Navervynish didn't bombard our rooftop." She shrugged her shoulders.

They followed Erethalie and Shonan up the gangway and into the craft, the hatch closing firmly behind them. They walked single file through a narrow corridor past several closed doors, their footsteps clicking softly against the smooth metal floor. They settled into the spacious cabin and stowed their things. Erethalie then moved into the cockpit, sat in the pilot's chair, and fastened her safety harness. Tenrai took the navigator's seat on her right, rested his bag beside him, and secured himself. Darshima, Sydarias, and Shonan sat behind them in a row of firm leather chairs.

As they secured the belts over their hips and shoulders, Erethalie set to work turning on the engines. Her delicate hands moved swiftly over the instrument panel, pulling levers, turning dials, and tapping a dizzying array of glowing symbols on a large bank of screens before her. The lights overhead flickered on, and the engines at the rear let out a deep roar as the craft came to life. The fuselage shuddered under the raw power of the engines and she pulled another lever, tempering their vibration to a soft hum.

"What if we get stopped by the Navervynish?" Darshima peered through the window beside him, his eyes following the bands of traffic soaring through the evening sky.

"They tried to regulate voyages between the cities of the realm after the invasion, but were met with further protests and work stoppages at ports on all of the moons." Erethalie grabbed the throttle and gently lifted the craft higher off the ground. With a soft mechanical whir, the struts retracted, and she grasped the hexagonal control wheel with both hands. She slowly guided the craft out of the hangar and into the debris-strewn field.

"How did they react to the protests?" Sydarias peered at her, leaning forward in his seat.

"Their soldiers lashed out violently and killed scores of protesters. The situation only worsened, and commerce between Navervyne and the moons ground to a halt. They couldn't sell their goods or collect taxes and were forced to relent." Erethalie tapped several icons on the screens before her and the craft hovered higher.

"That's remarkable," exclaimed Darshima. "So the protests are changing things?"

"Sometimes they seem to work, sometimes they don't." She steered the craft above the rooftop, toward the parapet of the building. "Though they are technologically superior, the Navervynish realize they are despised and outnumbered here."

"I've noticed that the soldiers look on edge when they patrol the streets," said Sydarias.

"They have conquered the realm and intimidated its people with violence. If they change things any further, they know that they risk a popular revolt." Tenrai gripped the armrests of his seat as the craft moved further into the field. "They are solidifying their hegemony, but are learning that the balance here is delicate."

A wave of nervousness came over Darshima as he listened to the conversation. His mind raced with conjectured images of clashing protesters and armed soldiers. A sense of hope rose within him as he mulled over Erethalie's account of events. Despite the violence they faced, he was encouraged to hear that people were collectively resisting the actions of the invaders.

"They have been stopping fewer vehicles at random. As long as we move with traffic, they shouldn't bother us." She glanced over her shoulder toward the rear of the cabin. "Is everyone secure?"

"We are fine back here," said Sydarias as he settled into his seat.

Erethalie turned back around and pulled on a lever beside her. The craft drifted beyond the edge of the parapet, gently rocking with the winds. With a sweep of her hand over the control panel, she aimed the vessel's conical nose toward the sky. The engines issued a deep roar, and they rocketed upward. Darshima sank forcefully into his seat, drawing in deep breaths as he felt the pressure of their acceleration against his chest. The airfield and rooftop fell away from view as they vaulted toward the clouds.

Darshima looked through the window beside him as they soared over the opposing peninsulas of The Vilides. Its countless lights, though dimmed, still shone boldly against the night sky. The craft rocked gently during its steep ascent, and the moonlit expanse of ocean spread before them. Erethalie brought the craft up to speed and merged into a wide band of outbound traffic heading toward the upper atmosphere.

"What is our destination on Iberwight, Tenrai?" She tapped a row of rotating symbols on the screens before her.

"We must go to my home village in Tiriyuud." Tenrai pointed through the windshield toward the shimmering white orb hanging above the dark ripples of the watery horizon.

"I've only heard about your kingdom. Its true location isn't precise on any maps." She gripped the control wheel with one hand and scrolled through a glowing array of navigational charts on the screens in front of her.

"I will show you the way once we get to Iberwight." He leaned back in his seat.

Darshima's pulse thudded nervously as he listened to Tenrai. Since his rescue, he had yearned to go home to Gordanelle, but Tenrai had warned him against it. Before their return to Ciblaithia, Iberwight had seemed like an abstract idea, but it was no longer the case. He stared at the icy orb, a cold sensation settling in his chest as they hurtled toward an uncertain future. He wasn't ready to go. His family's fate weighed heavily upon him and without answers, he wouldn't be able to continue.

"We must go to Ardavia first," blurted Darshima.

"I have delayed our return to Iberwight long enough. We have much yet to accomplish." Tenrai turned around and shot a piercing look at him.

"I must find out what happened to my family." Darshima nervously tapped his foot against the floor.

"Darshima, you must move on from your life on Gordanelle. It is long past." A fleeting look of confusion crossed Tenrai's face.

"I don't know what lies ahead for me on Iberwight. I need to find out if they survived." Darshima anxiously shook his head. Tenrai's gaze lingered upon Darshima and he then turned back around.

An uneasy silence filled the cabin, punctuated by the low roar of the engines and the rush of air as they ascended into the upper reaches of the atmosphere. They flew through a thin veil of clouds, the blackness of space looming beyond. An ache settled in the pit of Darshima's stomach. Though he was so close to home, he never felt so far away. He closed his eyes tightly and tried to stifle his disappointment. They had made time to deliver Sydarias to his family, to rescue Erethalie and Shonan, but there was no opportunity for him to see his family. He understood that visiting Gordanelle would delay them even more, but he couldn't bring himself to think of anything else.

Darshima felt a hand upon his shoulder and turned to meet Sydarias' sympathetic gaze.

"We must have faith that your family has somehow survived," he said softly.

Darshima glared at the floor and avoided Sydarias' stare. Memories of happier times on Gordanelle crept into his mind. His life hadn't been perfect there. He did not always get along with his parents or his brother, but they were still his family, and he missed them dearly. His suffering on Navervyne had given him perspective, and the disagreements he once had with them now seemed so trivial. He could not simply move on.

"You communicated with Erethalie's siblings, and when I asked you to do the same for my family, you rebuffed me." Darshima's pulse thudded as a sense of frustration welled up within him.

"Darshima..." Tenrai turned around and faced him, but Darshima continued.

"I cannot travel to Iberwight and help you fulfill your mission you unless I have some sort of confirmation about my family's fate. Sydarias and Erethalie have had theirs, please let me have mine." Darshima let out a frustrated sigh.

"This is no mere mission. It is our destiny." Tenrai held Darshima's gaze. "I have deferred to every one of your requests."

"This one is particularly important to me." Darshima's eyes grew damp, and Tenrai glared at him. A pensive frown crossed his lips as he registered Darshima's disquiet.

"I believe I have underestimated your worry," he sighed. "If you say that you cannot continue with me in good faith, then I must believe you."

"I need to know what happened to them." A tear streamed down Darshima's cheek.

"If you are to survive what lies ahead in Tiriyuud, there must be no doubt in your heart." Tenrai then turned to Erethalie. "We must change our plans and make a very brief stop in Ardavia."

"I will do whatever you ask once we leave Gordanelle." Darshima looked toward the cockpit, his pulse slowing as a sense of relief washed over him.

"I will get us there safely." Erethalie turned a series of knobs and pushed a lever toward the floor. Buffeted by the winds, the craft banked sharply to the right. They roared toward a narrow band of traffic arcing upward into the black void of space, the green orb of Gordanelle beckoning them.

Chapter Thirty Nine

Darshima sat beside the window of the craft, his face glued to the large pane of glass. Stark rays from the afternoon sun filtered through the windows, illuminating the interior of the ship. He shook his head, chasing away the remaining bits of slumber. They had voyaged through the Ciblaithian night and had just arrived on Gordanelle. He looked toward the cockpit and observed Erethalie's steady hands upon the controls, guiding the craft downward through the cloudy atmosphere.

"We will arrive at your home shortly, Darshima." Erethalie glanced briefly at a glowing array of maps, then back through the windshield. Tenrai sat up in his chair and faced forward. Darshima looked beside him to see Sydarias dozing softly, and Shonan asleep upon his shoulder.

They soared high above the vast cityscape, perched upon the line of rocky island plateaus at the mouth of the roaring Eophasian River. A fine mist shrouded some of the buildings and refracted the rays of late morning light in a myriad of vivid colors. In the distance, the sun hovered just above the scarred peaks of an ancient volcano.

Darshima's eyes swept over the city, his stomach sinking as he beheld the destruction. Ardavia, like The Vilides, had suffered dearly during the invasion. He could see that several of the prominent domes of the skyline had either collapsed or were pocked with gaping holes. Many of the once verdant parks were burned and remained littered with wreckage from the violent battles during the invasion. Darshima's eyes scanned the horizon for other signs of foreign occupation. His pulse raced as he spotted the familiar, fusiform shapes of the Navervynish fleets patrolling the skies between the bands of traffic. As he had seen in The Vilides, there was indeed no escape from their reach.

Darshima had waited so long for this day, the day of his return home. His heart stirred with a turbulent mixture of anticipation and worry. He looked at the city below, searching intently for the shining metal frame of the tower where he had once worked, pressing his face against the window for some sign. As the craft hurtled forward, he spied an enormous, glinting metal pile in the distance.

His jaw fell agape in shock when he realized that the structure was all that remained of the tower. The building had collapsed into a mound of charred and warped steel beams. A dense carpet of shrubs and weeds had grown over the site, their tendrils and branches wrapping around much of the foundation. His thoughts raced back to the countless hours he spent working with so many others to raise that structure. A lump formed in his throat as he beheld the ruins of the once prominent symbol of Vilidesian might and contemplated the forces that had torn it asunder.

Erethalie steered the craft past the central plateau and descended over the stately homes of the surrounding neighborhoods. As they drew nearer to the Eweryn home on the outer edge of the city, a familiar, sinking sense of fear crept back into Darshima's chest. It had been more than a year since he was torn from his family and forced to toil in those unforgiving fields on Navervyne. He prayed that they had somehow avoided a similar fate and made their way back. Nonetheless, he couldn't escape the feeling that something had happened to them.

Erethalie guided the craft toward a small field behind the neighborhood and hovered to a landing. As the engines powered down, she and Tenrai released their harnesses. Sydarias and Shonan awoke from their slumber, unfastened their belts, and they all disembarked from the rear of the vehicle. Darshima led them across the grassy field toward the rows of homes. A stiff breeze stirred the cool, humid air around them. Darshima threw his hood over his head to protect against the chill. He stepped onto the road, but Tenrai and the others stayed behind.

"Won't you join me?" Darshima beckoned them, but Tenrai and the others remained in the field.

"We will stay here," said Tenrai.

"But I want you to meet my family." Darshima's brow wrinkled in confusion at their reluctance to join him.

"We will accompany you this far, but we must stay with the craft. Give them our regards." Tenrai glimpsed over his shoulder at the vehicle.

"I don't understand..." Darshima's voice trailed off, his heart beating anxiously.

"If you face any danger, trust that I will be at your side." Tenrai rested a hand upon his shoulder.

"We will be waiting for you, Darshima." A worried frown crossed Sydarias' lips. Tenrai motioned toward the craft and the others followed him. Darshima's gaze lingered upon their shrinking forms as they walked back across the field. A pang of nervousness coursed through him as he turned around. He would have to make this journey alone.

As Darshima walked up the road, he noticed several rows of abandoned homes and razed lots. Many buildings stood with missing doors and broken windows. The once manicured gardens had become tangled and unkempt. Stone fences had crumbled and the once neat, cobblestone pavement had buckled. He saw his home at the end of the road, his heart rising into his throat at the sight. He rubbed his eyes with his hands, trying to make sure he wasn't dreaming.

Darshima bounded up the steps of the porch, an anxious knot growing in the pit of his stomach. Something felt different to him, and it was unmistakable. The house that once seemed so big to him as a child now looked smaller. The neatly maintained lawn and garden had become overgrown. He looked to his side, drawing in a stunned breath as he saw the neighboring home had been burned to the ground, its charred masonry and collapsed slate roof now sitting in a solemn pile.

Darshima stood still for a moment, then rapped his knuckles against the dusty glass. He peered through the thick panes into the darkened interior of the house and waited. A faint glimmer of light seemed to flicker deep within its recesses, but he wasn't sure. His heart bounded nervously with each interminable second, but there was no response. He knocked again but was met with silence.

Fine beads of perspiration broke out upon his forehead as he remained alone at the door. He anxiously clenched his jaw as his mind entertained the worst possible scenarios. Darshima closed his eyes and drew in a deep breath. His chest tightened as a wave of fear enveloped him. Worries that his family might have not survived the invasion stalked his mind.

"They have to be here," he whispered, trying to convince himself as a sense of panic began to grip him. As he opened his eyes, a shadow fell upon the house, cloaking everything in its darkness. The hairs upon the nape of his neck stood on end, and a bolt of fear coursed through him. He backed away from the door and looked up to the sky. A large formation of Navervynish ships glided above him, their grey bulbous frames blotting out the sunlight. He shook his head and drew in a breath, as harrowing memories of those ships cruising over The Vilides came back to him.

Darshima descended the porch steps and walked along the stone path beside the house that led to the rear garden. He was certain that he saw a dim light through the front door. He clung to the hope that someone might be home. As he approached the back of the house, he heard the distinct clatter of pots and pans coming from the kitchen windows. The air around him bore the rich, spicy scent of simmering food.

"Someone is here," he said aloud. Darshima's heart leapt into his chest, and he walked even faster. He came to a stop at the side entrance and peered through the slightly ajar door. He quietly pushed it open and stepped inside. His pulse thudded as he walked through, the house appearing much as it had before. A sense of familiarity washed over him as he breathed in the air and gazed at the walls. Darshima made his way through the dim hallway toward the kitchen. He froze in the doorway when he saw the silhouette of his mother and father, illuminated by dusty beams of afternoon sunlight.

Sovani stood at the stove and methodically stirred the contents of a large iron pan over the tongues of open flame. Clouds of thick steam rose from the searing meat, spreading out upon the ceiling and dissipating quickly. He had lost weight, and his red armless tunic and linen breeches hung slightly from his once strapping frame. His silky mane of black hair had begun to grey at the temples and hung at his shoulders. Darshima looked toward the oval table and saw Dalia, seated with her hands folded upon its wooden surface. A simple green patterned robe with the shoulders exposed draped her slender frame. She had grown thinner, and the fine features of her face were drawn into a wistful expression. Her long brown locks were tinged with grey and hung in a thick braid down her back. She quietly gazed through the window, a far-off look glimmering in her eye.

The air resonated with the deep timber of Sovani's voice as he recounted the details of his day to her. His voice seemed softer than Darshima remembered it. The clatter of Sovani dropping a spoon to the floor broke through the din of their conversation. Sovani let out an exasperated sigh, knelt down, and grabbed the spoon. He rose to his feet and turned to look at his wife, when his eye caught Darshima's silhouette at the threshold. A look of surprise crossed the hardened features of Sovani's face as he marched toward him.

"Show yourself!" He tossed the spoon aside and clenched his fists. Dalia let out a shriek as she moved out of her seat and crouched in a corner.

"I didn't mean to frighten you, but the door was open." Darshima stepped out from the shadows and pulled his hood away. The sunlight revealed his face and Sovani's scowl dissolved into a look of utter incredulity. Dalia rose to her feet, her eyes widened in shock.

"Is that you, Darshima?" Sovani shook his head in disbelief. He spoke haltingly, as if he had never expected to say that name again. He clasped Darshima by the shoulders and embraced him tightly, letting out a deep sigh of relief.

"I have returned," whispered Darshima, his voice caught in his throat. Overcome by the moment, he was unable to say anything more. Darshima then turned to Dalia and wrapped his arms around her. She held him closely as a wave of emotion swept over him.

"I've missed you so much," said Darshima. He peered into her eyes and felt hot tears well up in his own.

"I thought I would never see you again, Darshima." She gasped as she put her hands to his cheeks. She shuddered in disbelief, as if she were in the presence of a ghost.

"You are alive!" Sovani rested his hands upon Darshima's shoulders as if to convince himself that it was truly him. His expression of shock dissolved into one of earnestness. "Please Darshima, sit and eat with us." Dalia gently guided him toward the table. Sovani let go of Darshima's shoulders and hurried back to the stove. He returned with three steaming plates of stewed meat and vegetables and placed them upon the table.

"You have lost weight, please eat something." Dalia looked intently at him as they settled into their seats. As Darshima peered around the kitchen, he sensed a glaring difference. Something was missing. He snapped his head toward his mother and father.

"Where is Sasha?" he asked nervously, as a cold fear gripped his chest. Sovani's gaze fell toward the table and the color drained from his face.

"We don't know, Darshima. He was captured." His eyes glistened with tears. Darshima drew in a sharp breath as he processed the words, a turbulent sense of shock rising within him. He grew numb as the dreadful realization of Sasha's absence seared itself into his mind.

"This is my fault. I am so sorry." Darshima's eyes brimmed with tears as he spoke, memories of their argument at the palace coming back to him.

"It is not your fault." Dalia covered her face and let out a painful sob. "I miss him so very much."

"I should have never abandoned you at the palace," said Darshima, his voice cracking with despair. "I should have been there for him."

"Please don't blame yourself, Darshima. There is nothing we could have done." Sovani wrapped his arm around Darshima's shoulder and drew him nearer. "Do not punish yourself for that night, we would never hold it against you." Darshima wiped away his tears with the back of his hand.

"We are very happy that you have returned safely Darshima." Dalia dried her eyes with the corner of her robe and clear her throat. "It means so much to us." She reached out and gently squeezed his hand. "You have survived, and it gives us hope that he also might be alive."

Darshima sat beside his parents and stared blankly ahead. His appetite had disappeared and was replaced by an ache in the pit of his stomach. A profound sense of loss, mixed with feelings of hopelessness took his words. His worst fear had been realized. His tears falling, he pushed his plate aside and rested his face in his hands. Sovani and Dalia embraced him as they dried their eyes and stared at Sasha's empty chair.

Chapter Forty

Darshima rested upon a stone footstool across from his parents, who sat perched upon a wooden bench. Thoughts of Sasha weighing heavily upon their minds, they had retired to the terrace in the rear garden after dinner for some needed fresh air. The evening was clear and Darshima's skin pricked against the chilly wind. The tree boughs overhead swayed in the stiff breeze, their silvery leaves rustling softly amid the moonlight.

He glanced up at the inky expanse of sky above them, stippled with intricate swirls and bands of flickering stars. Darshima turned to the west, the darkness yielding to Benai's hazy glow. Out of the corner of his eye, he saw a fleet of Navervynish ships, their bold silhouettes steadily transiting against the vast grey sphere. He and his parents sat in each other's company amid the stillness of the evening. A great deal had happened since they separated, and his parents shared their struggle with him.

Fortune had not looked kindly upon the Eweryn family, and the brutal events of the invasion had forever changed their lives. As the troops laid siege to the palace, they witnessed the assassination of the emperor and empress, and the seizure of the prince and his guests. Seeking refuge from the violence, Sovani and Dalia grabbed Sasha and fled to a nearby exit. They ran through the hallways, trying to avoid the frantic crowds of guests and marauding bands of troops. Amid the confusion, they found themselves separated, and a group of soldiers captured Sasha. As they tried to save him, Dalia and Sovani were injured. To spare their own lives, they laid silently in the great hall, surrounded by dozens of wounded and dead guests.

As the sun rose, the soldiers had cleared out, and the fighting beyond the palace walls had abated some. Bruised and beaten amid the commotion, they escaped to the home of an old acquaintance.

They remained in the occupied Vilides for several months as they recovered, trying to make sense of what had happened, and to understand the incomprehensible circumstances facing them. After the articles of surrender had been issued, they returned to Ardavia and found that things had changed drastically. The invaders had captured the city and led a brutal conquest of Gordanelle that resulted in untold devastation. Many Gordanellans had been killed or taken captive. Daily life had become a struggle, and essential commodities like food and fuel had grown scarce.

As they tried to re-establish some sense of normalcy in their lives, Sovani and Dalia thought of Sasha and Darshima constantly, looking for some sign of their whereabouts. Sovani had asked around for them, but it had been futile. The normal lines of communication had been severed after the invasion. Countless other families were also missing their sons and daughters, and were unable to find them. It was all but impossible for him to learn anything.

"I tried my best to protect us, but I failed." Tears formed at the corners of Sovani's eyes. Dalia wrapped her arm around his shoulder and drew him closer.

"It is not your fault," she said firmly. "No one could have imagined such a calamity would befall us." He closed his eyes and rested his head against her shoulder. "We have tried to move on, but it has been so difficult," she sighed.

As the months passed, they tried to carry on some semblance of their former lives, wondering daily what had become of their sons, and what had brought this misery to their world. Dalia tended to the garden and grew vegetables for their consumption, bartering some for meat and other provisions with the neighbors. Sovani's construction firm had been charged with clearing debris and tearing down damaged buildings throughout the city.

"I am no longer a builder. Every day, I tear down the wreckage and clear the rubble. We do nothing more than continue the destruction that these invaders brought here." He shook his head with disgust.

Darshima's heart rose into in his throat as he listened to their account. During his captivity, he had hoped and prayed for the safety of his family, but his prayers had gone unanswered. He lowered his head as silence again enveloped them.

"However did you manage to survive?" asked Dalia. Darshima looked up at her and Sovani, who both eyed him curiously. He bit his lip, unsure how to respond.

"I am just thankful to be alive. I don't want to burden you with my circumstances," he said.

"You have survived amid this catastrophe, but so many have not. Please tell us how." Sovani gently rested his hand upon Darshima's knee.

"I cannot understand why or how, but somehow I did," replied Darshima.

Darshima recounted everything, from his first day wandering in The Vilides, to his week spent with Sydarias and his family. Their expressions turned noticeably darker when he spoke about the invasion. Darshima's voice grew heavy as he recounted the harrowing events. He had tried hard to forget those memories but discussing them brought back feelings that he wasn't yet prepared to handle. He relived his brutal capture, the long, difficult voyage to Navervyne, and his time laboring in servitude upon the fields. His eyes grew damp as he talked about their failed escape, and the lashings they received.

As he recounted Tenrai's rescue and their improbable flight from Navervyne, Sovani interrupted him.

"You said you were rescued, Darshima?" Eyebrows knitted, he leaned closer. Before he could respond, Dalia interjected.

"How many of you were rescued?" she asked in a low, serious voice that caught Darshima's attention.

"I was to be the only one, but at my insistence, Sydarias was also rescued," he replied. Expressions of disbelief upon their faces, Sovani and Dalia exchanged a worried glance then turned back to Darshima.

"Mother, father, is there a problem?" His pulse thudded as he sensed their unease.

"We have not heard of a single person being rescued from Navervyne. Please forgive our reaction, but this is very unusual." Sovani hesitantly cleared his throat. "Can you tell us more about the person who rescued you?" Darshima's chest tightened anxiously as he contemplated what to say. Tenrai had instructed him to remain quiet about their plans on Iberwight.

"His name is Tenrai Nax," said Darshima.

"That is an Omystikai name. Did an Omystikai rescue you?" Sovani's gaze narrowed into a hardened expression.

"Yes, he is from Iberwight." Darshima nervously clenched his jaw. Sovani glared at him and cleared his throat.

"You will have no dealings with this man or his traitorous kind." Sovani crossed his arms over his broad chest.

"What do you mean? He saved my life." Darshima's eyes widened in confusion as he pondered his father's unexpected reaction. Sovani cast his gaze toward the sky, his eyes damp in bitter reflection.

"The Omystikai are responsible for this invasion. They betrayed the entire realm," he whispered, his voice wavering with suppressed anger.

"That cannot be." Darshima shook his head, his heart growing numb at his father's accusation.

"There are rumors stating that they collaborated with Navervyne and helped them plan the invasion of the realm." Sovani grew visibly upset, and his voice turned into a bark. His amber eyes glinted like cooling steel under the moonlight. "I bet you did not see a single Omystikai slave while you were on Navervyne."

"There has to be an explanation," stammered Darshima, as he realized that he hadn't seen a single one.

"The Navervynish didn't destroy Iberwight like the other moons. It was the only part of the realm that was spared the devastation of their invading armies. Now, Gavipristine is one of their bases of operation. There are even reports of some Omystikai working alongside the invaders. What else could that mean?" asked Sovani, his voice cracking bitterly.

Darshima turned to his mother, whose expression had grown visibly darker. He tried to catch her eye, but she avoided his gaze. A distinct air of sadness crossed her face. It seemed as if she wanted to say something but couldn't find the words. Darshima drew in a sharp breath as feelings of disbelief came over him. He did not know what to make of Sovani's accusation. Tenrai had said nothing of Omystikai involvement during the invasion, nor had he mentioned anything of a betrayal.

Dalia and Sovani sat quietly as Darshima digested the news. The brutality of the invasion was still fresh in his mind. The possibility that a people from within the realm could have allied with Navervyne in their conquest was more than he could bear.

"I cannot believe that he is a traitor father. Why would he have risked his own life to save mine?" asked Darshima.

"You must trust me," replied Sovani.

"Father, he seeks to bring back peace, and he needs my help. He is no traitor." Darshima shook his head.

Sovani froze in his seat as he heard Darshima's words. A somber expression crossed his face and he grew noticeably paler. A frown formed upon Dalia's lips and she began to shudder. Sovani noticed the change in her disposition and put his arm around her, drawing her closer. Dalia peered into Sovani's eyes as if trying to communicate something. He nodded solemnly, and then she hesitantly faced Darshima.

"Darshima, there is something that we need to tell you, something you must know," she said, her voice wavering with unease. Darshima leaned in closer, his heart pounding anxiously. Sovani sat straight up in his seat and stared at Darshima. He briefly closed his eyes and his brow wrinkled in a look of anguish. Dalia let out a pained sigh.

"Please remember that we have always loved you and this is your home. We have raised you and have done our best to protect you, but you are no longer a child," she said haltingly, tears forming at the corner of her eyes. Darshima drew in an anxious breath as she struggled through the words. His palms grew sweaty as a feeling of fear enveloped him. Dalia let out a pained sigh as she wiped away her tears with the back of her hand.

"I wanted to tell you sooner, but I could never find the words," she whispered.

"I don't understand." Confused, Darshima shook his head.

"Darshima, I can no longer hide the truth, it has managed to find you," she said.

"What do you mean?" Darshima's eyes widened in bewilderment. Dalia grasped his hand and peered at him, her eyes glittering with searing intensity.

"Darshima, I am not your mother, nor is Sovani your father."

Chapter Forty One

Under the soft moonlight, Darshima slumped wearily against the tree at his old promontory. The rhythmic murmur of the crashing surf below filled his ears. A steady breeze stirred about him, tugging at the locks of his hair draped over his face. His mind drifting in a roiling sea of emotion, he didn't even bother to sweep them aside. He stared numbly ahead at the fragmented reflection of Benai on the dark rippling waters of the river. A cold wind rose around him, and Darshima and drew his garments against his shoulders. The tree boughs swayed above him, their gnarled branches weaving an abstract pattern against the vast field of stars.

His world had come undone. In a single moment everything that he believed, all that he had known to be true, had been revealed as false. "I am not their son," he whispered, the words torn away by the wind. He could barely bring himself to say them aloud, but deep down he felt that it was the truth. Dalia's revelation had left him so distraught, that he abruptly left her and Sovani in the garden and ran to the promontory.

Darshima's mind sifted through the details of their conversation. He tried to piece it all together into a coherent whole, but could barely grasp the surface. Since he was a child, he had sensed a distance between his parents, Sasha, and himself. Despite Dalia's struggle to bring them all together, it had only become more acute as he had grown older. Darshima had long tried to make sense of these feelings, but now it was clear.

He was not originally from Gordanelle, as he believed since childhood. Sovani and Dalia however, were born on Gordanelle, like countless generations of their ancestors. Both from modest families, they were raised in a rural community on the outskirts of Ardavia. They met each other at a young age and had a brief, but romantic courtship. With the approval of their families, they wed as young adults. Their marriage began happily but grew tense as they faced expectations to have children of their own. Seeking a greater degree of independence, they decided to move to The Vilides, against the advice of their families.

With their savings and a great deal of ambition, they left the only home they had ever known and settled in the capital, amid the lofty towers and bustling traffic. Within three months of their arrival, Dalia became pregnant with Sasha. Sovani had been working informal jobs but with the joyful, stressful news of a child on the way, he sought more stable work.

Sovani found a position as a sentry at an imperial shrine and was able to provide a good life for his wife. Dalia's pregnancy progressed, and later that year they traveled back to Gordanelle where she gave birth to Sasha. As per their tradition, Gordanellans always gave birth and raised their children among family. They believed that children born apart from their family would grow up without direction. Though they had moved away, Sovani and Dalia wanted to abide by at least a part of this important custom. After Sasha's birth, they returned to The Vilides and dedicated themselves to raising their son.

Their sense of optimism was tempered by a troubling turn of events in the capital. A thick cloud of suspicion hung over the palace, as several scandals came to light. The imperial dynasty, long plagued by corruption, stood accused of colluding with powerful industrial and commercial clans for financial gain. When the situation appeared as if it could get no worse, a coup was attempted upon the House of Fyrenos and the dynastic Omystikai counselors negotiated a resolution.

The counselors beseeched the emperor to abdicate and allow the ascent of a new ruler of their choosing, named Aximes. A scion of a wealthy industrial clan, his only link to the dynasty was through a distant cousin of the deposed emperor. His rise represented the first-ever break in the direct line of ascension. The city sunk into a period of turmoil as Emperor Aximes assumed power and replaced the imperial court with his allies.

The political and economic upheaval had made life difficult for the Vilidesians, and basic necessities became harder to obtain. There was a troubling increase in crime and violence. Worried for their safety, Sovani and Dalia decided to return to Gordanelle with Sasha. Sovani relinquished his position at the shrine, and they gave up their apartment.

On a clear night, they gathered their remaining possessions and fled with Sasha. Seeking to avoid unwanted attention in the city, they set out toward a small port in the outskirts, amid the dunes to catch a passenger ship bound for Ardavia. As they walked through the sands, Dalia spotted a bright, vivid light flickering in the distance. They approached the mysterious glow and arrived at what appeared to be an abandoned campsite, completely engulfed in flame.

Startled by the size of the fire, Sovani started to turn away, but Dalia was entranced by the flames. Claiming she heard the noise of a crying child, she drew nearer. Fearing she would be burned alive, Sovani grabbed her arm but to his surprise, she struggled against him. She handed Sasha over to Sovani and stepped into the clearing. The fire enveloped her, but miraculously she was not burned. As she walked to the center, a forceful gale blew through and extinguished the flames.

She neared the smoldering embers and was astonished to see a crying, naked infant boy. He lay in the middle of an inscribed circle in the sand, ringed by black stones. Dalia picked him up and cradled him in her arms, amazed to see that he was unscathed by the flames. She took off her shawl and swaddled him, immediately noticing the unusual markings on his right arm. Sovani entered the clearing to get a closer look at the child and was overwhelmed by a strong feeling of trepidation. He wanted to leave the child where he lay, but Dalia refused to abandon him. He reluctantly gave in to his wife's plea, and they took the baby with them.

As they walked out of the site, the thud of heavy footsteps and the metallic click of drawn weapons filled the air. Moments later, a band of armed, uniformed men emerged into the space. They surrounded the Ewеryn family with their pistols squarely aimed at them. They demanded Dalia put the child back where she found him. Startled by the troops and their guns, she fearfully moved back to the circle.

As she knelt down to place him back upon the sand, the loud rush of flapping wings rose above the commotion. Flocks of large, feathered raptors descended from the skies and swarmed around them. Their shrieks filled the clearing as they darted about, viciously attacking the men with their razor-sharp beaks and talons. Over the screeching, they heard the sounds of hoofbeats and felt the ground rumble underfoot. Four-legged beasts, both great and small galloped into the clearing, trampling the men and goring them with their horns. The animals formed a protective circle around the family. Their thick hides protected them from the artillery fire as they fought the advancing men. Sovani and Dalia stood paralyzed with fear as they witnessed the incredible scene.

When all of the men had either been either trampled or chased away, the beasts moved out of the site amid the dunes, nudging the family toward their destination. With Sovani holding Sasha and Dalia cradling the child, they fearfully walked upon the shifting sands, the animals guiding them forward. When they made it safely to the port, the creatures dispersed into the dunes and took flight, vanishing as suddenly as they had appeared. Sovani and Dalia quietly boarded the ship with the children and made their way back to Gordanelle, vowing never to share their unbelievable experience.

They arrived in Ardavia to a mixed reception. Their families were thankful to have them home, but unhappy with Dalia's decision to take in the mysterious child. Dalia usually heeded her family's advice, but she was particularly defiant when it came to the little boy. Sovani sided with their families' opinions and wanted to give up the child, but Dalia refused to send him to the orphanage. She declared him her son and they kept him. Unsure of the baby's origins or heritage, she had no idea what to name him. Not long after their arrival, she happened upon the child's name in a vivid dream. In the dream, she found herself back in the clearing amid the blaze, where peculiar tongues of flame spoke to her as she reached for the baby. When she awoke, she found herself whispering the name Darshima.

Though adamant in her decision to raise him, she had doubts about how life would turn out for him. He looked different from the rest of the family. They were of a copper-brown hue and had the dark silky hair and amber eyes common to most people of Gordanelle. His bronze complexion, brown, wavy hair and cobalt eyes were traits that didn't really belong to any one moon or people. Furthermore, there was the peculiar mark upon his forearm. A lingering mystery to Dalia, she sought Sovani's advice, but he avoided any discussion of it. Despite their misgivings, they raised Sasha and Darshima together as brothers, vowing never to reveal Darshima's mysterious origins to him until he was older.

Dalia did her best to avoid favoring one son over the other, but Sovani had a much harder time. His family had reproached him for raising a child that was not his own, but he respected Dalia's wishes and kept silent. Though he tried, Sovani could not emulate his wife's conviction. Sasha was his son, and Darshima was not. Despite growing up together, the differences between them became evident as they matured. Sasha was strapping and full of life. He shared the same interests, opinions, and pursuits as his father. Darshima was leaner, quieter, and more introspective, and had little in common with Sovani.

Through tear-stained eyes, Darshima glimpsed the faint streaks of orange sunlight emerging across the blue, starlit expanse of sky. His heart broken, he had found no rest and remained awake through the night. During his darkest moments on Navervyne, dreams of the day when he would return home had sustained him, but it had been futile. He was not their son, they were not his family, and Gordanelle was no longer his home. Sovani's distance all of these years finally made sense. His past had been torn away, and his future had never seemed more unclear to him.

Darshima struggled to understand why his parents had kept the nature of his past from him. The truth seemed as improbable as it was painful. He wanted to doubt their story, but he couldn't fathom them ever telling such a cruel lie to him. The truth brought up more far more questions than they could answer. He wondered why he had been abandoned at birth and left to die. Growing up he had often sat at the promontory, staring longingly up at the sky, yearning for something he couldn't name. For so long, he had questioned why he felt so much closer to those distant worlds rather than to his family here on Gordanelle. He now had his answer and was left feeling broken and bitter.

Amid his grief, Darshima couldn't stop thinking about Sasha. His heart ached as he pondered his brother's fate amid the tumult of the invasion. Though Darshima was not an Eweryn, they had been raised together. Sasha would always be his brother. He prayed that he was alive and that somehow he would find his way home.

Darshima sat still and listened to the dawn breeze as it whistled past his ears. Over the distant rush of water, he heard the rhythmic crunch of grass underfoot. He rose to his feet and turned to see Tenrai and Sydarias, closely followed by Erethalie and Shonan. With his shirtsleeve, he hastily wiped the tears from his face.

Tenrai joined him at the edge of the promontory and the others stood back a few paces. He and Tenrai faced each other, the stiff wind tugging at their clothes.

"Darshima, the truth is painful right now, but in time you will move past it." Tenrai gently brushed Darshima's locks away from his face.

"How am I supposed to believe any of this?" Darshima trembled as he spoke.

"Deep down, you know that they have told you the truth. You cannot change it, but you must accept it." Tenrai's eyes narrowed and a sympathetic frown crossed his lips.

Darshima felt Tenrai's hand gently guide him away from the promontory. He followed Tenrai and Shonan, numbly placing one foot in front of the other. Walking alongside him, Erethalie wrapped her arm around his shoulder. Fatigued, he leaned upon her for support.

"You are not alone, I am here with you." She drew him closer and gently squeezed him. Eyes growing damp with tears, he turned toward her, unable to find any words.

"I am here too." Sydarias moved beside him and rested a hand upon his other shoulder. Despite their welcome presence, he had never felt more alone. Darshima walked with them, unsure how to move forward.

Chapter Forty Two

Darshima stood at the doorway of his parent's home and felt the rays of the morning sun upon his back. Tenrai, Sydarias, Erethalie, and Shonan waited for him in the distance, at the edge of the field abutting the road. He would be leaving for Iberwight with them that morning. Darshima had stood at that doorway more times than he could remember, bidding goodbye to his family on the way to school or work. Before the invasion, he had never given as much thought to saying farewell as he did now. After each journey, he had always dutifully returned up those steps to the open arms of his mother. The events of the past year, of the past several days, had shown him that a farewell could indeed be forever.

Darshima faced Sovani and Dalia as they stood before him. The fabric of their black, threadbare clothes rippled in the steady winds.

"Mother, father I want to thank you for taking me in, for raising me." His heart rose into his throat as the words crossed his lips. He didn't know if he would ever get used to the fact that they were not his parents.

"There is no need to say that." Sovani cleared his throat as he tugged at the hem of his tunic. Dalia stepped forward and straightened the folds of her robe.

"You weren't born to us, but it does not matter. You are still our son. It was our duty to raise you." Tears streamed down her cheeks as she looked at him.

Darshima's eyes grew misty as he saw her cry. He moved forward, then hugged and kissed them. Despite their revelation, they were the only family he knew. As he stood with them, he could feel Tenrai's gaze upon him.

"I must get going," stammered Darshima as he stepped back. A part of him yearned to remain in Ardavia and resume his old life, but he knew that it was no longer possible.

As Darshima turned away, Sovani grabbed his shoulder.

"Darshima, you are leaving us again and I feel fortunate to have seen you," he said, his voice wavering. "I should have done more to raise and protect you, please forgive me."

"You don't have to apologize, father. You did your best." Darshima shook his head, his eyes glimmering with a look of understanding that gave Sovani pause.

"Your father and I may not see you again in this life, but we are still your family and we love you." Dalia shuddered as she wiped away her tears. Sovani's gaze lingered upon the brightening sky. He clenched his jaw and placed his hands in the pockets of his breeches, as he seemingly searched for the right words.

"The suffering you endured on Navervyne has made you stronger. I know you will find your way out there." He then turned back to Darshima. "If you happen upon Sasha during your journeys, tell your brother that we miss him dearly. We would do anything to have him back," he said haltingly through his tears.

Darshima rested a hand upon his father's shoulder, comforting him as he stood overwhelmed by grief. His throat tightened as a wrenching sadness came over him. Sasha was their beloved son and the only brother that Darshima had ever known. At that moment, his muddled emotions crystallized, and his duty became clear. He needed to rescue Sasha.

"I will find him and bring him back to you." He embraced Sovani. "You have my word." Sovani looked at him through his tears and offered a solemn nod.

With a wave, Darshima bid them farewell, descended the porch steps, and made his way down the road. As he walked away, he glimpsed over his shoulder to see Sovani and Dalia standing together, haggard and grief-stricken upon the porch. His heart brimming with sadness, he turned back around and faced the field, the haunting image searing itself into his mind. He couldn't bear to see them in such a state.

Darshima reached the edge of the field and met Tenrai and the others. They made their way through the grass, and Erethalie led them back aboard the ship. She and Tenrai settled into the cockpit while Darshima, Sydarias, and Shonan sat behind them in the cabin. As they secured themselves in their chairs, Erethalie fired the engines and the vessel rumbled to life. They steadily lifted off the ground and she pointed the vessel skyward. With a great rush, the craft vaulted upward through the morning mists veiling the city.

Erethalie eased up on the throttle and turned to Tenrai.

"I will go ahead and set our course to Iberwight. We should arrive in your kingdom in approximately four Ciblaithian days." She tapped a row of glowing symbols on the instrument panel and pulled a lever in the console beside her seat. She gripped the controls as the ship hurtled above the clouds and into the blue void.

"I will guide you once we breach the moon's atmosphere." Tenrai narrowed his eyes as he looked through the windshield, the blackness of space hanging just beyond the curvature of the horizon.

"Your kingdom has always been such a mystery, and I honestly don't know what to expect." Sydarias gripped the armrests of his seat as he adjusted to the velocity.

"You will find it to be very different from other regions of the realm." Tenrai's gaze shifted between the windshield and the instrument panel.

Darshima leaned back in his seat and closed his eyes. His mind sifted through the improbable events of the past day. He had come to Gordanelle seeking to reunite with whom he believed was his family, but he was not their son. A sigh escaped his lips as he struggled to grasp the incredulous notion. Nonetheless, the truth was slowly taking hold. His mind struggled to fit the shattered pieces of his life together, but their sharp edges left a raw and painful wound. His initial refusal to believe the truth steadily gave way as he mulled over his conversation with Dalia and Sovani. He could not refute the facts they presented.

An overwhelming sense of guilt gnawed at him as he contemplated his circumstance. Sasha remained a captive on Navervyne, yet he had somehow escaped. Darshima's heart filled with grief as he imagined Sasha, still suffering. He didn't know how he could move on while knowing Sasha was still a slave, toiling his life away. Though he was not an Eweryn, he was raised as one, and Sasha would always be his brother. He had made a solemn vow to find and bring him back to Ardavia.

As the vessel roared through the sky, Darshima could think of nothing else but Sasha, and what he needed to do to rescue him. He needed to tell Tenrai.

"I cannot go to Iberwight unless I find Sasha," he blurted. Tenrai slowly swiveled his chair around.

"Darshima, we will not go back to Navervyne, I cannot allow it." He faced Darshima, his eyes glowing intensely.

"Tenrai, I must rescue him. It's the least I can do." Darshima's pulse raced nervously as he challenged him.

"I will not allow you to put us all in danger to find him." Tenrai leaned forward in his chair.

"If I must, I will go by myself," said Darshima.

"However do you plan on getting there?" Tenrai's eyes widened in incredulity.

"You managed to find a way Tenrai, and so can I." Darshima folded his arms across his chest.

"You cannot go by yourself. We are fugitives there and will be caught," said Tenrai, his voice rising with an edge that caught Darshima by surprise.

Darshima leaned back in his chair as he reflected upon what was at stake. He understood that a return to Navervyne would put them all in peril, but for Sasha, it was a risk he needed to take.

"Darshima, your relationship with the Eweryn family is in the past. We must dedicate ourselves to the struggle ahead." Tenrai glared at him intently, the rumble of the engines filling the tense silence between them.

"They took me in and raised me as their son, and I will never forget it." Darshima clenched his jaw, upset at Tenrai's seeming ambivalence.

"Going back there would be dangerous and we could be killed. How would you even know where to find him?" Sydarias turned to Darshima, his eyes widened with concern.

"I don't have an answer, but I must try somehow." Darshima shrugged his shoulders. Erethalie's eyes swept over the screens of the instrument panel.

"I don't even know where to find that world. I am not sure if my ship can make it there and back." She briefly glimpsed over her shoulder at Darshima, nervously biting her lip.

"This plan is much too risky. I will not allow it." Tenrai turned his chair back around and faced the instrument panel. Darshima's heart sank in despair as he realized that Tenrai would not yield to his request.

"What about your brother, Tenrai?" asked Darshima.

"What do you mean?" Tenrai swiveled back around and looked at Darshima, his eyes narrowing in a guarded stare.

"You told us that you had a brother when you first introduced yourself, " replied Darshima. Tenrai's gaze softened a bit as he continued. "If your brother were in danger, wouldn't you risk your life to save him?"

"I had a brother, but he is dead," sighed Tenrai. He lowered his eyes as a solemn frown crossed his lips.

"I'm sorry," whispered Darshima, taken aback by Tenrai's unexpected reply. "I must rescue Sasha and see to his safe return, otherwise he might die."

"I will not allow it, Darshima. We don't even know if he is alive." Tenrai turned back around, then looked to Erethalie. "We will continue to Iberwight."

"I must try and find out what happened to him. I owe this much to Sovani and Dalia," said Darshima, undaunted.

"Darshima, the answer is no. I cannot let you risk our lives," said Tenrai as he briefly looked over his shoulder.

"They risked their lives to save mine when I was helpless and vulnerable. They raised me as their child, and I must honor that. It is more than my birth parents ever did for me," said Darshima, his voice bitter with resentment. Tenrai turned back to Darshima, his eyes widened in surprise. A look of sadness spread across his features. He opened his mouth to speak, but fell silent.

"How do you propose we find and rescue him, Darshima? Navervyne is a vast world. He could be anywhere." Tenrai closed his eyes and placed a finger upon his temple.

Darshima pondered the question and his heart sank. Despite having been in captivity there for more than a year, Navervyne remained a mysterious and forbidding place.

"I don't know how, but I will find him," said Darshima, his voice wavering nervously. "Can you at least tell me if he is alive?"

"It is much more difficult than it appears. You are not connected to him by lineage, so I am very limited in what I can see. Furthermore, we are not prepared in any way to search for him." Tenrai leaned forward in his chair, his stare piercing straight into Darshima. "You are a very special young man with rare abilities and talents that you do not yet fully understand. Let us go to Iberwight. You will live with the Order and we will teach you how to use them. When you master them, you will be prepared to rescue Sasha, and for so much more."

"I want to learn, Tenrai," said Darshima, his voice filled with hesitation. His face flushed, he stared at his feet. Though he was loathe to admit it, he knew Tenrai was right to reject his request. He couldn't risk all of their lives. If he had any chance of rescuing Sasha, he needed to be prepared.

Darshima looked around the cabin, a growing sense of fatigue clouding his thoughts. He had not slept at all during the previous night and he struggled to stay awake.

"Darshima, you look exhausted. You need to rest," said Tenrai.

"Shonan, take Darshima to the sleeping quarters." Erethalie briefly looked over her shoulder. Shonan got up from his seat, and Darshima followed him down the narrow corridor to a small room at the rear of the craft. Furnished with a small bed, lamp, and desk, it was sufficiently comfortable.

"Thank you," said Darshima as the boy politely excused himself, closing the door behind him. He collapsed onto the bed and let out a sigh, his feelings of frustration and fatigue easing only slightly. Eyes open, he lay still in the dim light. Through the trapezoidal window, he eyed the inky void of space. The icy crescent of Iberwight shone amid the swirls of stars.

Despite the quiet surroundings, his mind took no rest. His thoughts wandered through memories of the past and worries of the present. He ruminated over his conversations with Tenrai, who had spoken several times of his abilities. Darshima had initially doubted him, but now he believed Tenrai's words. So many strange things had occurred since his capture and rescue. Darshima thought of how close Sydarias had come to death back on

Navervyne, and how he had miraculously defied it. He knew that Sydarias had survived because of him.

Darshima thought of how Tenrai had come to Navervyne on a mission to rescue him alone. He mulled over their seemingly impossible escape from Stebbenhour and the unfathomable distance he had leapt onto that departing freight vessel. Tenrai was another mystery that consumed his waking thoughts. This Omystikai man had bravely traveled through the forbidding voids, risking his life to rescue him.

Darshima's forehead grew damp with beads of cold sweat, as thoughts of Iberwight and its unknown challenges crept into his mind. He hoped that he could live up to Tenrai's expectations.

The memory of the solemn farewell with his parents that afternoon drifted before his eyes. Darshima felt his heart rising into his throat as he reflected upon Sasha's absence. His chest tightened as his mind burrowed into its recesses, venturing toward the worst possible fates. He vigorously shook his head, trying to rid himself of the frightening thoughts. Darshima wanted desperately to bring Sasha home from Navervyne, but he didn't even know where to begin on that watery, polluted world. Even if he found Sasha, he didn't know if he could rescue him from his captors.

His heart thudded as a sense of frustration grew within him.

"What should I do?" He let out an angry shout, slamming his fists against the stiff mattress. Even during his yearlong toil in chains, he had never felt so helpless. He fitfully settled back down and let out an anguished sigh. There was no use in him getting worked up over something beyond his control. He needed to save his energy for the trials ahead on Iberwight. Fatigue soon overwhelmed him, and he closed his eyes. The sound of the rumbling engines faded, and he drifted into a restless slumber.

Chapter Forty Three

Darshima jolted out of his sleep in a cold sweat. His heart raced uncontrollably and his temples throbbed. Eyes fluttering open, he sat up and drew in a deep breath. He had just awoken from the grip of a bizarre, powerful dream. The details escaped him, but the dream had shaken him to his core. Darshima rubbed the sleep from his eyes and looked around the room. His vision came into focus upon a familiar, glowing blue gaze at the door, staring at him through the darkness. Darshima gulped nervously as a wave of apprehension passed through him, and faded when he realized that it was only Tenrai.

"What is troubling you, Darshima?" Tenrai stepped forward, closed the door behind him, and sat at the edge of the bed. Darshima reached over and turned on a gleaming metal lamp beside the headboard, and the room filled with a dim white light.

"Do you remember your dream?" Tenrai tilted his head, his eyes glittering with an inquisitive stare. Darshima looked down at his hands and mulled through his thoughts. Whatever it was, the dream had disturbed him enough to wake him from his sleep and leave him shaken.

"I can't remember. Do you know what it was about?" He looked up at Tenrai.

"I can't know your dreams Darshima. No one can, no matter how powerful they claim to be. Dreams are very personal and we can only know our own." Tenrai scooted closer to him.

"Then what brought you here?" asked Darshima.

"I can sense the conflict stirring within you. Are you worried about Sasha?" A contemplative frown crossed his lips. The name struck Darshima like a bolt of lightning. He had a strong feeling that his dream was about Sasha. As he was about to pronounce the name, he held his tongue, fearing Tenrai wouldn't want to hear any more about him.

"You did dream about him," said Tenrai.

"Yes," he replied cautiously and stared at the floor.

"Can you recall any details or feelings in particular?" asked Tenrai, in a hushed voice. Darshima thought hard, but nothing surfaced. He shook his head.

"Let me help you." Tenrai faced him and drew closer. "Now, turn toward me." As Darshima looked at him, Tenrai stretched out his hand and gently placed it upon Darshima's right temple. Before his very eyes, the walls of the room unexpectedly dissolved away into the black void of space, and Tenrai faded into nothingness.

"What's happening?" Darshima's pulse bounded fearfully as his vision unexpectedly shifted before him. He felt the pressure on his temple release and Tenrai's reassuring hand upon his shoulder. The dim lamplight immediately returned, washing out the inkiness of the space before him. The room rematerialized and everything was exactly where it had been.

"Be calm, I am only trying to help you remember your dream." He gently squeezed Darshima's shoulder.

"How did you make that happen?" Darshima nervously pulled away.

"Be silent, you must concentrate." Tenrai put his hand back upon Darshima's temple. The walls of the room again dissolved into the blackness of space. Tenrai's body disappeared, and his eyes faded into two piercing blue constellations in the starry firmament. Darshima looked around and was surprised to see that his own body had faded into a ghostly silhouette. "Just focus on the details of your dream and nothing else," whispered Tenrai, his voice sounding distant.

Darshima hung still in open space, then began to move forward. Though it was a dream, the sensation of weightlessness was unmistakably real. He steadily gained speed as if some strong, unseen force was pulling him. He hurtled through the void, past the spinning arms of galaxies, around stars, planets, and moons. Off in the distance, he spied a dim, pulsating sun that stood apart from the others. He vaulted toward the hazy sphere, and it rapidly grew in size.

He drew nearer to a lone, cloudy orb. Half bathed in stark light, half veiled in darkness, it orbited the star at a fair distance. A chill ran through him as he realized it was Navervyne. He came to a stop directly above the planet and looked upon its turbulent, all-encompassing ocean. Below the fragile layers of clouds, he spied the glowing mosaics of the floating cities and colonies scattered through the planet's atmosphere. Their angular forms hovered effortlessly in the sky, slivers of the watery surface revealing themselves between the platforms.

Darshima drifted downward toward the surface, the coldness of space giving way to the fierce winds of the upper atmosphere. He fell through the billowy layers of clouds and approached a particularly dense cluster of platforms in the shape of a four-pointed star. His heart pounded as the details of Stebbenhour became clearer. He plummeted toward the southern tip of the city, the winds howling past his ears. The clouds gave way to the complex geometric layout of streets and avenues, spreading before him in intricate patterns. His descent slowed as he drifted through the bands of traffic and between the lofty, glinting towers. He landed upon the street, his feet tingling as he connected with the ground.

"Stay focused," said Tenrai, his hushed voice echoing in Darshima's head.

Darshima peered around him, taking in the details of the place. Everything seemed so real.

"I can't believe this," he whispered. His heart fluttered with disbelief and fear, as memories of their recent escape came back to him.

Beams of light from the distant sun filtered through the clouds, straining to illuminate the towers and flowing lines of traffic above him. His feet moved forward, and he sensed something unknown, a force deep within guiding his steps. He made his way toward a gritty alley cast in shadow. A gigantic windowless building with large smokestacks loomed at the far end. Judging from the mechanical noise and glowing lights, it appeared to be a factory. Even before he realized it, he moved toward the building. He approached the entrance and felt a blast of hot, pungent air against his skin.

Darshima walked into the space and eyed dozens of men wheeling carts along the floor, scurrying away in several directions. The air was filled with the deafening clangor of metal and the echo of amplified voices in the incomprehensible Navervynish language. He came to a stop in the middle of a large atrium and peered around the multilevel interior. His shadowy arms rose up to his face, shielding his eyes against the showers of sparks and pulsating light. Between the bright flashes, he spied men and machines in feverish action.

He felt himself floating upward toward a flickering glow in the distance. As he drew closer, he made out a line of slaves standing at wide metal benches, wielding steel hammers. They struck rhythmically at large squares of metal in front of them, toiling in concerted fury. Each blow sent up a shower of sparks, momentarily illuminating their faces. Heads shaven and faces blank, they worked methodically at their benches. Over the boom of the hammering, Darshima heard the sound of clinking metal and looked closely at the captives. His heart sank in despair when he realized that their legs were chained to the stout posts of the workbenches.

Darshima drifted along the line, taking in every terrifying detail. As he reached the middle of the floor, he came to an abrupt stop beside a particularly fast worker. The man methodically arranged a piece of the smooth, lustrous metal upon the worktop. He then picked up the hammer dangling at the side of the bench, raised his arm, and landed a particularly hard strike. The piece of metal exploded beneath the hammerhead in a cascade of sparks and illuminated his intense gaze.

Darshima gasped when he saw Sasha's face. Through the flashes of light, he could see that Sasha had grown gaunt, and his youthful features were drawn up into an unfamiliar expression of resignation. Amid the glow of the sparks, Darshima could make out the silhouette of the man working next to him, but not much else. For some inexplicable reason, Darshima felt deeply drawn to him.

Instinctively, Darshima reached out to Sasha and his spectral hand passed right through him. He knew that it was a dream, but his senses told him that it had been something more. To his astonishment, Sasha shuddered and drew in a startled breath. He turned to Darshima and stared right through him, his eyes narrowing as if he were trying to distinguish something in the darkness. His shoulders slumped, he let out a pained sigh before turning back to his bench and resuming his task.

"Sasha!" Darshima yelled as he reached again, desperate to seize him. Without warning, the image faded to black and the room rematerialized. Darshima hunched over the edge of the bed and panted in fright.

"What do you remember?" Tenrai put an arm around Darshima's shoulder and helped him sit up.

"I almost had him," whispered Darshima, his eyes damp with tears. "At least he is alive."

"What did you see?" Tenrai gently shook his shoulder.

His pulse thudding, Darshima looked up at Tenrai and recounted the details of his dream. He recalled what he had seen as he walked through the city and entered the factory. Just as the details nearly faded, Darshima told Tenrai of Sasha toiling at the bench next to another person.

"It all seemed so real," he sighed.

"So you saw Sasha and the silhouette of a man beside him?" Tenrai's eyebrows knit into a perplexed expression.

"He was close to Sasha, but that's all I saw," replied Darshima.

"Can you remember anything else about him?" asked Tenrai, whose voice had an insistent tone that puzzled Darshima. He shook his head and Tenrai cast his gaze downward. A pensive silence fell over the two.

"May I ask you something?" Darshima turned to Tenrai. "I don't know how to explain it, but it feels like I have met you before." Darshima searched his memory for some past encounter that could prove it. Like a bolt of lightning, it hit him. He had seen Tenrai once before.

"It was back in The Vilides, just before the invasion, you were there!" exclaimed Darshima. A perplexed look crossed Tenrai's features as Darshima described the Omystikai man that he and Sydarias had seen that fateful night.

"You are unfortunately mistaken. I was not in The Vilides during the invasion." He shook his head solemnly.

"When you spoke to Erethalie before we left The Vilides, you mentioned that you didn't know her brother and sister so you couldn't use your abilities to find them." A frown crept across Darshima's lips and he stared at his feet. "You were able to find me on Navervyne, so you must've known I was there. How do you know me?" Tenrai's serious expression gave way to an earnest smile as he contemplated the question.

"You are right about one thing, Darshima. You have seen me before, and I have indeed seen you." His eyes narrowed wistfully.

Darshima closed his eyes in thought, searching for some memory of a past encounter.

"The night before I rescued you and Sydarias, I saw you standing upon the porch of the barracks, staring at the sunset as I made my way through the fields," said Tenrai.

"It was you who made the rustling sounds in the grass. You were the burst of light that I saw out of the corner of my eye," exclaimed Darshima, as the memory flashed before his eyes.

"Indeed, it was me." Tenrai nodded.

"May I ask you another question?" Darshima folded his hands in his lap, a somber frown crossing his lips.

"You may," replied Tenrai.

"I spoke with my father before we left. He said that the Omystikai were responsible for this invasion. Is it true?" Darshima turned nervously to Tenrai, unsure how he would respond to such an accusation.

"In no way was Tiriyuud responsible for this calamity. We knew there would be an invasion and tried everything in our power to stop it." Tenrai vigorously shook his head.

"I don't mean to make any false assumptions." Darshima bowed his head, his heart fluttering with a wave of embarrassment.

"You have a right to ask, but I can only speak for Tiriyuud. Our kingdom maintains little contact with the Omystikai dominions." He looked toward the window, a shadow of sadness crossing his features. "Though not to the same degree, the Omystikai have also suffered from this invasion."

"I understand." Darshima nodded, chiding himself for asking such a fraught question.

"There was an important message in your dream that we cannot ignore." Tenrai's eyes glowed with a startling seriousness. "We must make the risky journey back to Navervyne to rescue your brother. Afterwards, we will focus on your training in the kingdom."

"Why are you are allowing us to go back?" Darshima looked at him, his eyes widened in astonishment. Tenrai had categorically refused to return, and his sudden change of heart took Darshima by surprise.

"I did not plan for us to return under these circumstances, but you have found him. We have no other choice." Tenrai narrowed his eyes and peered at the stars beyond the window. He stood up and left the room, the door clicking gently as he closed it behind him.

Darshima sat for a moment amid the silence, mulling over Tenrai's unexpected change in plans. He then reached over, turned off the light, and lay back down, but he was no longer tired. His mind raced with the frightful images of Sasha toiling in chains and that mysterious silhouette hunched over beside him. Despite Tenrai's earlier protest, he was willing to let Darshima risk all of their lives to return to Navervyne. Darshima vigorously shook his head, trying to forget the images and assuage his fears. He had no other choice but to return and rescue Sasha.

Unable to sleep, he rose out of the bed, shuffled across the floor, and exited the room. He joined the others back in the cabin and sank in the seat beside Shonan who dozed softly. Sydarias stared silently through the window beside him, his lips wrinkled in a solemn frown. Iberwight's crescent hung amid the starry abyss, glowing in the reflected sunlight. The furthest moon from Benai, its orbit was nearly three times as long as Ciblaithia's, which was the closest. Gordanelle, then Wohiimai dwelled in the orbits between them. Tenrai sat next to Erethalie and reviewed images of their trajectory upon the screens in front of them.

"I don't know how this ship will be able to make such a journey with the current fuel reserves. From what you describe, Navervyne is so incredibly far." She tapped several buttons on the console, then turned to him. "I don't even have any maps to guide us there."

"There is a way that we can get there, but we must travel beyond Iberwight." Tenrai trained his gaze upon the stars ahead.

"You want me to take us to the stars beyond Iberwight?" Erethalie looked at him, her jaw agape in surprise.

"We once believed that there was nothing, but now we know what lies in the darkness," whispered Sydarias, his voice heavy with bitterness.

"As we move past Iberwight's orbit, there are swift-flowing currents that link our world to the voids beyond. These currents can be dangerous but they will take us there and back faster than any engine." Tenrai steepled his fingers as he stared ahead.

"I've never heard of such a preposterous thing. How is that even possible?" She shook her head in disbelief.

"Is it how the invaders reached us?" Sydarias looked toward Tenrai, his eyes glittering with curiosity.

"There are vagaries of time and space that the Vilidesians and the Navervynish have yet to understand," replied Tenrai.

"What does that mean?' Darshima peered through the window into the blackness, his mind recalling facts from the books he had read back home.

The Omystikai were known as the original astronomers of their world. Their ancestors had made celestial observations and discovered phenomenon had been lost to the ages. A chill ran down Darshima's spine as he contemplated Tenrai's words and the fact that his people might have preserved some of that knowledge.

"There are ways to travel great distances that don't require the force of mere engines." Tenrai pointed toward the screens. "Erethalie, set our course for just beyond Iberwight's atmosphere."

"This is so unfamiliar to me, but I have no choice but to trust you, Tenrai." She gripped the controls and aimed the craft toward a trajectory past the icy orb.

"Like our ancestors who voyaged among the stars, Tiriyuusians are guided by far more than simple charts and maps." Tenrai stared through the windshield at the space before them, his eyes narrowed. Darshima followed Tenrai's gaze into the field of distant stars and galaxies, his heart beating anxiously as he glimpsed the seemingly infinite depths.

Chapter Forty Four

Darshima, Sydarias, and Tenrai clung to their seats while Erethalie piloted the ship, her hands steadily gripping the controls. Darshima's stomach sank as the airframe carved its way through the atmosphere, shuddering with every turn. Shonan grimaced as the ship rocked, and held tightly onto Sydarias' arm.

"Please excuse the turbulence, this atmosphere is far more dense than back home." She flipped a row of switches overhead.

As they traveled through the ominous grey clouds, Darshima peered at the dark waters of the forbidding ocean stretching before them. The small white disk of the late afternoon sun hung above the churning waters. They vaulted toward the city of Stebbenhour, which appeared as an immense, glowing line floating above the horizon. Darshima gazed at the city, its innumerable lights burning through the mists. His pulse raced as memories of their treacherous escape came back to him. He had never wanted to see this place again, yet they had returned, and it was because of him.

The journey from Gordanelle back to Navervyne had been faster than they anticipated. Under Tenrai's direction, Erethalie had guided the ship far beyond Iberwight's gravitational pull, where they were swept up in an undetectable, raging current amid the void. None of her instruments had been able to identify the strange force, but Tenrai had somehow sensed it. The current swept them from the outer reaches of Benai's orbit and into open space, where they flew at a velocity far faster than the ship's engines could have ever carried them. To their astonishment, a journey that normally would have taken several weeks, lasted three Ciblaithian days, and required minimal fuel.

"I cannot believe that we traveled so swiftly. How is any of this is possible?" asked Erethalie as she steered the craft downward.

"The Vilidesians studied space and time in great detail, but their tools only allowed them to scratch the surface. We Omystikai know the cosmos deeply. A part of it flows through us, much like our own blood, our own lymph." Tenrai leaned back in his seat. A shiver coursed through Darshima as he pondered the words, wondering what other hidden knowledge the Omystikai held. He briefly closed his eyes, and memories of the astounding deserted temple on Ciblaithia that he and Sydarias explored those many months ago filtered through his mind.

The gleaming form of Stebbenhour encompassed the entire windshield as they made their approach. Erethalie guided the vessel downward through the fragile layer of clouds and into a fast-flowing band of traffic heading toward the city.

"I can hardly believe what I am seeing. This is where they came from," she murmured.

"This is their home." Tenrai leaned forward in his seat as if trying to glimpse through the mists.

"Where are the continents and islands? There's nothing but sea and airborne platforms." She pressed on the throttle, speeding past fleets of bulbous vehicles amid the swiftly moving traffic.

"There is nothing but fouled oceans and filthy skies here. It is a hostile world and we must be on our guard." Tenrai's gaze darted from side to side.

They peered through the windows as Erethalie navigated through the lanes of vehicles traveling over the city. The sun hung low in the sky, and dusk was approaching. Stebbenhour spread out before them as an immeasurably vast, floating metropolis of shimmering glass metal towers, and glowing spires.

"I don't understand how we remained unaware of these people." Sydarias glared resignedly at the floor between his feet.

"Our parents, their parents, and our ancestors were taught that everything but our four moons had been long been destroyed. No one ever thought to search the stars beyond our skies," said Darshima.

"Where are we heading?" Erethalie gripped the controls tightly, steadying the craft against the buffeting winds.

"From what Darshima described, the factory should be at the southern end of the city." Tenrai pointed toward a row of looming spires.

Erethalie nosed the craft toward the southernmost district, which converged at a point. She leaned forward in her seat and scanned the surface for any sign of the structure.

Darshima drew in a nervous breath as he looked at the city below, a creeping sense of guilt filling his heart. It was a miracle that he and Sydarias had been able to escape with Tenrai. Erethalie and Shonan had been fortunate to survive the invading armies and avoid the horror of this world. His dream had compelled them to return here, and he was putting them all in significant danger. Deeply humbled by their willingness to voyage to this unforgiving place, Darshima whispered a silent vow to do everything in his power to protect them.

Erethalie steered in and out of the bands of heavy traffic, when a large Navervynish ship unexpectedly descended directly in front of them. The lights on its tapered rear flashed red, and its sirens blared, the low-pitched wail reverberating through the fuselage. With a pulsating white glow from its pair of circular engines, the vessel abruptly decelerated in front of them. Erethalie released the throttle, and the craft shuddered as she slowed it to avoid a collision.

"What's happening?" She nervously flipped several switches and tapped at the screens in front of her.

"It's a Navervynish patrol vessel. Our craft is foreign, and they want to board and inspect it." Tenrai pointed toward the ship ahead. Despite his calm demeanor, Darshima could hear the tension in his voice.

She slowed the craft further and cautiously trailed the ship in front of them.

"When we meet the soldiers, I will speak on our behalf," said Tenrai. He looked upon all of them, his eyes glinting sternly.

The ship led them onto a vast platform hovering above the southern end of the city. Directly above them, Darshima saw multitudes of vessels descending from all directions. Dozens of ships were escorted to the platform by the Stebbenhouri vehicles policing the skies. The ship leading them slowed to a halt and settled upon the far edge of the platform. Erethalie deployed the landing struts and brought the craft down with a gentle thud. She powered down the engines and they unfastened themselves from their seats.

The rumble of vessels flying overhead punctuated the tense silence of the cabin.

"What is this place?" Shonan looked around nervously.

"We are far from home Shonan, just stay quiet." Erethalie toggled a pair of switches in a panel overhead.

The sharp sound of knocking at the hatch echoed through the craft.

"Remember to follow my lead." Tenrai stared at them, his serious expression softening into a reassuring gaze. He stood up and walked toward the rear of the craft. They rose from their seats and followed him. The hatch opened with a mechanical whir and they walked down the gangway. Darshima looked around the platform, his pulse racing anxiously as he saw groups of armed soldiers milling between the craft and inspecting rows of square cargo palates.

They stood in the cold, misty air as Tenrai approached a group of soldiers. He spoke with a male officer and a woman who appeared to be his deputy. Both dressed in grey overcoats, black trousers, and knee-high boots, they glared at Tenrai from under the brims of their black caps.

"What business do you have here on Stebbenhour?" asked the officer in stilted Vilidesian, his crimson eyes narrowing.

"I am currently in transit to Iberwight with these former Vilidesian subjects," said Tenrai.

The officer looked at Tenrai, his eyes widening with an air of incredulity. He then made a gesture to the deputy who moved closer to the group and scrutinized each one of them. Erethalie put a protective arm around Shonan's shoulder and drew him closer.

"They are clearly slaves. Where did you buy them?" asked the officer.

"These people are from the former realm, and they are traveling with me due to an informal arrangement." Tenrai folded his hands in front of him. The officer's brow furrowed into a look of disbelief.

"I cannot believe that you legally acquired theses slaves and have no bill of sale to prove it." He moved closer to Tenrai until they were practically face-to-face.

"I have nothing further to discuss with you." Tenrai stared at him intently, his eyes burning like flame.

Their gazes locked upon each other, and an uneasy silence ensued between them. With great difficulty, the officer tore his gaze away from Tenrai and stumbled unsteadily backward. He vigorously shook his head, as if he were trying to rouse himself from a trance.

"Let them go." He turned to his deputy, his voice thick with fatigue.

"We cannot trust him. He has no proof that these Vilidesians or this ship belong to him." The deputy looked upon Tenrai, a suspicious scowl spreading upon her lips. The officer's gaze was forcefully drawn back to Tenrai. He struggled to close his eyes, grimacing in pain as Tenrai stared unflinchingly at him.

"Just let them go," he held his head in his hands and stumbled forward. Without warning, his knees buckled, and he abruptly collapsed onto the ground in a motionless heap.

"What have you done?" The deputy shouted. With a wave of her hand, she summoned a group of soldiers stationed nearby.

"Confiscate the ship. Seize the Omystikai and the slaves." She pointed toward Tenrai.

"Just stay where you are." Tenrai called out to Darshima and the others.

Darshima's chest tightened in fear as he heard the thud of the soldiers' footsteps. They arranged themselves in a line facing Tenrai, their grey fatigues flapping in the gusts of wind and engine exhaust. The soldiers aimed their pistols, the sharp metallic clicks pricking Darshima's ears as they engaged.

"Raise your hands where I can see them." The deputy aimed her pistol squarely at Tenrai's forehead.

His stomach in knots, Darshima slowly raised his hands along with Sydarias, Erethalie, and Shonan. His heart pounded as he saw Tenrai stand calmly with his hands at his sides.

"Raise your hands, Omystikai!" shouted the deputy as her finger slowly pulled the trigger. Shonan trembled and moved closer to Erethalie.

Tenrai stared solemnly at the deputy and her soldiers. In one sudden motion, he threw his hands outward, palms facing the armed group. Before they could react, their bodies were seized by convulsions, and their pistols fell from their hands. They then tumbled to the ground in unison, as if struck by an overwhelming and unseen force. The officer, deputy and the soldiers lay stunned upon their backs, their weapons scattered about them.

Tenrai hurried toward Darshima and the others.

"Everyone head back into the craft." He pointed toward the hatch and they ran back up the gangway. Erethalie belted herself into the pilot's chair. She fired the engines as the rest of the group took their seats and secured themselves. The gangway retracted, and the hatch door clanged shut behind them with a thud.

"Is everyone unharmed?" Tenrai looked briefly over his shoulder as he settled in the navigator's seat beside Erethalie.

"We are fine," said Darshima. He and Sydarias nodded in unison as they cast a protective eye on Shonan, seated between them.

"Tenrai, how did you make that happen?" exclaimed Sydarias.

"I will explain later, but now we must leave." Tenrai leaned forward and peered anxiously through the windows.

"I'll get us out of here in no time." Erethalie yanked on the throttle. The engines issued a throaty growl and the craft lifted off the platform. Over the roar, they heard the sound of pounding footsteps. Darshima peered through the windshield to see a large group of soldiers come into view, forming a line in front of the ship. Weapons drawn, the men shouted, their voices muffled by the engine noise.

"Step on it Erethalie!" yelled Sydarias. She pulled the control wheel and the craft vaulted skywards. The thrust sent Darshima back in his seat and his heart sank to his knees. He winced as his ears filled with the sharp pinging sound of artillery fire against the fuselage.

"I'm not sure how much more fire my ship can take!" Her eyes narrowed, Erethalie warily scanned the horizon as she guided the craft.

The platform fell away as they made their ascent, shrinking into a glinting metallic blade. Her hands gripping the wheel, she steadily pulled it toward her, and the craft rocketed upward. She aimed further south, weaving skillfully through multiple layers of traffic, around buildings, and above floating platforms. As she started to ease up on the throttle, Sydarias frantically pointed to the window beside him.

"We're being followed!" His voice was barely audible over the loud mechanical drone of nearby craft filling the cabin. Darshima looked through the windows to see a fleet of ships descend in front of them.

"I know." Erethalie reached beside her seat and yanked at a small lever, then gripped the wheel. "I just activated the auxiliary engines, that should help." Without warning, a sonorous rumble shook the cabin, and the craft hurtled even faster toward the vessels ahead.

"What are you doing?" Tenrai whipped his head toward her.

"Planning our escape." She trained her gaze forward as the ships rapidly encompassed the entire windshield. Darshima gasped as the force of the acceleration pressed him firmly into his seat. Just before the impact, everyone instinctively threw their hands up to their faces. Erethalie however, slammed the controls forward and the craft skirted beneath the opposing ships, hurtling down to the streets below. When the impact never came, Darshima and the others removed their hands, astonished at what she had done. She released the lever and the acceleration eased some.

"What a bold move," exclaimed Sydarias.

"Where did you learn to fly like that?" Darshima reached out and patted her on the shoulder.

"That was much too close." She let out a relieved sigh as she guided the craft through the canyon of buildings around them. They cruised between the metallic edifices, gliding above the streets veiled in shadow. Its engines howling, Erethalie steered the craft through several hard turns, weaving around the towers as they escaped the trailing ships.

"A perilous, but nevertheless astounding maneuver." Tenrai turned to Erethalie, his eyes widened in surprise.

"I think we've lost them." She looked over to him briefly as they skimmed through narrow alleys, far from the traffic above.

Darshima strained to hear the drone of the Navervynish craft, but his ears were met with silence.

"They are gone, but not for long." Tenrai pulled his gaze from the windshield and turned to Darshima.

"Does any of this look familiar to you?"

Darshima peered out upon the city as they flew past, but everything appeared hopelessly foreign. He closed his eyes and set his thoughts on his dream. Most of the details had faded, but the one that remained was the resigned look on Sasha's face. Sasha had always been the strong and confident one. Seeing him chained to a bench, toiling in misery cut through Darshima's heart like a blade. He would do anything to find his brother.

Darshima's mind raced as he tried to recall some helpful detail from the dream. He opened his eyes and looked through the windows as they glided above the streets, speeding alongside the buildings and through busy intersections. Out of the corner of his eye, he spotted an orange glow in the distance. He turned toward the light and saw a group of large smokestacks just as they slid behind a cluster of towers. His pulse quickened as he recognized the place.

"Over there!" He pointed in the direction of the light. Tenrai turned toward him.

"Are you sure? If those ships come back, we may not have another chance."

"I am certain," he replied. He remembered the vivid orange glow from the dream, but more importantly, he sensed that it was the right place.

"I'll get us there in no time." Erethalie steered toward the incandescent haze.

The factory came into view as they hurtled forward, the smokestacks looming above them. She slowed the craft to a crawl and descended upon an abandoned lot in front of the entrance.

"Erethalie, please stay with the ship. We will return as soon as possible." Tenrai turned to her.

"If you see my brother and sister, please rescue them too," she said, lowering her gaze.

"I do not know where they are, but if they are here, we will try." Tenrai released his harness and rose from his seat. She rifled through a compartment in the console beside her and produced a photograph imprinted on a small paper card.

"This is the last picture we took together as a family." She handed the card to Tenrai, her voice growing heavy. "If you see them, please help." Tenrai held the photograph, his eyes scanning over its details

"We will do everything we can." He handed the card back to her and offered a solemn nod. "Now we must go." Tenrai motioned to Darshima and Sydarias. They rose from their seats, followed him to the rear of the craft, and marched down the gangway.

Chapter Forty Five

The ship humming quietly behind them, Darshima led Tenrai and Sydarias toward the glowing entrance of the factory. Thin shafts of sunlight filtered down to the alley, piercing through the shadows. Hot acrid gusts, heavy with the pungent scent of gunpowder emanated from the open gates. Darshima recalled the distinct odor from his dream. They stepped through the entrance, and Tenrai rested his hands upon their shoulders.

"We must remain out of sight." He grabbed their hands, and they walked through the gates. Tenrai turned to Darshima."You must take us to where they are."

"I'll show you the way." Darshima led them further into the darkness.

He looked around the vast space, his heart beating anxiously as a feeling of familiarity flooded his senses. It was just as it appeared in the dream, but empty.

They walked along the ground floor amid the eerie silence but found no sign of the slaves. Darshima looked all around him for a hint of the flashing lights but saw none. They moved deeper into the factory until they found themselves at the blind end of a desolate corridor.

"Where are you taking us?" asked Tenrai, his voice rising with a note of stress.

"It must be somewhere around here." Darshima faced Tenrai and Sydarias. He was sure this was the place, but something seemed amiss.

"We have to hurry before we are caught." Sydarias' eyes darted about nervously.

"I know." Darshima's chest tightened as feelings of frustration welled up within him. He was lost.

"Stay calm, and follow the signs from your dream. You will find them." Tenrai guided them away from the dead end.

Darshima scoured his mind, trying to think of any hint that would lead him to his brother. He remembered the bursts of sparks and the hammering, but he couldn't figure out where in the dream he had seen it.

The faint sound of metal grinding against metal broke through the silence, pricking Darshima's ears.

"Did you hear that?" Sydarias looked around, his feet shifting nervously.

"It sounded like grinding metal, almost like chains." Tenrai stepped away from them and peered around. Like a clap of thunder, Tenrai's words struck Darshima, and memories of Sasha's location came back to him. Images of his brother and the other captives bound in chains flashed before his mind. He lifted his head, the noise filtering down from the dark metal ceiling above.

"They are all chained together. We have to follow that sound." Darshima pointed above him as he ran toward the noise.

Tenrai and Sydarias followed closely behind Darshima. He roved about, trying to locate the sound, but it seemed to be coming from everywhere, all at once. The low wail of an alarm rose above the din, and the building came to life with an even louder chorus of rustling chains, grinding metal, and weary voices rising.

"They are trapped above us." Tenrai looked up toward the ceiling as it shook. "We must take the staircase over there." He pointed toward a dark entryway ahead of them, its stairs barely visible. They dashed through the opening, ran up the stairwell, and stepped onto another expansive floor.

Tenrai held onto their hands as they stood in the shadows, staring aghast at the harrowing scene before them. Men and women of all ages, many with their heads shaven, stood at workbenches and toiled in the dim light. Chains rustled at their feet as they labored.

The space rang out with a jarring din as they methodically hammered at pieces of metal arranged upon their benches. Showers of sparks flew about them, casting the room in a searing, pulsating orange glow.

Darshima scanned the room for any sign of Sasha. His eyes lingered upon each person, seeking some characteristic that would distinguish him. Toward the middle of the floor, amidst the flying sparks, his eye caught a silhouette that stood out from the rest. While the other captives were hunched over, this person stood straight up with broad shoulders. His heart pounding, Darshima knew at that moment, he was staring at Sasha. As he pulled away, Tenrai held onto him.

"You must lead the way, but be careful," he whispered.

"I will, trust me." Darshima let go of Tenrai's hand.

"Sydarias, you must stay hidden and not make a sound." With his right thumb, Tenrai brushed a series of strokes onto Sydarias' forehead and whispered an unintelligible phrase. "They will not find you." Sydarias nodded nervously, then crouched in the shadows near the stairwell.

Darshima and Tenrai stalked between the rows toward the center of the floor, unnoticed by the slaves at work. Darshima shook his head as he looked around, trying to convince himself that this wasn't a dream. He cautiously approached the upright silhouette and stood in from him. His eyes narrowed, Darshima tried to glimpse the man's features, when a shower of sparks erupted from his hammer.

The scattering blaze of light illuminated the man's face and Darshima drew in a stunned breath. It was indeed Sasha, and he appeared exactly as he had in his dream. His hair had been shorn at his neck, and was caked in grease and grime. He wore an oil-stained dark fabric vest and ripped trousers. His biceps bulging, Sasha hammered steadily as the sweat poured from his brow.

Darshima moved closer to Sasha who remained unaware of his presence. His pulse raced, and he felt his hearing grow sharper and his vision more acute.

“Go ahead, I will distract the others.” Tenrai stood behind him, closed his eyes, and cast his hands over the slaves.

Darshima walked toward the bench and stood beside Sasha. Speechless, he looked at his brother. He had ached for this very moment since his capture.

“Sasha, I am here to save you,” he called out, his heart rising into his throat. Sasha stood frozen in mid-strike with the hammer in the air.

“I know that voice...” stammered Sasha. His voice trailed off and his eyes grew wide with fright. A tear rolled down his stained cheek. “I must be going mad.” He brushed it away with his calloused, grimy hand. A burst of sparks illuminated his face as he resumed his hammering.

“It’s me, your brother.” Darshima reached out and touched Sasha’s shoulder. Stunned, Sasha’s fingers sprung open. The hammer tumbled from his hand and onto the table with a loud clatter. He turned toward Darshima and drew in an alarmed gasp when he saw who it was.

“Darshima, is that really you? How can it be?” A shudder ran through his sinewy frame, and he placed a hand upon the bench to steady himself. “This must be a dream.” His amber eyes gazed incredulously upon Darshima.

“You are not dreaming. I am standing here before you.” Darshima stepped closer.

“How is this possible?” His hand trembling, Sasha reached out and touched Darshima’s face. “How did you find me?”

“You will know soon enough, but I must get you out of here.” Darshima’s eyes welled with tears of disbelief as he felt his brother’s hand upon his cheek.

As Darshima grabbed his arm and started to pull him away, Sasha resisted.

"Sasha, we must hurry." Darshima turned toward him. His heart seized in fear as he looked upon his brother, still standing at the bench. Sasha stared downward toward his feet.

"I am trapped here, and cannot leave." He pointed toward the floor, a somber expression spreading upon his face. Darshima knelt below the bench and looked down to see Sasha's feet shod in rough fabric, amid dozens of others, bound at the ankle by heavy iron manacles. Sasha and the others were firmly chained to the ground. Darshima's heart rose into his throat at the cruel sight. He didn't know what to do.

A sense of despair overwhelmed him as his mind raced for a solution.

"Use your strength, Darshima," said Tenrai, his voice rising above the pounding hammers.

"I will try." Darshima looked over his shoulder to see Tenrai a few paces behind, staring intently. His pulse thudding uncontrollably, Darshima stretched his right hand toward the restraints, unsure what else to do.

"You are more than capable," said Tenrai, speaking with a sense of urgency.

"I don't know if I can do this." Darshima shook his head and cried out as he glared at the unyielding objects. Precious seconds slipping by, his heart sank as the manacles remained firmly closed.

"You must overcome the doubts that restrain you, if you wish to break the chains that bind him," whispered Tenrai.

Darshima looked over his shoulder and caught Tenrai's determined gaze. He turned back to the shackles, training his eyes intently upon them. With all his might, Darshima imagined the chains falling away, daring himself to will the impossible into existence. Just as his hope began to fade, a strange, tingling jolt passed through his fingers. He stretched his hands even further toward the manacles. As he was about to seize them, they abruptly clicked open, falling to the floor with a clatter.

"It is done," whispered Darshima, his chest tightening in surprise at the sound. His jaw dropped in disbelief when he realized what had just happened. He stood up and looked at Sasha.

"My brother, you are free." Darshima grabbed his hand and pulled him away from the bench, but again, Sasha resisted.

"I cannot leave without Khydius. Please, you must free him as well." He motioned weakly to the figure at the other end of his workbench. Shoulders rounded, the man continued to work, unaware of Darshima's presence. It was the same intriguing silhouette that had drawn Darshima's attention in the dream.

Tenrai emerged from behind Darshima and stood before Sasha.

"Whom do you speak of, Sasha?" Tenrai's brow furrowed in an intense expression.

"An Omystikai is with you?" Sasha gazed upon Tenrai, his jaw agape in astonishment. He pointed across the table to the silhouette. "It is Khydius, the Prince of The Vilides," whispered Sasha.

Darshima and Tenrai moved to the other side of the bench and stood before the figure. Darshima's heart thudded in disbelief as he glimpsed the man's features amid the glowing sparks. It was indeed Prince Khydius, and he was a terrible sight. His skin was caked with dust and oil, and his head had been shaven of its once beautiful locks. Like Sasha, he was clothed in tattered and filthy rags.

Darshima gently touched the prince's shoulder, and the vacant expression on his face turned into one of bewilderment.

"Your Highness, we are here to rescue you," said Darshima. The prince's cerulean eyes beheld Darshima and glimmered with an air of recognition.

"You must have come from The Vilides. However did you find me?" He shook his head in disbelief.

Darshima knelt at the prince's feet and offered a deferential bow. He then reached for the shackles at his ankles and held his breath. His hands tingled as they had before, and the unseen force snapped open the iron restraints. Darshima rose to his feet, his pulse racing in amazement. "My prince, you are free," said Darshima. Tenrai grasped Prince Khydius by the arm and Darshima grabbed Sasha's shoulder.

"We must hurry before we are seen," said Tenrai. They escorted the two captives away from the bench, back toward the stairwell.

"What about the others?" The prince whispered to Tenrai.

"We will come back for them someday, but we must hurry," he replied. Darshima stopped.

"They cannot survive like this. Is there nothing we can do?" Darshima stared desperately upon the slaves as they worked, memories of his own toil coming back to him.

"They may be killed if we attempt to save them now." Tenrai shot a stern glance at Darshima. "They will be rescued someday, but that can only happen if we remain alive. Now we must leave." Tenrai pointed toward the stairs. Darshima nodded solemnly, the prospect of leaving slaves behind weighing deeply upon him. He knew Tenrai was right. If they had any hope of one day rescuing those still enslaved, they needed to survive.

They moved stealthily toward the stairwell, amid the cacophony of hammering metal and blinding sparks. Sasha, weakened by the months of grueling labor leaned upon Darshima for support. Sydarias ran from the shadows and joined them, putting Khydius' arm around his shoulder.

"There are two people?" Sydarias' eyes widened in awe when he realized whom he was assisting. "It cannot be...is this the prince?" he stammered.

"Yes it is," whispered Tenrai. He glimpsed over his shoulder as he guided them down the stairs.

They arrived upon the ground level and dashed through the shadows toward the entrance.

Tenrai led them through the gates, back into crisp twilight air. Engines whirring, the ship sat on the steel pavement. As he waved to Erethalie, the engines roared to life. Darshima and the others followed Tenrai toward the deploying hatch, their clothes flapping wildly in the exhaust wake of the engines.

Just as the gangway lowered toward the ground, the air around them filled with the click of drawn weapons. Darshima's blood surged in fear as he heard the familiar sound.

"Step away from the craft," shouted a chorus of voices in rough Vilidesian. Darshima, Tenrai, and Sydarias whipped around to see several dozen armed soldiers dressed in grey fatigues approaching them. Weary and weak, Prince Khydius and Sasha slowly turned around, their tattered boots scraping against the ground. Darshima's heart thudded at the sight of the soldiers, fearful that their lone chance of freedom had slipped away.

"Stop at once," they shouted in unison. A powerful sense of anger and grief welled up within Darshima as the soldiers positioned themselves in front of him and the others. He had risked everyone's lives to come back and free his brother, and now they were being recaptured. They all had endured the pain of occupation and slavery. He could endure no more.

Darshima seethed at how they had been chained up and forced to work like animals. He turned to Khydius and clenched his jaw, as a deep and raging sense of humiliation surged through him. A prince of his world, the heir to the Vilidesian throne and the future emperor of their realm, had been reduced to a slave in this one. They all had suffered through too much to lose their freedom. He would not leave without them.

Darshima stood beside them and faced the soldiers, awaiting their next move. Darshima tried to catch Tenrai's gaze, but he stared straight ahead and trained his eyes upon the men. The soldiers pointed their weapons and flashed a series of hand signals to each other.

"Seize them all," yelled their leader.

Sasha let out a mournful groan that communicated more to Darshima than any words could.

"Never again," whispered Darshima through clenched teeth. He refused to be captured again.

Driven by an impulse deep within, Darshima marched boldly toward the troops. Tenrai reached out and tried to restrain him, but he could not hold Darshima back. He stood directly before the soldiers, his eyes glinting defiantly. His senses grew sharper and he felt a familiar, yet inexplicable lightness about him.

The men moved to encircle him, aiming their weapons squarely at his chest. Darshima's gaze hardened as he faced them.

"We will never surrender!" shouted Darshima. His voice boomed through the alley, echoing against the metal edifices.

In one swift motion, the soldiers engaged their weapons and braced themselves to fire. Darshima's pulse thudded in his ears as he anticipated the searing pain of their ammunition tearing through his flesh. Without warning, the leader of the group shouted.

"Seize him!" The contingent surged toward Darshima and the ground trembled beneath his feet. Instinctively, Darshima threw his hands out in front of him, toward the oncoming rush of soldiers.

"Darshima, wait!" shouted Tenrai at the top of his lungs, but Darshima didn't hear him. It was too late. The pent up rage from his and Sydarias' ordeal in the fields, the torment endured by Prince Khydius and Sasha in the factory, and the suffering that Erethalie and Shonan had experienced under the occupation seethed within him. The anger and humiliation at what Navervyne had done to them and their world, surged forcefully through his right hand in a searing flash of heat and blazing white radiance.

The soldiers shielded their faces against the blinding intensity, but their defenses were futile. A shattering burst of energy, and an extraordinary wave of empyrean light swept over them, engulfing the entire alley. In an instant, the soldiers were incinerated by the overwhelming force. A towering column of spectral flame enveloped them, reducing their flesh and bone to a raging cloud of smoldering ash. Their weapons fell to the ground and melted into pools of glowing, liquid steel. The air filled with their disembodied, dying screams, echoing loudly through the alley and up into the sky. As the light receded, the fading embers of their remains scattered amid the chilly evening breeze.

Chapter Forty Six

Darshima lay sprawled out upon the cool floor of the room at the rear of the ship. It had been approximately a day since they had left Stebbenhour, and everything since had felt like a blur. He remembered running away from the factory, rushing onto the ship with the others, and taking flight into the misty night sky. Once they had breached the atmosphere, he had left the cockpit and settled in the room.

Unable to rest, Darshima stared at the ceiling, numbly sifting through his thoughts. Like the plumes of glowing, charred human remains, they sifted around the corners of his mind on turbulent gusts of emotion. Every time he closed his eyes, he saw the image of that alley and those soldiers burning. It was as if it were happening again right before him. Their screams echoed in his ears, and his nostrils filled with the scent of their charred flesh. He wanted to believe that none of it had happened, that he wasn't responsible for their deaths, but he couldn't conceive of any other explanation.

Darshima shuddered uncontrollably at the thought of what he had done. Tenrai and everyone else in the group had seen what had happened. He wondered what they now thought of him. His heart filled with worries that they might fear him or worse, loathe him. He had taken several lives, and it had happened in a most violent and unnatural way. His eyes brimming with tears, he felt as if he were some sort of monster.

Fighting a lingering sense of fatigue, Darshima lifted his right hand to his face. He gazed at the markings upon his skin, the intricate patterns glimmering in the dim light. A wave of nausea came over him, and his stomach soured. His chest tightened in fear as he relived the fiery destruction that his hand had wrought. A shiver coursed through him, and his arm fell to his side. He closed his eyes and let out a desperate sigh.

A soft knock at the door broke through the steady drone of the engines. His eyes fluttered open, and he reluctantly faced the entrance, then looked back up at the ceiling. Darshima had heard the sound at least twice since they had left Stebbenhour, but he had not bothered to respond. The gentle knocking persisted, echoing throughout the room. Realizing that he wouldn't be left alone, he rose to his feet, walked toward the door and opened it. A familiar pair of glowing sapphire eyes greeted him.

"May I come in?" Tenrai gently pushed the door open. Darshima lowered his gaze and stepped aside. Tenrai entered and shut it behind him. Darshima followed him toward the opposite end of the room. They sat upon the floor beside the window and faced each other.

"How are you feeling?" The corners of Tenrai's lips wrinkled in a concerned frown.

"I don't know," mumbled Darshima as he rubbed his bleary eyes.

"You have been avoiding me and everyone else since we left Stebbenhour. We must talk about what happened back there." Tenrai cleared his throat.

"I don't want to think about it." Darshima vigorously shook his head.

"Darshima, when are you going to face the truth? What happened was tragic and brutal, but it cannot be changed." Tenrai's brow knitted in frustration. Darshima's eyes widened in a look of incredulity.

"Tenrai, I destroyed an entire group of soldiers with a mere wave of my hand. How can I be capable of such a thing?" he stammered, his voice raw with emotion. Darshima trembled as images of those dying men floated back into his mind.

"It is the truth, those men met their death at your hands." Tenrai folded his arms across his chest. "But Darshima, you saved our lives. We are all very grateful to you."

Darshima's shoulders slumped, and he cast his gaze downward as he contemplated Tenrai's words. He knew he had saved them all from being captured, but the shocking way that it had happened left him deeply frightened.

"If these are the powers that you've been talking about, the power to destroy and kill, I renounce them," said Darshima, his voice wavering. He felt Tenrai's hand nudge his chin, and he looked up at him.

"These are the powers that you have. Do not deny or curse them," said Tenrai. His voice was barely above a whisper, but his eyes bore an intensity that held Darshima's attention. "I warned you about rescuing Sasha before you were ready, before training with me on Iberwight."

"How was I supposed to know?" Darshima's eyes grew damp as a wave of apprehension came over him. "What am I?" He shook his head in disgust and stared at Tenrai, his eyes pleading desperately.

"There is no way you could have known." A solemn frown crossed Tenrai's lips.

"I don't know if I'm ready for any of this," said Darshima, his voice faltering.

"You are someone very special." Tenrai reached out and grasped Darshima's right hand. "You feel that your powers are evil and destructive, but they do not have to be." With his fingers, Tenrai delicately traced the markings upon his arm. Darshima's heartbeat slowed some, and a sense of calm returned to him. "I will teach you how to use them. Never again will they control you as they did on Stebbenhour."

"Why didn't any of these powers reveal themselves to me when I was growing up on Gordanelle?" Darshima shook his head in confusion.

"What the flames took from you as an infant, was rekindled amid the hallowed sands of Ciblaithia." Tenrai gently let go of his arm and then rose to his feet.

Darshima glared down at his hands in disbelief. Tenrai's words conjured memories of his mother's incredible story of finding him abandoned in a fire, amid the dunes. As he blinked, an image of the moment when he and Sydarias ascended the temple ruins during the Iberwightian eclipse came to him. He recalled standing upon that mysterious, frost-covered black stone, with its swirling golden particles. At that moment, he had sensed that something deep within him had changed, and now he understood.

"It can't be." Darshima looked up Tenrai, his pulse racing in astonishment as he made the connection. Tenrai looked upon him, his eyes glittering with a knowing gaze.

"It would be best if you stop hiding and join us. Sasha is eager to speak with you." Tenrai lingered for a moment, then left the room. Darshima watched the door close behind him, his mind ruminating over their conversation. During his time as a slave, Darshima had come to learn that he was different, but their escape from Stebbenhour put everything into startling relief.

Darshima's eyes drifted to the markings upon his right arm, folded across the other in his lap. The walls of doubt that had long encircled him steadily crumbled as Tenrai's words took root. It was evident that Tenrai knew more about him than he knew about himself. Darshima realized that he couldn't change who he was, but he needed to learn more about this mysterious power that dwelled within him. If he didn't, he feared that it would consume him.

Darshima picked himself off the floor, exited the room and made his way down the corridor toward the cockpit. He took a seat behind Erethalie, who guided the craft amid the starry abyss. Tenrai, seated beside her, looked briefly over his shoulder at Darshima and acknowledged him with an earnest nod. Darshima looked furtively around the cabin. Sasha, Sydarias, and Prince Khydius reclined in a row of chairs behind Tenrai. Shonan lay curled up in a chair behind them and slept quietly.

As Darshima was about to close his eyes, he felt a hand upon his shoulder. He turned to see Sasha staring at him with a warm smile.

"I am so glad to see you, brother," said Sasha as he leaned closer. "How are you feeling?"

"I am tired, but okay." Darshima looked at him, his heart beating anxiously. He blinked his eyes as he stared at Sasha, convincing himself that this wasn't a dream and Sasha was indeed beside him. Prince Khydius turned to Darshima and gave him a polite nod.

"I thank you for saving our lives," said the prince.

"I am glad to have helped, Your Highness." Darshima bowed his head in deference.

"We would not have survived there much longer." A somber frown crossed the prince's lips as he described their struggle.

The prince and many others from his party had been captured and sold as slaves to the owner of a weapons factory. They spent their days toiling away at the workbenches, fashioning the arms that the Navervynish soldiers used to suppress the Vilidesians.

"Most days, they starved and beat us if we slowed down." Sasha's eyes grew damp as he recalled the memory. "Some of our friends didn't survive."

"Whom are you speaking of?" asked Darshima, his pulse racing as images of familiar faces flooded his mind.

"Seth collapsed and died of exhaustion not long after we were brought to the factory." Sasha bowed his head and let out an anguished sigh as his tears fell. "He was my best friend."

"It cannot be."Darshima shook his head as he beheld Sasha's grief-stricken face, searching for any hint of misinterpretation.

His heart sank as memories of Seth's friendly greeting after his failed hunting expedition came back to him. A tear fell down his cheek as Sasha's devastating words settled within him. Darshima hastily dried his eyes, his heart thudding as a sense of anger displaced his sadness. Seth had been a good man, and he, like countless other people did nothing to deserve such a cruel fate.

"So many have perished under the most unimaginable circumstances, but we somehow survived." Prince Khydius put an arm around Sasha's shoulder and comforted him. As Darshima looked at them, his heart ached at the depraved irony of their circumstance. They had been held captive and forced to manufacture the weapons used against their own people.

Tenrai swiveled his seat and looked at all of them.

"We have been through a difficult ordeal, but we have indeed survived. I think it is best if we return Sasha to Gordanelle and take a day's rest there. We will then continue to Iberwight afterward."

"What is on Iberwight?" Sasha looked to Tenrai as he dried his eyes.

"There is much to do there, but we must focus on getting you back to Gordanelle." Tenrai turned toward the cockpit and looked at the instrument panel.

"I don't understand." Sasha's brow wrinkled in confusion.

"I will explain when we get home." Darshima put a hand upon Sasha's shoulder, and he fell silent.

"I think a moment of rest on Gordanelle would be good for all of us." Erethalie glanced over her shoulder, then back toward the windshield. She tapped several moving symbols on the instrument panel. "I will take us there safely." Darshima sank into his seat as the craft accelerated. He looked to the starry void before them, straining to see Benai and its four moons, but saw nothing.

"I am loath to see what the invasion has done to our realm." Prince Khydius gazed through the window beside him.

"You must join us on Iberwight, Your Highness. The Vilides is much too dangerous for you." Tenrai turned toward the prince. "You are the anointed Defender of Iberwight and will find sanctuary in Tiriyuud." "I trust you and your people, Tenrai." Prince Khydius solemnly bowed his head.

"We must not lose hope, Your Highness. There are billions back home who await you," said Sydarias. The prince let out a pained sigh and closed his eyes.

As the cabin fell back into silence, Darshima pondered Sasha's question about their subsequent journey to Iberwight. He didn't know how he would reveal the truth to him.

Darshima closed his eyes and drew in a deep breath, trying to calm himself. He accomplished what he had promised to do and had saved Sasha. The rescue of the prince was something wholly unexpected. The realm and the dynasty had fallen, but Prince Khydius had miraculously survived. Darshima didn't know how, but he was sure that the prince's arrival in his former realm would change everything. As with every harrowing moment before this one, Darshima felt that things would somehow fall into place. He opened his eyes and gazed forward as Erethalie piloted them through the dark, starless sky, toward Ardavia.

Chapter Forty Seven

Darshima and Sasha walked up the stone path toward their home, and the rest of the group followed a few paces behind them. Erethalie had landed the craft in a field beyond the Ewerryn family's neighborhood, near the pair of gleaming marble temples. The grounds where they landed during their previous journey to Gordanelle had been occupied by Navervynish soldiers, and they sought to avoid any interaction with them.

The day was growing late, and the sun hung low above the horizon, its soft rays receding as the darkening sky approached. A gentle breeze stirred through the trees, the temperature feeling a bit more as Darshima had remembered it. As they drew closer, Darshima noticed a difference in Sasha. He had rested during the trip and already regained some of his former vigor.

"I can't believe we're really here." Sasha trembled as the wind blew through his tattered uniform. He drew in a deep breath at the sight of home. His expression grew somber as he beheld the devastation and neglect that had befallen their neighborhood.

"Welcome back, Sasha," said Darshima as they approached the front porch. "Ardavia has changed since the invasion, but it is still home."

They climbed the steps onto the porch and faced the doorway. Sasha looked around anxiously and noticed that Tenrai and the others remained upon the road behind them.

"Please come inside, I would like you to meet our parents." Sasha waved to them.

"We will join you, but first take some time with your family. " Tenrai stood with his arms folded across his chest, the corners of his eyes wrinkled in a sincere expression.

"Tenrai..." started Sasha, but Tenrai shook his head. Sasha fell silent and turned back around.

Darshima raised his hand to the door and knocked firmly. The darkened interior flooded with soft light and his heart leapt into his throat. His parents were still there. The muted sound of heavy footsteps growing louder, Sasha clenched his jaw and took one deep breath after another.

"Am I dreaming?" He turned to Darshima, his eyes brimming with tears.

"You are really here." Darshima put a reassuring arm around his shoulder. Through the thick pane of glass, they saw Sovani's form approaching the entrance.

Darshima gently pushed Sasha forward as Sovani disengaged the locks, and pulled the door open. Dressed in an armless red tunic and black breeches, he stepped past the threshold. With a hand, he shielded his eyes against the setting sun and stared at the two figures upon the porch. His somber expression dissolved into one of stunned surprise when he realized who stood before him.

"My son, Sasha?" Sovani gasped, turning ashen as the color drained from his face. He held onto the doorframe for support.

"Father, I thought I'd never see you again." Sasha rushed forward and embraced him. They stood for a moment, silently crying tears of joy.

"Darshima, I cannot believe it," stammered Sovani. "How did you ever manage to find him?" Sovani reached toward Darshima and drew him into the embrace. Darshima's heart rose into his throat, overcome with emotion as he felt Sovani's warmth.

The faint thud of footsteps came from the interior of the house and Dalia emerged into the hallway, her orange robe fluttering behind her. She peered through the doorway, and a look of bewilderment spread upon her face as she saw Darshima.

"Darshima, you've returned?" Her eyes darted from him to Sovani, then to Sasha. When she realized who stood before her, she paused mid-step.

"Sasha!" She exclaimed. Her knees grew weak and she faltered, reaching toward the door for support. Darshima moved beside her and caught her in his arms. Sasha reached over and held her tightly, her small frame shuddering as she sobbed.

"Is it really you, Sasha? You are home!" She looked toward him, her voice brimming with disbelief. Sovani turned to Darshima, then cast his tear-filled eyes up to the sky.

"Darshima, I will never find a way to thank you," he spoke haltingly.

"I am only one of several who helped free him." Darshima made a sweeping gesture with his hand, toward Tenrai and the others who stood patiently upon the road.

"You found him as you said you would. We are forever grateful to you." Sovani pulled Darshima into another warm embrace, then let go.

"He is my brother, and I couldn't rest until I found him." Darshima placed his hand upon Sasha's shoulder. They stood together in a poignant moment of silence, grateful for the inconceivable circumstance of their reunion. Sovani peered over his shoulder at Tenrai and the others.

"Please join us. You are friends of Darshima and Sasha, therefore you are friends of ours," he called out.

"Thank you for your kindness sir, madam," said Tenrai. He and the others walked along the pathway, bounded up the steps, and filed through the entrance.

Sovani closed the door as Dalia ushered them through the house and into the dining room. Darshima and the others took their seats around the large glass table, and Dalia and Sovani stepped into the adjoining kitchen. Moments later, they entered the dining room with a wooden tray bearing glasses of cold water. They served everyone and returned to the kitchen. The metallic clatter of pots and pans, and the sounds and smells of stewing meat emerged from the kitchen.

As the pots of food simmered, Sovani and Dalia rejoined them at the table and listened to the conversation. Tenrai recounted the details of Sasha's rescue on Navervyne, and Sovani and Dalia sat spellbound as he spoke. They were devastated to hear what Sasha had gone through as a slave on Stebbenhour, but were proud of the courage and bravery that Darshima and the others had shown in rescuing him.

When the meal had finished cooking, they went to the kitchen and returned with bowls of stewed meat and boiled roots. They placed them in front of their guests and sat beside Darshima and Sasha. Darshima and the others had not eaten much for the day and heartily tucked into the meal

"You all have won a special place in our hearts, but we don't know your names or where you are from." An embarrassed smile crossing her lips, Dalia looked around the table.

"I am Tenrai Nax, of Tiriyuud." Tenrai politely rested his fork down, clearing his throat as he spoke.

"I am Sydarias Idawa, of The Vilides." Sydarias offered an earnest smile.

"We are Erethalie and Shonan Danthe, of Pelethedral. Thank you for your hospitality," said Erethalie as she and her brother politely bowed their heads. Dalia and Sovani then turned toward Prince Khydius. They had not paid much attention to him since he had arrived in their home, but their gaze was focused squarely upon him.

"I am Khydius, of The Vilides," he said, his voice faltering slightly. He nervously adjusted his threadbare garments. Dalia squinted and leaned forward.

"Is it truly him?" said Dalia, her voice wavering in disbelief. "The Prince of the Vilides is alive?" Her eyes widened in utter disbelief as she recognized him. His jaw agape, Sovani exchanged a stunned glance with his wife.

"It cannot be...are you indeed Prince Khydius?" stammered Sovani. He and Dalia moved away from the table and then dropped to their knees before him as a sign of respect.

"Madam, Sir, please resume your seats," said the prince, his face flushed with embarrassment.

"Please, Your Highness, we must show our respect." Sovani looked up at him.

"The people who invaded our realm, captured and sold me as a slave did not care about my titles. I am simply Khydius, of The Vilides." Khydius stared at them, a resigned frown crossing his lips. A somber hush fell upon the room. Their gazes deferred, Sovani and Dalia resumed their seats and they all finished their meal in silence.

Chapter Forty Eight

As they once did on clear nights, Darshima and Sasha sat beside each other upon the wooden bench in the garden behind their home, relaxing under the starlit sky. They had finished dinner a while ago, and everyone else had retired for the evening. Darshima looked upon the horizon, the shattered domes and spires of Ardavia glimmering boldly in the moonlight. His heart was filled with a bittersweet gladness at the marred but familiar sight. It had been so long since they had sat together, and he was simply content to be in his brother's presence.

"Darshima, thank you for saving me and Khydius. We would've died without you." Sasha looked up at the sky, his voice wavering.

"You are my brother and I could do no less. Sydarias and I also toiled together on Navervyne," said Darshima. His voice struck a solemn note as the painful memories from the fields came back to him.

"During the voyage, Sydarias told us what you both endured." Sasha looked at his hands folded in his lap.

"Like you and Prince Khydius, we depended on each other to survive." Darshima rested his hand upon Sasha's shoulder, and he nodded in agreement.

"How were you able to find us?" Sasha lifted his head and stared at him.

"I had a hunch about it." Darshima nodded, his eyes twinkling with a knowing gaze.

"However you managed to do it, you showed a degree of bravery that I've never seen in you before." Sasha shook his head in astonishment.

"I'm simply glad you are home." Darshima leaned back in his seat and breathed a sigh of relief.

"I am grateful to be back. There's so much I want to do." Sasha gazed toward the moons above as he enumerated his plans. He wanted to complete his studies, find work as an engineer and hopefully start a family of his own.

"That all sounds wonderful." Darshima smiled as he saw Sasha's face light up.

"I also want to take you back out on the hunt. I know you will be able to catch a powilix this time." Sasha made a motion with his arms as if he were firing an imaginary bow and arrow. Darshima's heart sank as he watched. He lowered his eyes, and his expression grew noticeably darker.

"I understand things are different now." Sasha stared at Darshima, a worried frown crossing his lips.

"Ardavia is not the same place." Darshima shook his head. "Our home is a conquered land. So much had been destroyed, and so many people are still missing."

"But we must persevere in our own lives. We have the fortune of being together again." The corners of Sasha's eyes wrinkled wistfully. "Father and mother will need our help with repairs around the house."

Darshima's chest felt heavy with numbness as he listened. The time had come for him to tell Sasha the truth. It was only recently that he had accepted Tenrai's unbelievable words and his parents' incredible story. His heart thudded anxiously as he contemplated how to tell Sasha.

"You're not saying very much, and you seem distant. What's wrong?" Sasha turned to him.

"So much will always be the same between us, but some things are different now," he sighed nervously.

"What are you talking about?" Sasha's brow furrowed in confusion. Darshima looked up at the stars, searching for the right words. Never in his life had he ever had to deliver such difficult news.

“Sasha, I don’t know of an easy way to tell you this,” began Darshima.

“Tell me what?” said Sasha, his voice rising with apprehension.

“You will always be my brother, but I am not an Eweryn.” Darshima held his gaze. Sasha drew in a sharp breath and shook his head in disbelief.

“What nonsense is this? You are my brother,” stammered Sasha, the tone of his voice betraying his incredulity. “You are part of this family.”

“I was not born to Dalia and Sovani,” said Darshima. The soft rustling of the evening wind through the trees filled the painful silence between them.

“I don’t believe it.” Sasha stared numbly ahead, his jaw clenched.

“They told me in their own words,” said Darshima. His voice broke as he revealed the truth. He bowed his head, overcome by the weight of the moment.

“Why didn’t they ever say anything?” Sasha shook his head in disbelief.

“They did their best to understand where I came from, but the truth was difficult.” He solemnly bowed his head as he recalled their words.

Darshima then shared Sovani and Dalia’s incredible story with Sasha. He told Sasha about their life in The Vilides and how they had found him abandoned in the sands during their flight from the turmoil in the capital.

“None of this is true.” Sasha folded his arms across his chest and looked away from him.

“This is no easier for me than it is for you, but it is the only truth, Sasha.” Darshima grasped him by the shoulders and looked him in the eye. He then let go of Sasha and slumped against the bench, his eyes lingering upon the ground. "If only it weren't," he whispered, his words barely audible.

"What does this mean? Why are you telling me all of this?" Sasha clenched his jaw.

"It means that I don't belong here anymore." Darshima looked up and met Sasha's intense gaze. "Tomorrow, I am leaving for Iberwight with Tenrai and the others."

Sasha's lips parted as a mournful expression crossed his features. He closed his eyes and buried his hands in his face. Darshima's heart rose into his throat, and a wave of sadness filled him. Darshima couldn't bear to see his brother so upset, but he had no choice but to tell him the truth.

"I'm sorry." Darshima reached out to comfort Sasha, but he pulled away.

"Why are you leaving us?" Sasha glared at the ground.

"Tenrai needs me, and I must go with him." Darshima nervously gripped the armrest of the bench.

"We need you here. We are your family," replied Sasha, his voice wavering with wounded anger.

"I know, but I am needed somewhere else. I must train with Tenrai's order and learn their ways so that we can one day be free from Navervyne's rule." Darshima looked at Sasha, who avoided his gaze.

"You belong here with us Darshima, not with them." Sasha visibly shaken, glared at the grass beneath his bare feet.

"This is hard for me too, but I must go." Darshima rested his hand upon Sasha's shoulder.

"Why would an Omystikai man need your help?" Sasha's shoulder tensed, and he stared intently at Darshima. "Does this have anything to do with what happened during our escape?"

Darshima's blood ran cold and he shivered. He had tried hard to forget the memories of that harrowing day, but Sasha's words brought back the images of those soldiers as they burst into flaming ash.

"Yes, it does." Darshima forced himself to look at Sasha and offered a hasty nod.

"I understand." Sasha turned his gaze toward the expanse of sky overhead.

"Tenrai rescued Sydarias and me from Navervyne. I owe him my life, Sasha. I must help him with whatever he needs. Please don't be angry with me." Darshima's heart thudded as he spoke.

"What if I join you?" asked Sasha, his eyes widening in curiosity.

"I cannot let you. You must stay here with mother and father, they need you more than ever." Darshima shook his head. Dalia and Sovani were getting older. They would eventually need Sasha's help. His absence had nearly destroyed them, and Darshima didn't know how they would cope if he were to leave again.

"I could be of help to you." Sasha gripped his arm.

"You have so much work to finish here Sasha. Now is your time to do it," said Darshima. Sasha lowered his gaze and released his grasp.

"What will become of you, Darshima?" Sasha's eyes brimmed with concern. Darshima didn't have an answer. His existence on Navervyne had shown him that nothing was guaranteed, and had given him the habit of living his life from day to day. Since their rescue, he hadn't given much thought to his future beyond the journey to Iberwight.

"I don't know, but I will be okay." Darshima moved closer to Sasha, then embraced him.

"You have become your own man, and I know that I cannot change your mind," whispered Sasha as a tear fell from his eye.

"Leaving you all is the hardest thing I have ever done, but I must do it." Darshima's eyes grew damp.

"Promise me you will take care of yourself out there." Sasha held him tightly.

"I will take care of myself and the others," replied Darshima.

"You cannot leave us without a proper sendoff. We must prepare something." Sasha let him go and cleared his throat.

They sat back upon the bench and looked up at the stars in silence, contemplating the uncertain future that lay ahead of them both. The mysterious stroke of fate that had brought them together as children was now pushing them on separate paths as men. Faint rays of sunlight streaked the dark sky, heralding the dawn. They rose to their feet and made their way toward the house.

Chapter Forty Nine

Darshima stood in the field with Tenrai, Khydius, Sydarias, Erethalie, and Shonan. They basked in the fiery rays of the late afternoon sun. Erethalie's craft stood several paces behind them, its engines whirring softly. Balmy gusts of wind gently stirred the blades of grass at their feet. That morning, they all had gotten a much-needed chance to bathe, to wash their clothes, and to rest. Like Darshima and the others, Khydius had fled Navervyne with nothing but his tattered uniform. As he had done for Darshima and Sydarias, Tenrai had given Khydius a black hooded shirt, a pair of trousers and split-toed boots to wear for the journey to Iberwight, the last of the items he had brought with him from Tiriyuud.

Darshima took in the scene, his pulse thudding as a deep sense of nostalgia came over him. The field was home to the pair of majestic temples hewn in stone that had somehow managed to survive the invasion. Standing opposite each other, their white marble domes rose toward the sky, blending in with the billowing clouds. An image of him and Sasha at rest upon these lawns after his failed hunt flashed before his eyes. He shook his head in disbelief at how much had changed since then.

The large, dark wooden doors of both temples were flung wide open. He caught a glimpse of the enormous golden idols within, their human figures wreathed with chains of colorful flowers. The verdant grounds were crisscrossed with cobbled paths, lined with stone lanterns that burned brightly with tongues of orange flame. The fragrant smoke of incense and ash enveloped the atmosphere in a rich haze. A lump formed in Darshima's throat as cherished memories from his youth, of ceremonies both festive and solemn, came back to him. The ringing sound of harmonious chimes rose into the air, filling his ears. The deep thud of syncopated drumbeats rumbled in his chest. Over the pleasing tones, Darshima heard the melodic chants from several dozen bearded priests. They wore orange robes with the right shoulder exposed, and their long hair was wrapped in elaborate white turbans. Chains of red and blue glass beads hung about their necks, glittering in the rays of sunlight. They stood in a row upon the steps of the temples and surveyed the grounds. A dozen percussionists in similar attire stood behind them. Some with silver tambourines in hand and others with oblong wooden drums strapped to their shoulders, they pounded out increasingly complex rhythms that echoed amid the approaching dusk.

Darshima beheld his family standing before him upon the path between the temples, his heart stirring with both joy and sadness. Dalia wore a crown of flowers and a ceremonial red robe with the shoulders exposed, its rich fabric billowing about her in the light gusts. A chain of white, glistening beads graced her delicate neck. Sasha and Sovani were bare-chested and wore traditional Ardavian red skirts with a pleat in the front that fell just above their ankles. They stood barefoot upon the grass, beside Dalia. Their cloth headbands, decorated with amber beads and colorful feathers fluttered in the winds. Chains of flowers draped their necks, shifting gently as they moved. Sovani, Dalia, and Sasha's faces were marked with a vertical dash of glowing red paint under each eyelid, a ceremonial expression of sadness for a departing loved one. A lump formed in Darshima's throat as he recognized the powerful Gordanellan symbol. He would miss them, as much as they would him.

About three dozen people from their neighborhood, both young and old joined them. The woman wore beads about their necks and red and orange robes similar to Dalia's. Like Sovani and Sasha, the men stood bare-chested with chains of flowers hanging from their necks and wore red ceremonial skirts. Lining the cobbled path, the men and women waved wreaths of flowers and green, leafy fronds to the steady drumbeats. They chanted in rousing harmonies, their voices blending in with the priests.

As Darshima learned earlier that day, Sasha had told Dalia of his imminent departure for Iberwight. She had informed their neighbors about Darshima's improbable journey and his rescue of Sasha. Word quickly spread about this seemingly impossible feat. The neighbors wanted to commemorate the occasion and had organized a traditional Ardavian farewell.

Darshima had been hesitant about having the ceremony. He wanted to keep their arrival and their plans secret, but Tenrai encouraged him to accept his community's sendoff. As he took in the scene, Darshima was grateful that he had. Many of their neighbors had lost their children to the invasion and hoped that a miracle like Darshima and Sasha's return would happen for them. With the permission of the temple, Sasha and Dalia had hastily arranged a ceremony to send off Darshima and his friends.

The congregation of priests descended the temple stairs in a procession and stood before them. They placed chains of fragrant flowers upon Darshima and the others' shoulders and waved a pair of silver censers that belched pungent tendrils of red and white smoke. The priests clasped their hands, issued rousing chants, then embraced each of them. Their voices rose in a melodious, ancient Gordanellan incantation, pleading for their safety and health. Darshima's heart rose in a bittersweet emotion as he listened to the familiar blessing. The priests concluded the rite, and their procession wended its way back to the temple stairs.

The Eweryn family bid farewell to Tenrai and the others, thanking them for their bravery in rescuing Sasha. Amid the drumbeats, Sasha stepped forward and faced Darshima.

"There's nothing I can do or say so that you'll stay?" he asked, his trembling voice blending with the melodious chants of their neighbors.

"I wish I could, but I must go." Darshima lowered his head as his chest tightened with grief. Had the invasion never happened, he would've stayed in Ardavia. With the truth that Dalia and Sovani had revealed, Darshima felt that his home was no longer there. He knew that greater things awaited him in the worlds beyond Gordanelle.

Sovani and Dalia beheld Darshima, their faces drawn in somber expressions.

"I wish you would stay with us my son, but who am I to keep you?" Dalia stepped forward and held his hands. "Just as your origins are a mystery to me, so is your future." She dashed a tear from her cheek. Darshima felt his throat tighten as the waves of sadness roiled within him.

"I will come back and visit you one day," he whispered as he embraced her tightly. "They will keep me safe." He gestured to Tenrai and the others behind him.

"Please take care of yourselves out there," she said. Darshima nodded at her words and gazed upon his family, letting out a contented sigh. He had set out to reunite them and had succeeded.

Sasha stepped toward him and grabbed him gently by the shoulders.

"I am losing both you and Khydius today. It is so much to bear." He closed his eyes and clenched his jaw, trying to fight back his tears. Sasha cleared his throat and regained his composure. "Thank you for finding us, Darshima," he said, his voice filled with sadness. "I don't care about the truth. You will always be my brother, and our bond is stronger than blood."

"We are family, and that will never change." Darshima embraced Sasha. "Please take care of mother and father."

"You have my word." Sasha nodded.

Dalia cupped Darshima's cheeks with her hands. "You will always have a home here with us in Ardavia. We will be waiting for you with open arms." She hugged him and kissed his forehead. She then let go as the tears streamed down her face. Sovani then moved over to him. They stared at each other, unsure of what to say.

"I have returned Sasha to you as I promised." Darshima beheld his father. Sovani gazed upon him, his amber eyes glinting with tears.

"Your mother and I will never find a way to thank you for bringing us together again. I am proud of you, Darshima." Sovani reached out to Darshima and drew him closer. They stood face to face.

"Sasha is my brother, and I love him. I couldn't continue on, knowing that he was still enslaved," said Darshima, his voice heavy with emotion. As he moved away toward the group, Sovani held him for a bit longer.

"You have shown so much courage and honor, under the most difficult circumstances. You are a great man in my eyes. I want you to know that." Sovani wrapped his arms around Darshima in a tight embrace. "Please take care of yourself, my son." Sovani reluctantly let him go, then rejoined Dalia and Sasha.

Overcome by the moment, Darshima stepped back, his eyes lingering upon his family. Fighting his tears at Sovani's unexpected words, he turned away from them. He joined Tenrai and the others as Erethalie led them along the path from the temple grounds toward the craft. The chants and the drumbeats increased in intensity as they approached the ship, echoing in his ears.

As he made his way, Darshima waded through his swirling thoughts. He had succeeded in rescuing Sasha and reuniting the Eweryn family. The journey ahead would be filled with perils yet unknown, but at least he had fulfilled his duty as their son. His heart fluttered with an anxious sensation, as he felt the stirrings of a new beginning in his life.

As they neared the ship, he felt an arm rest gently upon his shoulder.

"We are the lucky ones, Darshima," whispered Sydarias, who walked closely beside him."We were rescued from our servitude. We got the chance to reunite and to say goodbye to our families. It would be selfish if we were the only ones to do so. We must help the others."

"You are right," Darshima nodded, the corners of his eyes growing damp.

They arrived at the rear of the ship, its polished airframe glinting a deep blue in the waning sunlight. Darshima's pulse beat along with the fading sounds of the drums and chants. With a soft whirr, the hatch opened and they boarded single file. Darshima, the last in the line upon the gangway, lingered behind everyone else. He walked slowly up the ramp, his heart heavy with the weight of the unknown before him.

Darshima looked over his shoulder toward the temple grounds to see his family and his neighbors standing along the torchlit path, waiting for him to board. He could just make out their bright robes in the receding rays of daylight. Feelings of sadness came over him, and his heart rose into his throat as he saw them. This was indeed goodbye, and it was much harder than he had imagined. With a wave, Darshima saluted them for a final time. His family and his neighbors waved back heartily, responding with rousing cheers that echoed in the twilight. He closed his eyes and then turned back to the ship.

Darshima stepped aboard and the hatch closed behind him, the drum beats and the harmonious chants fading into silence. He took his seat behind Tenrai and stared blankly forward as he secured himself. The rising rumble of the engines broke through the quietness of the cabin. He sank in his seat as they vaulted skyward, his stomach lurching as they accelerated. The craft shuddered and a tear escaped his eye. As they broke the bonds of gravity, the magnitude of what he was setting out to do hit him. He buried his face in his hands and let out a pained sigh, unsure if he was ready.

A hand rested upon his shoulder and he lifted his face to meet Khydius' gaze.

"Be strong Darshima. We will make it through this together. We have no other choice," he said, a thoughtful expression gracing his features.

"I will try my best, Your Highness," replied Darshima. The words struck him, and he deferentially bowed his head. The prince sank back into his seat under the force of the acceleration and gazed through the windshield in front of them. Darshima closed his eyes and focused on the prince's words. There was indeed no other choice. He could not stay on Gordanelle when there was so much suffering in their midst. The shuddering subsided and the cabin again fell silent.

"I will set our course for Iberwight," said Erethalie, as she tapped the glowing chart upon her screen. "Everyone get settled and get some rest. At Gordanelle's current orbital position, it will take us approximately five Vilidesian days to get there."

"Thank you, Erethalie. Once we arrive, I will show you the approach to Tiriyuud." Tenrai turned toward her.

Darshima peered through the window beside him. Ardavia steadily drifted away, its scarred edifices shimmering in the morning light as they ascended. They passed through the atmosphere in a flash of white vapor, and the emerald green sphere of Gordanelle steadily receded into the depths of space. Erethalie toggled a control above her and steered the craft toward the small white crescent of Iberwight, hanging before them in the black abyss. Darshima turned to the window beside him, and through his tears, let out a melancholy sigh. He cast a longing gaze at the verdant orb that had raised and nurtured him, vowing to himself that it would not be his last.

Chapter Fifty

Darshima gripped the armrests of his chair, his heart pounding in fear as the airframe shuddered violently. He looked toward the cockpit as Erethalie guided the craft, her knuckles taut as she gripped the control wheel. They had arrived on Iberwight at dawn after a nearly five-day voyage from Gordanelle, and were making their final approach. She desperately tapped at the instrument panels as the glowing screens faded to black. The interior lights around them flickered and dimmed in rapid succession. Alarms and horns wailed in a jarring cacophony, grating his ears. The engines let out a terrifying growl as they churned through the frigid atmosphere.

Darshima peered through the window at the thick blanket of grey clouds and snow squalls surrounding them. Brilliant veins of blue and white lighting bolted through the air, their branching glow searing into his eyes. The earsplitting clap of thunder rattled him, and he covered his ears against deafening noise. He looked below the billowing wisps and saw no land amid the choppy waters.

"What is happening?" Khydius held onto his seat as the craft lurched back and forth.

"We've hit severe turbulence and none of my instruments are functioning." Erethalie flipped several pairs of switches overhead. "The engines cannot take much more of this." She yanked at the throttle.

"Please make it stop." Sydarias gripped his seatbelt and closed his eyes.

"We are going to survive, right?" Darshima leaned forward and grabbed the back of Tenrai's seat for support. His stomach lurched as the craft rocked with the buffeting winds, gaining then losing altitude at a moment's notice.

Amid the tumult of the cabin, Tenrai sat calmly as Darshima and the others braced themselves against the vessel's violent tremors.

"Erethalie, let go of the controls and allow me to guide the ship." He turned to her.

"But there are no controls at your seat." She tightened her grip upon the wheel.

"I do not need them." Tenrai shook his head. Erethalie turned to him, her eyes widening in incredulity.

"I don't understand." She looked down at the controls, then back at him.

"I will guide us for this part of the journey," he said calmly, his voice rising amid the creaking shudders of the fuselage. She glared at him, her eyes narrowing as she contemplated his unusual request.

"I have no choice but to trust you." She let out a nervous sigh and loosened her grip.

"You have my word." He gently placed his hand upon hers. She hesitantly let go of the wheel, then folded her hands in her lap.

"What is happening?" Darshima's eyes darted between the two as they spoke. "We are running out of time."

"Everyone stay calm. We are approaching the Kingdom of Tiriyuud," said Tenrai.

The craft pitched sharply to the right and the engines made a mournful sputter, then cut out. The airframe creaked and rocked violently as they plummeted, nose-first toward the ocean. Darshima sank into his seat as they fell, struggling to breathe as the force of the acceleration pressed against his chest.

"Tenrai, you must do something!" shouted Khydius as he gripped his seatbelt.

"Are we going to die?" Shonan grabbed onto Sydarias' arm.

"Stay calm, Shonan." Erethalie glanced over her shoulder, and offered him a reassuring nod, despite the worried frown upon her face.

"We are almost there." Tenrai extended a hand toward the windshield and whispered a string of cryptic phrases in his unfamiliar language.

Darshima crouched in his seat and awaited the impact, images of his family flashing through his mind.

"We're too close to the ocean Tenrai!" shouted Erethalie.

Darshima closed his eyes, bowed his head, and braced himself for the crash. As he drew in what he thought would be his final breath, the shuddering unexpectedly ceased. The cabin became still, and the soft whistle of wind over the fuselage filled his ears. The pressure against his chest disappeared, and he could breathe once again. He opened his eyes to see Tenrai with his hand still extended toward the windshield. The craft swayed gently amid the clouds, as if it were a leaf in a gentle gust. Darshima shook his head in disbelief as they descended. Moments ago, they faced certain doom, but now they were gliding smoothly upon the wind.

"What just happened, Tenrai?" asked Darshima.

"My apologies for the turbulence, but our defenses make it nearly impossible for foreign craft to approach," he replied.

"How did we manage to survive?" Khydius leaned back in his chair and let out a deep sigh of relief.

"There are ways to navigate foreign craft around the perpetual storms surrounding the kingdom. Only we Tiriyuusians know how." Tenrai drew his hand back from the window.

"So that is why you needed to take control of my ship." Erethalie's jaw dropped in surprise.

"It is a matter of understanding the forces surrounding your ship, and letting them guide us." Tenrai rested his hand upon his knee. "Sometimes you must let go to find a way through."

"That was incredible," whispered Sydarias, his voice filled with awe.

"We are now safe. You may take us in for landing." Tenrai reclined in his seat.

"Thank you, Tenrai." As Erethalie put her hands back upon the controls, the screens flickered on, and the engines roared back to life. "That was unbelievable." she shook her head in astonishment.

"The members of my Order know that you all are here and will grant us entry," said Tenrai.

"But how? You haven't even contacted them," remarked Sydarias, pointing to the instrument panel.

"Tiriyuusians have ways of communicating and navigating beyond your Vilidesian electromagnetic radios or sensors." Tenrai tapped a finger against his temple.

A shiver coursed through Darshima as he heard Tenrai's words. He couldn't understand how someone could communicate across distances without modern equipment. He shook his head as he remembered all of the seemingly miraculous things that had happened since he had met Tenrai. In his presence, the impossible seemed quite normal. Darshima peered through the window beside him to see that the tempest had dissipated into bands of puffy clouds and serene blue skies.

Erethalie navigated the craft toward a chain of immense, mountainous islands rising from the ocean.

"Welcome to Tiriyuud." Tenrai looked over his shoulder and peered at Darshima, then turned back to Erethalie. "My home is just over that summit. There will be a place for us to land." He pointed toward a valley hemmed in by a jagged line of peaks. She guided them over the mountains and through the billowing clouds as they descended.

As Tenrai described, they had reached the northernmost island of the kingdom and would soon arrive in his ancestral village of

Foseidem. A lonely, mountainous archipelago of eight principle islands arranged in the shape of a crescent, Tiriyuud lay upon Iberwight's northern hemisphere, in the middle of its largest ocean. Amid the driving snowfall, Darshima spotted a gleaming, black octagonal surface. They soared over the valley and approached the airfield.

Buffeted by the frigid gusts, Erethalie landed the craft upon the field with a gentle thud. The snowfall vaporized into thin clouds of steam as it hit the clean, paved surface. They grabbed their things and disembarked through the rear hatch. Darshima narrowed his eyes against the fierce winds as Tenrai led them across the paved field. Before they stepped into the surrounding, snow-covered expanse, he stooped down and hoisted Shonan upon his back.

Darshima's skin stung against the biting cold as they walked upon the frozen ground. He trudged through the knee-high snowbanks along with the others, his hair and shoulders soon covered in the powdery cold flakes. His senses overwhelmed, he drew in an icy breath and shivered.

"We are headed to the dwelling just over there." Tenrai pointed toward a large, square wooden arch at the foot of a gently sloping hill, nestled against the mountains. His words came out in steaming puffs of air.

Darshima braced himself against the rising gusts as they trudged amid the snowdrifts. Though it was morning, the rays of sunlight offered neither warmth nor comfort against the cold. Tenrai trudged a few paces ahead of them, seemingly unfazed by the inclement weather.

"Are we almost there?" Sydarias' teeth chattered as he drew his garments around him.

"It is not much further." Tenrai glanced over his shoulder.

"I don't know how much more of this cold I can take." Erethalie shivered and rubbed her hands together.

"The weather here isn't so terrible. My duties required me to spend several months a year in Gavipristine." Khydius looked toward Erethalie and Sydarias as he dusted the snow from his shoulders.

"You are the sworn Defender of Iberwight. You'll have to teach us how to survive here." Darshima stared at him.

"Those days are no more." Khydius glared back, his lips curling into a resigned frown.

"This weather will toughen all of you," said Tenrai, as he led them through the snow. "We are nearly there."

As they walked, Darshima rubbed the back of his arms and tried to stave off the stinging cold. He peered over his shoulder and saw Erethalie's ship in the distance, standing as a mere sliver of blue metal upon the frigid horizon. The visibility diminished by the snow squalls, he looked around and tried to gain some sense of the foreign terrain. The gently rolling hills were covered in a thick blanket of fluffy white snow. Large outcroppings of jagged, multicolored crystals jutted through the powdery layer like fingers, glittering in the muted rays of the morning sun.

In the near distance, beyond the hills, vast tracts of primeval forest carpeted the land. An immense range of snow-capped mountains and glaciers punctuated the distant horizon. Upon the hilltops he eyed stately wooden homes perched upon stout, stone foundations. They were among the only signs of civilization amid the frozen splendor. Rising several stories tall with tiled, sloping roofs and chimneys that belched white vapor, they stood boldly against the snowy landscape.

Further afield, a line of enormous, octagonal stone and glass pyramids rose between the forests and mountains. Their glowing apices seemed to nudge against the clouds.

"What are those pyramids?" Darshima pointed toward the horizon. They were unlike anything he had ever seen.

"That is how we grow our food," said Tenrai.

"You don't import your provisions from Wohiimai like the other peoples of the realm?" asked Sydarias.

"We grow plants for food in the taller ones and rear livestock in the shorter ones." Tenrai gestured toward the impressive structures in the distance. "We believe that self-sufficiency is of utmost importance."

"Unlike the dominions, Tiriyuud perfected this technology and obviated the need to import food." Khydius pointed toward the line of pyramids.

"How were they able to figure it out?" asked Erethalie.

"Though Iberwight remains frozen the whole year round, there is ample sunlight and hydrothermal vapor. The pyramids trap heat from the sun and steam, which warms the soil enough for us to farm and rear animals," replied Tenrai.

"That's remarkable." Darshima narrowed his eyes as he took in the details of the structures, amazed that Tiriyuusians had found a way to support agriculture upon the frozen terrain.

The sun traced an arc across the cloudy sky as they approached the multilevel dwelling. Darshima's chest tightened with a wave of anxiety as he eyed the imposing home. Everything that happened since Tenrai rescued him from Navervyne had been leading to this moment. Tenrai had promised to answer his questions and assuage his fears once they arrived on Iberwight. Darshima's heart pounded a bit harder with each step, his anticipation only growing.

They stopped under the base of the large square arch and caught their breath amid the heavy snowfall. Ornately carved, its triple cross beam stood boldly against the snowdrifts. A cast bronze bell hung from its center. Tenrai stooped down and Shonan hopped from his back, shaking the snow from his clothes.

Tenrai stood in front of the structure and whispered a few words in his mysterious language. He bowed his head, clapped his hands twice then walked through, beckoning them to join him. Darshima, followed by Erethalie, Shonan, Sydarias, and Khydius passed through to the other side. In a single-file line, they climbed a long stone staircase carved into the snow-covered hill. Tenrai bounded upward two at a time, surefooted in his ascent. Darshima and the others, tired from the long trek followed at a more moderate pace.

At the top of the stairs, they stepped into the manicured, coniferous garden of a handsome wooden home. Tenrai led them onto the broad porch and stood before a large pair of dark wooden doors with an array of geometric carvings.

"Welcome home." Tenrai gripped the iron knobs and pulled the doors open. A blast of warm air greeted them as he ushered Darshima and the others inside.

"Thank you for bringing us here safely." Darshima brushed the snow from his clothes and gratefully soaked up the warmth.

"We will be comfortable here," said Tenrai, the doors groaning as he pushed them closed.

Tenrai led them from the entrance into the spacious interior. White woolen rugs woven with colorful, tessellated designs covered the polished, dark wooden floors. An enormous, inviting brick hearth roaring with white flame sat at the opposite end of the room. Large glass windows spanned from the floor to the ceiling high above. Muted sunlight streamed in and gave the room an airy ambiance.

"Your home is beautiful." Darshima's gaze lingered upon the rich details of the space.

"It has been in the family for generations." A wistful smile came to Tenrai's lips as his eyes swept over the room. "This home was built seven centuries ago and passed down through the ages. When my father and mother died, they left me as the caretaker." Darshima's eyes widened in surprise as he contemplated the age of the building.

Tenrai ushered them into the spacious drawing room and toward the hearth. A row of comfortable leather cushions and an oval, low profile obsidian table sat before the inviting flames. Darshima and the others walked to the windows and peered at their surroundings. Beyond the snow-covered hills and forests, the jagged mountains yielded to a wide bay, leading out to the expansive, calm blue ocean stretching toward the horizon.

"The landscape here in Tiriyuud is unlike any other place." Tenrai joined them as they gazed at the scenery through the muted, monochromatic haze of the snowfall.

"I have never seen anything like it," exclaimed Darshima as he took in the details.

"It's so different from The Vilides." Erethalie leaned against the glass as she studied the surroundings. Like the others, Darshima had grown up in a more urban part of the realm. He was accustomed to the jarring bustle of traffic and humid skies crowded out by buildings. The forbidding landscape spread out before him, glistening under the cloudy skies in frozen majesty. He wondered if he would ever get accustomed to living upon this moon.

"Why don't you all sit down and rest." Tenrai gestured toward the hearth. They sat down upon the cushions before the table, and enjoyed the warmth from the fire. Tenrai politely excused himself and left the room. Darshima stared at the tongues of white flame as the others chatted around him. He was impressed by Tenrai's home and felt a sense of peace emanating from every corner.

The clatter of dishes rang out from the kitchen, and Tenrai returned with a metal tray bearing a porcelain kettle of tea and cups, cured meats, pickled roots, and utensils. He knelt down, rested the tray upon the table before them and sat beside Darshima.

"How long will we be here?" asked Sydarias as he reached for a piece of meat with a wooden skewer.

"Only for the night. We will set out for the capital in the morning." Tenrai poured the tea into the delicate cups and passed them around.

"What is the name of the capital?" asked Erethalie, her brow furrowed in curiosity. Seated beside her, Shonan leaned forward and helped himself to the tray of food.

"They call it Chryshaihem. It is virtually cut off from the outside world." Khydius sipped slowly from his cup.

"Why is it so isolated?" asked Darshima as he picked up his cup, the tendrils of steam tickling his nose.

"Restricted engagement with the outside world is how Tiriyuud has managed to survive over the ages." Tenrai sipped his tea and set his cup down.

"How will we get there?" Sydarias reached for another piece of meat and took a bite.

"We must cross overland. Aerial traffic is not permitted there." Tenrai settled in his seat and gazed through the window.

"How long will that take?" asked Darshima.

"Weather permitting, our trek will last a day," he replied.

As they finished their meal, Tenrai described what they would be doing in the coming weeks. Once they arrived in the capital, they would meet the members of Tenrai's order and begin their training. They would hone their minds, bodies, and souls, and learn the ways of the legendary Tiriyuusian guardians. The training would be difficult for them, but Tenrai believed that they would succeed. Once fully trained, they could then begin their struggle against Navervyne.

Chapter Fifty One

Darshima lay upon a downy, low profile bed in a well-appointed room. Like the other rooms of the home, its bright, wooden interior was comfortably furnished and offered a sweeping view of the bay and mountains in the distance. It was still morning, but the richness of the food and the exhausting journey had taken its toll on him. He and the others had retired to their quarters for some much-needed rest.

Though fatigued, Darshima was too anxious to sleep. His mind raced through the events of the past several days. He had left everything he had ever known back on Gordanelle for the frozen expanses of Iberwight. Apart from Tenrai's vague description, the days ahead remained a mystery. His thoughts turned to Tenrai, who had done so much for them. Despite significant danger, he had delivered them from Navervyne and the occupied Vilides, and had now brought them to the protected shores of his kingdom.

Despite Tenrai's bravery and selflessness, Darshima's heart fluttered with a kernel of doubt. He understood that Tenrai sought to help him cultivate his abilities in service of the kingdom, but he wondered to what end. Darshima shuddered as the memory of the destruction he had wrought on Stebbenhour flashed before his eyes. He shook his head, trying to rid himself of the frightful memory. Though he was beginning to accept what happened back there, the gruesome images stalked the corners of his mind, seizing him when he least expected it. Darshima knew that he would need guidance in learning about this newfound and terrifying ability. He hoped that Tenrai would show him how to control this part of himself and use it to help, not to harm.

Darshima tossed and turned in the bed, but could find no rest amid his troubling thoughts. A sigh escaped his lips, and he heaved himself off the mattress. He walked toward the window and stared at the rippling waters of the bay lapping at the curving shore. As his eyes lingered upon the falling snowflakes, his mind drifted back to his family at home on Gordanelle.

Darshima couldn't help but think about how different his life would have been had the realm never been invaded. Somehow, he would have found a way to earn a living back home in Ardavia. He and his father would have found a way to reconcile their differences. He would have made himself useful, helping Dalia around the garden, and supporting Sasha as he continued his studies. Maybe he would have even finished reading those books given to him by his professor.

As Darshima's mind boldly framed an alternate scenario of the past, the reality of his present situation violently broke through. His chest tightened as the hard and painful facts resurfaced. The invasion and its aftermath had revealed that he was in truth, an orphan abandoned in the desert sands, who had mercifully been taken in by a kindhearted family. There was no use mourning the loss of what could have been. Navervyne's conquest had disrupted everything in his life, and things would never be as they once were.

A tear escaped Darshima's eye and he wiped it away with his palm. He let out an anxious sigh and tried to focus on the days ahead. His pulse thudded as Tenrai's description of the training regimen filtered through his mind. He and the others were considered outsiders to Tenrai's Order, and their foreignness would make teaching them more difficult. They needed to be just as strong as the Tiriyuusians, and would have to prove their loyalty to the kingdom beyond any doubt.

Like the snowdrifts in the distance, Darshima's gaze shifted aimlessly as he peered through the window. He had spent many a night back on Gordanelle staring up at the evening sky, pondering the desolate, frozen expanses of Iberwight. He never imagined visiting this moon, nor did he fathom the circumstances that would have eventually brought him here.

The sound of soft knocking at the door echoed through the room. Darshima peeled his eyes away from the window, walked toward the door, and slid it open. Khydius stood patiently outside.

"May I come in?" Khydius stared at him, a contemplative frown upon his lips.

"Please, join me." Darshima opened the door further and the prince stepped past the threshold, his eyes drawn to the dramatic view. Khydius walked to the opposite end of the room and Darshima followed him. They sat beside the window and faced each other.

Since their return from Stebbenhour, Darshima had not said much the prince. His mere presence both intimidated and intrigued Darshima. Memories of their first encounter at his birthday celebration back in The Vilides came back to him. Khydius had seemed so imposing to him back then. Darshima sat in anxious silence, deferentially bowing his head and keeping his eyes upon the ground.

Darshima was at a loss for words as he sat face to face with Khydius, the heir to the throne. At times, he struggled to fully comprehend the aftermath of the invasion but seeing the Vilidesian prince seated before him, dressed in simple clothing on a world away from their own put everything in devastating relief.

"How are you, Darshima?" Khydius cleared his throat and folded his hands in his lap.

"I am as fine as can be expected, Your Highness." Darshima looked up at the prince.

"Please, call me Khydius." He raised a hand to Darshima.

"If you insist, sir." Darshima nodded nervously.

"We have not said much to each other since we left Navervyne." A polite smile crossed Khydius' lips.

"We all have been through so much, and I didn't want to trouble you with my worries." Darshima deftly gazed toward the window, avoiding his stare.

"I must personally thank you for rescuing me. If it weren't for you, Sasha and I wouldn't have survived for much longer," said Khydius, his voice wavering with emotion.

"I am glad that I was able to help." Darshima's demeanor softened a bit, and he turned back him. "If I may ask, why do you insist that we no longer call you Prince Khydius? Why have you renounced your title?"

"What difference does it make?" Khydius shook his head, a look of sadness spreading upon his face.

"You're the Prince of the Vilides," whispered Darshima, barely able to hide his disbelief.

"The people who murdered the emperor and empress, and enslaved me didn't care that I was a prince." His eyes glinted in the sunlight.

Regretting his question, Darshima felt his cheeks grow hot. He stared at the floor as they fell into an uneasy silence.

"My apologies, Khydius." Darshima bowed his head. He chided himself for his harsh tone, remembering that he wasn't the only one who had suffered during the invasion.

"Darshima, I am not the same person that you encountered in The Vilides. I have changed, just as you have." Khydius cleared his throat and straightened his posture.

"You remember who I am?" asked Darshima.

"I certainly remember you. Sasha attended my birthday celebration. You were at the palace assisting him with his things. He told me that you chose the gift of those two birds." Khydius' lips curled into a thoughtful smile.

"He is a good brother." Darshima chuckled to himself as he recalled the gift.

"I wouldn't have survived on Navervyne without Sasha." Overcome with emotion, Khydius closed his eyes and let out a sigh. "He spoke of you every day during our toil in the factory, and he feared that you had died."

"I feared the same for him and our parents." Darshima's pulse raced as fiery images of the invasion and the siege at the palace came back to him.

"He was consumed with finding you and your parents and returning to Gordanelle." Khydius leaned forward and peered intently at him.

"Thank you for being there for Sasha." Darshima's eyes grew damp as he thought of his brother.

"Darshima, you are Sasha's brother, therefore you are my friend. We must get along." Khydius wrapped his arms around him in a warm embrace, and Darshima returned the gesture.

They spoke about their time thus far in Tiriyuud, and how different it was from the rest of the realm. His apprehension soon disappeared and he began to feel at ease around Khydius. Back in Ardavia, he had noticed how close Sasha and Khydius were. Much like him and Sydarias, the pair had survived their terrible ordeal together as slaves in the munitions factory on Navervyne. If Sasha had found a friend in Khydius, he certainly could.

"What do you think of Tenrai?" Darshima leaned closer to Khydius.

"He is a good man, but there is something that seems unknowable about him." A pensive expression crossed Khydius' face.

"I feel that he is keeping something from us." Darshima bit his lip as the lingering doubts crept back.

"What do you mean?" Khydius' eyebrows arched in curiosity.

"He remains a mystery to me." Darshima's heart thudded anxiously as he told Khydius about Tenrai's daring voyage to Navervyne. He revealed how Tenrai had only planned on rescuing him, and how he had called him by his name during their first encounter.

"I sense it too, but we must trust his judgment," whispered Khydius. An abrupt shiver coursed through him and his skin momentarily flushed. Khydius then closed his eyes and put a hand to his chest, as if he were in pain.

"Are you okay?" Darshima reached out to him.

"Answer the door, someone is approaching." Khydius's eyes fluttered open and he looked up at Darshima, his eyes glittering with a spark of recognition.

As Darshima turned toward the entryway, he heard a soft knock. Startled, he jumped to his feet, hurried toward the door and slid it open to find Tenrai waiting in the hallway.

"How are you?" asked Tenrai.

"We're fine." Darshima shifted nervously as he stood at the threshold.

"Darshima, Khydius will you come with me?" His eyebrows wrinkled in a serious expression. "There is something I have been meaning to show you."

They nodded in unison at Tenrai's request, and Khydius joined them at the doorway. Tenrai led them down the dim hallway, and Darshima let his fingertips grace the smooth, wood-paneled walls as they made their way through the shadows. Apart from the distant noise of the howling winds outside, the house was completely silent. They reached a door at the end of the hall, and Tenrai slid it open.

They climbed the wooden steps of a narrow staircase until they reached another door. Thin beans of sunlight escaped through the seams, partially revealing Tenrai's face. He drew in a deep breath, slid it open, and stepped through. A cascade of light spilled forth, completely enveloping him. Shielding their eyes against the brilliance, Darshima and Khydius followed him and closed the door behind them.

They entered a large, octagonal room, with a dark wooden floor and sloping glass walls that converged above them in a pyramid. Through the glass, Darshima eyed the arresting views of the surrounding wintry landscape. The snows had momentarily abated, revealing the cloudless blue sky above. The space was sparsely furnished, save for a tall, ornate cabinet in the center, and eight woolen, white rectangular rugs arranged around it in a neat circle.

Darshima and Khydius walked across the polished floorboards and joined Tenrai, who stood in front of the striking, cuboidal object.

"Darshima, Khydius, I sense that I am losing your trust." He rested a hand upon its dark wooden surface. "Please know that my intentions have always been pure. I would never do anything to mislead or harm you."

"I believe you Tenrai, but there is so much I want to know." Darshima anxiously cast his gaze toward the ground.

"You have shown great courage in rescuing us. We just want to know more about you." Khydius stepped closer to Tenrai.

"As you wish. You both have a right to know everything." Tenrai turned toward the cabinet. "So that you believe me, it is time for me to share something very important with you."

Tenrai retrieved an eight-sided, engraved golden card from a pocket in his trousers. He then inserted it into an octagonal relief between the two doors of the cabinet. The cabinet issued a melodious, polyphonic chime, and the card disappeared in its recesses with a gentle plink.

The sound of turning gears and disengaging tumblers filled the room, and the doors slowly opened. Tenrai stepped behind the two young men and gently pushed them closer to the object. To Darshima's surprise, it was not a storage cabinet as he had presumed, but an intriguing work of art. The parted doors revealed an enormous, carved slab of red wood whose polished surface bore a dizzying array of lines, symbols and script, inlaid in gold and crystal.

"What an exquisite object," whispered Khydius as the doors disappeared into concealed pockets in the sides of the wooden chest.

"This is more than a mere object. Please step closer and examine it." Tenrai gestured with his hands.

Darshima's gaze swept over the surface as he tried to make sense of the complex tableau. It appeared to be an intricate map of abstract emblems and symbols connected by a dizzying, ramified web of lines. A glittering gemstone and a row of script written in gold stood underneath each carved symbol. He scoured through the diagram, attempting to distinguish anything familiar. His eyes scanned the top of the slab, where he saw a line of gracefully hashed marks etched deeply into the wood. Unfamiliar with the written Omystikaiyn language, he turned to Tenrai,

"What does the heading say?" Darshima pointed to the script.

"It says Siono Nax, or the Nax Clan," said Khydius, his voice brimming with confidence.

"You can read Omystikaiyn?" Impressed, Darshima turned to Khydius.

"I studied the language as a child." His eyes darted about the polished surface as he whispered a string of foreign words. "This is a much older dialect than what my counselors taught me."

"Is this your family tree?" Darshima turned to Tenrai.

"Yes, it is. You can find my symbol here." Tenrai pointed out a complex series of curving lines and shapes carved into the wood, accented with a large sapphire stone, and a line of gold script inlaid beneath.

"Nax-Foseidem, Tenrai," murmured Khydius.

"As Tiriyuusian Omystikai, we are assigned a gemstone and a symbol. They are both equally important to a person. The name reflects a family's ancestral village and heritage. The stone represents qualities of that person's inner spirit." Tenrai pointed to the diagram as he spoke.

"What about the symbol?" asked Darshima.

"The symbol is unique and reflects many things, such as character and ability." Tenrai's fingers gently swept over the decorated wooden slab.

"How do you choose them?" asked Khydius, his eyebrows raised in curiosity.

"After we are born, our families partake in several days of ritual fasting, celestial observation, and meditation. They decide which stones and symbols must be chosen, and then place the ink upon our skin during a ceremony. Like one's spirit, the stone is immutable. Like one's character, the symbol is indelible." Tenrai furrowed his brow and searched their eyes. He then unfastened the top buttons of his shirt, and the black garment slid down his muscular shoulders. An intricate, almost calligraphic design of shimmering blue and black ink stood out upon the smooth, porcelain skin of his back, spanning from the left shoulder blade all the way to the right.

"This my symbol," he said.

"It's beautiful." Darshima gazed at the markings, trying to take in every detail. It was an exact match to the symbol that he had shown them upon the wooden slab.

"Darshima, Khydius, look carefully at the symbols near mine and you will find the answer to your questions." Tenrai pulled his shirt back over his shoulders.

His heart pounding, Darshima turned toward the chart and scoured the names connected to Tenrai's. He gazed at Tenrai's ancestors but the emblems were hopelessly foreign to him. He looked at Tenrai's parents, and again saw nothing familiar. His eyes drifted down one generation and he saw Tenrai's name and symbol, which stood solitarily. There appeared to be no wife or children.

Darshima looked at the name beside Tenrai's. His eyes lingered over the strange emblem, accented with an emerald. He drew in a nervous breath when he realized it was Tenrai's deceased brother. He moved in closer and examined the names surrounding it. An elegant seal, unlike any other on the chart was connected to it with a golden arc, denoting his wife.

Darshima's finger slid down the line, to their descendants. It appeared as if they had two children. His finger slowly traced the gleaming line connecting to the symbol on the right, accented with a fiery ruby. His eyes nearly passed over it when something unexpected caught his eye. He looked closely at the symbol's intricate marks, his pulse racing with an unmistakable sense of familiarity.

He pulled his finger away from the chart and yanked up his right sleeve. His heart thudding with bewilderment, he glared at his right arm. The symbol on the carving was an exact match to the swirl of markings on his right arm. His chest tightened as a bolt of utter surprise struck him.

"It cannot be..." His hand trembling uncontrollably, Darshima again traced his finger along the line from Tenrai's symbol to his, when his finger unexpectedly nudged against Khydius. Darshima looked over to see Khydius' finger poised upon the symbol adjacent to his, accented with a glittering diamond.

"*Nax-Foseidem, Khydius...*" he stammered, his voice barely above a whisper. Khydius then slid his finger over to Darshima's symbol. "*Nax-Foseidem, Darshima.*"

Darshima drew in a halting breath, and his sight grew dim. He turned toward Khydius, whose stunned gaze met his. Khydius had torn his shirt open, exposing an intricate blue marking upon the golden brown skin of his bare chest. Darshima's eyes darted between the mark on Khydius's smooth skin and the carved emblem, and they were the same. Khydius' eyes scanned the marking on Darshima's arm and the identical symbol etched into the wood. Overcome by a wave of disbelief, Darshima faced Tenrai and looked him squarely in the eye.

"Is this the truth, Tenrai?" he whispered, barely able to find the words.

"Yes, it is." Tenrai stepped closer to them. "Do you understand what this means Darshima and Khydius? Do you finally understand why I rescued you?" Darshima stood in stunned silence, trying to digest the true meaning of the diagram before him.

"This is impossible," exclaimed Khydius, his eyes widened in shock.

"As it is written, it is so." Tenrai pointed to the chart. "When you were infants, your father and I chose those symbols and placed them upon you both."

"But how?" stammered Darshima, his mind racing as it struggled to fit the inconceivable pieces together.

"Darshima, Khydius, our past is complicated. I will share more of it when you are ready, but trust that I have known you both for a very long time." The corners of Tenrai's eyes grew damp as he spoke.

Tenrai then turned to Darshima. "In all Tiriyuusian Omystikai, there is a fiber of strength that runs deeply within our being. It is intertwined with the stars and the interstices between. It connects us to each other and to forces beyond what we can see, hear, and feel. This strength is very distinct in you, Darshima. I was fortunate to sense it and find you. Without your strength, we would have struggled greatly to find Khydius." An earnest smile crossed his lips. "Do you now understand why you both are here in Tiriyuud with me?"

"Yes, I understand," whispered Darshima. His pulse bounded in disbelief as Tenrai's words took root.

"Darshima and Khydius, behold our heritage." Tenrai gestured toward the diagram.

The unmitigated shock of Tenrai's revelation had left Darshima numb. He looked at Tenrai and then bowed his head. "Why didn't you tell us sooner?" asked Darshima.

"You would have never believed me," he replied.

Despite the gravity of Tenrai's words, Darshima could no longer deny their truth in the face of such overwhelming evidence. He resembled nothing of an Omystikai or a Tiriyuusian, save for his cobalt eyes. Khydius perhaps bore more of a resemblance with his fairer skin and cerulean eyes. Nonetheless, Darshima would have never believed Tenrai if he had not shown any proof.

"I am a descendent of the House of Fyrenos, how can this possibly be?" Jaw agape, Khydius stared at the floor.

"You are both of Tiriyuusian and Vilidesian ancestry. As it has been documented upon this tablet, our heritage is marked upon your skin, flows in your blood, and is etched upon your soul." Tenrai put his arms upon their shoulders and embraced them. "This is our family's lineage, and in time, you both will come to embrace it." Darshima's heart rose into his throat as the unalloyed truth settled within him. Through teary eyes, he gazed upon the intricate lines of their family tree. Khydius was his brother, and Tenrai was their uncle.

Chapter Fifty Two

Under the pale evening light of Benai, Tenrai led the group across the frozen landscape. With Shonan hoisted upon his back, they walked steadily through the knee-deep snow. They had started their trek at dawn and journeyed for the entire day. Darshima pulled the black wool coat over his shoulders, thankful for its warmth. Before setting out, Tenrai had outfitted them all with sturdy leather boots, gloves, and Tiriyuusian clothes made of special fibers that easily withstood the cold.

Eyes trained on a dense line of trees upon the horizon, Tenrai searched for the secluded gate leading into the capital. Though the last rays of sunlight had long ceded their brilliance to the vast starlit sky, the night was clear and they could see for a great distance around them. For the first time since their arrival, the chilly air stood still, and the powdery flakes of snow gently stirred about their feet.

The group was on their way to the capital to meet with the members of Tenrai's Order, where they would be inducted as members and begin their training. Tenrai insisted they travel by foot and under the cover of darkness. Their presence as foreigners in the kingdom was highly unusual, and Tenrai sought to avoid attention from the people in his village.

Darshima walked a few paces behind Tenrai, beside Khydius. Erethalie and Sydarias trudged steadily behind them, the snowdrifts brushing against their knees. Darshima's mind was strangely calm this evening. He couldn't recall a time since the invasion when he had felt more at peace. The truths that Tenrai and his adoptive parents on Gordanelle had revealed to him were slowly but steadily taking hold. He and Khydius were half Tiriyuusian and half Vilidesian. Darshima was the elder brother, having been born one year before Khydius. Their lineage was a unique exception, as the Omystikai never intermarried with the other peoples of the realm.

Their father, Tenrai's older brother was called *Nax-Foseidem, Rion* or Rion, and had died when they were very young. As Darshima and Khydius were his only sons, they were considered kin and would be accepted into the Order. Their mother was a Vilidesian noblewoman. Beyond these facts, Tenrai hesitated to elaborate, as their tragic past remained a deep source of grief for him. He agreed to share their history in due time, but he first wanted to help them acclimate to their new life on Iberwight.

There were so many questions that Darshima had yet to ask or even think of. His life had shifted so profoundly, and he was struggling to adjust to the changes. At times, he could hardly believe that he had once led a normal existence in Ardavia. As they walked onward, Darshima's mind sifted through the tumult and toil of the past several months. He had lost everything, yet somehow he had gained so much. His full-blooded brother was the prince and heir to the now defunct Vilidesian Realm, and his long-lost uncle was a Tiriyuusian Knight. As he had in the past, he would strive to accept the truth, no matter how painful or unbelievable it was.

Adrift in his thoughts, he found himself falling behind the group. Darshima hurried his pace to catch up with Tenrai, whose fleeting footsteps disappeared in the shifting snow.

"How are you doing over there?" Darshima looked over to Khydius on his right.

"The snow is deep, but I'm managing." Khydius offered him a polite nod, and adjusted the black woolen scarf covering his nose and mouth.

Darshima focused his gaze ahead and trudged through the snowdrifts. His heart fluttered with a mixture of joy and astonishment as he contemplated the truth of their blood relation. Tenrai's proof was incontrovertible and had shaken Darshima to his core. Khydius' features bore little resemblance to the House of Fyrenos, and like Darshima, the true origins of his markings had been revealed and claimed by an Omystikai man. Like times before, Darshima would strive to find stability amid the changing circumstances, but he couldn't imagine how difficult it was for Khydius. He had been torn from their world and enslaved in another, with no regard to his royal heritage. As Khydius had told him, the experience of laboring with his former subjects had transformed him.

Darshima looked over his shoulder toward Erethalie and Sydarias. They shivered and huddled together under the falling snows as they trekked forward. That morning, he and Khydius had told them the truth of their relation. They were at first stunned, but then recognized their resemblance and understood why Tenrai had risked so much to find them. Darshima mulled over what they both had given up to accompany him on this unknown journey. Sydarias had left behind a life of wealth and security to be with him. Erethalie risked her and Shonan's lives to serve as their pilot. He didn't know if he could ever repay them for their devotion.

The winds picked up as they trudged through the snowy landscape. Tenrai came to a stop and turned toward Darshima and the others.

"We are almost there," he said, his sapphire eyes glowing in the night.

"Do you want me to carry him?" Erethalie pointed toward Shonan, who had fallen asleep upon Tenrai's back.

"He is no burden at all." A wistful smile crossed Tenrai's lips.

"Tenrai, what will your people think of us?" She lowered her gaze as the snow drifted around them. "We have no Tiriyuusian heritage like Darshima and Khydius. Will they accept us?"

"Darshima has accepted you, and so have I." The corners of his eyes wrinkled in an earnest expression. "I will beseech the Order to admit both of you. Shonan is much too young to train. We will find a family in the capital who will take good care of him and raise him as a son."

"I understand." She bit her lip nervously.

"You and Sydarias have demonstrated much strength and bravery during this difficult time, but you both must earn your welcome, just like Darshima and Khydius." Tenrai gestured toward his nephews.

"I will do my best." Sydarias bowed his head.

"Let us continue." Tenrai pointed toward the line of trees.

As his feet crunched over the snow, Darshima ruminated upon Erethalie's concern. When they set out that morning, she had told him her misgivings about joining Tenrai's Order, and he understood. Many Vilidesian subjects saw the Omystikai as a peculiar band of isolationists with a secretive culture, obscure past and purported unnatural powers. They had often been blamed for turmoil in the realm, and their influence in The Vilides had been largely unwelcome outside of the dynasty.

Darshima had once viewed the Omystikai with skepticism, but his feelings were now different. Half of his lineage came from these mysterious people. Nonetheless, the suspicion that Sovani had shared of Omystikai involvement in the invasion nagged at him. Despite Tenrai's assurance that Tiriyuud played no role, his uncertainty persisted.

During their journey to Tiriyuud, they had flown over the Dominion of Fauridise. He had seen no traces of devastation in their territory. Furthermore, he couldn't recall seeing a single Omystikai slave during his time on Navervyne. Darshima knew that there had to be some rational explanation for it all. His thoughts racing, he shook his head and tried to rid himself of the creeping doubts. He gazed up at the clear night sky, searching the stars for some hint of the uncertain future that lay before them. Moving against the strengthening winds, he walked with Tenrai and the others, over the hills blanketed in snow and through undulating valleys, bearing the weight of his feelings.

In the night's darkest hour, they finally reached the edge of the forest. The snow-covered trees loomed high above and were much larger than any that Darshima had ever seen. Tenrai led them toward a large wooden gate, virtually identical in design to the one outside of his home. Darshima peered through the structure and saw nothing but a dense wall of impassable trees, their needle-shaped leaves covered in a thick layer of snow. Tenrai faced them.

"We have arrived." He looked at each of them as he stooped to let Shonan down, who was now fully awake.

"There is nothing beyond but forest." Darshima pointed at the gate, a perplexed frown spreading upon his face.

"You will enter this gate and one day reemerge, reborn as Tiriyuusian Omystikai." Tenrai ushered Darshima and the others forward. "You will belong to the Order of The Gilded Moon. You will be fully trained in our traditions and ways. You will become one of us." He beckoned them with a wave of his hand, stepped through, and disappeared into the snow-covered foliage.

Darshima hesitantly passed through the wooden gate and into the forest, bracing himself for a collision with the snowy wall of trees. To his astonishment, he felt neither branches nor thorns, but the chilly breeze. The forest before him vanished to reveal a tree-lined road, with Tenrai standing at the edge.

"What kind of illusion is this?" Darshima anxiously reached out and grasped the air before him. In the distance, he saw the glowing lights of an enormous city surrounded by the rippling waters of a vast lake.

"Keep walking and you will arrive." Tenrai looked over his shoulder and called out to the others.

"I never thought I would see this place in my lifetime," exclaimed Khydius, as he joined them. Erethalie, Shonan, and

Sydarias stepped through the gate, looking around them in wonderment.

"We have just passed through one of several hidden entrances to the city." Tenrai pointed to the open air behind them.

"Where are we?" Shonan rubbed his eyes, his brow furrowing in a look of confusion.

"Welcome to Chryshaihem." Tenrai beamed at him.

Tenrai led them down a sloping, cobbled path that led toward the water's edge. An icy mist wafted up from the dark, rippling surface. As they approached, Darshima gained a clearer sense of their unique location. An immense group of five hilly islands rose majestically from the lake, the waters lapping at their rocky shores. The city stood as a veritable fortress with walls and ramparts wrapping along its lower perimeter. Several arched stone bridges spanned the rivers flowing between the fortified islands. Upon the steep terrain stood clusters of soaring buildings, glowing temples, and ornate shrines. Beyond the city, toward the horizon, Darshima spotted a range of rugged mountains encircling the lake. Chains of waterfalls spilled from the rock faces, their cascades crashing to the water's surface.

Against an inky sky awash with starlight, the large, shimmering golden orb of Ciblaithia hung just above the sloping, tiled roofs of the buildings. Stunned by its beauty, Darshima held his breath at the stirring sight. They reached the entrance of an immense, wrought-iron bridge leading onto the main island. The lengthy span hung from radiating webs of cables bound to several pairs of elegant, cantilevered towers. Like pointed arrows, their oblique forms rose boldly from the waters and aimed toward the sky.

With Tenrai at the lead, the group made their way across the bridge toward the sacred city of Chryshaihem, the capital of Tiriyuud and home to the Order of the Gilded Moon. Perched upon a large snow-swept hill in the center of the city, the octagonal, multi-tiered towers of the main temple complex loomed magnificently above the metropolis. As they drew nearer, Darshima eyed the sloping, snow-capped roofs ornamented in gold leaf and glittering shards of crystal.

They walked along the length of the bridge, over the rippling dark waters amid the tranquil moonlight. A steady dusting of snow fell from the frozen sky, covering the road beneath them. They left their footprints in the untouched powder as they walked past the thick cables of the hanging span. Tenrai led them onto the main island, and they came to a stop at a pair of immense iron gates guarding the entrance. Their black facades were cast in an abstract array of complex symbols and script that Darshima had never seen in his life.

They waited anxiously as Tenrai stood still and closed his eyes. After a moment, he whispered a few words in his native tongue. A light gust of wind abruptly stirred around them, taking his words away into the night. His eyes fluttered open, and the large doors issued a deep groan as they parted, revealing a cobbled, tree-lined avenue. The thoroughfare was flanked by stately, multilevel buildings of wood and stone, capped by sloping roofs of fluted ceramic tile. Chains of glowing, polygonal crystals hung from the eaves, casting their porches in a soft, ethereal glow.

Despite the early hour, the streets were anything but empty. Sentries dressed in pleated black trousers, knee-high boots, stiff black overcoats with creased sleeves and dark blue hoods stood watch as Tenrai led Darshima and the others past. They wore black scarves that covered the lower half of their pale faces against the icy cold, revealing only their brilliant, sapphire eyes. Under the starlight, they stood completely still. The only movement came from the rustling of their garments in the steady breeze. Their hands clad in black leather gloves, they held wooden lanterns burning with white flame toward the street, softly illuminating the path ahead.

The sentries bowed their heads in deference as the group walked by, casting their glowing gazes downward in a gesture of respect. Under the snowfall, Darshima and the others moved silently along the streets, taking in the striking scene before them. They walked toward the cluster of temples, their spires, and sloped roofs reaching gracefully toward the sky.

Despite all he had witnessed during his journey thus far, Darshima had never set his eyes on such a place. The stark silence and foreign beauty of their surroundings had an indescribable, yet tangible sense of antiquity. It was almost as if the ancient winds of change that had swept through every corner of the realm upon the rise of The Vilides had died long before they had ever made it to these hidden shores.

They approached the broad stone staircase leading toward the temple complex, flakes of snow gently drifting over the ornately carved steps. Darshima looked up at the imposing, majestic structure gleaming under the soft rays of moonlight. His pulse slowed, and a profound yet unmistakable feeling of peace flooded his senses. For a moment, his worries disappeared, and he felt neither fear nor sadness. There would be no more hiding and no more running. He was finally home.

Golden dunes hollowed by Firmament's breath
Time's pendulum sways between life and death
Fragile sands witness nascent creation
Heaven observes in silent ovation
Worlds rise beneath distant constellations
Civil orbs yield to the might of nations
Wealth of ages corrodes a gilded throne
The ancient dusts whisper in coded stone
Buried eons whose mysteries abound

Echoes of an empire's collapse resound
A child of fire whose destinies helm
Fate's augury upon a faded realm
Armies presaged in cryptic emblems cast
Cavalcades fury smites heritage past
Revered bastions bearing armaments proud
Arrows aflame pierce through the star-crossed shroud
Ordained mortars rain down upon damned shields
Soaring apses falter on bequeathed seals
Diadems crushed against scepters broken
Spectral voices chant scriptures awoken
Deafening skies roil as hallowed grounds quake
Tides of destruction whose thirst cannot slake
Ashes fall upon fractured azimuths
Warring banners reveal unguarded truths
Austere winds quell a newly conquered land
Oppressed souls submit to an unknown hand
A people besieged whose spirits opine
All that is mortal cedes to the divine
Foretold fragments of a most sacred rune
Herald the Exiles of a Gilded Moon
-Dustin R. Cummings

• • • •

-THE END

About the Author

Dustin R Cummings is an author who lives in New York, NY. Originally from Michigan, he is an avid fan of science fiction and fantasy. In his spare time, he enjoys reading, piano, and long walks. He is an assistant professor of surgery in New Jersey.

The first installment in his epic fantasy series *Exiles of a Gilded Moon Volume I: Empire's Wake* chronicles the incredible life of Darshima, a young, inquisitive man finding his place in the world, who faces the unexpected - the invasion and destruction of his homeland.

He can be found on Twitter @dorenavant2020 or at dustinr-cummings.com

CPSIA information can be obtained
at www.ICGtesting.com
Printed in the USA
LVHW111627221220
674907LV00001B/33